"The notion of mixing basketball and crime seems totally predictable— a natural combination, like ham and eggs, Laurel and Hardy, yin and yang. It would be difficult to think that a group of fiction writers, people who make up stories, could find a way to write about crime and criminals in a way that surpasses the real-life adventures we can all read about in the tabloids, but the assembled team of top-notch writers has done just that. This Dream Team of outstanding authors has put together a game plan that will keep you at the edge of your seat right up to the last second."

—Otto Penzler, from the Introduction

PRAISE FOR *DANGEROUS WOMEN*, EDITED BY OTTO PENZLER

"I'm not usually given to superlatives, but *Dangerous Women* may be the best, most varied, and colorful mystery anthology of all time."

—Janet Evanovich

"Wow, what memorable dames! What terrific short stories! *Dangerous Women* is a winning collection."

—Susan Isaacs

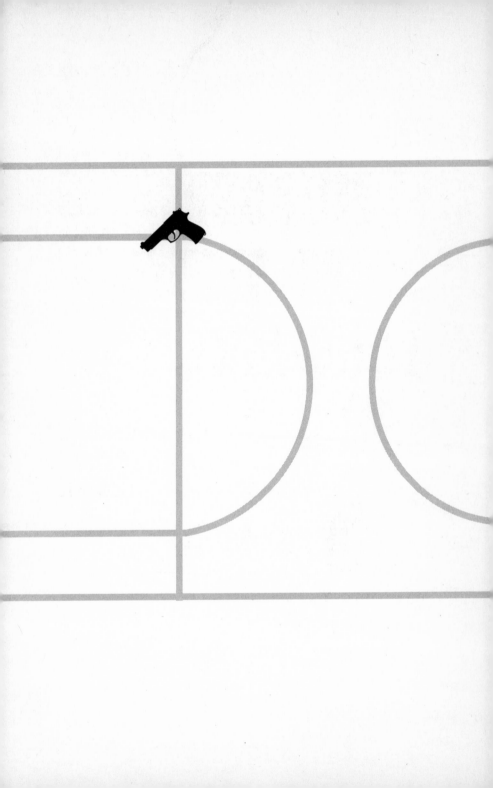

MURDER AT THE FOUL LINE

EDITED BY
OTTO PENZLER

NEW YORK   BOSTON

The events and characters in this book are fictitious. Certain real locations and public figures are mentioned, but all other characters and events described in the book are totally imaginary.

Mysterious Press
Warner Books

Time Warner Book Group
1271 Avenue of the Americas, New York, NY 10020
Visit our Web site at www.twbookmark.com.

The Mysterious Press name and logo are registered trademarks of Warner Books.

Printed in the United States of America
Published simultaneously in hardcover by Mysterious Press

First Trade Edition: January 2006
10 9 8 7 6 5 4 3 2 1

Library of Congress Cataloging-in-Publication Data

Murder at the foul line / edited by Otto Penzler.
    p. cm.
    ISBN 0-89296-016-7
    ISBN 0-446-69631-5 (pbk.)
    1. Basketball stories. 2. Detective and mystery stories, American. I. Penzler, Otto.

PS648.B39M87 2006
813'.087208—dc22   2005047996

In affectionate memory of Evan Hunter
And for his wife, Dragica,
with thanks for making my friend so happy

CONTENTS

INTRODUCTION

Otto Penzler

Basketball was a little different when I was growing up, which is just before James Naismith reputedly invented the game in 1891.

First, most of the players were white. I don't know if they *could* jump, but I do know they *didn't* jump. Dunking was something you did with a doughnut and a cup of coffee. There was such a thing as a two-handed set shot. I'm not making this up. Hook shots were common, and soon some of the better players developed a jump shot. Foul shots were frequently taken underhanded, with two hands guiding the ball toward the hoop. Eventually, to help speed the game up, the twenty-four-second clock was invented.

Second, players actually played by the rules, mainly because the referees called fouls and other violations. Traveling, for example, was called if a player carried the ball for two steps. Today it's called only if he carries the ball to another city. Basketball was described accurately back in the Dark Ages as a noncontact sport. If you bumped into a player, you were called for a foul. Today the foul is called only if you hit someone repeatedly, generally with a blunt instrument.

Also, players seemed tall but human. Today the guys who used to be the "big" forward (now known as the power forward) are the speedy little guys who bring the ball up the court. The big guys seem descended from another planet.

Don't get me wrong. I'm not some old fogey who thinks players were better when I was a kid. I'm an old fogey who thinks basketball players during the past quarter century or so are the best all-around athletes in the world. They just don't play the same game. I'm not sure when it went from being a team sport to being a game played by five individuals to a side, but it was probably when ESPN's *SportsCenter* started to show highlights every night and 95 percent of them were dunks (just as most baseball highlights on that show are home runs, and there's nothing more boring than watching one long fly ball after another landing in the seats).

But perhaps the biggest difference in the game is the level of criminal activity. One of the big crime stories of the 1950s was when some Manhattan College, CCNY, and Long Island University players conspired to fix games so that certain gamblers could make a killing. The scandal rocked the sport for years, and those teams, then national powers, never recovered.

Today, of course, that would be looked upon as kid stuff. Now we're really talking. Stars are commonly arrested for drug abuse, drunk driving, wife (and girlfriend) battering, barroom brawling, rape, and so many other acts of violence and criminality that it is difficult to keep track.

There was a time when I thought Kermit Washington's brutal punch of an innocent and unsuspecting Rudy Tomjanovich, caving in his face, fracturing his skull, breaking his jaw and nose, and causing a potentially lethal spinal fluid drip from his brain, was the most disgusting thing I'd ever seen on a basketball court, but that was before Ron Artest and fellow thugs on the Indiana Pacers brawled with fans in Detroit. Now, I'll quickly concede that some guy who throws a cup full of beer into the face of a six-foot-eight-inch tower of muscle is so stupid that he probably deserves a good whipping, but still . . .

Even this pales when compared with Latrell Sprewell's attempted murder of his coach. Not merely in the heat of the moment, mind you. He grabbed P. J. Carlesimo, put his big hands around his throat, and choked him until he was pulled away. He left, came back about twenty minutes later, and *did it again*! (Well, Sprewell explained later, it's not like he couldn't breathe *at all*.) Because he's a star athlete, he didn't do a single day in jail. Instead, he got traded to the New York Knicks and became a crowd favorite. When he left the team as a free agent, he spurned a $29-million offer, explaining that it wasn't enough, that he had to feed his family.

Jayson Williams, a great basketball player and a charming man, was not convicted of killing his chauffeur.

In a never-ending headline story, Kobe Bryant was arrested for rape but admits only to being stupid and an adulterer. Allen Iverson, who has all the charm of a Mexican snuff film, was arrested with illegal weapons—again. Charles Barkley cold-cocked a pencil-thin opponent in the Olympics for no discernible reason. There *was* a perfectly good reason for him to throw someone through a barroom window. He'd been hassled by the idiot. When asked if he had any regrets about the incident, Barkley said yes. He was sorry they hadn't been on a higher floor.

The notion, then, of mixing basketball and crime in this collection seems predictable—a natural combination, like ham and eggs, Laurel and Hardy, yin and yang. Or, to put it more darkly, it's a predictably unnatural combination, like Michael Jackson and little boys, S&M, Paris Hilton and farm animals, and the team of buffoons (sorry, self-described "idiots") known as the 2004 World Champion Boston Red Sox.

It would be difficult to think that a group of fiction writers, people who make up stories, could find a way to write about crime and criminals in a way that surpasses the real-life adventures we can all read about in the tabloids, but the assembled team of top-notch mystery writers has done just that. This Dream Team of outstanding authors has put together a game plan that will keep you at the edge of your seat right to the last second. Here is the lineup of superstars:

Lawrence Block has received the highest honor bestowed by the Mystery Writers of America, the Grand Master Award for lifetime achievement, and received the equivalent prize, the Diamond Dagger, from the Crime Writers' Association of Great Britain. He has produced more than sixty novels, mainly about such series characters as the tough alcoholic private eye, Matt Scudder; his comedic bookseller/burglar, Bernie Rhodenbarr; and the amoral hit man who appears in this volume, Keller.

Jeffery Deaver is the author of twenty novels, many featuring Lincoln Rhyme, including *The Bone Collector,* which was filmed starring Denzel Washington. Deaver has been nominated for four Edgar Allan Poe Awards and an Anthony and is the three-time recipient of the Ellery Queen Reader's Award for Best Short Story of the Year. *Garden of Beasts* won the 2004 Ian Fleming Steel Dagger Award by the Crime Writers' Association of Great Britain for the best thriller in the vein of James Bond.

Sue DeNymme has a rich bloodline of storytellers, embellishers, and exaggerators, including fishermen, pirates, and royalty. She has traveled extensively, studying language and culture, and has earned degrees from several prestigious universities. When she began writing, she immediately won a poetry prize. Now that she has decided to write the tallest possible tales, she chose mystery fiction for her career. In fact, she is in the process of writing a crime novel and cannot wait to read it.

Brendan DuBois is the author of seven novels, one of which, *Resurrection Day*, is planned as a major motion picture. He has produced numerous short stories, three of which have been nominated for Edgar Allan Poe Awards and two of which have won Shamus Awards. His story "The Dark Snow" was selected for *Best American Mystery Stories of the Century*, edited by Tony Hillerman.

Parnell Hall is the author of the critically acclaimed Stanley Hastings series about an inept and cowardly private eye, and the Puzzle Lady novels that involve crossword puzzles as clues, voted the Best New Discovery by members of the Mystery Guild. He has been nominated for an Edgar Allan Poe Award by the Mystery Writers of America and the Shamus Award by the Private Eye Writers of America.

Laurie R. King writes stand-alone thrillers, a series about San Francisco homicide inspector Kate Martinelli and, most notably, a series about Sherlock Holmes and his wife, Mary Russell. Her first novel, *A Grave Talent*, won the Edgar and the John Creasey Awards from the (British) Crime Writers' Association. *With Child* was nominated for an Edgar.

Mike Lupica is one of the best-known and most accomplished sportswriters in America, a regular on ESPN's *The Sports Reporters*, as well as the author of fifteen books of fiction, non-fiction, juvenile and mystery fiction. His first mystery, *Dead Air*, was nominated for an Edgar and was later filmed for CBS as *Money, Power and Murder*. His most recent novel, *Too Far*, was a national best-seller.

Michael Malone has written three mysteries, *Uncivil Seasons, Time's Witness*, and *First Lady*, as well as several mainstream novels, notably such modern classics as *Dingley Falls, Handling Sin*, and *Foolscap*. He was the head writer for various daytime drama series, including *One Life to Live*. His short story "Red Clay" won the Edgar and was selected for *Best American Mystery Stories of the Century*.

Joan H. Parker is the coauthor, with her husband, Robert B. Parker, of *Three Weeks in Spring*, the moving story of her battle with cancer, and *A Year at the Races*, a pictorial journal of their adventures with horse racing. She and her husband also collaborated on several scripts for *Spenser*, the television series based on the Boston P.I.

Robert B. Parker, acclaimed as the contemporary private eye writer in the pantheon of Hammett, Chandler, and Ross Macdonald, won an Edgar for *Promised Land*, the fourth in the series of instant classics involving Spenser, the tough, wise-cracking Boston P.I. who was the basis for a network television series in the 1990s. Parker was recently named a Grand Master by the Mystery Writers of America.

George Pelecanos, one of the most critically acclaimed crime writers in America, is the author of a dozen novels with several different series characters, most notably Nick Stefanos and the team of Derek Strange and Terry Quinn. *Hell to Pay* won the Los Angeles Times Book Award, and *The Big Blowdown* won the International Crime Novel of the Year Award in

France, Germany, and Japan. He is currently a writer and producer of the HBO series *The Wire*.

R. D. Rosen has written for *Saturday Night Live* and several CBS news shows, but he claims that his novels about Harvey Blissberg, a professional baseball player turned private eye, are closest to his heart. His first book, *Strike Three, You're Dead*, won the Edgar in 1984 and was recently named "one of the hundred favorite mysteries of the century" by the Independent Booksellers Association.

S. J. Rozan is one of the most honored mystery writers of recent years, winning two Edgars (for Best Short Story and Best Novel), as well as a Shamus, Macavity, Nero, and Anthony. Her series characters are Lydia Chin, a young American-born Chinese private eye whose cases originate mainly in New York's Chinese community, and Chin's partner, Bill Smith, an older, more experienced sleuth who lives above a bar in Tribeca.

Justin Scott is the author of more than twenty novels, including such huge international best-sellers as *The Shipkiller, The Widow of Desire,* and *A Pride of Royals*. His humorous mystery *Many Happy Returns* was nominated for an Edgar in 1974. His most recent series of novels, recounting the adventures of Benjamin Abbott, a real estate agent in the charming Connecticut town of Newbury, includes *HardScape, StoneDust,* and *Frostline*.

Stephen Solomita has received an extraordinary amount of critical acclaim, being compared to Elmore Leonard and Tom Wolfe (by the *New York Times*), to Joseph Wambaugh and William J. Caunitz (by the Associated Press), and to John Grisham (*Kirkus Reviews*). He is the author of nearly twenty books under his own name, many about Stanley Moodrow, a tough New York City cop, and under the pseudonym David Cray.

So let the games begin. Oh, one more thing. While it is generally accepted that James Naismith invented the game of basketball in 1891 by cutting out the bottom of a peach basket and nailing it to a wall, in fact a very similar game had been played hundreds of years earlier. The object was to put a rubber ball through a ring. The stakes were pretty high, as it was possible that the captain of the losing team would be beheaded. Maybe we shouldn't let this become common knowledge. Some of the thugs in the NBA might think it's a good idea to reinstate the custom.

—*Otto Penzler*
January 2005, New York

MURDER AT THE FOUL LINE

KELLER'S DOUBLE DRIBBLE

Lawrence Block

Keller, his hands in his pockets, watched a dark-skinned black man with his shirt off drive for the basket. His shaved head gleamed, and the muscles of his upper back, the traps and lats, bulged as if steroidally enhanced. Another man, wearing a T-shirt but otherwise of the same shade and physique, leapt to block the shot, and the two bodies met in midair. It was a little like ballet, Keller thought, and a little like combat, and the ball kissed off the backboard and dropped through the hoop.

There was no net, just a bare hoop. The playground was at the corner of Sixth Avenue and West Third Street, in Greenwich Village, and Keller was one of a handful of spectators standing outside the high chain-link fence, watching idly as ten men, half wearing T-shirts, half bare-chested, played a fiercely competitive game of half-court basketball.

If this were a game at the Garden, the last play would have sent someone to the free-throw line. But there was no ref here to call fouls, and order was maintained in a simpler fashion: Anyone who fouled too frequently was thrown out of the game. It was, Keller felt, an interesting libertarian solution, and he thought it might be worth a try outside the basketball court, but had a feeling it would be tough to make it work.

Keller watched a few more plays, feeling his spirits sink as he did, yet finding it oddly difficult to tear himself away. He'd had a tooth drilled and filled a few blocks away, by a dentist who had himself played varsity basketball years ago at the University of Kentucky, and had been walking around waiting for the Novocain to wear off so he could grab some lunch, and the basketball game had caught his eye, and here he was. Watching, and being brought down in the process, because basketball always depressed him.

His mouth wasn't numb anymore. He crossed the street, walked two blocks east, turned right on Sullivan Street, left on Bleecker. He considered and rejected restaurants as he walked, knowing he wanted something spicy. If basketball depressed him, highly seasoned food put him right again. He thought it odd, didn't understand it, but knew it worked.

*　*　*

The restaurant he found was Indian, and Keller made sure the waiter got the message. "You tone things down for Westerners," he told the man. "I only look like an American of European ancestry. Inside, I am a man from Sri Lanka."

"You want spicy," the waiter said.

"I want very spicy," Keller said. "And then some."

The little man beamed. "You wish to sweat."

"I wish to suffer."

"Leave it to me," the little man said.

The meal was almost too hot to eat. It was nominally a lamb curry, but its ingredients might have been anything. Lamb, beef, dog, duck. Tofu, shoe leather, balsawood. Papier-mâché? Plaster of paris? The searing heat of the cayenne obscured everything else. Keller, forcing himself to finish every bite, loved and hated every minute of it. By the time he was done he was drenched in perspiration and felt as if he'd just gone ten rounds with a worthy opponent. He felt, too, a sense of accomplishment and an abiding sense of peace with the world.

Something made him call home to check his answering machine. Two hours later he was on the front porch of the big old house on Taunton Place, sipping a glass of iced tea. Three days after that he was in Indiana.

★   ★   ★

At the Avis desk at Indy International, Keller turned in the Chevy he'd driven from New York. At the Hertz counter, he picked up the keys to the Ford he'd reserved. He carried his bag to the car, left it in short-term parking, and went back into the airport, remembering to take his bag with him. There was a fellow waiting at baggage claim, wearing the green and gold John Deere cap they'd said he'd be wearing.

"Oh, there you are," the fellow said when Keller approached him. "The bags are just starting to come down."

Keller brandished his carry-on, said he hadn't checked anything.

"Then I guess you didn't bring a nail clipper," the man said, "or a Swiss Army knife. Never mind a bazooka."

Keller had a Swiss Army knife in his carry-on and a nail clipper in his pocket, attached to his key ring. Since he hadn't flown anywhere, he'd had no problem. As for the other, well, he had never minded a bazooka in his life, and saw no reason to start now.

"Now let's get you squared away," the man said. He was around forty, and lean, except for an incongruous potbelly, as if he'd swallowed a small watermelon. "Quick orientation, drive you around, show you where he lives. We'll take my car, and when we're done, you can drop me off and keep it."

The airport was at the southwest corner of Indianapolis, and the man (who'd flipped the John Deere cap into the backseat of his Hyundai squareback, alongside Keller's carry-on) drove to Carmel, an upscale suburb north of the I-465 beltway. He made a few efforts at conversation, which Keller let wither on the vine, whereupon he gave up and switched on the radio. He kept it tuned to an all-talk station, and right now two opinionated fellows were arguing about the outsourcing of jobs.

Keller thought about turning it off. You're a hit man, brought in at great expense from out of town, and some gofer picks you up and plays the radio, and you turn it off, what's he gonna do? Be impressed and a little intimidated, he thought, but decided it wasn't worth the trouble.

The driver killed the radio himself when they left the interstate and drove through the treelined streets of Carmel. Keller paid close attention now, noting street names and landmarks and taking a good look at the house that was pointed out to him. It was a Dutch Colonial with a mansard roof, he noted, and that tugged at his memory until he remembered a real estate agent in Roseburg, Oregon, who'd shown him through a similar house years ago. Keller had wanted to buy it, to move there. For a few days, anyway, until he came to his senses.

When they were done, the man asked him if there was anything else he wanted to see, and Keller said there wasn't. "Then I'll drive you to my house," the man said, "and you can drop me off."

Keller shook his head. "Drop me at the airport," he said.

"Oh, Jesus," the man said. "Is something wrong? Did I say the wrong thing?"

Keller looked at him.

" 'Cause if you're backing out, I'm gonna get blamed for it. They'll have a goddamn fit. Is it the location? Because, you know, it doesn't have to be at his house. It could be anywhere."

Oh. Keller explained that he didn't want to use the Hyundai, that he'd pick up a car at the airport. He preferred it that way, he said.

Driving back to the airport, the man obviously wanted to ask why Keller wanted his own car, and just as obviously was afraid to say a word. Nor did he play the radio. The silence was a heavy one, but that was okay with Keller.

When they got there, the fellow said he supposed Keller wanted to rent a car. Keller shook his head and directed him to the lot where he'd already stowed the Ford. "Keep going," he said. "Maybe that one . . . no, that's the one I want. Stop here."

"What are you gonna do?"

"Borrow a car," Keller said.

He'd added the key to his key ring, and now he stood alongside the car and made a show of flipping through keys, finally selecting the one they'd given him. He tried it in the door and, unsurprisingly, it worked. He tried it in the ignition, and it worked there, too. He switched off the ignition and went back to the Hyundai for his carry-on, where the driver, wide-eyed, asked him if he was really going to steal that car.

"I'm just borrowing it," he said.

"But if the owner reports it—"

"I'll be done with it by then." He smiled. "Relax. I do this all the time."

The fellow started to say something, then changed his mind. "Well," he said instead. "Look, do you want a piece?"

Was the man offering him a woman? Or, God forbid, offering to supply sexual favors personally? Keller frowned and then realized the piece in question was a gun. Keller, relieved, shook his head and said he had everything he needed in his carry-on. Amazing the damage you could inflict with a Swiss Army knife and a nail clipper.

"Well," the man said again. "Well, here's something." He reached into his breast pocket and came out with a pair of tickets. "To the Pacers game," he said. "They're playing the Knicks, so I guess you'll be rooting for your homies, huh? Tonight, eight sharp. They're not courtside, but they're damn good seats. You want, I could dig up somebody to go with you, keep you company."

Keller said he'd take care of that himself, and the man didn't seem surprised to hear it.

★　★　★

"He's a witness," Dot had said, "but apparently nobody's thought of sticking him in the Federal Witness Protection Program, but maybe that's because the situation's not federal. Do you have to be involved in a federal case in order to be protected by the federal government?"

Keller wasn't sure, and Dot said it didn't really matter. What mattered was that the witness wasn't in the program, and wasn't hidden at all, and that made it a job for Keller, because the client really didn't want the witness to stand up and testify.

"Or sit down and testify," she said, "which is what they usually do, at least on the television programs I watch. The lawyers stand up, and even walk around some, but the witnesses just sit there."

"What did he witness, do you happen to know?"

"You know," she said, "they were pretty vague on that point. The guy I talked to wasn't a principal. He was more like a booking agent. I've worked with him before, when his clients were O.C. guys."

"Huh?"

"Organized crime. So he's connected, but this isn't O.C., and my sense is it's not violent."

"But it's going to get that way."

"Well, you're not going all the way to Indiana to talk sense into him, are you? What he witnessed, I think it was like corporate shenanigans. What's the matter?"

"Shenanigans," he said.

"It's a perfectly good word. What's the matter with shenanigans?"

"I just didn't think anybody said it anymore," he said. "That's all."

"Well, maybe they should. God knows they've got occasion to."

"If it's corporate fiddle-faddle," he began, and stopped when she held up a hand.

"Fiddle-faddle? This from a man who has a problem with shenanigans?"

"If it's that sort of thing," he said, "then it actually could be federal, couldn't it?"

"I suppose so."

"But he's not in the witness program because they don't think he's in danger."

She nodded. "Stands to reason."

"So they probably haven't assigned people to guard him," he said, "and he's probably not taking precautions."

"Probably not."

"Should be easy."

"It should," she agreed. "So why are you disappointed?"

"Disappointed?"

"That's the vibe I'm getting. Are you picking up on something? Like it's really going to be a lot more complicated than it sounds?"

He shook his head. "I think it's going to be easy," he said, "and I hope it is, and I'm not picking up any vibe. And I certainly didn't mean to sound disappointed, because I don't feel disappointed. I can use the money, and besides that, I can use the work. I don't want to go stale."

"So there's no problem."

"No. As far as your vibe is concerned, well, I spent the morning at the dentist."

"Say no more. That's enough to depress anybody."

"It wasn't, really. But then I was watching some guys play basketball. The Indian food helped, but the mood lingered."

"You're just one big non sequitur, aren't you, Keller?" She held up a hand. "No, don't explain. You'll go to Indianapolis, you lucky man, and your actions will get to speak for themselves."

★   ★   ★

Keller's motel was a Rodeway Inn at the junction of Interstates 465 and 69, close enough to Carmel but not too close. He signed in with a name that matched his credit card and made up a license plate number for the registration card. In his room, he ran the channels on the TV, then switched off the set. He took a shower, got dressed, turned the TV on, turned it off again.

Then he went to the car and found his way to the Conseco

Fieldhouse, where the Indiana Pacers were playing host to the New York Knicks.

The stadium was in the center of the city, but the signage made it easy to get there. A man in a porkpie hat asked him in an undertone if he had any extra tickets, and Keller realized that he did. He took a good look at his tickets for the first time and saw that he had a pair of $96 seats in section 117, wherever that was. He could sell one, but wouldn't that be awkward if the man he sold it to sat beside him? He'd probably be a talker, and Keller didn't want that.

But a moment's observation clarified the situation. The man in the porkpie hat—who had, Keller noted, a face straight out of an OTB parlor, a coulda-woulda-shoulda gambler's face—was doing a little business, buying tickets from people who had too many, selling them to people who had too few. So he wouldn't be sitting next to Keller. Someone else would, but it would be someone he hadn't met, so it would be easy to keep an intimacy barrier in place.

Keller went up to the man in the hat, showed him one of the tickets. The man said, "Fifty bucks," and Keller pointed out that it was a $96 ticket. The man gave him a look, and Keller took the ticket back.

"Jesus," the man said. "What do you want for it, anyway?"

"Eighty-five," Keller said, picking the number out of the air.

"That's crazy."

"The Pacers and the Knicks? Section 117? I bet I can find somebody who wants it eighty-five dollars' worth."

They settled on $75, and Keller pocketed the money and used his other ticket to enter the arena. Then it struck him that he could have unloaded both tickets and had $150 to show for it, and gone straight home, spared the ordeal of a basketball game. But he was already through the turnstile when the thought came to him, and by that point he no longer had a ticket to sell.

He found his seat and sat down to watch the game.

★   ★   ★

Keller, an only child, was raised by his mother, who he had come to realize in later years was probably mentally ill. He never suspected this at the time, although he was aware that she was different from other people.

She kept a picture of Keller's father in a frame in the living room. The photograph showed a young man in a military uniform, and Keller grew up knowing that his father had been a soldier, a casualty of the war. As a teenager, he'd been employed cleaning out a stockroom, and one of the boxes of obsolete merchandise he'd hauled out had contained picture frames, half of them containing the familiar photograph of his putative father.

It occurred to him that he ought to mention this to his mother. On further thought, he decided not to say anything. He went home and looked at the photo and wondered who his father was. A soldier, he decided, though not this one. Someone passing through, who'd fathered a son and never knew it.

And died in battle? Well, a lot of soldiers did. His father might very well have been one of them.

Growing up in a fatherless home with a mother who didn't seem to have any friends or acquaintances was something Keller had been on the point of addressing in therapy, until a problem with his therapist put an end to that experiment. He'd had trouble deciding just how he felt about his mother, but had ultimately come to the conclusion that she was a good woman who'd done a good job of raising him, given her limitations. She was a serviceable cook if not an imaginative one, and he had a hot breakfast every morning and a hot dinner every night. She kept their house clean and taught Keller to be clean about his person. She was detached, and talked more to herself than to him—and, in the afternoons, talked to the characters in her TV soap operas.

She bought him presents at Christmas and on his birthday, usually clothing to replace garments he'd outgrown, but occasionally something more interesting. One year she bought him an Erector set, and he'd proved quite hopeless at following the diagrams in an effort to produce a flatbed railcar or, indeed, anything else. Another year's present was a beginner's stamp collecting kit—a stamp album, a packet of stamps, a pair of tongs to pick them up with, and a supply of hinges for mounting them in the album. The Erector set wound up in the closet, gathering dust, but the stamp album turned out to be the foundation of a lifelong hobby. He'd abandoned it after high school, of course, and the original album was long gone, but Keller had taken up the hobby again as an adult and cheerfully poured much of his spare time and extra cash into it.

Would he have become a stamp collector if not for his mother's gift? Possibly, he thought, but probably not. It was one more reason to thank her.

The Erector set was a good thought that failed, the stamp album an inspiration. The biggest surprise, though, of all the gifts she gave him was neither of these.

That would have to be the basketball backboard.

★ ★ ★

Keller hadn't bothered to note the seat number of the ticket he sold to the man in the porkpie hat. His own seat was 117, situated unsurprisingly enough between seats 116 and 118, both of them unoccupied when he sat down between them. Then two men came along and sat down in 115 and 116. One was substantially older than the other, and Keller found himself wondering if they were father and son, boss and employee, uncle and nephew, or gay lovers. He didn't really care, but he couldn't keep from wondering, and he kept changing his mind.

The game had already started by the time a man turned up and sat down in 118. He was wearing a dark suit with a subtle pinstripe and looked as though he'd come straight from the office, an office where he spent his days doing something no one, least of all the man himself, would describe as interesting.

The man in the porkpie hat had paid Keller $75 for that seat, which suggested that the man in the suit must have paid at least $100 for it, and perhaps as much as $125. But, of course, the fellow had no idea that Keller was the source of his ticket, and in fact paid no attention to Keller, devoting the full measure of his attention to the action on the court, where the Pacers had jumped off to an early lead.

Keller, with some reluctance, turned his attention to the game.

★ ★ ★

Across the street and two doors up from Keller's house, a family named Breitbart filled a large frame house to overflowing. Mr. Breitbart owned and ran a furniture store on Euclid Avenue, and Mrs. Breitbart stayed home and, for a while at least, had a baby every year. The year Keller was born she gave birth to two—twin sons, Andrew and Randall, the names no doubt selected so that their nicknames could rhyme. The twins were the family's only boys; the other five little Breitbarts, some older than the twins, the rest younger, were all girls.

Every afternoon, weather permitting, boys gathered in the Breitbart backyard to play basketball. Sometimes they divided into teams, and one side took off their shirts, and they played the sort of half-court game you could play with a single garage-mounted backboard. Other times, when fewer boys showed up or for some other reason, they found other ways to compete—playing Horse, say, where each player had to duplicate the particular shot of the first player. There were other games as well, but Keller, watching idly from across the street, was less clear on their rules and objectives.

One night at dinner, Keller's mother told him he should go across the street and join the game. "You watch all the time," she said—inaccurately, as he only occasionally let himself loll on the sidewalk watching the action in the Breitbart yard. "I bet they'd love it if you joined in. I bet you'd be good at it."

As it turned out, she lost both bets.

Keller, a quiet boy, always felt more at ease with grown-ups than with his contemporaries. On his own, he moved with an easy grace; in group sports, self-consciousness turned him awkward and made him ill at ease. Nonetheless, later that week he crossed the street and presented himself in the Breitbart backyard. "It's Keller," Andy or Randy said. "From across the street." Someone tossed him the ball, and he bounced it twice and tossed it unsuccessfully at the basket.

They chose up sides, and he, the unknown quantity, was picked last, which struck him as reasonable enough. He was on the Skins team, and shucked his shirt, which made him feel a little self-conscious, but that was nothing compared to the self-consciousness that ensued when the game began.

Because he didn't know how to play. He was ineffectual at guarding, and more obviously inept when someone tossed him the ball and he didn't know what to do with it. "Shoot," someone yelled, and he shot and missed. "Here, here!" someone called out, and his pass was intercepted. He just didn't know what he was doing, and before long his teammates figured out as much and stopped passing him the ball.

After fifteen or twenty minutes, the Shirts were a little more than halfway to the number of points that would end the game when a boy a grade ahead of Keller showed up. "Hey, it's Lassman," Randy or Andy said. "Lassman, take over for Keller."

And just like that, Lassman, suddenly shirtless, was in and Keller was out. This, too, struck him as reasonable enough. He went to the sidelines and put his shirt on, relief and disappointment settling over him in equal parts. For a few minutes, he stood there watching the others play, and relief faded while disappointment swelled. Well, I better be getting home now, he planned to say, and he rehearsed the line, rephrasing it in his mind, giving it different inflections. But nobody was paying any attention to him, so why say anything? He turned around and went home.

When his mother asked him about it, he said it had turned out okay, but he wouldn't be going over there anymore. They had regular teams, he said, and he didn't really fit in. She looked at him for a moment, then let it go.

A few days later he came home from school to see two workmen mounting a backboard and basket on the Keller garage. At dinner he wanted to ask her about it, but didn't know how to start. She didn't say anything either at first, and years later, when he heard the expression "the elephant in the living room that nobody talks about," he thought of that basketball backboard.

But then she did talk about it. "I thought it would be good to have," she said. "You can go out there and practice anytime you want, and the other boys will see you there and come over and play."

She was half right. He practiced, dribbling, driving toward the basket, trying set shots and jump shots and hook shots from different angles. He paced off a foul line and practiced foul shots. If practice didn't make perfect, it certainly didn't hurt. He got better.

And the other boys saw him there, she was right about that, too. But nobody ever came over to play, and before long he stopped going out there himself. Then he got an after-school job, and he put the basketball in the garage and forgot about it.

The backboard stayed where it was, securely mounted on the garage. It was the elephant in the driveway that nobody talked about.

*　　*　　*

The Pacers won in overtime, in what Keller supposed was an exciting game, although it didn't excite him much. He didn't care who won, and found his attention drifting throughout, even at the game's most crucial moments. The fact that the visiting team was the New York Knicks didn't make any difference to him. He didn't follow basketball, and his devotion to the city of New York didn't make him a partisan follower of the city's sports teams.

Except for the Yankees. He liked the Yankees and enjoyed it when they won. But he didn't eat his heart out when on rare occasions they lost. As far as he was concerned, getting upset over the outcome of a sports event was like getting depressed when a movie had a sad ending. I mean, get a grip, man. It's only a movie, it's only a ball game.

He walked to his car, which was where he'd parked it, and drove to his motel, which was where he'd left it. He was $75 richer than he'd been a few hours ago, and his only regret was that he hadn't thought to sell both tickets. And skip the game.

*   *   *

Grondahl had a backboard in his driveway.

That was the target's name, Meredith Grondahl, and when Keller had first seen it, before Dot showed him the photograph, he'd supposed it was a woman. He'd even said, "A woman?" and Dot had asked him if he'd become a sexist overnight. "You've done women before," she reminded him. "You've always been an equal-opportunity kind of guy. But all that's beside the point, because this particular Meredith is a man."

What, he'd wondered, did Meredith's friends call him for short? Merry? Probably not, Keller decided. If he had a nickname, it was probably Bud or Mac or Bubba.

Grondahl, he figured, meant *green valley* in whatever Scandinavian language Meredith's forebears had spoken. So maybe the guy's friends called him Greenie.

Or maybe not.

The backboard, which Keller saw on a drive-by the morning after the basketball game, was freestanding, mounted on a post just a couple of feet in front of the garage. It was a two-car garage, and the post was positioned so that it didn't block access to either side.

The garage door was closed, so Keller couldn't tell how many cars it held at the moment. Nor was anybody shooting baskets in the driveway. Keller drove off picturing Grondahl playing a solitary game, dribbling, shooting, all the while considering how his testimony might expose corporate shenanigans, making of basketball a meditative experience.

You could get a lot of thinking done that way. Provided you were alone and didn't have to break your concentration by interacting with somebody else.

*　*　*

South and east of downtown Indianapolis, tucked into a shopping mall, Keller found a stamp dealer named Hubert Haas. He'd done business with the man in the past, when he'd managed to outbid other collectors for lots Haas offered on eBay. So the name rang a bell when he came across it in the yellow pages.

He'd brought his Scott catalog, which he used as a checklist, so he could be sure he wasn't buying stamps he already owned. Haas, a plump and owlish young man who looked as though his chief exercise consisted of driving past a health club, was happy to show Keller his stock. He did almost all of his business online, he confided, and hardly ever had a real customer in the shop, so this was a treat for him.

So why pay rent? Why not work out of his house?

"Buying," Haas said. "I've got a presence in a high-traffic mall. That keeps the noncollectors aware of me. Uncle Fred dies, they inherit his stamp collection, who do they bring it to? Somebody they heard of, and they not only heard of Hubert Haas, they know he's for real, because he's got a store in the Glendale Mall to prove it. And then there's the walk-in who buys a starter album for his kid, the collector who runs out of hinges or Showgard mounts or needs to replace a lost pair of tongs. Helps with the rent, but buying's the real reason."

Keller found a comforting quantity of stamps to buy from Haas, including an inexpensive but curiously elusive set of Venezuelan airmails. He walked out imbued with a sense of accomplishment and took a few minutes to walk around the mall, to see what further accomplishments might be there for the taking.

The mall had the sort of stores malls usually have, and he found it easy enough to scan their window displays and walk on by. Until he came to the library.

Who had ever heard of a public library in a shopping mall? But that's what this was, occupying substantial space on the second and third levels, and complete with a turnstile and, yes, a metal detector, its purpose unapparent to Keller. Was there a problem of folks toting guns in hollowed-out books?

No matter. Keller wasn't carrying a gun or anything metallic but a handful of coins and his car keys. He entered without raising any alarms, and ten minutes later he was scanning back issues of the *Indianapolis Star,* learning all manner of things about Meredith Grondahl.

*   *   *

"It's pretty interesting," he told Dot. "There's this company called Central Indiana Finance. They buy and sell mortgages and do a lot of refinancing. The stock's traded on Nasdaq. The symbol is CIFI, but when people talk about it, they refer to it as Indy Fi."

"If that's interesting," she said, "I'd hate to hear your idea of a real yawner."

"That's not the interesting part."

"No kidding."

"The stock's very volatile," he said. "It pays a high dividend, which makes it attractive to investors, but it could be vulnerable to changes in interest rates, which makes it speculative, I guess. And a couple of hedge funds have shorted the stock heavily, along with a lot of private traders.

"Let me know when we get to the interesting part, will you, Keller?"

"Well, it's all kind of interesting," he said. "You walk around in a shopping mall, you don't expect to find out this stuff."

"Here I am, finding it out without even leaving the house."

"There's this class-action suit," he said. "Brought on behalf of the Indy Fi stockholders, though probably ninety-nine percent of them are opposed to the whole idea of the suit. The suit charges the company's management with irregularities and cover-ups, that sort of thing. It's the people who shorted the stock who are behind the suit, the hedge fund guys, and their whole reason for bringing it seems to be to destroy confidence in the company and further depress the price of the stock."

"Can they do that?"

"Anybody can sue anybody. All they risk, really, is their legal expenses and having the suit get tossed out of court. Meanwhile the company has to defend the suit, and the controversy keeps the stock price depressed, and even if the suit gets settled in the company's favor, the short interests will have had a chance to make money."

"I don't really care about any of this," Dot said, "but I have to admit you're starting to get me interested, although I couldn't tell you why. And our quarry's going to testify for the people bringing the suit?"

"No."

"No?"

"They subpoenaed him," he said. "Meredith Grondahl. He's an assistant to the chief financial officer, and he's supposed to testify about irregularities in their accounting procedures, but he's no whistle-blower. He's more of a cheerleader. As far as he's concerned, Indy Fi's a great company, and his personal 401(k) is full of the company's stock. He can't really damage either side in the suit."

"Then why would somebody decide to summon you to Indianapolis?"

"That's what I've been wondering."

He thought the connection might have broken, but she was just taking her time thinking it over. "Well," she said at length, "even though this gets us interested, Keller, we're also disinterested, if you get my drift."

"It doesn't change things."

"That's my drift, all right. We've got an assignment and the fee's half paid already, so the whys and wherefores don't make any difference. Somebody doesn't want the guy to testify about something, and as soon as you nail that down, you can come on home and play with your stamps. You bought some today, didn't you tell me that earlier? So come on home and you can paste them in your book. And we'll get paid, and you can buy some more."

★   ★   ★

The next morning, Keller got up early and drove straight to Grondahl's house in Carmel. He parked across the street and sat behind the wheel of his rented Ford, a newspaper propped on the steering wheel. He read the national and international news, then the sports. The Pacers, he noted, had won last night, in double overtime. The local sportswriter described the game as thrilling and said the shot from half-court that fell in just as the second overtime period ran out demonstrated "the moral integrity and indomitable spirit of our guys." Keller wished he'd taken it a small step further, claiming the ball's unerring flight to the basket as proof of the Almighty's clear preference for the local heroes.

Reading, he kept an eye on Grondahl's front door, waiting for Greenie to appear. He still hadn't done so by the time Keller was done with the sports pages. Well, it was early, he told himself, and turned to the business section. The Dow had been up, he learned, in heavy volume.

He knew what this meant—he wasn't an idiot—but it was something he never followed because it didn't concern him or hold interest for him. Keller earned good money when he worked, and he didn't live high, and for years he had saved a substantial portion of the money that came into his hands. But he'd never bought stocks or mutual funds with it. He tucked some of it into a safe-deposit box and the rest into savings accounts. The money grew slowly if it grew at all, but it didn't shrink, and there was something to be said for that.

Eventually he reached a point where retirement was an option, and realized that he'd need a hobby to fill the golden years. He took up stamp collecting again, but in a far more serious fashion this time around. He started spending serious money on stamps, and his retirement savings waned as his collection grew.

So he'd never managed to get interested in the world of stocks and bonds. This morning, for some reason, he found the business section interesting, not least because of an article on Central Indiana Finance. CIFI, which opened the day at

$43.27 a share, had fluctuated wildly, up five points at its high for the day, down as much as seven, and finishing the day at $40.35. On the one hand, he learned, the shorts were scrambling to cover before the ex-dividend date, when they would be liable for the company's substantial dividend. On the other, players were continuing to short the stock and drive the price down, encouraged by the pending class-action lawsuit.

He was thinking about the article when the door opened and Meredith Grondahl emerged.

Grondahl was dressed for the office, wearing a dark gray suit and a white shirt and a striped tie and carrying a briefcase. That was to be expected, it being a Thursday, but Keller realized he'd unconsciously been waiting for the man to show himself in shorts and a singlet, dribbling a basketball.

In the driveway, Grondahl paid no attention to the basketball backboard but triggered a button to raise the garage door. There was, Keller noted, only one car in the garage, and a slew of objects (he made out a barbecue grill and some lawn furniture) took up the space where a second car might otherwise have been parked.

Grondahl, given his position in the corporate world, could clearly have afforded a second car for his wife. Which suggested to Keller that he didn't have a wife. The fine suburban house, on the other hand, suggested that he'd had one once upon a time, and Keller suspected she'd chosen to go away and had taken her car with her.

Poor bastard.

Keller, comfortable behind the wheel, stayed where he was while Grondahl backed his Grand Cherokee out of the driveway and drove off somewhere. He thought about following the man, but why? For that matter, why had he come here to watch him leave the house?

Of course, there were more basic questions than that. Why wasn't he getting down to business and fulfilling his contract? Why was he watching Meredith Grondahl instead of punching the man's ticket?

And a question that was, strictly speaking, none of his business, but no less compelling for it: Why did somebody want Meredith Grondahl dead?

Thinking, he reminded himself, was one thing. Acting was another. His mind could go where it wanted, as long as his body did what it was supposed to.

Drive back to the motel, he told himself, and find a way to use up the day. And tonight, when Meredith Grondahl comes home, be here waiting for him. Then return this car to Hertz, pick up a fresh one from somebody else, and go home.

He nodded, affirming the wisdom of that course of action. Then he started the engine, backed up a few yards, and swung the car into the Grondahl driveway. He got out, found the button Grondahl had used to raise the garage door, pressed it, got back in the car, and pulled into the spot recently vacated by the Grand Cherokee.

There was a small boulder the size of a bowling ball standing just to the right of Grondahl's front door. It might have been residue from a local avalanche, but Keller thought that unlikely. It looked to him like something to hide a spare house key under, and he was right about that. He picked up the key, opened the door, and let himself in.

★   ★   ★

There was a chance, of course, that there was still a Mrs. Grondahl and that she was home. Maybe she didn't drive, maybe she was an agoraphobe who never left the house. Keller thought this was unlikely, and it didn't take him long to rule it out. The house was antiseptically clean, but that didn't necessarily signal a woman's presence; Grondahl might be neat by nature, or he might have someone who cleaned for him once or twice a week.

There were no women's clothes in the closets or dressers, and that was a tip-off. And there were two dressers, a highboy and a low triple dresser with a vanity mirror, and the low dresser's drawers were empty, except for one which Grondahl had begun to use for suspenders and cuff links and such. So there had indeed been a Mrs. Grondahl, and now there wasn't.

Keller, having established this much, wandered around the two-story house trying to see what else he could learn. Except he wasn't trying very hard, because he wasn't really looking for anything, or if he was, he didn't know what it might be. It was more as if he was trying to get the feel of the man, and that didn't make any sense, but then what sense was there in letting yourself into the house of the man you were planning to kill?

Maybe the best course of action was to settle in and wait. Sooner or later Grondahl would return to the house, and he'd probably be alone when he did, since he was beginning to strike Keller as your typical lonely guy.

Your typical lonely guy. The phrase resonated oddly for Keller, because he couldn't help identifying with it. He was, face it, a lonely guy himself, although he didn't suppose you could call him typical. Did this resonance get in the way of what he was supposed to do? He thought it over and decided it did and it didn't. It made him sympathize with Meredith Grondahl, and thus disinclined to kill him; on the other hand, wouldn't he be doing the poor bastard a favor?

He frowned, found a chair to sit in. When Grondahl came home, he'd be alone. And he'd be relieved to return to the safe harbor of his empty house. So he'd be unguarded, and getting taken from behind by a man with a club or a knife or a garrote—Keller hadn't decided yet—was the last thing he'd worry about.

It'd be the last thing, all right.

★　★　★

The problem, of course, was to figure out what to do with the day. If he just holed up here, it looked to be a minimum of eight hours before Grondahl returned, and the wait might well stretch to twelve or more. He could read, if he could find something he felt like reading, or watch TV with the sound off, or—

Hell. His car was parked in Grondahl's garage. That assured that the neighbors wouldn't see it and grow suspicious, but what happened when Grondahl came home and found his parking spot taken?

No good at all. Keller would have to move the car, and the sooner the better, because for all he knew, Grondahl might feel the need to come home for lunch. So what should he do? Drive it around the block, leave it in front of some stranger's house? And then he'd have to return on foot, hoping no one noticed him, because nobody walked anywhere in the suburbs and a pedestrian was suspicious by definition.

Maybe waiting for Grondahl was a bad idea altogether. Maybe he should just get the hell out and go back to his motel.

He was on his way to the door when he heard a key in the lock.

Funny how decisions had a way of making themselves. Grondahl, who had returned for something he'd forgotten, was insisting on being put out of his misery. Keller backed out of the entrance hall and waited around the corner in the dining room.

The door opened, and Keller heard steps, a lot of them. And a voice called out, "Hello? Anybody home?"

Keller's first thought was that it was an odd thing for Grondahl to do. Then another voice, pitched lower, said, "You better hope you don't get an answer to that one."

Had Grondahl brought a friend? No, of course not, he realized. It wasn't Grondahl, who was almost certainly doing something corporate at his office. It was someone else, a pair of somebody elses, and they'd let themselves in with a key and wanted the house to be empty.

If they came into the dining room, he'd have to do something about it. If they took a different tack, he'd have to slip out of the door as soon as the opportunity presented itself. And hide in the garage, waiting for them to emerge from the house and drive away, so that *he* could drive away, too.

"I think the den," one voice said. "House like this, guy living alone, he's gotta have a den, don't you think?"

"Or a home office," the other voice offered.

"A den, a home office, what the hell's the difference?"

"One's deductible."

"But it's the same room, isn't it? No matter what you call it?"

"I suppose, but for tax purposes—"

"Jesus," the first voice said. It was, Keller noted, vaguely familiar, but maybe that was just because the speaker had a Hoosier accent. "I'm not planning to audit his fucking tax returns," the man said. "I just want to plant an envelope in his desk."

Out the door, Keller told himself. Let them plant whatever they wanted in whatever they decided to call the room with the desk in it. He'd be gone, and they'd never know he'd been there in the first place.

But when he left the dining room, something led him not to the door but away from it. He tagged along after the two men and caught a glimpse of them as he rounded a corner into the living room. He saw them from the back, and only for a moment, but that was time enough to note that they were both of average height and medium build and that one was bald as an egg. The other might or might not have hair; you couldn't tell at a glance, because he was wearing a cap.

A green cap with gold piping, and when had Keller seen a cap like that? Oh, right. Same place he'd heard that voice. It was a John Deere cap, and the man wearing it had met him at the airport and given him tickets to that goddamn basketball game. Depressed the hell out of him, ruined his first evening in Indianapolis, and thanks a lot for that, you son of a bitch.

Keller, oddly irritated, padded silently after the two of them and lurked around a corner while they stationed themselves at Meredith Grondahl's desk. "Definitely a home office," the bald man said. "You got your filing cabinets, you got your desk and your computer, you got your Canon desktop copier, you got your printer and your fax machine—"

"You also got a big-screen TV and a La-Z-Boy recliner, which shouts den to me," the man in the Deere cap said. "Look at this, will you? The drawer's locked."

"This one ain't. Neither's this one. You got seven drawers, for chrissake, who cares if one of 'em's locked?"

"This is incriminating evidence, right? Dangerous stuff?"

"So?"

"You got a desk with a locked drawer, don't you think that's the drawer you're gonna keep the shit in?"

"The cops in this town," the bald man said, "they find a

locked drawer, they might just decide it's too much trouble to open it."

"Point."

Keller, out of sight in the adjoining room, heard a drawer open and close.

"There," the Deere cap said. "Right where they'll find it."

"And if Grondahl finds it first?"

"I figure that's in the next day or two, because he's not gonna wait that long."

"The shooter."

"A real piece of work."

"You told me."

"I tell you how he walks up to a car in the airport lot and drives off with it? Has a master key on his ring, pops the lock like it was made for it. 'I'll just borrow it,' he tells me."

"Casual son of a bitch."

"But how long is he gonna drive around in a stolen vehicle? I'm surprised he hasn't made his move already."

"Maybe he has. Maybe we go to the bedroom, we find Grondahl sleeping with the fishes."

"That'd be in the river, wouldn't it? You don't find fishes sleeping in beds."

Oysters, Keller thought. In oyster beds. He retreated a few steps, because there was no longer any reason to stick around. These two worked for the client, and they were just planting evidence to support the same end as Grondahl's removal. They could have let him plant the stuff himself, all part of the service, but they hadn't thought of that, or hadn't trusted him, so—

The bald guy said, "It's not really finished until he's dead, you know."

"Grondahl."

"Well, that, obviously. No, I mean the shooter. He's killed, and he's the one took out Grondahl, and he's tied to Indy Fi's management. Then you got them good."

Jesus, Keller thought. And he'd almost walked away from this. They were moving, the two of them, and he moved, as well, so that he could wind up behind them when they headed for the door.

"All part of the plan," Deere Cap said.

"But if he just goes and steals another car and flies back to wherever he came from—"

"Portland, I think somebody said."

"Which Portland?"

"Who cares? He ain't making it back. What I did, I stuck a bug on the underside of his back bumper while he was showing me how slick his key worked. He went to that basketball game, incidentally. Guy loves basketball."

"Who won the game?"

"You'd have to ask him. That Global Positioning shit is wonderful. He's at the Rodeway Inn near the I-69 exit. That's our next stop. What we'll do, I got a pair of tickets for tomorrow night's game, and we'll leave 'em at the motel desk for him. What I figure—"

It might have been interesting to learn how the basketball tickets were part of the man's plan, but they were almost at the door at this point, and that was as far as Keller could let them get. Following them, he'd paused long enough to snatch a brass candlestick off a tabletop, and he closed the distance between him and them and swung the candlestick in a sweeping arc that ended at a patch of gold braid on the green John Deere cap. It caught the man in midstride and midsentence, and he never finished either. He dropped in his tracks, and the bald man was just beginning to take it in, just beginning to react, when Keller backhanded him with the candlestick, striking him right across his endless forehead. The scalp split and blood spurted, and the man let out a cry and clapped a hand to the spot, and Keller swung the candlestick a third time, like a woodsman with an ax, and brought it down authoritatively on the back of the bald man's neck.

Jack be nimble, he thought.

It took Keller a moment to catch his breath, but only a moment. He stood there still holding on to the candlestick and looked down at the two men lying a couple of feet apart on the patterned area rug. They both looked dead. He checked, and the bald man was every bit as dead as he looked, but the guy in the cap still had a pulse.

Keller, waiting for him to regain consciousness, did what he could to clean up. He washed and wiped the candlestick and put it back where he'd found it. He wasn't going to be able to do anything about the blood on the rug, and couldn't even make an attempt while the two of them were lying on it.

He stationed himself alongside them and waited. Eventually the Deere cap guy came to, and Keller asked him a couple of questions. The man didn't want to answer them, but eventually he did, and then there was no need to keep him alive anymore.

The hardest part, really, was getting the two bodies out of the house and into their car, which turned out to be the same Hyundai squareback that had picked him up at the airport. It was parked in the driveway, and the keys were in the Deere cap guy's pocket.

He could see how it was all going to work out.

★   ★   ★

"Like we don't have enough to contend with," Dot said. "You do everything right and then you get killed by the client. This business isn't the bed of roses people think it is."

"Is that what people think?"

"Who knows what people think, Keller? I know what I think. I think you better come home."

"Not just yet."

"Oh?"

"One of the fellows gave me a name."

"Probably his very last words."

"Just about."

"And you want to get together with this fellow?"

"I probably won't be able to," he said. "My guess is he'll be overcome by fear or remorse."

"And he'll take his own life?"

"It wouldn't surprise me."

"And it wouldn't start me crying, I have to tell you that. All right, sure, why not? We can't let people get away with that crap. Do what you have to do and then come home. We got half in front, and I don't suppose there's any way to collect the back half, so—"

"Don't be too sure of that," Keller said. "I've been think-ing, and why don't you see how this sounds to you?"

★   ★   ★

When Meredith Grondahl pulled into his driveway around five-thirty, Keller was parked halfway down the block at the curb. He got out of the car and stood where he could watch the Grondahl driveway, and after five minutes Grondahl emerged from the house. He'd changed from a suit and tie to sneakers and sweats, and he was dribbling a basketball. He took a shot, missed, took the ball as it came off the backboard, and drove for a layup.

Keller headed up the driveway. Grondahl turned, saw him, and tossed him the ball. Keller shot, missed.

They played for a few minutes, just taking turns trying shots, most of which failed to make it through the hoop. Then Keller sank a fade-away jump shot, surprising both of them, and Grondahl said, "Nice."

"Luck," Keller said. "Listen, we should talk."

"Huh?"

"You had a couple of visitors earlier today. They got into an argument, and they bled all over your rug."

"My rug."

"That area rug with the geometric pattern, right when you come into the house."

"*That's* what was different," Grondahl said. "The rug wasn't there. I knew there was something, but I couldn't put my finger on it."

"Or your foot."

"You said there was blood on it?"

"Their blood, and you don't want that. Anyway, you get a lot of blood on a rug and it's never the same. So the rug's not there anymore."

"And the two men?"

"They're not there anymore, either."

Grondahl had been holding the basketball, and now he turned and flipped it at the basket. It hit the rim and bounced away, and neither man made any move toward it.

Grondahl said, "These men. They came into my house?"

"Right through the door over there. They had a key—not the one you keep under the fake rock, either."

"And then, inside my house, they got into an argument and . . . killed each other?"

"That's close enough," Keller said.

Grondahl thought about it. "I think I get the picture," he said.

"You probably get as much of the picture as you need to get."

"That's what it sounds like. Why did they come here in the first place?"

"They were going to leave an envelope."

"An envelope."

"In a desk drawer."

"And the envelope contained . . ."

"A motive for a murder."

"My murder?"

Keller nodded.

"They were going to kill me?"

"Their employer," Keller said, "had already hired someone else for that job."

"Who?"

"Some stranger," Keller said. "Some faceless assassin flown in from out of town."

Grondahl looked thoughtfully at him, the way one might look at a putative faceless assassin. "But he's not going to do it," he said. "At least I don't think he is."

"He's not."

"Why?"

"Because he happened to learn that once his job was done, they were planning to kill him."

"And pin everything on the Indy Fi management," Grondahl said. "I was killed to keep me from giving testimony I never had any thought of giving in the first place. Jesus, it might have worked. I can imagine what must have been in the envelope. Is it still around? The envelope. Or did it disappear along with the two men?"

"The men will turn up eventually," Keller said. "The envelope is gone forever."

Grondahl nodded, retrieved the basketball, bounced it a few times. Keller could almost see the wheels turning in the man's head. He was bright, Keller was pleased to note. You didn't have to spell things out for him, you gave him the first paragraph and he got the rest of the page on his own.

"I owe you," Grondahl said.

Keller shrugged.

"I mean it. You saved my life."

"I was saving my own at the time," Keller pointed out.

"When the two of them, uh, had their accident, I'll concede that was in your own self-interest. But you could have just walked away. And you certainly didn't have to show up here and fill me in. Which leads to a question."

"Why am I here?"

"If you don't mind my asking."

"Well, actually," Keller said, "I have a couple of questions of my own."

★   ★   ★

"I think I get it," Dot said. "This is a new thing for me, Keller. I wrote it down, and I'm going to read it back to you, to make sure I've got it all straight."

She did, and he told her she had it right.

"That's a miracle," she said, "because it was a little like taking dictation in a foreign language. I'll take care of it tomorrow. Can I do it all in a day?"

"Probably."

"Then I will. And you'll be . . ."

"Biding my time in Indianapolis. I switched motels, by the way."

"Good."

"And found the bug they put on my bumper, and switched it to the bumper of another Ford the same color as mine."

"That should muddy the waters nicely."

"I thought so. So I'll do what I have to do, and then I'll be a couple of days driving home."

"Not to worry," she said. "I'll leave the porch light on for you."

★ ★ ★

It was a full week later when Keller drove his rented Toyota through the Lincoln Tunnel and found his way to the National garage, where he turned it in. He went home, unpacked his bag, and spent two full hours working on his stamp collection before he picked up the phone and called White Plains.

"Come right on up," Dot said, "so I can turn the light off. It's attracting moths."

In the kitchen of the house on Taunton Place, Dot poured him a big glass of iced tea and told him they'd done very well indeed. "I was wondering at first," she said, "because I bought a big chunk of Indy Fi, and the first thing it did was go down a couple of points. But then it turned around and went back up again, and the last I checked it's up better than ten points from when I bought it. I bought options, too, for increased leverage. I don't understand how they work exactly, but I was able to buy them, and this morning I sold them, and do you want to know exactly how much we made on them?"

"It doesn't have to be exact."

She told him, down to the last decimal point, and it was a satisfying number.

"We're about that much ahead on the actual stock we bought," she said, "but I haven't sold that yet, because I kind of like owning it, especially the way it's going up. Maybe we can sell half and let the rest ride, something like that, but I figured I'd wait and see what you want to do."

"We'll work it out."

"My thought exactly." She sat forward, rubbed her hands together. "What really kick-started things," she said, "was when Clocker killed himself. His hedge fund had been shorting Indy Fi's stock all along, and he was behind the lawsuit they were going through, and when he was out of the picture, and in a way that put the cloud right over his own head, well, the price of Indy Fi's stock could go back where it belonged. And the price of his hedge fund . . ."

"Sank?"

"Like a stone," she said. "And we sold it short and covered our shorts very cheaply and made a killing. It's nice to make a killing without having to drive anywhere. How did you know how to do all this?"

"I had advice," he said. "From a fellow who couldn't do any of this himself because it would be insider trading. But you and I aren't insiders, so there's no problem."

"Well, I've got no problem with it myself, Keller. That's for sure. You know, this isn't the first time you've wound up killing a client of ours."

"I know."

"This one brought it on himself, no question. But usually it costs us money, and this time we came out way ahead. You're going to be able to buy a veritable shitload of stamps."

"I was thinking about that."

"And we're a giant stride closer to being able to retire, when the time comes."

"I was thinking about that, too."

"And you bonded with what's-his-name."

"Meredith Grondahl."

"What do his friends call him, did you happen to find out?"

"It never came up. I'm not sure he's got any friends."

"Oh."

"I was thinking I ought to send him something, Dot. I had an idea of how to make money in the market, but he spelled the whole thing out for me. I didn't know a thing about options, and I never would have thought of shorting the hedge fund."

"How big a share do you want to send him?"

"Not a share. He's pretty straight-arrow, and even if he weren't, the last thing he wants is cash he can't explain. No, I was thinking more of a present. A token, really, but something he'd like to have and probably wouldn't ever buy for himself."

"Like?"

"Season tickets to the Pacers home games. He loves basketball, and a pair of courtside season tickets should really do it for the guy."

"What's it cost?" Before he could answer, she waived the question away. "Not enough to matter, not the way we just made out. That's a great idea, Keller. And who knows? Next time you're in Indianapolis, maybe the two of you can take in a game."

He shook his head. "No," he said. "Leave me out of it. I hate basketball."

NOTHING BUT NET

Jeffery Deaver

He's stupid. And he makes three million a year."

"And you won't feel guilty getting a stupid man mixed up in a deal like this?" T. D. Randall asked.

Andy Cabot shook his head, sipped more beer and glanced out the greasy window as an ambulance eased through Midtown traffic. "I don't feel guilt. Never have. It's inefficient."

"Yeah?"

"The point I was making is, since he's stupid he's going to be more likely to go for it."

Cabot and Randall were in Ernie's, a small bar near Madison Square Garden. The place, a total dive, was a relic; there used to be dozens of these old sports bars in the neighborhood but they'd been squeezed out by the same fast-food franchises populating strip malls all over the country. Andy Cabot didn't really like it here but he couldn't see planning a deal like they were working on now while sitting next to the salad bar at Ruby Tuesday.

Randall called for another Stroh's. "I hear you talking, Andy. But the thing is, I don't know sports that good. Is this guy really the one we want? Danny Wa—"

"Shhh." Cabot waved his hand to shut the man up. Ernie's was a bastion for serious sports people and the name Danny Washington would turn a few heads, the sober ones at least. If the deal went south and people heard that Washington had been caught up in a scandal, someone might just remember that these two skinny white guys, unshaven, dressed in scuzzy jeans and T-shirts, had been whispering about the player.

"I mean, how good is he?" Randall asked.

"Don't get any better than him when it comes to free throws and treys."

"What's a trey?"

"Three-point shot. You know, from outside the arc."

"Whatever."

Cabot was amazed that Randall didn't know about Washington or about treys. He probably didn't know what the arc line was either.

"But how do you know he's stupid enough to go for it?"

"I joined the gym where he works out. And I got—"

"You're in a gym?" Randall laughed, glancing at the man's scrawny frame.

Cabot ignored the put-down. "I got to talking with him. Washington can hardly hang a sentence together. He lifts iron, he jumps rope. He stands on the free-throw line on the half-court and lobs basketballs for, like, two hours straight. Never gets bored. You ask him a question and he looks at you for a minute like you're from Neptune or something. And it takes him another minute to figure out an answer."

"But didn't he go to college?"

"Nope. He got drafted right out of high school. And he's a free agent. There's nobody looking over his shoulder."

"You think this deal'll work?" Randall asked.

"I *know* it will."

Andy Cabot, lifelong resident of Hell's Kitchen, on the west side of New York, had had three or four dozen jobs in his life. He'd tried his hand at a hundred different hustles. Some worked out, some didn't. He'd made some good money, lost more. He'd owned two houses, lost one to an ex and one to the bank. And, having just stepped blindly into middle age, he'd recently spent copious time reassessing his life situation and had come to the conclusion that he wanted more out of life than a disability payment of two thousand bucks a month for a faked back injury and twelve thousand in the bank. This introspection, goosed by massive quantities of Old Milwaukee one night, led ultimately to his asking the question: How do people make real money?

And the answer, he realized, was that it didn't matter exactly *what* they did as long as it involved something they loved. That was the key to success.

So Andy Cabot came to a decision. He abandoned the slip-and-falls, the shoplifting, the rigged poker games, the real estate hustles, the knockoff polo shirts . . . Fom now on, his only "deals"—his word for scams—would be in a subject he loved and knew a lot about: basketball.

One day when he'd been channel surfing, he'd watched an ESPN interview with Danny Washington, who'd just thrown more than two thousand free throws in a row as part of a benefit for St. Vincent Hospital's Children's Unit. When asked why he didn't try to shoot another four or five hundred and beat the world record, the big man had said, blinking, that he'd thought it'd be more fun to go hang out with the kids.

Stupid, thought Andy Cabot, irritated that while the man probably had the skill to break the world record he simply didn't have the brains.

But then Cabot got to thinking that the fact that this rich basketball player was stupid was a good thing, something he could *use*. And he'd come up with the plan he was now pitching to T. D. Randall, a wannabe mafioso from Bay Ridge, Brooklyn, he'd met last month here at Ernie's.

Cabot now ordered another beer and continued. "He doesn't know squat about *any*thing. All he cares about is his mother, grandmother, brother and sister. They live in Maryland, where he grew up. He doesn't hang out with the rest of the players, doesn't have a girlfriend. There're three things he feels passionate about: his family, playing basketball and . . ."

Randall looked at Cabot, who'd let the sentence dangle tantalizingly. "What?" Randall asked with faint exasperation.

". . . and complaining about taxes."

"He complains about taxes?"

"We're shooting the breeze the other day and the next thing I know he's going on and on about taxes. Sounds to me like when he started making real money he never knew the government'd take so much. I mean, maybe he never had a job before this and didn't even know about taxes. I wouldn't be surprised."

"Is that, like, a significant fact? About him and taxes?"

"Oh," Andy Cabot said slowly, "it's very significant."

*   *   *

Andy Cabot opened the door of his apartment on West Forty-fourth Street, near the Hudson River. The skinny five-foot-six man looked up into Danny Washington's eyes, way above his, and said, "Hey, Danny, come on in. You want a beer?"

"Don't drink."

The player, in workout clothes, followed his host down the

corridor of the old, dusty apartment, looking around with cautious eyes as if he were staring at Donald Trump luxury. A ceramic eagle Cabot had bought at a street fair on Columbus Circle and a three-foot-high cigar store Indian—plastic and made in Taiwan—got approving looks. One print, in a Woolworth's frame, stopped Washington cold.

"I like that," the player said in his infuriatingly slow voice. "The guy who did it, he live 'round here?"

"Van Gogh? No, he's dead."

Washington leaned forward, studied the stained picture. "Man, too bad. What happened?"

"He lived a long time ago."

"Oh. You know, I don't like pictures of flowers as a rule. But that one's okay. You ever wanna sell that, you let me know."

"I will, Danny. Come on in the living room. This is my friend Tommy Randall."

The big man folded his massive hand around Randall's.

"T. D. lives over in Brooklyn." Cabot said this with special emphasis on the borough. Suggesting that Randall had some connections with one of the crime organizations there—to impress Washington. But the player didn't get the connection. He said slowly, looking at the floor, "Brooklyn. I been there a few times. To see the Mets."

"That's Queens," Randall said, glancing uncertainly at Cabot.

Washington paused a moment. Then he frowned. "I thought Shea Stadium was on Long Island."

"It *is* on Long Island. Queens and Brooklyn're both on Long Island."

"Oh."

Another man, older, with thinning curly hair, sat in the corner of the living room. He was dressed in a navy-blue suit, white shirt and tie. Two briefcases sat in front of him. The man didn't say anything and Cabot didn't introduce him.

Cabot sat and gestured Washington into a chair. It creaked under his weight. According to the stats he was six-eight and weighed 245 pounds but in this small apartment he seemed a lot bigger than that.

"Sure you don't want a beer?"

"Nope."

Cabot said to Washington, "You know much about me, Danny?"

"Not too much. I seen you 'round the gym in the last month or so. And I seen you hanging 'round the Garden."

"You know what I do?"

"Most people hang out 'round the Garden, either they're scalping tickets or taking bets on the games, you know. I'm guessing you do some betting."

Cabot said, "That—and a few other things. Mostly I make money for people."

Washington's face broke into a slow smile. "That's a good job."

"You've got a good job too. And you're good at it. I saw you last week. Against the Bulls. Twenty-four points."

"I guess."

"Is that good?" Randall asked.

Cabot laughed and rolled his eyes, said to Washington, "My friend from Brooklyn here knows all about lending money and all about getting paid back. But he doesn't know sports."

"I know baseball," Randall said defensively.

"The Mets," Washington said, squinting to see if this was an appropriate comment.

"That's my team." The man from Brooklyn offered a smile to his huge new buddy.

Cabot nodded toward Washington and said to Randall, "Danny's a two-guard. Same as Michael Jordan. His speciality's free throws and treys. He's one of the best in the NBA."

"I'm not too good under the boards," the player said slowly.

"Who cares?" Cabot asked. "You can shoot the long ones like nobody's business."

"I guess." A cautious glance toward the man in the corner, who still said nothing and just stared at the tall man. At every pause in the conversation the rustling sound of traffic racing through Hell's Kitchen filled the room, punctuated by horns and shouts.

"How come you're such a good shooter?" Cabot asked.

"I dunno. Just got some kind of sense," the big man said.

"Like Psychic Friends Hotline?" Randall suggested.

The big player didn't get the joke. He said seriously, "Naw, naw, not that stuff my grandma goes for. I can't explain it good. See, I'm not too smart—I got drafted by the Hawks right outta high school. I was probably gonna flunk out anyway. So I was thinking that maybe when you're like that you get this sixth sense or something. Somehow I just know things on the court before they happen. Like knowing when somebody's going to foul me. Or knowing, when I throw the ball, whether it'll be a miss or it'll be nothing but net."

"What's that mean?" Randall asked. "Nothing but net."

Cabot explained, "A perfect swish—the ball doesn't even hit the rim, just drops right through. All it touches is the net. And that's what Danny's treys and free throws do most of the time."

Washington shrugged. "It's not that hard. All's I'm doing is putting a nine-inch ball through a eighteen-inch hoop." He frowned in concentration as he thought. Then, after a long pause, he said, "The thing is, it's not just shooting—it's *seeing*."

"Seeing?" Randall asked.

"Yeah. Lotta players got good hands. But they don't have the eye." He pointed a huge finger at his right eye. "That's one thing God gave me. Maybe I didn't get a lotta brains but He gave me an eye." He lowered his hand and glanced at Cabot. "So what you ask me up here for?"

"You and me were talking in the gym the other day, Danny."

"Yeah, I remember."

"And you were saying you didn't like it that the government took half your money."

"All them taxes . . . Don't seem fair."

"And you were saying that makes you mad."

"Hells yeah, it makes me mad. But not much I can do about it."

"Maybe there *is* one thing you can do about it," Cabot said.

"What's that?"

"Make more money."

Washington nodded. "Might happen. My contract's up next year. Maybe my agent can get me more."

"Well, Danny, since you brought it up, there's something I have to show you."

Cabot took a piece of paper from a stained envelope and handed it to the player. "I've got a friend who works in the office of your team. He got his hands on a copy of this."

Washington took it uncertainly and Cabot had a moment's panic thinking that the man might be illiterate. But the player squinted and read over the sheet. As he struggled over the words his face grew troubled.

From: Head Coach Arnold Hopper
To: Management
Re: Daniel Washington
    This confirms our decision not to offer Washington a new contract for next year. He's shown some promise but his talent at shooting is offset by his lack of skill in making jump shots, not to mention his turnover record inside the wings. I'm also very troubled by his refusal to socialize with his teammates.

"Man," he said, shaking his head. "Arnie wrote *this*? This's bullshit. What's he mean, socialize?"

"Get along with the other players."

"It's not that . . . I like 'em all right. It's just I like to go home after playing. Watch TV, talk to my brother on the phone. And when I get a couple days off I go visit my mother and grandmother and my sister and her kids."

"I'm sorry, Danny. They don't seem to care."

Washington tossed the memo angrily on the floor. "This means I'm getting dropped?"

"I'm afraid so, Danny."

"Hell . . . what'm I gonna do?"

Finally the man in the corner spoke up. "Danny, what do you think of the Lakers?"

"That's a good team."

"How'd you like to play for them?"

"I always wanted to play for L.A." A grin broke out on his face. "Weather's nice out there."

"Nicer than here," the man said.

"If I played for them I could move my grandmother out there. She's eighty-two this month. Lives outside Baltimore. She don't like the cold." Then he frowned. "But the Lakers got Bob Klinger—that big kid from Carolina. He shoots treys real good. They don't need me."

Cabot glanced at the man in the corner and said, "Danny, this is Mr. Pettiway."

"Hello, sir."

Pettiway nodded.

"He's sort of an agent."

"Sort of?"

Pettiway nodded again. "Danny, the Lakers're prepared to offer you a three-year contract. They'll up your salary to four million the first year, five the second, six the third. I think we can even convince them to move your grandmother out there if you want."

"They'd do that?"

"They would, yes. They'd like you on the team real bad."

"This's sounding pretty good," Washington drawled.

Pettiway fell silent. Then Cabot nodded at him and the man continued. "Well, Danny, there *is* a little something else."

"What's that?"

"You're playing them tonight, right?"

"The Lakers? Yessir."

Pettiway said, "I could arrange for this contract for you— but the Lakers have to win."

"Man." Danny Washington shook his head. "I don't know if that's gonna happen. Doug Hamilton, their center, he's benched—his knee's out. And Sammy Johnston, he's back from that wrist surgery—first time he's played for months. Everybody's saying we'll win by twenty . . ." Then his eyes narrowed. "Wait . . . wait . . . You're saying you want me to do something to . . ."

The big player couldn't bring himself to say "throw the game," but he wasn't so stupid he didn't understand Pettiway's meaning. "The *Lakers* want me to do that?"

"No, no," Cabot said. "The team doesn't know anything

about it. This is something Mr. Pettiway and I've been working on. I told you my job is making money for people. We've got a lot of money tied up in bets on this game tonight. With Hamilton out and this being Johnston's first game in two months, you're right—the odds are real good for your team. So if the Lakers win we're going to make a lot of money. If that happens then Mr. Pettiway'll pull some strings at the Lakers and get you that contract. We can guarantee it."

A blank look filled the player's face as he looked around the room. His eyes settled on the van Gogh. What was he thinking? Cabot wondered. Anything at all?

Finally the player turned back to Pettiway. Washington squinted and said, "You guarantee it in *writing*?"

Cabot looked at Pettiway and grinned. "I told you Danny knows what he's about. Just 'cause a man talks slow doesn't mean he *is* slow."

Pettiway pulled a document out of one of his briefcases and slid it toward the player, who read it slowly, his lips moving. He read it again. Then once more. "Some of this I can't scope out. Maybe I should have my lawyer look it over. I get into trouble sometimes if I don't do that."

"Um, Danny," Pettiway said delicately, "we probably don't want to do that, now, do we? Not with the talk of making sure your team loses that game tonight."

"Oh, right. That'd be bad."

"Yes, it would."

Washington took the pen and looked over the paper again. "I don't know. I never done anything like this before."

At a glance from Cabot, Pettiway opened his second brief-case, revealing stacks of hundred-dollar bills. "Here's a signing bonus, Danny. Half a million. You were saying you didn't like

NOTHING BUT NET • 49

paying taxes? Well, since this's cash, you don't have to pay a penny in tax. It's yours if you sign now."

Washington's eyes slid to the memo from the head coach. "I gave the team everything I got and they treat me like that? Man, that's low." He gripped the pen in tight fingers.

"Go ahead, Danny," Cabot said.

The big man signed the letter. Then Pettiway did too and gave Washington a copy.

They shook hands.

Cabot grinned and said, "Maybe you don't drink beer, Danny, but I've got some champagne in the fridge. How 'bout we celebrate?"

But before he got halfway to the kitchen T. D. Randall pulled what looked like a walkie-talkie from his pocket and shouted, "I need backup, now!" He leapt to his feet, drawing a pistol from the back of his waistband and training it on Cabot.

"Jesus," Cabot gasped, eyes wide.

Pettiway stood up, confusion on his face. "What're you—"

And then the apartment door burst open and two men in suits, also brandishing guns, pushed inside. Badges hung from their necks.

Cabot snapped, "What the hell's going on?"

Pettiway looked horrified. One of the policemen—a short, muscular man—grabbed him and shoved him against the wall. "Don't move." He roughly frisked the man and cuffed him. The other did the same to Cabot, then to Washington.

The taller of the cops said, "I'm Detective Harvey, Midtown Vice." Then he recited, "You men are under arrest for conspiracy to alter the outcome of a sporting event and for wagering on the outcome of said event."

"You!" Cabot turned to T. D. Randall. "You're undercover?"

Randall's only response was to read the men their rights. He then took a tape recorder out of his pocket. Harvey played a portion of the tape. All their voices were clearly audible.

"Oh, man," Washington said. "I don't understand. What's this mean? What's—"

"It means you're going to jail, big fella," Harvey said.

"No, I can't—"

"You lying son of a bitch!" Cabot snapped at Randall.

The little man said evenly, "You say your job's making money, Andy? Well, mine's arresting people when they do it illegally."

A third man in a suit, a badge around his neck too, walked into the room. Balding and pudgy, he surveyed the men in the room. "Hey, Lieutenant Grimsby," Harvey said. "We got the contract, the tape and the perps." He laughed and looked at Washington. "The case's a slam dunk."

The lieutenant followed Harvey's eyes to the basketball player, who stood, with his hands cuffed in front of him, staring miserably at the floor. Then the lieutenant frowned. He said, "Wait a minute, that's Danny Washington? I didn't know *he* was the guy. The warrant only listed a John Doe."

Randall shrugged and said, "The warrant was issued last week—before Cabot decided on Washington."

Grimsby looked Washington up and down. He said to Harvey and his partner, "I'll take over from here. You guys can go."

"But—"

"It's okay. I'll call for transport. Officer Randall, you stay here."

"Sure thing, Lieutenant."

When the two detectives were gone the lieutenant gestured Randall into the corner of the apartment and they spoke for a minute or two. Randall glanced at Washington a couple of times and nodded.

"Officer," Pettiway muttered, "I want a lawyer. I'm entitled to one!" The policemen ignored him. Cabot sat miserably on the couch.

Randall and Grimsby finished their discussion and Grimsby walked up to Washington. He looked his unfortunate prisoner over once more, then said, "Let's step into the hall for a minute, son."

* * *

"You got yourself into a mess here, didn't you?" the lieutenant asked, lighting a cigarette.

"Yessir, I did."

Grimsby offered a Marlboro to Washington, who shook his head. "I read that story about you. In the *Times.* How you take care of your mother and grandmother. You go home regularly to see them. You stay off drugs and out of those gangsta clubs in Midtown. You lead a good life . . . Why'd you get mixed up with Cabot?"

"My team was going to fire me and I—"

The lieutenant gave a sour laugh. "You believed that? Cabot and Pettiway faked it all. That memo in there? Cabot probably wrote it himself."

"What?"

"The team'd be crazy to drop you. They find another two-guard could shoot like you?"

"Why'd Cabot do that?"

"He had to make you mad at your team so you'd agree to throw the game. Otherwise, you wouldn't have, right?"

"Course not."

"They had their bets all lined up in Atlantic City and Vegas. Put a ton of money on the Lakers. They stood to win two million if your team lost."

Washington's face twisted into an angry frown. "And they fooled me. Damn! That's why they picked me, 'cause I'm stupid. Oh, man, now what'm I gonna do?"

"You never been in any trouble with the law before?"

"No, sir."

The lieutenant smiled sadly. "My son and I go to nearly every game. We love watching you make those shots."

"I love making 'em."

The cop's eyes took in the cheap, stained wallpaper, focused on the corpse of a spider crushed against the wall a long time ago and never cleaned off. "Danny, your name's not on the warrant. There's a possibility I may be able to make this go away—if you promise you never get in any trouble with the law again."

"Lord, sir, you've got my word on that."

"But it'll cost you."

"Cost me?"

"I'll have to take care of those other cops who were here, Harvey and his partner. Officer Randall too. Then I'd have to make sure the evidence gets lost—permanently. And then the judge who issued the warrants is going to wonder why nothing ever happened with the case. If he asks questions I'll have to pay him off. His clerk too."

"You can do that?"

"I wouldn't otherwise, Danny, but you're a legend here in town. A lot of kids look up to you."

"I like it when there're kids in the bleachers. If I disappointed them 'cause of this, man, I'd feel so bad . . . How much money would it take, you think?"

"Probably all of your savings."

"Man, I'm using that money for my family back in Maryland. My mother and grandmother . . . My nieces—I'm making sure they're going to college."

Grimsby shook his head. "Well, Danny, you're going to have to make a choice here. You don't have to get me that money but then you'll go to jail. And what're your mother and grandmother going to do then?"

"Man, that'd be terrible."

"And if you stay out of jail," Grimsby pointed out, "you'll be able to make more money."

"That's true. I will. What about Cabot?"

"Have to let him go too. But this probably shook him up bad. He may just change his ways—at least for a little while. So what's it gonna be, Danny?"

The big man looked down at his hands for a long moment, then held up the cuffs for Grimsby to unlock.

★   ★   ★

Three hours later Teddy Grimsby walked up the sour-smelling hallway of Andy Cabot's apartment building.

The duffel bag he carried was heavy and he was out of shape. Still he moved quickly; you don't want to dawdle when you're carrying a million dollars in cash through Hell's Kitchen. Washington had come through. They'd met at his gym an hour ago and the player had—almost tearfully—given Grimsby his entire savings account.

Grimsby now came to Cabot's apartment. The door was open and the man walked inside, to find himself in the middle of a celebration. Cabot was pouring Asti Spumante into Styrofoam cups and passing them out to the crew from Ernie's—Mike O'Hanlon and Sedd the Greek, who'd pretended to be

Harvey and his partner, the vice cops. Here was Tony Benotti, who'd swallowed his Queens drawl long enough to play "sort of" sports agent Pettiway from L.A.

Sitting on the couch was T. D. Randall, who'd spent all night rehearsing his critical role by shouting, "I need backup, now!" and leaping up from a table in his Brooklyn apartment about fifty times.

"I got it," Grimsby said, gasping from the effort of carrying the money. He opened the duffel bag and dumped a portion of the contents out onto the table. The packets spilled across the stained wood and onto the floor.

"Jesus," Randall muttered, picking up one and smelling it. "Ain't that pretty."

"The big dumb shit . . . Know what he did?" Grimsby asked, taking a cup. "I meet him in the middle of the locker room of his gym, right? And he says, right in front of everybody, 'Hey, Detective, I got the money.'"

"I'll bet somebody's got to tie his Nikes for him," Cabot said, and started distributing stacks of Washington's million dollars.

It had been Cabot and Randall's idea to lay the scam on Washington. So they split $600,000 between them. The others divvied up the rest but nobody complained—they were all just punks and barflies, mostly in debt, and were delighted to be involved in a deal that both made good money and featured a victim who wasn't going to go to the cops.

As Cabot dug the last of the cash out of the bag, he frowned and said, "Hey, what's this?"

He lifted a little black box from the bag.

"Looks like a pager," Grimsby said. "It's Washington's bag. Must be his."

Pettiway took the device. "Naw, it's no pager." Then his eyes grew wide in alarm. "Hell, it's a GPS tracer!"

"Oh, shit," Cabot spat out. He leapt up, just as, for the second time that day, the door to his apartment burst open. This time, however, the law enforcement officers who pushed inside were very real.

And far more numerous than before.

In sixty seconds the gang was cuffed and sitting on the floor. A detective from the real Midtown South Vice Unit read them their rights while the crime scene team started collecting evidence: Randall's "informant" tape, the fake badges, the guns, the phony contract and letter from the coach, the briefcase containing the signing bonus—which wasn't $500,000 at all but stacks of play money, each one topped with a single hundred-dollar bill. One cop started counting Washington's cash.

A moment later a furious and frightened Andy Cabot heard heavy footsteps on the stairs and two men entered the room. One was Danny Washington. The other was a middle-aged man in a suit. His ID card identified him as Detective Tim Getz. "Are these them, Danny?" the cop asked.

"Yeah. All of them. Those two played they was detectives. And he was an undercover cop, the one with the tape recorder. That guy there, Pettiway—he was playing at being some agent or something for the Lakers, and"—Washington angrily pointed at Cabot—"he was playing at being a asshole."

Cabot muttered to Grimsby, "What the hell did you do to tip yourself off?"

"Nothing!" the faux cop protested. "I did just what you told me to!"

Getz ignored the bickering. He said to Washington, "The

whole thing was a setup, Danny. From the start. They tricked you into agreeing to throw the game, they tricked you into thinking you were arrested, they tricked you into giving up your savings as a bribe. It almost worked too. Except you had the guts to come to us. A lot of people wouldn't have."

The cop inventorying the money finished and looked up. "The serial numbers on the first million match." He looked around. "Where's the rest?"

"Rest?" Cabot's head turned slowly to the duffel bag.

"The other five million."

"*What* six million?" Grimsby asked. "Washington only gave me a million."

"No, man," Washington said, frowning. He nodded at Grimsby angrily. "He said to fix it so I wouldn't go to jail, I had to pay him *six* million. My whole savings account."

One of the cops nodded. "That was the withdrawal receipt from the bank. Six million."

Cabot coldly asked Grimsby, "You got six from him? You told us you asked for one million."

"I *did* ask for one!" the man protested. "And that's what he gave me."

Washington blurted, "He said he wanted six million or I'd go to jail and never play basketball again."

"No, no!" Grimsby said. "He gave me one million. He must've skimmed the rest himself."

Getz laughed. "Why the hell would he skim money from *himself*? That doesn't make a lot of sense, now, does it, Grimsby?"

"I don't know. But he *had* to. I didn't do it."

Cabot snapped at Grimsby, "You gave it to somebody on the way over here, didn't you? Who was it? Was it that scumbag Lorn Smales you're always hanging around with? Or maybe your slut girlfriend? Who? You son of a bitch, you're going down—"

Getz waved his hand at Cabot to silence him.

"Where's my money?" Now it was Danny Washington who was raging. "That was for my mama and grandma! That was my whole savings account—all everything I saved up playing ball!"

"I don't know what you're talking about!" Grimsby said.

"We'll track it down," Getz said to Washington to calm him. "But for now let's book these losers."

The gang of extortionists was led outside into paddy wagons for the ride down to central booking.

The police searched Grimsby's car, his office at BQE Auto Parts, his and his girlfriend's apartments and the home of his bewildered friend, Lorn Smales, a skinny druggie living in a walk-up in the East Village. They found no sign of the missing five million. Getz came to the conclusion that Cabot and Grimsby together had probably skimmed the money and hidden it someplace.

"I'm sorry for your loss, Mr. Washington," the detective said. "We'll do what we can but if we can't recover the money . . . well, you better prepare yourself for that. You have insurance?"

The player said miserably, "Only fifty thousand or something like that—you know, enough to replace my stereo and TV and watch and stuff if my apartment got broke into. I never thought I'd get robbed this much—five million."

"We'll do everything possible, Danny."

"Thanks, Detective."

The cop started to leave, then paused and turned back.

"Hey, Danny, one thing . . . I hate to ask at a time like this . . . but . . ."

Washington's face broke into a wan smile. "You want an autograph?"

"For my kid, you understand."

"Sure. What's his name?"

★ ★ ★

A week later Danny Washington was getting ready for a game against the Detroit Pistons. The two-guard had limbered up with a run and plenty of stretches and had just donned his uniform when one of the assistant coaches called him over to the phone.

He took the receiver.

"Danny?" the man's voice asked.

"Yeah."

"It's Detective Getz. I just wanted you to know. That last lead about the cash didn't pay off."

"Oh, man," Washington muttered.

"It's still an open case but the way it usually works is that if we don't find stolen cash by now, it's probably gone for good. I'm sorry."

"Well, it's nobody's fault but my own," the player said, sighing. "I shouldn't ever've listened to somebody like Andy Cabot. That was stupid. And I'm paying for it now."

"Good luck tonight. I'll be watching the game."

"I shoot a couple of treys for you, Detective."

After they'd hung up, Washington leaned his head against the locker room wall for a moment. Then he picked up the phone again and placed a call. This one was to his accountant at the man's home in Manhasset, Long Island.

"Jerry? It's Danny Washington."

"Danny, how you doing?"

"Gotta go play some hoops in a minute but I got a question for you. Had this thing happen to me last week." He explained about the scam and the money.

"Oh, Danny, that's terrible. They got five *million*?"

"Yeah, it hurt," the player said. "Anyway, you know I've been working on my degree in business during the off-season."

"I remember."

"Now if I read the tax code right it looks to me like, on my Schedule A, I can take a theft-loss deduction in the amount of the money stolen. Well, less that exclusion—ten percent of adjusted gross income, of course."

"That's absolutely right."

"Okay, my question is—since the loss is five million and I'll only have three million income this year, can I carry the other two million loss forward and offset most of *next* year's income too?"

"I'll have to check. But I'm pretty sure you can."

"So basically," Washington summarized, "I'll hardly be paying the IRS any tax for two years."

"That's right."

"Well, now, that's good to hear."

The accountant said, "It's still a bummer you had to lose all that money to get out of paying taxes, though."

"A damn shame, Jerry," said the ballplayer, and hung up, thinking: Well, it *would* be a shame except that the five million, which he'd hidden in a second locker at the gym before he gave the duffel bag to Grimsby, was currently earning sweet interest in an offshore banking account he'd opened years ago in his and his mother's names.

Of course he'd known from the minute that little weasel Andy Cabot approached him in the gym more or less what the scam artist had in mind. The two-guard had foreseen the plan unfold as clearly as he could anticipate a 1-3-1 offensive alignment against a 2-3 zone defense.

Somehow I just know things on the court before they happen. Like knowing when somebody's going to foul me. Or knowing, when I throw the ball, whether it'll be a miss or it'll be nothing but net.

He looked at his battered Casio. Five minutes until game time. He made one more phone call—to the men's detention center in downtown New York, where Andy Cabot and T. D. Randall and those coconspirators who couldn't post bond—which was most of them—were awaiting trial.

The chief night guard snapped to attention immediately when Washington identified himself. The player and the guard chatted about a recent game, then Washington said, "Can you do me a favor?"

"Sure thing, Danny, anything you want. Everybody down here, we're all big fans of yours."

"Make sure the prisoners watch the game tonight."

"We don't usually let 'em watch TV after six but I'll make sure it's on. Just for you."

"Thanks."

That night, toward the end of the game, Danny Washington found the moment he'd been waiting for. He'd just got possession of the ball from his center, who'd fired him a distant lob after a rebound from a missed shot by the Pistons. All alone, Washington jogged fast toward the net and could've gone in for an easy dunk but he suddenly braked to a stop outside of the arc. Turning toward the nearest ESPN cameraman filming him, he glanced into the lens of the camera, offered a faint smile and pointed toward his right eye. Then he sank down real slow, leapt high into the air and let fly a long trey. The instant the ball left his hands, he looked away from the hoop and jogged back down the court to take up his defensive position.

BANK SHOTS

Sue DeNymme

Manny swallowed the last drop of tequila and wiped his mouth on his sleeve. So his wife was going to kill him, what else was new? He couldn't afford to worry about it now. He couldn't afford much of anything after last night's game. Besides, he didn't have the energy. His drinking binge had made him ill, and the wife would be home any minute. Time to get the hell up and cover his ass.

He stumbled to the toilet and heaved, then heaved again, his insides swirling like water down the drain as he sank to his knees in front of the bowl and prayed for the room to stop spinning.

Then it came to him, the only way out.

He pushed himself off the tiles and shuffled to his wife's dressing bureau. Undergarments slipped through his fingers until he worked his hands to the far corner of her lingerie drawer where she'd hidden the last valuable thing in the apartment: a costly diamond bracelet recently inherited from her grandma's estate.

As he inspected the glistening band that his wife had cherished, his forehead felt damp and hot. His heart throbbed in his chest, and his palms felt clammy, but he took a deep breath and swiped the bracelet anyway.

Even if Becky could forgive him for losing their nest egg on last night's basketball game, she'd definitely kill him for this.

He crammed the heirloom into the pocket of his jeans, slinked across the hall and slipped down the stairs of the walk-up where they lived.

Scanning the street for any sign of his wife, he clutched the bracelet in his jacket and headed toward the river. There was always a chance that he could plead for mercy and beg his way out, but that would be up to Tony the Ear.

Every basketball season, which in New York meant whenever there wasn't actually snow on the ground, the Ear sat courtside at Riverside Park, watching the talented local kids play hoops with such concentrated energy you'd think their lives depended on it. With a notebook and pen at the ready, he liked that spot on his favorite bench, and everyone knew where to find him. His tiny feet were planted on the ground, sun warming the back of his neck.

"Tony." Manny caught his breath. "I have to get my money back from last night's bet."

Tony didn't say a word. His eyes were fixed on the kids shooting, running, passing and banging bodies.

He was dressed, as usual, in an old satin New York Knicks jacket that probably predated the Walt Frazier, Willis Reed glory years, when the Knicks still played in the old Madison Square Garden at Fiftieth Street and Eighth Avenue. His jeans last saw soap and water a decade before he got the jacket, and his sneakers belonged in the Smithsonian.

"Tony," Manny said again, a little more urgently, but the

bookie never moved, never took his eyes off the game. He knew Tony could hear perfectly well with his one good ear, but he didn't turn around and didn't answer.

Manny tried not to stare at Tony's strange left ear, but he could never get used to the pea-sized lobe that popped out from that indentation where his ear should have been. The story was that an overeager doctor had torn off his ear with the forceps as he wrenched Tony out of the birth canal. Then the doctor smoothed it all over with skin from the right side of his face, and that's why his nose was slanted and his mouth was scrunched to the right, so that he always looked as if he were speaking in asides.

Finally, he stepped directly in front of the Ear. "Tony, I need my money back."

"What are you talking about? You bet, you lost, game over. Get outta my way. I'm watching a game here."

"Listen," Manny pleaded. "Can't you just forget it? I mean, pretend I never made the bet? Give me my money back?"

"Sorry, kid." Suddenly, he jumped up to get a better view of the court as a cornrowed kid in a lime-green T-shirt stole the ball and led a fast break. "Run," he screamed, "move your damn ass." Probably since his lips were permanently sphinctered on his right cheek, Tony spoke with a lisp. He turned to look Manny in the eye. "I really am sorry for you." He nodded and looked at the ground. "Maybe you should borrow some money. You got friends."

"Whose friends have that kind of cash? Besides, they only laugh when I ask." Manny watched one of the players score from the charity line. "My own wife pushes for Gamblers Anonymous."

"I know." He smirked out of the side of his mouth. "I used

to get that line myself." Tony peered around Manny's torso, and Manny turned to see the same kid take two huge steps from the foul line and dunk over two taller kids without shirts.

Manny stumbled, still a little tipsy from his self-pity binge. "Why don't you give me back the money I bet? I'll never ask again."

Tony sat down. "I don't have it, pal." He ran a hand over his filthy jeans. "You wanna play? You gotta pay. Ain't that our deal?" Tony raised a finger. "Have you hit up your mother?"

"She won't give me a dime. I already owe her forty grand." He put a hand on Tony's shoulder. "You gotta help me. I'm desperate here."

Tony brushed away Manny's hand. "What you need is a shower and a shave . . . and brush your stinking teeth because you smell like a goddamn dump."

"Give me a break." Manny shrugged, palms in the air. "I'm dying."

"Did you see that shot?" Tony shouted and pointed at the court. "Unbelievable."

Manny snorted and clenched his fists. "You don't give a fuck about anyone but yourself."

"What do you mean?" He pointed at the home team. "I bought their uniforms."

"What? A dozen T-shirts?" Manny shoved a finger in his face and poked out the words. "Give me back my cash."

"Take it easy, pal," Tony yelled. Palms up, he motioned him back. "Relax."

Manny wiped Tony's spittle off his cheek. "I don't want to relax." He pushed Tony back down to the bench. "You think I'm gonna go easy because you're some kind of cripple? I oughta do you a favor and kick that mouth back to the other side of your head where it belongs." He fisted Tony in the chest. "You, pal, are gonna give me back my money. Now."

Tony reached into his jacket and pulled out a pocketknife.

"What the fuck is that?" Manny's eyes skittered from the blade to the basketball decal on the handle, then back to Tony's face.

"What we're gonna do"—Tony waved the knife like a nun waving a ruler—"is sit the fuck down and take a minute to sort things out." He patted the seat with the blade. "You want to turn your luck around or you want to stand there whining like some kinda pussy?"

One of the players missed a bounce pass, and the ball popped off the court and hit Manny in the back of his head.

"Sorry, Tony!" A sinewy Puerto Rican kid scooped up the ball and dribbled back to the game.

"Hopeless." Tony took an apple from the brown paper bag on the bench.

"I can't believe my rotten luck." Manny crumbled to his seat and leaned his forehead on his hands. "When did you get a knife?" He rubbed his neck and asked, "And when did you start pulling it on your pals?"

"You take yourself too serious." Tony shrugged and cut into the apple. "I can't stand the sight of blood." He stuck his chin out and took a deep breath. "I was only making a point."

"What point?"

"Listen up, 'cause I'm the smartest guy you know. Everything goes in one ear and stays there."

Manny chuckled. "You're nuts."

Tony offered him a slice of fruit. "You want your money back. Well, it's all a zero-sum game. Somebody has to lose for somebody else to win. So what are the odds for you, my friend?"

Tony chewed a slice and swallowed. His Adam's apple rose like a ball in his throat. "The odds are nil if you're out of the game. Am I right or am I right?"

Manny nodded, pretending to understand.

"You got no hope if you're out of the game." He swallowed again. "If you're out, it's your own fault. Luck has nothing to do with it. So you gonna die by the odds here? You gonna let them slaughter you or will you jump up swinging?" He paused for effect. "And here's the most important piece of advice you will ever get in life. Never ever let the odds get you down. You're gonna die by the odds or you're gonna live by the odds."

"That's your big tip?" Manny clicked his tongue against the roof of his mouth. He sprung to his feet. "You gotta be kidding me."

"Where do you think you're going?" Tony wiped his crazy mouth with a paper napkin. "I can help you make back your losses, but what you really want is college money, right? Have you thought about that?" Tony flicked the knife closed and stuck it into his pocket. "You gotta act like a man now that you're playing with the big boys."

"That's what I'm trying to do."

"Then you gotta think like Casanova. You know? The greatest lover in the world had it all figured out, see." Tony turned his face toward Manny. "Know how Casanova won at gambling?"

Manny shoved his hands into his pockets. "How?"

"If Casanova lost, he redoubled his bet until he won." He tapped his finger on the bench. "So that's Casanova. Now, who the fuck are you?"

"I just want to get back what I lost." Manny shook his head and scanned the park, seeing everything and nothing at once.

"Sit down here." Tony nodded at the bench. "You're out of the game now, right?"

Manny nodded and sat.

"Well, how can you win if you're out of the goddamn game?" Tony paused. "Now, what do you say?" He leaned toward Manny with the only ear he had. "You got nothing to say. So sit the fuck down." Tony cleared his throat. "You want a chance to get that money back?"

"I have to get that money back."

"I'm telling you how to get your money back, kid. That's all. You got a pretty wife, new baby. You're young and you got your health. Everything to live for. I can help you. Your timing is right on the money, believe it or not." Tony leaned toward Manny and grinned. "So." Tony wiped his hands on his pants. "You wanna be a loser for the rest of your life or do you wanna win big this time? It's up to you."

Manny stared at his squashed-up mouth. "What the hell are you talking about?"

"You know basketball. You know the line on tonight's game at the Garden, right?"

Manny nodded.

"Go double or nothing tonight." Tony crumpled the empty bag and made a nice arcing shot into the can.

"You're kidding."

Tony chuckled. "Serious as cancer. Listen to me. I'm the smartest guy you know, remember?"

Manny spat on the ground. "What if I lose again?"

"Tonight's the Connecticut game, and everyone loves that team, right? Well, the competition's gonna shoot the lights out. Think of the odds."

"Not a chance." Manny shook his head. "UCLA's been shooting bricks for years now."

"So what? You think life's random? It all runs in cycles, kid, even the NCAA tournament. I do the charts. It's a technical analysis, see? It's all in the cycles. Let the cycles call the shots and you can bank on them like you can bank on the stock market." Tony raised a brow and stared Manny in the eye. "Now, you know this and I know this, but nobody else knows this. I even put a grand down for myself."

"This is my house we're talking about. The down payment on my house." Manny kicked the dirt. "I can't."

"How long have we been doing this and how many times have we won? A lot, right? So you had a temporary slump. You're only a loser if you take yourself out."

Manny stood and looked around. He lifted his Knicks cap and wiped down his hair before returning the hat to his head. "It's a long shot."

Tony stood and slurped the last sip from his straw. "I gotta get back to the sports desk. What's it gonna be?"

"Can you front me the money?"

"What do I look like, your father?"

Manny took the gold band from his wedding finger. "This is worth at least a hundred."

Tony snorted. "That wouldn't cover the vigorish."

Manny pulled the bracelet from his shirt pocket. "It's my wife's inheritance." He moved it in the light. "Platinum and diamonds. The real deal."

Tony snapped up the jewelry and fingered the pieces in his palm. "I'll do you a favor this time, kid. I'll check these at Sal's, and whatever he gives me, I'll put that down for you."

Manny took the bottle of mouthwash from his pocket and chugged some down. He held it out to Tony.

Tony grabbed the bottle. "Forty-five cents a pint?" Bright green liquid sloshed around the bottom. "What the hell is this?"

"Thirty percent alcohol. That's what. A giant Yankee julep."

Tony handed it back. "Looks like puke and backwash to me."

"Thanks." Manny smiled.

"Don't worry about it."

"And don't forget the pawn ticket. I gotta get the jewelry back once the deal is done."

Tony smiled. "Have I ever let you down?"

⋆ ⋆ ⋆

On the way back to the newspaper office, Tony stopped at Sal's Pawnshop by the deli a few blocks uptown.

The pawnbroker buzzed him in. Flashy in a Vegas sort of way, Sal overdressed most of the time, and today the pits of Sal's shirt were circled in sweat despite the cool spring weather.

"What can I do you for?" Sal's double chin jiggled as he stood up from the stool behind the counter. "How's your pretty mama?" He reminded Tony of a Cuban pimp he once met on a hot Miami Beach, running the numbers with a silver-plated smile. "Did you tell her I asked about her?"

Tony crossed to the glass display case where Sal was leaning. "Yeah, I told her." He smiled as nicely as he could with his grotesque mouth. "She says hello." He lied. "She's just so busy with the charities and all. Too busy to socialize much outside of church." He scanned the gem-stuffed display case. "Don't you already have a girl?"

Sal raised his brows. "If one's good, two is better."

Tony forced his jaw open so he wouldn't grind his teeth. He took a deep breath and said, "I got twenty grand says UCLA wins with the points tonight."

"Long shot." Sal laughed. "So what do you want me to do about it?"

Tony shrugged. "I gotta lay off the bets."

Sal raised a brow. "Street says you can't pay your medical bills since they diagnosed your tumor. How do I know you're still good for it?"

"I guess I better be, right?" Tony let out a nervous laugh before producing the bracelet and gold band that Manny had given him. He laid them out to glisten on the black velvet cloth that lay atop the display case.

Sal ambled back to his desk to get a loupe. Then he got personal with the diamond bracelet. A minute passed, and Sal grunted. He scratched his chin and took another look.

The canned lights buzzed in sync with Tony's nerves. "You know me for years, Sal. You also know the house always wins." Tony wiped the sweat from his brow. "And you should know I got a stack of bearer bonds for you if you don't like the produce here."

"Good." Sal's gut jiggled as he chuckled. He put the loupe down and sat on his stool. " 'Cause this is some kind of joke."

Tony nodded. "I swear I'm good for it, Sal. Help a guy out."

Sal examined the bad side of Tony's face. "If I help you out, it's only 'cause I like your mother." He pushed the cloth away and waved his hand at it. "Two grand would be generous."

A bead of sweat raced down Tony's spine. "Then we have a deal."

Sal licked his lips. "I gotta warn you." Spittle flew from the corner of Sal's mouth. "My brother isn't happy with you. You still owe for last time, and you're a credit risk what with the cancer. Can't let you slide on this one." He tapped the loupe on the countertop. "Remember what happened to your reporter friend who thought he was cute and tried to renege?"

Tony nodded. "Mack never came back to the sports desk."

"Right. And don't let it slip your memory." Sal reached underneath a case and brought up an envelope that he pushed across the glass to Tony.

Tony took the envelope and leafed through the bills to count them.

"We get the cash back tomorrow." Sal buzzed the door open. "That gives you twenty-four hours."

Tony smiled and hurried out the door. "Thanks, Sal."

★　★　★

The morning after Manny won, he felt like he'd won the lottery. Tony had been right! His luck would never have changed if he hadn't been in the game. UCLA got killed, as everyone figured they would, but a last-minute flurry of meaningless points from a reserve guard meant that UConn didn't cover the spread.

Manny raced through the drizzle to the newspaper building. He bounded the stairs from the subway stop and sprinted down the block through the revolving door to the *Breaking News*.

Inside, his footsteps echoed off the marble as he walked to the island in the middle of the lobby, where he greeted the receptionist, who watched him closely. "Hello, sweetheart."

Young and attentive, the Latin receptionist spoke into her mouthpiece, pushed a few buttons on the switchboard and followed his fidgety fingers with her eyes. "May I help you?"

His grin felt so big that he was sure he looked like a mental patient. "I came to see Tony the Ear."

"Tony Morelli." She looked down and ran a finger down her clipboard, then shook her head and picked up a pencil. "Mr. Morelli hasn't come in yet. Would you like to leave a message?"

Manny moved aside for an old lady who stepped in front of him, eyed him and whispered to her poodle. "I'll just wait," he said. He shifted from one foot to the other.

"You can't stand there," the receptionist told him. "This isn't a waiting area."

"Well." Manny looked past her at the clock on the wall. "It's eleven-thirty. What time does he come to work?"

"He usually gets in at nine o'clock." She juggled a few calls, then said, "If you have his number, I would try him at home."

Manny's breath quickened. What if the Ear had taken off with all his winnings, his wedding band and his wife's bracelet?

"I don't have his number on me. Can you look it up?"

She answered after taking a phone message. "I'm sorry, sir, but we can't give out any private information."

"This is an emergency." Fear turned to anger, and his voice was getting louder. "Just give me the number and I'll go."

A security guard tapped Manny on the shoulder. "I'm afraid you'll have to leave now, sir. Would you like me to show you the way?"

"All right. All right." Manny stepped back. "I'm going."

On the street in front of the *Breaking News,* taxis and limos splashed up and down the wet streets. People rushed past on the sidewalk, fumbling not to impale him or one another with the metal ends on their umbrellas.

Manny pulled the collar of his Knicks jacket over his head

and ran into a covered stairwell by a deli. At the counter a guy who looked like a derelict sipped something steamy.

Manny sucked down the last drop of his mouthwash. He didn't even have enough for a double espresso. He needed to get his winnings, but where the hell was Tony?

Tony wasn't hard up for money. He'd been banking his vigorish all those years, and he always made good on his bets. Everyone trusted Tony.

Half an hour after standing in the chill, Manny slicked back his hair and went back to the *Breaking News*. His wet sneakers squeaked on the marble floor.

"No luck." The receptionist looked up between calls. "Tony never came in."

"Well, can you find out if he's sick or something? Did he call someone? His boss or his secretary? I just need a little help here. Tony doesn't answer his cell phone. He's not at our usual haunts. He just up and disappeared."

The receptionist squinted. "It's only been a day, you know. Call tomorrow morning."

"Hey." A young redheaded guy stepped up to the reception desk. "You a friend of Tony's?"

Manny nodded. "Who are you?"

"I work with him on the sports desk." The guy frowned. "Did you try him at home?"

Manny shrugged. "I don't have his number in the Bronx."

"That's ancient history, pal." The copyboy shook his head. "Tony moved in with his mom near Riverside Park. She was taking care of him after they found his tumor."

"What tumor?"

The guy backed up and lowered his palms like he was pushing down the trunk of a car. "You knew he had cancer, didn't you?" The guy led Manny to the revolving door. He whispered and wrote on the back of his business card. "I'll do you a favor if you call me when you find him. I need to collect on a debt." He handed Manny the card. "Try this address. His mom will be able to help."

★   ★   ★

Manny approached Tony's modern high-rise as the security camera watched from its perch atop the intercom.

He rang the buzzer next to Tony's last name.

"Yes?" A woman's voice came through the box.

"Hey. I came to see Tony. Is he okay?"

"Who are you?"

"Manny. A friend of Tony's from way back. He has something for me."

"Oh, I know exactly what you mean." She said, "I'll be right down."

A minute later she was standing in the doorway with him. Slim and petite, she was too darn sexy, Manny decided, to be anybody's mother. "Pleasure to meet you." He took her hand. "Are you Tony's sister?"

"Oh, another charmer like my Tony." She looked Manny up and down. "I'm his mother, of course. And I know he didn't go to work today. I called the office." She frowned. "Gee, your breath smells minty. Anyway, I called his girlfriend, but she said they broke up last week. Do you know his girlfriend Diana?" She didn't wait for an answer. "It's just not like Tony to take off, especially what with the chemo appointment. This is the first one he's missed after all this time."

Manny's heart thudded against his chest. "You mean you don't know where he is?"

"The police won't help because it hasn't been twenty-four hours since he went missing, but he didn't come home last night. I have a bad feeling, Manny." She crossed her arms. "Tony didn't call me this morning. Whenever he sleeps out, he always calls me in the morning."

Manny felt his shoulders droop.

"I found this on his dresser. It's got your name on it, see?" She held out a wooden cigar box.

Manny took the box and stepped back. "Thanks." He wanted to rip into it, but if his winnings were in there, it was just too much cash to flash on the street.

Her eyes glistened with urgency. "You can come upstairs if you want to open it inside." She shifted in place. "I'm dying to know if there's anything in there about where he went, and my friend Sal told me I should look through everything, but I just—do you know Sal? He has been so nice lately, but since my Tony left this with your name on the package, I couldn't open it and go rifling . . ." She stopped and smiled sweetly. "I just made coffee. Why don't you come up?"

"Thanks." Manny stowed the box under his arm and edged his way backward. "I'm running late, or I would."

"Are you sure?"

Manny stepped onto the sidewalk. "I'll call if I find Tony. I promise I will."

Disappointed, she pursed her lips together. "Don't forget. Maria Morelli. I'm in the book."

He sprinted down the sidewalk, sneakers splashing in the rain.

Manny felt someone watching him before he turned and saw the man. Manny looked back. The guy was definitely tailing him. He was overweight with a silver front tooth, and Manny knew he could outrun him if he had to.

He cut through a public passage and came out on the next street. He looked behind him. Not only was the guy still there, but now Manny thought another guy was following. He wished he had his bike.

He tripped over a crack in the sidewalk.

The box clattered open. Its contents scattered on the ground.

Manny crawled on hands and knees in the pouring rain. He saw the wedding band and grabbed it. Then he scooped up five bundles of hundreds before he finally found the diamond bracelet.

The guy with the silver tooth stood over him, rain dripping down his face. "Those things are mine."

"Who the hell are you?" Manny clutched the cash to his chest.

"The name is Sal, and this game is now over." Sal flipped out a pocketknife and held it in front of him. "Tony could never pay his debts, see? I bet he didn't tell you how I broke two of his fingers the last time he tried to be cute." Sal knelt down and sat on his haunches. "Now, give me my money."

"Hey." Manny noticed the basketball decal on the handle. "That's Tony's knife. What the hell did you do to Tony?"

Sal's shoulders rose in a kind of shrug. "Don't worry about it."

Manny took a deep breath and grabbed Sal's wrist as he lunged at him with all the force he could muster. He wrenched Tony's knife from Sal's hand and kicked him in the groin.

"Shit!" Sal fell to the ground and grabbed his crotch.

"Tony would want me to have this." He flashed the blade so it gleamed in the light. "Game over."

"What the hell are you doing?" Sal sneered as he pushed

himself up from the sidewalk, but Manny kicked his elbow out from under him and stashed the loot in his pockets.

"Don't worry about it." Holding the knife out in front of his hip, Manny jogged backward until he got some distance between them.

Sal waved a fist in the air. "You can't hide from me, punk. I'll find you, and you'll end up like your friend."

"Well . . ." Manny winked and shot him a nod. "We all gotta live by the odds."

THE TASTE OF SILVER

Brendan DuBois

I t was a Monday morning, a week after Labor Day, and most of the tourists had left the wooded shores of Walker's Lake, leaving the wide blue waters quiet for a change. Glen Jackson stood on the rear steps of his summer cottage, looking down the long dirt driveway that eventually led out to Mill Street, the road in from town, a small village of about four hundred or so. He folded his lanky arms and waited, staring down at the empty dirt lane. To the right was a basketball court that he had installed here, over a decade ago, when they had bought the place. It had been a nice summer but now this warm season was down to mere hours. Marcia had gone home to Boston with their two granddaughters three days ago. She had wanted to stay but he was insistent: "No, I'll be fine closing it up. You take the kids and have fun back home. I'll be right along."

And he wasn't sure how women did it—was it genetic? trained into them by their mothers?—but she knew right from the start that he had been lying about something. But that special sense of hers also quickly determined that his fib wasn't part of a plan to sneak in some beach bunny for the night. No, she knew him well enough to know that those wild days of his were gone, long gone, since he had exchanged vows with her more than twenty-five years ago. He grinned. Of course, not that there weren't some good wild times to think over at three a.m., trying to get back to sleep . . .

He turned and looked out to the cove, where some of the cottage owners had already dragged in their docks and had put wooden shutters up over the windows, to protect them from the harsh winds and snows due in a couple of months. His own shutters were on the porch, ready to go, numbered for each spot on the windows. He really should have started putting up the shutters a few hours ago, but there was a finality to it that he hated. With each shutter going up, less light came into the cottage, until finally, at noon, he had to have every light inside blazing to see what was going on. And that marked the official end of summer, no matter what day was on the calendar. Out on the water a couple of fishermen hung on in their expensive bass boats, and he could hardly wait for them to leave so he could get everything done. Everything that had to be done to mark another year gone by.

Ugh. He went down the steps, picked up a basketball from the ground, the pebbled leather against his large palms bringing back muscle memories of the hundreds of thousands of times he had picked up a similar ball, from his neighborhood in Philly to the local high school to Temple U to the Olympic team and then six glorious years in the NBA, two championship rings to wear . . . He dribbled a few times, getting the feel of the court, and then just started working from one side to the next, ball going up, *swish*—nothing but net, thank you kindly—and just getting into the groove of hearing the *slap* of the ball in his hands, the *whisper-clang* as it went through the hoop, the solid *thunk* as it hit asphalt. He kept looking at the net as he went back and forth, back and forth, thinking of the different courts he had played on, from the cracked and stained asphalt, starting out as a kid, through all the polished wood in all the different arenas, right up to the famous parquet floor at the old Boston Garden. Downstairs in the basement at home in Boston he had lots of souvenirs, and one of his faves was a piece of the old parquet, doled out just before the idiots destroyed that creaky old shrine to the Celtics.

Another three-point shot. How sweet, even though the three-point rule hadn't been in effect during his career. And, of course, this little half-court was probably the most pleasant one he had ever played on. It was framed by old pine trees, and through the underbrush one could make out the cool waters of Walker's Lake. Boston was nice enough most times of the year, but when the sun grew higher in the sky and the air got thick and hot, there was nothing he loved more than just coming up here to the cool breezes and warm summer nights, Marcia and he growing older and older and—truth be told—happier and happier. He had been at this cottage once, years ago, during one of those "Fresh Air" experiences for city kids, back when he was twelve. He had made a vow then, during those special two weeks, that if he could, he would buy this place when he got older. Which he did. It was now a good life, one he never thought would end.

Boom. Another three-pointer. He grabbed the ball and as he was moving around for another shot, there was the sound of a car engine coming up his driveway. He waited, conscious of how heavily he was breathing, how his knees and wrists were complaining, and how damn old he was getting.

There. Visible past the saplings and brush. A dark blue car, coming up. He put the ball in the crook of his arm, hardly even thinking about it, as the car came into view.

A police cruiser.

He took a breath. Waited.

★ ★ ★

The cruiser came to a polite halt near his own vehicle, a silver Lexus SUV. It was the local police and he tried not to smile as the young officer stepped out, looking so polished and serious in his uniform. A guy like that, back in his old Philly neighborhood, would have lasted maybe ten minutes with his corner gang before being dumped back at the local station house, stripped naked except for his socks. The officer came up to him and nodded and said, "Mr. Jackson?"

"The same," he said, wondering if this young pup even shaved more than three times a week.

"I'm Tom Colter, the police chief," he said, actually holding out his hand, which Glen shook, all the while thinking, M'man, if you were in Philly like this, they'd even take your socks before dumping you back at your station house.

"Sure, I've seen you around town," Glen said. "What can I do for you?"

The young chief looked embarrassed, like he was apologizing for interrupting his practice or some damn thing. "I'm investigating a missing person case."

Glen moved the ball back into his hands, dribbled it a few times on the asphalt. "Really? Anybody I know?"

"Oh, I sure do think so," he said. "Marcus Harrison. A teammate of yours, am I right?"

Glen said, "Yeah, a former teammate. He was up here a couple of days ago, stopping by. Shit. You say he's missing?"

Colter said, "Yes. And you're saying he was here?"

"Uh-huh," he said, bouncing the ball back up and down. "Stayed for a day and a night. Last time I saw him, yesterday morning, I drove him back into town, at the Greyhound stop, by Frye's General Store. You mean he never got back down to Queens?"

"That's what we're trying to figure out," Colter said. "You see, his wife was expecting him back yesterday evening, and he never showed up. And Greyhound is claiming that he never got on the bus when it stopped in town. So it looks like you might be the last one to see him."

"Wow," he said, bouncing the ball up and down some more and then suddenly stopping. "C'mon inside, I'll get you something to drink. I'll tell you everything you want to know."

"Gee, thanks," the chief said, and Glen moved quick, turning his head so the kid couldn't see him smile.

*   *   *

Glen didn't bother offering anything alcoholic to the chief, so he poured them both glasses of lemonade and went into the dining room, which had great views from the windows that overlooked the lake. Nearby was the dock and moored to the dock was his light blue powerboat, with a gray canvas tarpaulin covering it. The fishermen were gone and there was now just a solitary sailboat, out on the south end of the lake, catching one last sail before wintering in some boathouse somewhere, and Colter said, "View must be nice once the leaves start changing."

Glen sat down at the round oak dining room table, letting his long legs stretch out. "Sure, but we don't come up that much during the fall. Summer's our playtime, and when we get back to Boston, there's plenty of work to be done."

"And what exactly do you do now, Mr. Jackson?" And with

that, the polite young chief sat down, took out a little note-book and opened it up on the dining room table. "You haven't played for the Celtics for a very long time, right?"

"Promise not to laugh?" he asked.

"Sure. Promise not to laugh."

"Good. I give motivational speeches, that's what I do." He couldn't help himself, he smiled at the chief, who was gracious enough to smile back. "You see, the thing is, once you're out of basketball, what's left? I didn't have the voice for doing an-nouncing work. I was okay in doing some advertising spots, but that kind of work didn't last long. You see, things have changed since back when I was tossing the ball around. Back then, there weren't the endorsements, the contracts, the TV work. Today's guys can earn a couple of million by just show-ing up in the right sneakers. Wasn't like that when I was their age."

"So you give speeches?"

"Yep. About a dozen a year, on how to be better managers, better team players, work together for the same goal. That sort of thing. Not lots of money, but enough to make a living. Hey. Wanna hear a secret?"

The chief smiled but there was something in those eyes that said he liked hearing secrets very much. "Sure. Go right ahead."

Glen said, "Truth is, most of the time, I'm just stealin' their money. Companies get in trouble, they have morale problems, they tend to look outside for a solution. They don't think about looking inside. So I come by and give 'em a nice pep talk, everything's jazzed up for a week or so after I'm gone, and then the same lousy managers and overworked employees fall back into their ruts, while I'm waiting for their checks to clear."

Colter didn't write anything down, which was fine. Glen said, "Secret's safe with you?"

"Sure is," the chief said.

Glen said, "All right, enough about me. What do you want to know about Marcus?"

"Did he play with you on the Celtics?"

Glen looked at that smooth face and those unblinking eyes, wondering if the guy was trying to play some sort of game. "No, he didn't."

The chief said, "But he was a teammate of yours, right?"

"Right. But not on the Celtics."

"Oh. I'm sorry. Where, then?"

Maybe the boy was just dumb. Could it be? Glen said, "On the Olympic team, that's where. Marcus and me and ten other guys, we played for the United States back in '72."

"All right, then," the chief said, making a note. "The 1972 Olympic team. Okay. Now. When did Marcus come up here?"

"Today's Monday. He came up here Saturday, spent the night, and I dropped him off at the bus stop yesterday morning."

"Was there anybody else in your house at the time?"

"Nope."

"And what did the two of you do while he was here?"

Glen shrugged. "Played some hoops for old time's sake. Talked about the old days. Had a barbecue and some beer."

Colter took a careful sip from his lemonade. "Were you expecting him?"

"Excuse me?"

Colter said, "He's only up here for a day and a half. He took a bus up from Queens, in New York. It seems like a lot of work to get up here for just a quick visit."

Glen said, "Yeah, I was expecting him. But he only gave me a day's warning."

Colter's eyes were now fixed on him. "So why the quick visit? Why did he come to see you, Mr. Jackson?"

Now he knew that the young boy was pretty sharp. "Money."

"He had money problems?"

"Shit, yes. Poor guy's about to be kicked out of his apartment, he's had maybe a half dozen jobs over the years, everything from selling cars to real estate . . . like I said earlier, Chief, things are so much different now than it was back then. You get a guy like him or me, in our fifties . . . time's running out if you didn't plan real serious back when you were younger for your financial future."

"Did you help him?"

Glen thought for just a moment, shook his head. "I offered to, but he wouldn't take any of my money. But he had other ideas."

"Like what?"

"The silver medal, that's what."

"I'm sorry, the what?"

He paused, judging the face, recalled all the times he had seen opponents' faces on the court, trying to read who they were and where they were coming from. This one was trying to be the Mayberry hayseed, sort of be the dummy cop, and Glen was going to play along with the game. Thing about games is that it's only fair when both sides know that it's being played.

"The silver medal," Glen said. "Marcus decided it was time to get it, and me and the other team members, we didn't want him to. He came up here to try to convince me otherwise."

Colter tried a smile and said, "You're getting me even more confused, Mr. Jackson. Look. I'm sorry to hurt your feelings and all, but I'm not a basketball fan. I don't know much about you or the game, or the Olympic team. I'm more of a Red Sox fan myself."

"Okay. No problem there."

"So I'm afraid I don't know what you mean, the silver medal. Did your team win the silver medal at the Olympics?"

"Sort of."

"And why doesn't Marcus have the silver medal?"

Glen shook his head. "Because none of us does, and none of us will. Look, you really meant that, about not knowing anything about basketball?"

A quick nod. "Hardly a thing."

He ran a thumb across the top of his lemonade glass. "You in the mood for a history lesson?"

"Will it have something to do with Marcus?"

"It'll have a lot to do with Marcus, and me, and the other guys, and what happened in '72. Look. Back in 1972, the Olympics were in Munich, okay? First time they had been in Germany since Berlin, back in '36. Which was one hell of a co-incidence, because back in 1936, that was the first time basketball was an Olympic sport. The U.S. won the gold medal then, and won the gold medal at every other Olympics since then, right up to 1972. You know what our record was, the U.S. Olympic team record?"

"No, I don't, but I'm sure you'll tell me," Colter said with a smile.

"Okay. Sixty-two and oh. That means almost over four decades, in six different Olympics, the United States had never lost a single basketball match. Not one. So we were favored, going into Munich, even though the Soviets were tough bastards and had been wanting to nail us for years. Okay. Munich. That Olympics mean anything to you?"

Colter rubbed at his chin. "The Israeli athletes, right?"

"Right you are. Eleven of those poor guys got killed by terrorists. Most Americans, you mention the Munich Olympics, they remember three things: the Israelis, Mark Spitz getting seven gold medals, and the way we guys on the basketball team got robbed."

"How did you get robbed?"

Another shrug. "We just did. Look, imagine what it was like, being back there, most of us in our teens or early twenties. Our coach was Hank Iba, a legend. He had coached the Olympic teams in '64 and '68 and got a gold medal both times. We went through years of work and training and practice to be picked as part of the team. You know? And when we marched through that stadium with everybody else on the U.S. team, representing our friends and families and everyone back home . . . well, it made your hair stand up on end."

"Marcus, too?"

"Sure, Marcus and everybody else. Then we started playing and we just blazed through everybody that was in our way. I mean, Christ, we beat Japan 99 to 33. We met other players, fans . . . it wasn't like today, with the dream team playin', every player demanding his own hotel suite. Nope, we bunked together in the dormitories, just like everybody else. And then the Israelis got killed and the Olympics were postponed for a day. It was awful, it was chaos, lots of rumors . . ."

Colter said, "And when did you get robbed?"

Glen took a breath, fascinated at how it was all coming back, like the damn thing had just happened last week. "We made it to the finals against the Soviet Union. There we were, college kids mostly, going toe-to-toe with guys that had their entire nation and entire sports ministry behind them. All they had to worry about was basketball, basketball, basketball. That was it. And we played them late on September 9, the damn game didn't start until eleven-forty-five p.m. Can you believe that? The gold medal finals, starting almost at midnight."

"Why?"

"Because the schedule and everything else got tossed up in the air after the Israeli massacre, that's why. So we were playing late, everybody was still jazzed up over the massacre, and pretty soon we were losing to the Russians, and losing bad. I mean, at one point, those guys were ahead by ten points. We couldn't believe it, that our team, *our* team, would break a winning streak that had been in place for thirty-six years. We felt horrible."

Colter kept pen to pad, though nothing had been written in a while. "I take it you and Marcus and everybody else fought back."

"Uh-huh," he said, and now the old emotions, the old memories, were racing right through him . . . the smell of sweat and the court, the yells and chants from the crowd, the squeaking of sneakers on the court, the coach yelling and pointing and keeping them together, those damn Russians, staring at them, like they just wanted to crush these college kids and sweep them aside. "We fought back. Man, how we fought back, and at the very end, one of our guys tossed in two free throws, and the score was U.S. 50, U.S.S.R. 49. And there was just three seconds left on the clock. Three seconds. One, two, three. That's it. And even then, the Russians—with some help—managed to steal it from us."

"How?"

Another breath, another amazement of how the old feelings of shock and betrayal were rumbling through. "Three times . . . the Russians were allowed to put the ball into play three times, can you believe that? The first two times, the clock was reset in their favor. And the third time, one of their guys— Belov—managed to make a basket, even though there were two violations against the Russians that the refs didn't call. Third time was a charm for the bastards, and the score ended up being 51 to 50."

"Wow," Colter said. "I'm sorry, it's just that my parents hadn't even gotten married by 1972 . . . this is the first time I've ever heard of it. What happened then?"

"Well, protests were filed and a five-judge panel reviewed the results, and since three of the judges were from Cuba, Hungary, and Poland, it was a done deal who they were going to rule in favor of—their Russian buddies. Our whole team voted to boycott the medal ceremony, and not one of us agreed to receive our silver medal. We went home thinking we were winners, while the world thought we were losers. So that's how it's been for thirty years."

Colter now made a note in his pad. "And Marcus, he wanted to get his silver medal, all these years later? For the money?"

Glen looked out at the now-empty waters of Walker's Lake, where all the boats had finally left the waters in peace. "Yeah. Sorry to say. The silver medals are in a bank vault somewhere, still controlled by the International Olympic Committee, and every few years, they've asked us if we wanted to have them, finally. And each time, every one of us said no. We went into the Olympics as a team, we left as a team, and by God, we're still not going to accept the fact that we got robbed. Those medals can gather dust until all of us are dead."

"But Marcus changed his mind."

"Debt can do that to a man," Glen said. "Thing is, he had an idea. Get the medal and put it up at auction on eBay or something. He figured he could make enough money off that to live quite well, and you know what, he's probably right. But dammit, thirty years later, we're still not taking those medals. Some of us are even in worse shape than Marcus, and the fact that we're still hanging in there, still not letting those medals come into our hands, well, for some of us, that's the only thing we've got going. One guy takes a medal, then the whole team is broke up. That's the point."

Another notation in the notebook. "I take it that's what the two of you talked about?"

"Yep." He continued to look out on the waters, just letting the words come out mechanically. "I told Marcus not to do it. I told him that I'd give him some money, that I'd contact a couple of other team members . . . get a package or something together. Just to avoid him taking the medal."

"And what did he say?"

He kept his view on the lake. "Ol' Marcus, he wasn't buying what I was selling. He wanted to do this on his own, and he didn't want to listen to what I had to say."

Colter flipped through a page in his notebook and Glen looked at him. The chief glanced up and said, "One thing I don't understand. Why did he come to see you?"

"Excuse me?"

Colter said, "What was the point of getting on a bus and coming all the way up here? Why not just contact the IOC and say he agreed to take the medal, and leave you out of it?"

Exactly, he thought, and he said, "Thing is, Chief, I'm sort of the guy that keeps in touch with the other guys, you know? I wasn't team captain or anything, but I'm the one who sort of keeps everybody's address and phone number up to date. Marcus came up here, sort of looking for permission. Said that if I didn't make a fuss, then maybe the other team members would cut him some slack."

"And what did you tell him?"

He took a breath. "I told him that he shouldn't do it. That he'd be betraying the memory of our team and our coach to do it, that one thing we had going for us was the fact that we had stuck together, had boycotted the awards ceremony, had boycotted the medals for thirty years. I told him that we could help him out, but only if we stuck together. And I reminded him what silver tasted like."

"I'm sorry, I didn't catch that."

Glen nodded. "Sorry. Just a phrase we had, back in Munich. That gold had the best taste of all. And then we talked some more, had a barbecue, and then changed the subject. Marcus said he had to do what was right for him and his family. I said I could see his point. And that was that."

"Uh-huh." The pen made a few motions across the small notebook. "Then what?"

He shrugged. "Up at dawn. Quick breakfast of coffee and toast. Drove him into town, to Frye's. It opens up at six. Got there about fifteen minutes early. He was going to get into the store at six, buy a ticket for the six-fifteen bus. Last I saw him, he was standing by the front door of the store."

"And was anybody else around?"

"Chief, you know what it's like in town. Some days at noon the place is empty. Nope, nobody was there."

Colter said, "Which is strange, because nobody at the store saw him, Mr. Jackson. The owner opened up at six a.m. on the dot, and nobody was waiting for him. Which means that something happened to him in those fifteen minutes."

"Sure sounds like that, doesn't it?"

"Did he say he was going to see anybody else? Or stay another night in town? Or anything?"

"No, not at all. He was just going to get on the bus, head to Boston and then back to Queens."

"Is there anything else you can think of that can help us in our investigation?"

He shook his head. "No, I wish I could help. Jesus. I mean, what do you think? Somebody picked him up? He wandered off?"

The chief closed his notebook. "We're not sure, but we'll be looking into everything." Colter stood up and so did Glen, and the chief said, "Thanks for the cooperation. And the lemonade. I guess I'll be going."

They went into the living room and the chief sniffed the air, said, "Smells like you've had a fire in the fireplace."

"Yeah, last couple of nights, it's been chilly here. Nothing like a fire to keep the damp out of a room."

By the doorway, as they were walking out, the chief pointed to a collection of sports gear in the corner. "It doesn't look like everybody plays basketball who comes up here, does it?"

Glen stood quite still, looking at the mess in the corner. The hockey sticks for street hockey on the asphalt, the soccer balls, Frisbees, baseball gloves, baseballs, and footballs. "That's right," he said. "My grandkids come up here, they sure like to play with other stuff. They get tired of Grandpa beating them on the basketball court."

Colter laughed and just as he was getting ready to leave, just as he was getting ready to step out of the room, he said, "Oh, one more thing."

Oh, how fake, Glen thought. How fake can you get? "Sure, what is it?"

Colter's smile disappeared. "I'd like to take a look around. If you don't mind."

"Here? The house?"

A crisp nod. "Yes. Your house. If you don't mind."

He certainly did mind but he shrugged and said, "Go ahead. Knock yourself out."

So they spent the next fifteen minutes as the chief went through the closets, checked out the attached utility room that held the water heater and oil furnace, went back into the living room and kitchen and then upstairs. The cottage had no basement. More poking through the closets and in the bathroom and the master bedroom and the two spare rooms—"Marcus spent the night in this one," Glen said, pointing out the spare room that had a view of the lake—and then they came to the last room in the small house, at the end of the hallway.

Colter said, "What's in here?"

"My office, that's all."

"I'd like to take a look at it, if you don't mind."

Glen said, "It's just an office. Nothing in there at all."

Colter said, "Please. Open the door, Mr. Jackson. Or I'll come back here with—"

"Oh, for God's sake, here," Glen said, opening up the door. "Look as much as you want."

The office was small, another spare room that had been converted. There was a desk and office chair and filing cabinets, and a closet that the chief looked into. Glen stood perfectly still. Near his desk was his ego wall, a twin of the one back home, in his larger office. Framed certificates, photos and plaques, and one large framed uniform from his last season with the Celtics. Colter closed the closet door and then looked up at the ego wall. Glen did not move, tried not to show a thing. Colter said, "Lots of photos up there."

"Yeah, well, you tend to get those over time."

Colter stepped forward and Glen closed his eyes, imagined the questions that would come his way once Colter looked at the photos and the inscriptions and what was there, but Colter said, "Hey, I recognize this guy. Red Auerbach, am I right?"

Glen opened his eyes. "Yes. You're absolutely right."

Colter turned away from the wall and said, "Well, I guess it's time to go."

Another handshake outside and then Colter headed to his cruiser. "Thanks again for your cooperation, Mr. Jackson, and for the history lesson. You're not offended that I'm not a basketball fan, are you?"

Glen tried to keep the relief out of his voice. "Not at all. Tell me—I'm heading home to Boston tomorrow—can you keep me informed on how the investigation is going?"

"Sure," he said, "but . . . well, I don't know. It just seems so damn strange, like the earth just opened up and swallowed him. Quite strange."

"Yeah," Glen said. "Strange."

* * *

Twelve hours after the police chief had left him, Glen was out on his powerboat, alone, just past midnight, in the middle reaches of Walker's Lake. He had slowly motored out here and then waited, and switched off the engine and the running lights, letting his eyes adjust to the darkness. He sat on the seat and leaned back and looked up at the stars. It was a quiet night and the water was still, and he had no worries of drifting or being swamped.

Out in the distance a loon called out to its mate, the trilling sound making the back of his hands tingle, and he thought of Marcus's wife, back there in Queens, alone and wondering what had happened to her husband.

He sighed, shifted some in the seat, and then stood up, the boat weaving back and forth. He said in the darkness, "I bet she misses you, though I don't know why, you rotten son of a bitch."

But there was no reply, no sound coming back from the plastic-wrapped object in the stern of the boat, secured on both ends with concrete blocks. He went to the back of the boat and waited, still looking at the dark stretches of the shore-line. Aloud he said, "Just my luck he wasn't a basketball fan, ol' boy. He stood in my office and looked at my plaques and tro-phies, and it was staring right at him. My old nickname on the court. The Enforcer. That was me, Marcus the Enforcer, and that's why you shouldn't have come to see me. 'Cause I was going to enforce our agreement. Man, even somebody as young as that chief should have seen that."

Part of the story was true, about the discussion and the beer and the barbecue, but he had left out the part when ol' Marcus, hair gone gray and stomach gone thick, had got into a screaming match, saying screw you, screw the team, I'm on my own, it's been thirty years, the hell with you all, and when he started storming out of the cottage, saying he was going to walk to town and catch a cab or do something to get him back home and get that silver medal in his hands, well, Glen was not going to allow it. Not for a moment. And when Marcus got to the door, he had reached into the sports gear and picked up a baseball bat and creamed the back of Marcus's skull.

The baseball bat that he had burned in the fireplace later that night.

And dammit, if it hadn't been for all those fishermen, hanging out all those hours, Marcus would have been gone before the chief showed up. Shit, that had been a close-run thing.

One more look around the dark waters, and then he bent down and grunted and picked up the body and dumped it into the water. It didn't make much of a noise, hardly even a splash, and as it disappeared from view, he thought about the fall coming up quick, and then the ice, and then the long winter, and by the time spring came 'round, Marcus would be gone.

"Thing is," he said again to the darkness, "the chief forgot to ask me one more question. About the taste of silver. And this is what I would have told him: that the taste of silver is the taste of losers. That's it. And I ain't no loser."

With that, he went forward and started up his powerboat and headed back to his cottage, thirty years later, still feeling like a winner, no matter what.

FEAR OF FAILURE

Parnell Hall

He was tall, black, and dead. A bad combination. And for an ex-Celtics fan, one that conjured up images of Len Bias and Reggie Lewis. I say ex-fan because it was about then that I stopped following the team, when Bird, McHale, and Parish retired, to be replaced by a crop of young players I did not know who did not win.

Since then I've followed the Knicks, an interesting exercise, to be sure, recalling just the sort of heartbreak I'd grown used to from years of watching the Red Sox. A disappointing but interesting team, the Knicks: I was in Madison Square Garden when Starks made the dunk, and watched on TV that seventh game of the Finals when he threw up brick after brick. I listen now, in the post-Ewing era, when people in the elevator of my Upper West Side apartment building maintain that while they like Marcus Camby, he's a forward, not a center, and what are the Knicks going to do now? And I realize after twenty years I am finally assimilated.

I am a New Yorker.

But I was talking about the boy.

And here I have to be careful. A word I shouldn't use for an African American. Just as I shouldn't use *girl* to refer to a young woman. But it was hard not to think of him as a boy.

He was only eighteen.

Grant Jackson was six foot ten, 280 pounds, all muscle. He collapsed and died during a preseason practice of the varsity basketball team of Cedar Park College, a small Brooklyn school with big aspirations. Without Grant the team had rarely posted a winning season. This year they had hoped to reach the NIT playoffs.

That would not happen.

It was up to me to find out why.

"No, it isn't," Richard Rosenberg insisted. He got up from his desk, hooked his thumbs in his suspenders, and strutted back and forth as if he were making an argument in front of a jury.

Richard Rosenberg was the negligence lawyer I work for. A little man, with an inexhaustible source of nervous energy, he loved beating opposing attorneys down. With none in sight, he was happy to pick on me.

"Stanley," he said, "I don't know how to impress this on you. Your job is *not* to find out why this happened. Your job is simply to record the fact it *did*. Take down the information. Have the mother sign the necessary release forms. That's the reason you're there. To get her to sign the retainer. So see that she does."

"What about the father?"

"If he's there, sign him. It's the mother who called. I think it's a single mother. I certainly hope so."

"Richard."

"Well, I'll get a bigger settlement. A poor woman, raising her children alone. Trust me, there won't be a dry eye in court."

"I'm sure there won't. Pardon me, Richard, but just who do you intend to sue?"

"I don't know. The school, the coach, the EMS, the doctors, the hospital. That's not your problem, that's my problem. Just sign the kid up. There's always someone to sue. Now, get going before Jacoby and Meyers gets wind of this and aces me out."

★ ★ ★

Grant's mother lived in Bedford-Stuyvesant in one of those housing projects I always dread and always seem to get. Steel outer doors with smashed locks and windows, dimly lit lobbies, and odd/even elevators, at least one of which was never working, invariably the one I wanted. In this case it was the odd, a sure thing, since the Jacksons lived on seven. I rode up to eight in the company of a young man in a do-rag wearing half the gold in Fort Knox, who looked as if he'd like to mug me if it weren't for the nagging suspicion I might be a cop. I walked down a stairwell that reeked of urine and stale marijuana, then tried to find apartment J, not an easy task since the letters had fallen off half the doors. Eventually I located apartment F and counted down. I rang the bell, heard nothing, tried knocking on the door.

It was opened by a young black man with the word *hostile* tattooed on his forehead.

"You the lawyer?" he demanded.

A moment of truth.

Richard Rosenberg's TV advertising, besides promising "free consultation" and "no fee unless recovery," boldly proclaims, "We will come to your house."

He wouldn't, of course. He would send me. I would come

walking in in a suit and tie, saying, "Hi, I'm from the lawyer's office," and if people wanted to assume I was an attorney, that was just fine, and it didn't really hurt anybody, since a lawyer couldn't do any more than I could at that juncture anyway. But I never lied to the client, I never claimed to be a lawyer, and if directly asked, I would explain that I was actually the investigator hired by the lawyer.

Only, this didn't seem to be that time. The gentleman, whoever he was, was not the client, and it occurred to me it was probably not wise to get into a philosophical conversation with him. So I tried a simple deflection. "Hi," I said, "I'm Stanley Hastings. I'm here to see Mrs. Jackson. I believe she called Rosenberg and Stone."

While that did not appear to please him, it worked. He turned, hollered, "Hey, Ma, is the lawyer," and walked off, giving me the choice of standing there like a jerk or trailing along behind.

I followed him into a living room where a large black woman sat on a couch bouncing a baby boy on her knee. In a playpen in the corner, a baby girl was chewing on a Miss Piggy doll. A third small child was building a tower on the rug.

The room reeked of poverty. The furniture could have been gathered off the street. Only the children's toys looked new. And the baby's diapers were fresh Pampers. Clearly all money was spent on the kids.

"Mrs. Jackson?" I said.

She looked up at me with big brown eyes. Hurt, pained, yet still polite. "Yes?"

"I'm Mr. Hastings from the lawyer's office."

"Oh, yes. Come, sit down."

She patted the couch next to her, which would have been

my first choice. For one thing, she had to sign papers. For another, I wouldn't have to look at her, see her grief.

I sat down, put my briefcase on the coffee table, snapped it open, took out a fact sheet.

"All right, Mrs. Jackson," I said. "Your son's name was Grant?"

"That's right."

"Grant Jackson?"

"Yes."

I filled his name in the blank. Grant Jackson, though dead, was still the client. His mother was filing suit in his behalf. I put down his particulars, then hers.

As Richard had surmised, Grant's father had left the family picture years ago. I inquired of the brothers and sisters, all of whom would benefit in the event of a successful suit. There were nine, ranging in age from the baby on her knee to the young man who had opened the door, whose name turned out to be Lincoln. Indeed, the chronological list of Mrs. Jackson's children mapped a cultural evolution, from Grant and Lincoln to Jamal and Rasheed.

The preliminaries out of the way, I took a breath. "All right," I said. "Can you tell me what happened?"

Mrs. Jackson snuffled once, bounced the baby automatically. "Grant was at practice. He always at practice. He work him hard. Too hard."

"Who worked him hard?"

"Coach Tom."

"Who's Coach Tom?"

"The coach."

"What's his name?"

"Coach Tom."

I didn't want to get impatient with a woman in her grief, but I wasn't making much headway. "Does Coach Tom have another name?"

"Suppose. But everyone call him Coach Tom."

"He was Grant's basketball coach?"

"Yes, and he work him too hard."

"Ma, take it easy," Lincoln warned. He was prowling the room as if suspicious I might be trying to rip his mother off.

She pierced him with her eyes. "Easy? I should take it easy? My boy. My poor boy."

"Grant collapsed during practice?"

"That's right. He had a bad heart. No, not a *bad* heart. A *weak* heart. And Coach Tom knew. That's the thing. Coach Tom knew."

"Grant had a heart condition?"

"Yes, he did."

"He'd been to the doctor for this?"

"Tha's right. Said he had arrhythmia. Not bad if he careful. If he don't play ball."

"Not what he say," Lincoln contradicted. "He don't say don't play ball. He just say take it easy."

"Same thing. Shouldn't have played. I tell him that. I tell him don't play. Grant, he don't listen."

"Did your son play ball before? In high school?"

"Course he did. Course we don't know. We don't know nothin' wrong. Till the physical. The college physical. Doctor find out what the pediatrician miss." Her voice quivered in outrage. "Can you believe that? Pediatrician see him every year, don't know a thing."

"What's the pediatrician's name?" I asked. It occurred to me Richard was right, there were a lot of people to sue.

She gave me the information and I wrote it down.

"So what'd the doctor say? The one who found the arrhythmia?"

"The doctor say he can play. He got a heart condition, but he can play. He just gotta take it easy. How you take it easy playin' ball? I tell him, Grant, don't do it. I tell him no. My boy, he got a big heart." She broke down. "Oh, why I say that? But it's true. He had a plan. Can't talk him out of it. Gonna be a star, claim hardship, jump to the NBA. Signin' bonus, get us outta here. I tell him no, but he won't hear. He won't hear."

A sob racked her body, and her eyes filled with tears.

It was a relief when my beeper went off. It startled the baby, made him cry, snapped his mother back to the present.

"Wha's that?" she said.

"Sorry. It's the office, paging me. I have to call in."

"Phone's inna kitchen. Lincoln, show the man."

I got up, followed Lincoln Jackson into a kitchen where cockroaches scurried about in plain sight. I picked up the receiver of the wall phone, punched in the office number.

"Rosenberg and Stone," came the voice of Wendy/Janet.

Wendy and Janet were Richard's switchboard girls. They had identical voices, so I never knew which I was talking to.

"It's Stanley. What's up?"

"Where are you?"

"Grant Jackson's apartment, signing up the mother."

"Forget it," Wendy/Janet said. "I got a case for you in Queens."

I blinked. "Excuse me?"

"A case in Queens. The guy's waiting for you. Head out there now."

"I'm just getting started here." I lowered my voice. "She hasn't signed the retainer yet."

"It doesn't matter. We're dropping the case."

I blinked again. "Why?"

"I don't know, but Richard said to send you out to Queens."

I groaned. Besides a voice, Wendy and Janet shared an intelligence. Between them, they had the I.Q. of a fireplug. I had learned from bitter experience any fact they gave me was apt to be wrong.

This had to be one of them.

"I'll have to hear it from Richard," I said.

"Very well," Wendy/Janet said acidly, taking my request for the rebuke it was, and put me on hold.

Moments later Richard Rosenberg came on the line. "Stanley. Why are you giving the girls a hard time? Take down the information and get out to Queens."

"I'm not done here."

"Yes, you are. We're dropping the case."

"How come?"

"It'll be on the evening news. A friend of mine leaked me the autopsy report. Grant Jackson died of a drug overdose."

"You're kidding."

"Not at all. Pretty stupid, huh? A guy with a weak heart shouldn't be messing around with cocaine."

I looked up, saw Lincoln standing there staring at me.

"You wanna run that by me again, Richard?"

"Of course," Richard said sarcastically. "God forbid you should merely follow instructions without making me justify my decisions. The point is, Grant Jackson with a bad ticker made the rather unwise career choice of mainlining a rather large dose of rather pure coke. Under the circumstances, the number of people I can sue has dropped from everybody and his brother to one, the guy who sold him the drugs. Whom I would suspect of being unlikely to be found. So I'm dropping the case. So wrap it up and get out to Queens. Hang on, I'll transfer you back, you can get the address."

Wendy/Janet came back on the line and gave me the info. A Frederick Tucker of Forest Hills had tripped on a crack in the sidewalk and broken his leg, giving him a cause of action against the City of New York. I took down the details, told Wendy/Janet I'd get right on it.

I didn't.

I figured a guy with a broken leg wasn't going anywhere. Frederick Tucker could wait. First I finished signing up Mrs. Jackson.

* * *

"That's awful," Alice said as we watched the report on the evening news.

"It certainly is," I told her.

"So there's no case, but you signed it up anyway? Just so you wouldn't have to tell the woman Richard had turned her down?"

"That's right."

"As a humane gesture, to spare her feelings?"

"No," I said. "As a cowardly gesture, not wanting to be the one to tell her."

"Instead you spent a half hour filling out forms."

"Fifteen minutes. No big deal."

"So the woman's signed up?"

"Yes, she is."

"What does that mean?"

"It means she'll have to get a note from Rosenberg and Stone, telling her we're no longer handling the case."

"I don't think so."

I looked at Alice. She was lying on the bed propped up on her elbow. She looked bright, attractive, alluring, fetching, radiant.

I was in trouble.

I took the zapper, flicked the TV on mute. Leaned back in the overstuffed chair. "Alice, what am I missing here?"

"You told me all about this woman and her umpteen children and her squalid apartment. Her dead son wanted to get her out of there. *She* wants to get out of there. That's why she wants to sue. You know the reason that won't work. You knew it, but you signed her up anyway."

"I told you why."

"Yeah, but I know you. You're a nice guy. You see this woman with her kids, and you wanna help her. You figure maybe there's a loophole even Richard doesn't know. You figure there's gotta be a way."

I'm not entirely sure I figured all that. As I grow older and more cynical, any resemblance between me and a knight in shining armor is entirely coincidental and not to be inferred. If asked for an objective self-evaluation, I would have said I chickened out. Being a devout coward.

Of course that goes double for my wife. Don't get me wrong—I don't mean she's a coward—I mean when confronted with her, that's what I become. Anyway, faced with Alice's placid assurance that my motivation was clearly to help the woman, I found myself, as I usually do when dealing with my wife, ill equipped to contradict her. In short, helping the woman had become the coward's way out.

★ ★ ★

Cedar Park was a small college nestled within a single city block. Its facilities consisted of a series a crumbling stone buildings, all of the same vintage and architectural design. Clearly no wealthy graduate was springing for a new theater or science lab.

The gymnasium turned out to be on the fourth floor of the history building. I determined this by going in what appeared to be the administration building and looking in vain for any sort of office, then going back outside and asking some students, who were leery of me, making me for a cop. Eventually I got the right building, found the stairs. Halfway up the last flight, I was rewarded by the sound of a bouncing basketball.

The Cedar Park College basketball court was small, as I'd expected, but surprisingly well maintained. The parquet floor gleamed. The keys and three-point lines had been stenciled on with care. The wooden backboards were freshly painted white. The orange rims were new, as were the white and blue nets.

The court was about three-quarters of the length of a regulation floor. There were no bleachers for fans, just a single row of benches along the narrow side walls, which might have led me to believe this was just a practice gym, were it not for the score clock on the wall. The clock looked older than me, which cast doubts as to whether it actually worked. Taken together, a pair of depressing thoughts.

There were ten men on the court, playing a practice game. Five wore red pullover jerseys, five did not. All were black. Most were lithe and thin. Some were tall. Some were broad. All had moves. None were dominant.

Watching the action was a wizened old black man with horn-rimmed glasses, a whistle in his mouth, and a perpetual frown. As I watched, he blew the whistle, stopped action, strode onto the court.

"No, no, no!" he complained, shaking his head. He addressed a lanky young man with an open mouth and a *who, me?* expression. "Clyde, what was that play? That was a pick-an'-roll. You pick, but you din't roll. Floyd got the ball, two defenders on him, nowhere to go. All you do is bring another man to cover Floyd. Now, is that *helpful*? Is that *useful*? Is that what you were *tryin'* to do?"

Players from both teams grinned and snickered while Clyde shuffled his feet and muttered, "No."

"No," the man with the whistle said. "Tha's right, Clyde. Good answer. So we learnin' here. So the next time you pick an' roll, you *roll*."

Play started up again.

I moved around the court, approached the man. "Coach Tom?"

He spoke without looking or taking the whistle out of his mouth. "Yes?"

"I'm here about Grant Jackson."

He exhaled hard enough to blow the whistle slightly. Heads turned on the court, but he waved it off. "Play on." He turned to me, aggrieved. "What about him? Not bad enough I lose my star player, I gotta answer questions too?"

"Yeah," I said. "It must be hard. But it's harder for his family. For their sake, could you help me out?"

Coach Tom squinted up his eyes and turned his back on the action on the court. "Just what you mean?"

I was treading a fine line here, what with Richard rejecting the case. "I'm trying to help out Grant's mom. See if there's any insurance money to be had. It's probably a long shot, but the woman had ten kids. If you can see a way to help me out."

"How could I do that?"

"I understand Grant collapsed during a practice. Was that up here?"

"Course it here. You think we got some other gym we use for games? This here's it. Always has been, probably always will. 'Specially now."

"You mean without Grant?"

"Made a difference, that he did. Expectations were high."

"Justifiably so?"

He squinted. "Wha's that?"

"Did *you* think Grant would have made a difference?"

"Yes, he would. How much is hard to say, but he certainly would." He jerked his thumb. "These are good boys, but without him they just another team."

"How will they do?"

"Same as usual. Not too good, not too bad. Couple of schools we always beat, couple always beat us. Bunch inna middle. Same thing every year."

"How long have you coached this team?"

"Twenty-six years now."

"Ever had a player like Grant?"

"I had good players. But like Grant? No, not like Grant. Damn shame."

"How did it happen?"

"We havin' a scrimmage, just like this. He goes up for a rebound. Come down holdin' his side. I thought he got elbowed. By the guy in front. I'm giving him what-for 'bout boxin' out, he fall down on the floor."

"Any chance he did take an elbow to the ribs, something might have hurt his heart?"

"Sure there is. But that's not what killed him. Not accordin' to the TV."

"That surprised you?"

"What?"

"That he was taking drugs?"

"Yes and no."

"What do you mean by that?"

Coach Tom scratched his nose. "You gotta understand. I seen 'em come, I seen 'em go. All types of kid. I never seen a kid as good as Grant. But I seen kids like him. I know how they think."

"And how is that?"

"You wouldn't understand."

"Try me."

He tapped his glasses. "You can see it in their eyes. The fear. The fear of failure. They got all the goods they need to succeed, and they afraid it's not enough. They scared to death to get out there, have to prove themselves." He shrugged. "So they turn to junk. You think Grant the first star player I had took to drugs? What planet you live on?"

"Grant was a special case. He had a heart problem. He knew drugs could kill him."

"Drugs could kill anybody. Sometimes do. They still take 'em. Kid got the fear, like Grant, he not thinkin' that. He don't care. I'm not sayin' he tryin' to kill himself. But it's not a deterrent, you know what I mean? Grant decide to take a toot, stuff don't agree with him, there you go. Shame, but there you be."

Coach Tom watched the action up and down the court. "*Bounce*-pass, Larry. *Bounce*-pass."

"Grant never used drugs before?"

"How should I know?"

"I don't know. The college have a drug policy?"

"Sure they do. Make me run drug tests." He snorted. "What a joke. Guys pee in a cup. Big deal. Pass the cup around. Guy who's not high pees for 'em all."

"You don't supervise 'em?"

He gave me the evil eye. "You like to hold that cup? They say test 'em, I test 'em. They don't like it, jus' too damn bad."

"So Grant passed his drug screen?"

"That he did. Did he pass it on his own, I couldn't say."

"If he was gettin' high, who was giving it to him?"

He gave me another look. "How the hell should I know?"

I shrugged. "You strike me as a man don't miss much. I bet you could tell me the most likely source on your team for coke or grass."

"Oh, you think so?" Coach Tom blew the whistle. "No, tha's a turnover. You can palm the ball all you want, no one care anymore, but you carry it like that, you gonna get called. Red ball onna side." He turned back to me. "You talk a good game. You start talkin' to my boys about drugs, they're gonna think you a cop, no matter what cover story you give. You don't need that, and neither do I. And you ain't a cop. You got no authority to do it, so you don't."

He stuck his finger in my face. "So lemme put it 'nother way. How will knowing where Grant got his drugs help you get some insurance money for his mom? Riddle me that."

I couldn't.

★ ★ ★

MacAullif smiled when I walked in the door.

I stopped, blinked, wondered if I was in the wrong office.

"Hi, how you doin'?" MacAullif said.

I looked at him suspiciously. "Just fine. How are you?"

"Couldn't be better."

I was concerned. If things couldn't be better, something was definitely wrong. Under normal circumstances Sergeant MacAullif treated my entrance into his office as an intrusion on his valuable time. If he was pleased to see me, the world was out of whack.

"I'm glad to hear it," I said. "I'm wondering if you have time to discuss a case."

"As long as you can be calm."

"Calm?"

"Yes. And don't get riled up. And don't get *me* riled up. Do you think you can do that?"

"Why would I get you riled up?"

"Because you always do," MacAullif flared, and immediately pulled back.

"Jeez, MacAullif," I said. "You mind telling me why you're trying so hard to keep calm?"

MacAullif exhaled through his teeth. He sounded like a steam locomotive. "Blood pressure. I got high blood pressure. I had my physical, the doc says it's dangerously high. Gotta avoid stress. Gotta avoid tension. Tough assignment, the work I do, but there are ways and there are ways. The main way, Doc says, is don't take it personally. It may be a homicide, but it's just a job. You handle it and move on. So the bottom line is, while I'd much prefer you didn't bring me any more stress, I'm not gonna let it bother me if you do. So how about it, can you handle this on your own?"

"I could use some help."

A frown crossed MacAullif's face, was instantly replaced by

a smile. "Of course," he said. "Pray tell me what you want. So I may help you with it before getting back to the three homicides I am coordinating. Among five detectives, as one is out with the flu." He considered. "I said that very calmly. I should get points for that."

"You should get points just for saying *among*. Most cops would say *between*."

MacAullif gave me an utterly baffled look. "Excuse me?"

"Sorry," I said. "I didn't mean to intrude on your calm. I was just wondering if you had anything on the Grant Jackson case."

MacAullif frowned. "What made you wonder that?"

"The mother called Rosenberg and Stone."

"Indeed," MacAullif said. He didn't sound happy. "Well, it happens to have crossed my desk. It is not one of the three homicides I mentioned. It is in *addition* to the three homicides I mentioned. It is a closed case I was hoping to clear, for, as I say, manpower is short."

MacAullif took a cigar from his desk, began twirling it through his fingers, a nervous habit he had when thinking something out. "The Grant Jackson case is rather straightforward. A kid with a bad heart shoots a lethal dose of coke. It's a no-brainer. It's a slam dunk. The type of case you pray for with a case overload. Just this morning I was quite thrilled at the prospect of having chalked it up and not having to deal with it again."

"I'm not asking you to deal with it. I'm just wondering if you could discuss it."

MacAullif took a breath, then smiled what had to be the most forced smile this side of the *Mona Lisa*. It occurred to me if he were working any harder at being relaxed, his jaw might crack. "Of course," he said.

"You get anything from the autopsy report?"

"Just what I said. Kid OD'd. Shame, but it happens all the time."

"The kid a user?"

"No, he wasn't. Not according to the M.E. No track marks. He might have snorted before, but he never shot. And for good reason. Guy with a heart condition mainlinin' got to be suicidal."

"Think it was?"

"What?"

"Suicide?"

MacAullif's face contorted in what could only be preparation for a barrage of sarcasm. He re-collected himself, composed his features. One could almost hear him reciting a mantra. "I would think you could rule out suicide. Suicides kill themselves. They don't get high and go play ball."

"What do you think of the theory he was trying to get himself up for practice?"

"I don't like it, but I'd take it over suicide."

"What do you think of the theory someone did him in?"

He raised one finger. "That theory I don't like at all. That theory takes the Grant Jackson case out of my inactive file and places it in my pending file. That theory gives me *four* homicides and five detectives. You do the math."

"I see your point."

"Do you? Tell me something. Why are you pushing this?"

"If the kid OD'd, the mother doesn't get a dime."

MacAullif squinted at me sideways. "Richard kicked the case?"

"I was signing up the mother when we got the report that—"

"Richard kicked the case?"

"When we found out that the kid OD'd and—"

"Richard kicked the case?"

"You're getting all worked up."

He took a deep breath, blew it out slowly. "I'm not getting all worked up. I'm fine. Let me know if I understand you correctly. You came in to bother me about a case you are not even working on?"

"I didn't say I wasn't working on it."

"Is anyone paying you to work on it?"

"No."

"Well, how delightful." MacAullif spread his arms. "Is there anything *else* I can do for you?"

"Actually there is."

"I might have known. Pray what might that be?"

"Well, I know you scrutinized this case carefully before you decided it wasn't worth your notice. I imagine you checked out where Grant might have copped the cocaine. Did that investigation bear fruit?"

"Oh, sure," MacAullif said. "We had people linin' up claimin' to be the dope dealer who sold him his last toot. Would you like a list of names?"

"Good, MacAullif. You're getting better at calm sarcasm. Actually I was wondering if you pulled the rap sheets on his friends, family, and teammates."

MacAullif had.

Of the gentlemen in question, there were two with prior drug busts.

One was Larry White, one of Grant Jackson's teammates.

The other was brother Lincoln.

★ ★ ★

Lincoln Jackson met me at a small coffee shop near the project in Bed-Stuy. He had no reason not to. As far as he knew, I was still working for his mother. He slid into the booth, propped his elbows up on the faded Formica table, and demanded, "Why we meetin' here? Why not up there?"

"Don't you want coffee?"

"I don' want coffee. I want to know what's going on."

"I want to talk with you. I didn't want to disturb your mom."

"She interested."

"I know she is. I wanted you to be able to talk freely."

He glared at me suspiciously. " 'Bout what?"

"I think you know 'bout what."

"No, I don't. I don't 'preciate this." He turned, yelled to the waitress. "Hey, we get some coffee here?"

I didn't remind him he didn't want coffee. "Your brother died of an overdose. I bet the cops wanted to know where he got it."

He muttered something about the integrity of the police force in general and one detective in particular. The waitress shoved a cup of coffee in front of him. He didn't notice. He looked at me as if I were a cockroach he was about to step on. "They talk to me 'cause I got a prior. Is that stupid or what? That I'd give my own brother junk when I know he got a weak heart."

"You knew that?"

"Course I did. Grant don't want to tell, can't hide nothin'. Face like a road map. He come back from the doctor, we all knew somethin's wrong."

"You dealin' coke?"

His face twisted into a snarl. "I jus' tol' you, wasn't me."

"Yeah, but if it was in the house, Grant could have got his hands on it. Say if he wanted a boost, to play better."

Lincoln snorted. "Play better? Tha's a good one. You never seen him play. Grant didn't *need* to play better. Grant was the *best.*"

"That bother you?"

"What?"

"That your brother was the star and not you?"

Lincoln took a sip of coffee. Like MacAullif, he seemed to be composing himself, holding himself in, framing a moderate response. "Do I wanna be Grant, sure I wanna be Grant, but I ain't, Grant's Grant, so I'm glad of that. When I find out who *did* give him dope, that sucker in trouble." He jabbed a finger in my face. "You hear me? You hear what I say?"

"I hear you," I said.

I'm not sure I believed him.

★　★　★

Larry White was suspicious. "You a cop?"

"No, I'm not."

"You sure?"

"I think I'd know."

"If you a cop, you gotta say."

"I'm not a cop."

"If you a cop, I ask you direct, you gotta say. Tha's the law. You don' say, you can't bust me anyhow, don' matter what I do."

"I don't wanna bust you."

His eyes widened. "You a cop? Then you can't bust me, even if I whip out a *ki*-lo, ask you if you wanna *buy.*"

"Is that right?"

"Truth. Leroy say so."

"Savvy guy."

"Damn right. He been *aroun'*. He done *time*."

I blinked in despair over a generation that regarded a jail sentence as a qualification, had to remind myself I liked Robin Hood as a boy.

"Now we got that out of the way, you mind answering a few questions?"

"You make it quick. I gotta get to class."

I knew that. I had located the administration building, looked up his schedule, and ambushed him coming out of math. He'd been easy to spot. He was the one who had to duck to get out the door.

"You were there when Grant Jackson collapsed?"

"Course I was. Durin' practice."

"What did you see?"

A girl with a Cedar Park College sweatshirt put her book bag in one of the metal lockers lining the hallway. She flashed us a look as she went by.

Larry White frowned. "Hey, man," he said. "Maybe you can't bust me, but *she* think I'm talkin' to a cop."

"That bad for business?"

He frowned. "Hey! What you mean?"

"Lemme speed things along for you, Larry," I said. "I pulled your record. You got drug busts. I don't give a damn, except how it relates to Grant. If Grant got coke from you, I gotta know."

He shook his head. "No way!"

"And if Grant got works from you, I gotta know."

His head kept shaking. "No way!"

"The medical examiner says Grant was a virgin, never shot

before. If he wanted to shoot coke, he wouldn't have the equipment. He'd have to get a hypodermic. I'm wondering if he got it from you."

"No way! Christ, man, you say you not a cop, then you come on like this. I ain' talkin' to you. I get my lawyer."

"That would be a very bad move."

"You ain' seen my lawyer."

"No, I haven't, but that's not the point. Let me say it one more time. I'm not a cop. I'm a private investigator trying to get insurance money for Grant's mom. You talk to me, that's as far as it goes. You tell me what I need to know, and that's that. No one hassles you.

"If, instead, you go and get your lawyer, you got trouble. Then I got no right to ask you questions, 'cause I'm not a cop. So then I gotta *get* a cop. And I gotta tell the cop that you won't answer questions. Then the cop will ask you, and your lawyer will advise you, and the whole thing will be out of my hands. But you'll be happy. At least you'll be dealing with a routine you know.

"If you wanna do that, fine. If you *don't* wanna do that, you got another choice. You talk to me, and I go away. And no one asks you any more questions. Sounds like a pretty good deal. Particularly since you know even if I were a cop, nothing you say could hurt you anyway. So come on, let's do this. I don't wanna make you late for class."

Larry frowned, glanced at his watch. It was a gold Rolex. If the obvious display of riches embarrassed him any, he didn't show it. "You got two minutes."

"Did Grant Jackson ever do drugs?"

"No way."

"If he had, would you know it?"

Grudgingly. "Suppose."

"Is there any chance he got the stuff from anyone else on the team?"

"No way."

"If it wasn't you, it was no one?"

"Hey, look—"

"No offense meant."

"Is that so?" His nostrils flared. He bent down in my face. "Now, see here. I don' do drugs. No one on the team do drugs. You got that? We got drug screens. Wit' a no-tolerance policy. You flunk one, you done. A guy was usin', he be on the bench."

"I thought you had a designated pisser."

He started to flare up, then smiled. "Tha's good. Gotta use that."

"Feel free. The point is, you guys know how to fake drug tests. So don't give me the everybody's clean. Coach Tom knows better than that."

Larry's eyes narrowed. "He rat me out?"

"Not at all. He just suggested you guys were in the habit of sharing urine samples when somebody was high."

He banged the door shut on a metal locker. Not violently, just absently, casually. Still, I felt the hall shake. "That so bogus, man. That happen two, three times, big deal. Not like somebody hidin' a *lifestyle,* know what I mean. Junkie got a problem, junkie don' get by. But there *ain'* no junkie. There be a junkie, he be on the bench. Coach Tom nail his ass."

"How, if he keeps faking the urine sample?"

"Yeah, but they do blood test too."

"Oh?"

"Yeah, and there ain' no way to fake that. A needle in your arm, ain' no way to go borrowin' no blood."

"If you were friends with the nurse, and she mislabeled a test tube or two?"

He shook his head. "Ain' no nurse. Coach Tom do it hisself. And, trus' me, he ain' gonna mislabel nothin'."

"Not even to protect his star?"

" 'Specially then. Few years back, he give a drug test, two guys flunk. Both starters, one a high *scorer*. An' he sat 'em down. Din' let 'em play. Championship year."

"Championship?"

"Coulda been. Only, Coach Tom sat his stars."

"How long?"

"Month. Missed the NIT playoffs."

"He sat 'em for a whole month?"

"Tha's the rule. You *fail* a blood test, you sit till you *pass* a blood test. And he don't give 'em more'n once a month. Tha's a fact. Blood test, I mean. Pee cup happen alla time."

I frowned. I didn't like what I was hearing. "Let me be sure I understand this. The urine test happens all the time, but you can fake 'em. However, once a month you get a blood test that there's no way to fake. And Coach Tom gives it. So if Grant was doing cocaine, Coach Tom would know. On account of the blood test."

"That's right."

"When's the last time you had one?"

*   *   *

I found Coach Tom in the gym, working on the parquet floor. He had removed about a three-foot-square section of boards and was cleaning and sanding them. He didn't look up when I came in, just continued to inspect the groove on the side of a board. I wasn't even sure if he knew I was there.

He did.

"Buckles," he said. "Wood floor's a sweet thing, but the wood swells and the floor buckles. Forms an air pocket, makes a little bump. You gotta take it up, put it back down. Don't know how many hundred times I done this, one spot or another."

"You want to talk about Grant Jackson?"

"I'd rather talk about my floor."

I figured that was true. "I'm sorry," I said. "But there's some things I need to know."

"And I suppose they're so all-fired important you gotta ask. Boy's dead, can't you leave it be?"

"I'm afraid I can't. I understand you gave blood tests, as well as urine. Tests that were impossible to fake."

"Oh, you understand that, do you?"

"You did it yourself. You were in complete control. If someone tampered with someone's blood sample, you were the only one who could have done it."

"Never happened."

"No, I don't suppose it did. In fact, it's legend. You sittin' down your star players when you had a shot at the NIT."

"Ain' nothin' to it," Coach Tom said. "Rule's a rule."

"Yes, it is," I said. I set my briefcase down on the parquet floor, snapped it open, took out a sheaf of papers. "And I know you're a stickler for playing by the rules." I thrust the papers on the floor in front of him. "You know what these are? They're lab reports. Going back the last ten years. Lab reports on the blood samples you had processed."

"So?"

"There's none for the day Grant Jackson died. According to the players on the team, you took blood that day."

"What if I did?"

"According to the lab, you never turned it in."

He shrugged. "Maybe I didn't. With Grant collapsin', it would be easy to forget."

"You're saying you forgot to turn it in?"

"If that's what the lab says, must be."

"Then where are those samples now?"

"How the hell should I know?"

"If you didn't turn 'em in, you must still have 'em."

"So?"

"So let's go take a look."

"Let's not. What's with you? First you say you're workin' for the mother, then you come around you want blood. What's the deal?"

"If you have a vial of blood you took from Grant Jackson on the day he collapsed, that would be rather valuable evidence."

"Well, I don't."

I nodded. "Yeah, I didn't think you did." I picked up the papers, flipped through. "February 3, 1994. Drug screen for Harold Wilks and Alan Powers. Positive for cocaine. You sat them both, in spite of the fact you had a great team that year, with a shot at makin' the NIT. It's legend. All the players know it. Gives you a terrific hold over them."

"That's not why I did it."

"Yeah, I know." After a pause I added, "I'm probably the only one who does."

He looked up at me from his seat on the floor. "What you mean?"

"This drug test in '94 that sat your stars. According to the lab reports, it was three weeks after the last test. Only three weeks, when you always give four. A sudden, surprise test that netted two of your biggest stars. And knocked you out of the NIT."

He may not have heard me. He bent over, fitted a board back into the floor.

"See, you talk a good game, Coach Tom. That's what bothered me. You talk *too* good a game. The bit about fear of failure. That was pretty damn good. That sounded plausible. It took a while for me to figure out that if it sounded that good, it probably wasn't. And, sure enough, that's the case. Fear of failure wasn't the problem. It was fear of success.

"It happened first in '94, when a team got a little too good, went a little too far. Gonna get in the playoffs, get some national exposure. Get the alumni all excited. Raise money. Hire a name coach. Build a new gym.

"I'm not sure which scared you more. Someone trying to replace you, or the thought of losing this.

"Grant Jackson, same thing, only worse. He's not just a great player, he's a marquee player. He's the type of player gets your team in the papers and on TV. And this gym isn't set up for TV, is it?"

"I don't know what you're talking about."

"I think you do. You're very comfortable in your little gym, with a .500 team. It's not just a job, it's your whole life. Which Grant Jackson threatened to destroy." I referred to the sheets. "Which is why, once again, we have a blood test a little early. It's not on these sheets, but according to the guys on the team, it was the same day Grant Jackson died. Three weeks since the last one. A week early, just like before."

I shook my head. "A blood test that never got to the lab, where the blood disappeared." I lowered my voice. "It must have been a tough thing to do. But I'm sure you thought you had no choice.

"So there you are, with a needle in Grant's arm, taking blood. Filling test tubes. Easy to switch; instead of an empty tube, a full hypodermic you squeeze back in. For a boy with a heart condition, a lethal dose of coke. Because Grant Jackson didn't do drugs. Under any circumstances. Even before he knew about the heart condition. There was no way he would fall for a setup, like the coke you planted on your boys in '94. That they found in their locker and couldn't resist. And why would they? The drug screen wasn't due for another week. Surely it would be out of their system by then."

He frowned, looked up at me. There were tears running down his cheeks. "Why you doin' this?"

I didn't have an answer. I couldn't say "It's my job," because it wasn't. And I couldn't bear to say something clunky and holier-than-thou like "Because it's right."

I turned and motioned to the door, where Sergeant MacAullif was waiting. He came in, introduced himself to Coach Tom, and delivered what had to be the calmest Miranda warning in the history of the NYPD.

★　★　★

Richard was dumbfounded. "Grant Jackson's a homicide?"

"That's right."

"His coach killed him because he would have made the team too famous and cost him his job?"

"That's a bit of an oversimplification."

"But he's under arrest?"

"That he is."

"Which makes it a brand-new ball game." Richard rubbed his hands together. "Suddenly everyone's liable again. The coach, the college, the doctors. Maybe even the police."

"Let's not go overboard," I said. I could envision MacAullif's blood pressure if he got named as a defendant.

"You signed this woman up. Even though I told you not to."

"I admit I exceeded my authority."

"Yes, you did, and it couldn't have worked out better. You're even entitled to the hundred-and-fifty-dollar initiative bonus for bringing me a new case."

"Two hundred and fifty."

"What?"

"It went up to two hundred and fifty last year."

"Are you sure?"

"That kid, Patrick, who worked here for a month, brought you a case and wouldn't give it to you for less."

"That was a special case."

"Oh, come on. You're trying to justify paying a kid out of college more than the investigator who's worked for you for years?"

Richard paused, considered, probably realized the number of cases I brought him could be counted on the fingers of one hand. "Of course not, Stanley," he said magnanimously. "Two hundred and fifty bucks it is. And a damn fine job." He riffled through the fact sheet I'd given him. "The woman has nine dependents, no husband, lives on welfare, has no other visible means of support. Cruelly deprived of her only source of income. The insurance companies are going to fall all over themselves trying to settle this."

I figured that was probably true. Richard's reputation as a fearsome litigator was well known. Opposing counsel were used to throwing large sums of money at him to keep him out of court.

"So," Richard said, "you get your bonus, I get a nice case, and a woman with nine dependents gets some much-needed relief. All in all, it couldn't be better."

I sighed.

I was thinking of Coach Tom, down on his hands and knees, meticulously, lovingly replacing the boards of his parquet floor.

"Yeah," I said flatly. "Couldn't be better."

CAT'S PAW

Laurie R. King

You girls got the balls," Lauren shouted at the girls on the court. Marisol bumped against Pilar with a stifled giggle while their coach pretended not to notice. This was a long-established, straight-faced game she played with her teams, or maybe with herself, an important part of which was keeping them in doubt as to whether their repressed spinster of a coach actually intended these outrageous double entendres, or if she was just a complete tongue-klutz.

This particular Monday afternoon, the game was proving something of an effort. Lauren's heart wasn't in rude jokes. It wasn't even in the practice, which at the moment involved an intricate figure eight pattern of dribbling and passing, an exercise two of the players had worked out themselves following the Globetrotters field trip the spring before. The girls had come up with the idea, but it needed close supervision to keep it from disintegrating into a pileup, and frankly, their coach wasn't up to it today.

The third time the tight configuration of weaving figures (one, two, three, and pass; one, two, three—) had collided and dissolved into chaos and irritation, Lauren gave up and set them to a simpler shooting practice. That was better. The rhythm and noises of their shoes and voices soothed her, allowing her eyes and mind to follow their skills and personalities, looking at both with an eye to the beginning of the season in a couple of weeks. Saturday's informal preseason game, she saw, had helped draw them together, given them the unity of purpose she'd hoped for. The day had been a disaster in other ways, but in this it had been a success.

After a while, she called them over for a brief talk about strategy (which boiled down to *Teamwork!*), then allowed them a short practice game before dismissing them for the day. She watched them snag their bags and chatter their way out the doors to their waiting rides, feeling pride and affection despite her grinding fatigue. Good team, she thought. Good bunch of girls. God, I'm tired.

At the dinner table that night, bent over her solitary plate of overcooked pasta, Lauren squinted through gritty eyes as she made notes about the team. Her job was teaching social studies and history, but her love was coaching, especially basketball. It was not the girls themselves that gave her pleasure, although she had no doubt that they speculated furiously about her—she was scrupulous about avoiding physical contact, just in case. She was, however, not a lesbian. She was something far more rare, a twenty-nine-year-old virgin, and the pleasure she took in her girls was not for their bodies, but for their freedom. She craved their overheard conversations about hair and parents and boys, much as a prisoner craves a window, and if her own iron bars were made of emotional distance and a firm concentration on the game, she nonetheless secretly reveled in the social interaction of teenagers such as she had never been.

She also drew comfort and pride in knowing that she was, if not exactly liked, then at least respected and (although they might not realize it, or admit it if they did) needed. Junior high school girls were so vulnerable, so adrift on a sea of hormones and insecurities, confusion and energy, that giving them a team to cling to was far more important than just something healthy to do after school. Lauren gave them self-respect and a sense of their own strength, as individuals, as a group, and as a sex. She was aware, always, of the irony involved in their learning this from her, of all people. Hence, for her own amusement, the were-they-or-weren't-they jokes, those faint overtures from the Lauren who might have been. *Marisol coming on nicely,* she noted on her pad: *cocaptain? Tina,* on the other hand, was getting just a bit too self-important for the team's good: *sit the bench for a while?*

By ten o'clock she was aching with fatigue and her eyes felt as if she'd been through a sandstorm. Pushing away the twinge of apprehension, she filled her cat's bowl, set up the coffeemaker for the morning, and went to bed.

And for the third night running, came awake within the hour, heart pounding over the noise that wasn't there. She fumbled for the clock and groaned at the reading of its luminous hands. What the hell was going on, anyway? She hadn't had insomnia for years, but for the last three nights she had. Ever since the cat.

With thought of the cat, all hope of sleep shriveled up and crept into a corner to hide. Lauren threw off the covers, felt for her slippers, and pulled on her warm robe as she passed through the dim hallway to the kitchen. By the light of the open refrigerator door she filled a mug with milk and stuck it in the microwave for a minute, added a splash of cheap brandy and a shake of nutmeg, and went to turn on the Weather Channel on the television.

Storms lay over the nation, although it was calm enough here. Timson, her arthritic Siamese, grumbled in to ask what the hell she was doing up this time of night. He sniffed in disapproval at the corruption of the good honest milk in her mug, curled into her legs, and went to sleep.

The other cat had been black, or maybe a dark tabby. On the fateful Saturday morning, not even seventy-two hours ago, she'd been driving through San Jose with four of her girls, heading for a preseason meet with a middle school up in the Bay Area that was famous as the home of three actual, real-life professional women players. Somewhere behind Lauren's car was a minivan with the rest of the team, driven by one of the moms. It was a clear, sunny autumnal morning: ho hum, another beautiful day in the paradise that was Northern California, and the girls were pretending to scorn the sixties and seventies rock of Lauren's tape collection, although they seemed to know most of the words. Traffic was moving easily enough to allow the driver's mind to wander, moving forward to the coming game, then back to the meeting she'd had a few days earlier with a prospective sponsor for the team. She was mulling over his proposal to grace their new uniforms with the name of his software company in letters larger than the girls' own when the cat appeared.

And it did simply appear, on the road ahead of her, as if it had been dropped from the cloudless blue sky—or more probably, she realized much later, launched from the bowels of the plumber's truck two vehicles ahead of her. The truck was big and red and bristling with cranes, nozzles, storage tanks, and various fixtures whose purpose Lauren couldn't begin to guess.

For one cat, however, one dark, bedraggled, desperately bewildered feline, the truck had been a place of refuge against the chill of the previous night, its nooks and crannies welcome shelter.

Until the truck reached sixty on the freeway and started to bounce and rattle.

The animal hit the ground running, or trying its damnedest to run, all four feet skittering across the concrete at sixty miles an hour, its paws working automatically to find some kind of traction that would enable it to lunge for safety. It was not tumbling head over heels; its head was bolt upright, revealing eyes popped and staring with astonishment, fur spiked awry with wet or grease. Every fiber of the creature's being was fighting to make sense of the impossible concrete and steel maelstrom into which it had been ejected, every sinew and cell in its body battling valiantly to stay upright, to find the safe haven that it knew had to be there somewhere in the hell bearing down on it, to gather itself up from the loud/fast/huge confusion and leap in haven's direction, to survive, to *live*.

All this—its attitude and its youth, the wide-staring eyes and the state of its dark fur and the way its delicate paws were trying for something they could comprehend—printed itself on Lauren's mind in about two seconds. The cat simply materialized—it hadn't wandered out across two lanes of traffic from the shoulder, that would have been impossible—it just appeared, having passed miraculously without harm under the rattletrap old Chevy that separated Lauren from the plumber's truck, skating down the roadway between that oblivious car's four tires and shooting out from under the back bumper like some macabre version of Bambi on ice. It had not been afraid, she decided on the tenth or hundredth time those two seconds replayed themselves in her mind's eye: it wasn't fear that had bugged those eyes and given such desperate strength to its fragile muscles. Somehow she knew that there had been no time for fear in the moments allotted to it, just astonishment wedded to a frantic and determined hunt for solution. She also knew, queasily, that had there been a vehicle in the next lane, half a dozen cars and a girl's basketball team would have come to wrenching, steel-tearing grief on top of the cat. Fortunately there had been no car to meet her unthinking yank on the wheel.

The girls hadn't seen the cat, just shrieked in reaction to the abrupt swerve and started gabbling questions at her. Lauren did not answer. She clenched the steering wheel with white-knuckled hands, slowing so dramatically the car behind her blared its horn in protest, and she kept her eyes glued to the rust-speckled bumper of the rapidly retreating Chevy. She did not look into the rearview mirror; she did not have to. She knew what her eyes would see there if she did look, knew that the only possible ending to the cat's story had borne down on it with metal teeth bared and rubber wheels pounding, to give the animal's valiant efforts a casual, two-ton swat and drive on. Lauren kept her own wide-staring eyes fixed on the road ahead of her and turned deaf ears on the demands of the girls, moving with infinite caution into the exit lane, off the freeway, and into the first convenient parking lot.

Her four girls were gibbering frantically; in a moment the minivan carrying the rest of the team swerved behind them into the lot. All the occupants of both vehicles went abruptly quiet when Lauren flung open her door, stumbled over to the ivy strip bordering the lot, and vomited up her breakfast.

The girls subsided and let the other adult take over. Gwen

jumped out of the minivan and trotted over to Lauren's side, where she stood with one hand on the coach's sweating back until she was sure the spasms were finished. Then she went back to the van, dug a bottle of water from the cooler, and came back to hand it to Lauren.

"Thanks, Gwen," Lauren managed when the icy clean water had reduced the awful taste to a burning in the back of her throat.

"Are you coming down with something?"

"You didn't see it?"

"See what?"

"The cat. It just . . . appeared in front of me on the road." As soon as the words left her mouth, Lauren realized how pitiful they were: for this she had endangered the lives of four students? But Gwen seemed inclined to be sympathetic rather than disapproving; after all, nothing had happened.

"Oh, how awful," she said. "I ran over a dog once, I know how you feel."

"Just the shock of it," Lauren said. Gwen thought she was saying that she'd run over the thing herself. Let it be, Lauren thought: her extreme reaction might be more easily understood if guilt were thought to be the culprit, not the weird, almost anthropomorphic link of empathy she'd felt for the animal during those two terrible seconds.

"You going to be okay?"

"Oh, yeah," Lauren said heartily, standing straight to add assurance.

"I could run my load up and come back for yours; it's only about twenty minutes away."

"No, I'm fine. Really."

And she was. She downplayed the death of a stray cat for

the girls and turned the conversation to the game ahead, she drove at a normal speed the rest of the way, she greeted the other coach (a high school acquaintance) with the right balance of friendliness and good-humored threat, and she worked her girls up into enough of a lather that they bounced out onto the court with that attitude she loved. And if she hugged her jacket around her in the warm auditorium to stifle the shivers running up and down her arms all that day, no one commented.

Her girls didn't win, but the final score was by no means humiliating, and they sure as hell learned a lot from the others. They even loved the funky pizza parlor the two teams had taken over for the afternoon, and left town with a dozen new best friends and an exchange of phone numbers and e-mail addresses.

In the excitement of the day, the cat was forgotten. Lauren drove her quartet of tired players back over the hills, dropped each at the correct front door, and wearily steered herself home. She let herself in, gathered up old Timson, and buried her face into his fur for a minute until he mewed his bones' protest, then walked into her kitchen, dug through the cupboards for the dusty bottle of brandy, and poured a generous two fingers into a glass and down her throat.

After a while the trembling sensation under her skin subsided.

You're such a wimp, she told herself. *Cats die all the time, sad but true.*

Except that she wasn't a wimp. She'd done hard things when necessary: she'd once beheaded and buried an agonized, broken-back garter snake that some kid had run over on the sidewalk, and she had no particular squeamishness when it came to trapping mice or performing first aid to the goriest of cuts.

Low blood sugar, she decided. She slopped a couple of eggs around in a frying pan and ate them on toast, and felt better. She took another jolt of the brandy to the television and fed an old favorite movie into the VCR; that, too, helped. Pleasantly woozy from the unaccustomed booze, she scrubbed the day away beneath a hot shower, towel-dried her short hair, and fell blithely into bed before the clock's hands rested on ten.

Only to find the cat waiting for her, riding the undulating concrete on four outstretched paws like a water strider riding the surface of a fast, deep river. Under something it flew—car bumper? tree limb?—with a look of startled, outraged confusion on its near-human features. One front paw came up in a gesture of supplication, and then a sharp noise somewhere in the reaches of the house jerked Lauren out of the nightmare to stare into the dark room, feeling all the cat's panic on her own face.

Cat: noise. Timson must be—but no, Timson was asleep against her feet. She sat frozen among the tangled sheets, the threat of vomit raw in the back of her throat, straining her thudding ears for the sound to repeat itself. After a minute she got up, took her old hockey stick out of its corner, and crept through the house to see what had invaded. She found nothing, and when she got back to her bedroom again, she saw that the ever-nervous Timson was still fast asleep, which he would not be if there was a stranger anywhere in the house. She propped the stick back in the corner of the room, went back to bed and eventually to sleep.

The doomed cat came through her dreaming mind twice more before dawn, and Lauren spent the next day in a thick-limbed daze, alternating between empty-minded half-sleep over the Sunday paper and unnecessarily vigorous housecleaning. By evening she had barely enough energy to perform her always-on-Sunday task of the phone call to her mother.

She did so at the kitchen table, knowing that if she listened to her mother's endless monologue from a comfortable chair, she'd soon be snoring. As it was, she drifted in and out of awareness with her chin resting on her hand, grunting responses into the pauses provided and wondering how long this creepy cat thing would take to fade.

When she had fumbled and nearly dropped the phone twice, she cut into her mother's epic narrative of the retirement center's inefficient postman, told her she'd call again Wednesday, and went to bed.

The cat was waiting for her.

In the morning she felt so utterly wretched at the idea of the new week that she thought about calling in sick. Except that she was not sick, she was haunted, by an idiotic feline who hadn't had enough sense to know an unsafe resting spot when it found one. For some ungodly reason, those vivid moments had been seared onto Lauren's mind as if it had been her own life passing before her eyes. She groaned, held an ice-filled cloth to her inflamed eyelids while the coffee brewed, and went to work.

Monday afternoon: a bleary and out-of-control practice session; Monday night: a third set of sessions with the unknown cat. Three nights of broken sleep that reduced her to a nervous wreck—or maybe her nervous state had reduced her to sleeplessness, she could not be sure. She could not, in fact, be too sure of her own sanity. The next night was the same; following that, she knew something had to be done. During

Wednesday's prep period, Lauren picked up the phone to call for help.

Unfortunately, the only psychotherapist she knew, the woman she'd seen a decade before when she'd been an insomniac college student, couldn't see her before Friday. Lauren's desperation did, however, make an impression on the receptionist, because Dr. Minerva Henry herself called back twenty minutes later. Greetings, a brief catch-up, Lauren's halting and by now embarrassed description of the cat episode and its consequences, and Min's regrets that she had no free time until Friday.

"That's all right, I understand," Lauren told her. "I'm sure I'll be okay until then. It's just so . . . silly."

"It doesn't sound at all silly."

"I mean, to be so upset by such an inconsequential event. I really am a very stable kind of a person. Or I was until Saturday."

"This episode has clearly driven a wedge under some firmly shut door in your mind. You may remember, I recommended ten years ago that you remain in therapy. I take it you did not."

"But I was fine," Lauren protested.

"You were functioning well," the doctor corrected her gently. "Now you're not. We'll sort it out beginning Friday."

"Two more nights like I've been having, you might want to book me a padded cell," Lauren remarked. As an attempt at dry humor, it fell completely flat, leaving Min Henry to take it as a cry for help. In truth, it was.

"Avoid caffeine," the good doctor recommended. "And no alcohol, either. Eat well, get some nice healthy outdoor exercise, and drink a glass of warm milk before bed. You might also take a pen and paper to bed with you, to write down any words or images that come to mind when you wake up. We'll talk about those on Friday."

The mere suggestion that the problem might be sorted out was a comfort, and helped Lauren make it through the day and the practice session. She ate a balanced dinner, corrected the stack of exam papers, and phoned her mother to listen to the endless trickle of gentle complaints about the workers and neighbors in her quite comfortable retirement home.

"Mother," she said at one point, interrupting a detailed description of the tragedy inflicted by the cook on a poor, unsuspecting piece of beef. "Did anything ever happen to me as a child that involved a cat?"

"A cat, dear?"

"Yes. The other day I saw a cat get . . . hurt, and it's given me nightmares. I just wondered if maybe something similar happened when I was small, that I forgot about."

"Oh, dear, how terrible for you. One of the ladies down the hall has bad dreams, she talks in her sleep so you can hear every—"

"Mother? The cat?"

"We never had cats, dear. Your father didn't like them."

"But did I—oh, never mind. How is Mrs. Peasley's leg doing?"

She hung up twenty minutes later, knowing more than she cared to about the pernicious results of circulatory problems but little the wiser about cats. However, mention of her father, an uncomfortable topic at the best of times, seemed to drive another section of wedge into the gap opened by the cat. That night's dream found her sitting not behind the wheel of her car as the frantic man-faced cat spun around and around on the surface of the roadway, but rather on a hard bench of a seat beside her long-estranged father. He seemed enormous in her dream, as he had not been in life, bristling with the self-importance she had believed in until college freed her of illusions, the father of her youth.

As it turned out, it was Father who took up most of the Friday session with Min Henry, not the list of words and images she had jotted down in the still of the night (*wet fur* and *fast current;* also *mouth "O" in surprise* and *too fast for fear* and *thunk!*). Her ambiguous feelings toward her parent, his peculiar combination of the ineffectual and the quick to anger, her jumble of respect and love and fear that must, it occurred to her, be very like the feelings her mother still bore for the man who had abandoned her with two small children and a mountain of debts.

What did all that have to do with a cat? she asked the therapist at the close of the session.

Patience, the woman said. And maybe we should meet twice a week.

The nightmare retreated a fraction, in frequency if not intensity. Once or twice a night instead of every couple of hours: cat/panic/bench, father/thud/wake.

The following Wednesday, Lauren forced herself to ask her mother again about what might lie in the past.

"The cat again, dear?"

"When I was with Daddy." *Daddy?* she thought; *I haven't called him that since I was eight.*

"Oh, sweetie, I wouldn't know. I mean, your father often took you and your brother off for a while so I could go to the hairdressers' or some such thing. You'd go to the beach or the country club. He liked to show you off. But I'd have thought that if something happened during one of those outings, he'd have mentioned it. Then again I suppose he could have told me and I've forgotten it, I do forget so much. But not usually from the past—isn't it funny how I can forget where I put my book down but I can remember what dress you wore to your fifth-birthday party? No, I think I'd remember if something happened to a cat while you were out with him. There was the time your brother cut his hand at the racetrack, I remember that. And you were frightened once when you got separated from your father for a few minutes at the county fair; you clung to my skirts for a week after that. I suppose you could have seen a cat get hurt during that time, although what a cat would be doing wandering around a crowded fairground I can't think." (*Dropping out of a shiny red tractor, maybe?*) "And there was the time, when was that? Just after your brother was born, that's right, when your father took you for the day. You went fishing with him and, um, Arty. You remember Arty?" Lauren's antennae pricked at the casual tone of her mother's voice. Arty? But her mother was rushing on. "I wasn't too keen on the idea of you in a boat, you were awfully young, but your father promised me he'd keep your life vest on you every second, and with both of them to keep an eye on you, you'd be fine. Which you were."

"Arty? I don't remember—wait a minute. Was he a man with a red face and a mustache?"

"That's right, fancy you remembering that! And he was always smoking a cigar. It had a lovely smell, I thought, but your father wouldn't let him smoke in the house. You loved the smell, always followed him around, even when he went outside to smoke. He called you his little shadow," she said wistfully. "You missed him so when he left, moped around for days." *I* missed him, Lauren heard in her mother's voice.

"Where did he go?"

"They told me he'd gone to Montana."

Lauren waited for more; when nothing more came, she found herself sitting forward, as if to pull information out of the telephone. Her mother's uncharacteristically brief answer seemed to echo down the line.

"Did he?" she prompted.

"Oh, dear," her mother replied with a sigh. "I don't know. I suppose he must have, although at the time, well, I thought he'd maybe had an accident, out hiking somewhere. He was a great one for hiking."

"Didn't anyone go looking for him?"

"No, honey, that was only for a couple of days. And then he called your father to tell him he was quitting—a middle-aged crisis I guess they'd call it today. Anyway, he just quit, threw it all over of a sudden and left town. It must have been right after that fishing trip, come to think of it. That's right—your brother was just born, you were moping around and having tantrums at the drop of a hat, your father was even more short-tempered than usual. We thought it really was very thoughtless of Arty, to leave him in the lurch like that, and at such a difficult time. Then a few weeks later the accountant found that Arty'd been siphoning off cash. He was your father's manager, you remember. Young for the job, but capable. Later the police decided he'd panicked, thinking they were on to him, and that was why he left in such a hurry. He probably moved to Mexico or something—your father had a few phone conversations with him, asking him to take care of some things, but those stopped after a few months."

"I might have seen something that day he took me on the boat?" Lauren asked, trying to tug the conversation back to where it had begun.

"You might have, I suppose. I wasn't in any shape to take notice of much right then. I'd had all these stitches, down there, you know, and they were so uncomfortable, and then you were going through this phase of being jealous of your new brother and so kept waking me up at night with your bad dreams and forgetting your toilet training and bursting into tears at the least thing. Which was perfectly normal with a new baby in the house," she hastened to say, "even if maybe a little extreme. In the end I had to agree with my mother and your father that the best way to let you get over your naughtiness was to ignore it as much as possible. And you did settle down, after a while. In fact, you became a new child, so quiet and obedient. You were always so good with your brother, too."

Her mother dithered on for a while, recounting in intimate detail the extensive difficulties the stitches had caused, even going so far as to speculate aloud (*Does she even remember that she's got her daughter on the other end of the phone?* Lauren wondered) that the lingering discomfort, and at a time when her husband needed her most, what with the embezzlement and Arty's treachery and all, had contributed to the divorce.

Lauren interrupted desperately, before her mother could go into any greater detail. "Well, think about it, Mother, see if you can remember anything traumatic involving a cat."

"I'll try, dear. You could call your father and ask him. I have a number for him somewhere."

Lauren cut her off, knowing that she was about to take the phone over to the desk and begin a search. She had no intention of asking her father about it; she hadn't talked to him in so long she'd forgotten the sound of his voice, and she wasn't about to resume their relationship with a revelation of her psychic distress. Maybe her mother's approach was best and would work as well now as it had then. Ignore it, and it'll go away.

Her mother's approach, to ignore distress. Look at their conversations centering around the cat: She'd been fond of Arty, that was obvious, but expressed neither resentment nor even puzzlement at his abandonment. Then must have come a hellish time—a newborn and a jealous three-year-old, a demanding husband and the first threats of bankruptcy, the revelation that a trusted friend (or more than a friend?) had stolen them blind. Creditors, an abrupt change in lifestyle, a husband fleeing infamy and leaving her behind to raise two children on a secretary's pay. Lauren's father, meanwhile, had salvaged enough out of the whole mess to afford a nice house on a tropical island, complete with a twenty-four-year-old "housekeeper."

Ignore it, and it'll go away. Only it didn't. The nightmares continued. Not every night now, but at least every other, she would see the spinning cat with the human face, hear a startlingly loud and completely imaginary thud, and come heartpoundingly awake in the dark. It was beginning to make her angry. And just a little bit worried. Insanity didn't run in her family, so far as she knew—although come to think of it, her father's final loss of stability had come when he wasn't much older than she was now.

Another Friday and Monday in Min Henry's soothing office, a Sunday and a Wednesday correcting papers and grunting replies while her mother rambled on in her ear, practice three afternoons and the beginning of the season on Saturday, plus her regular schedule of classes. A person could grow accustomed to anything, Lauren said to herself; even being haunted by a cat. Still, regular as clockwork it came: hard bench under her bottom, cold wind on her face, wet fur and the "O" of shock, a thud and the roaring sound of blood beating through her ears in the still house. Then the following Monday, Min Henry tapped the wedge in a little further, with a couple of questions.

"Tell me again about the sound you hear in your dream," she said in this, their sixth session. "Was it the car behind you hitting the cat?"

"In my imagination, maybe—I didn't actually hear anything. I couldn't have, since I know I didn't hit it, and the car windows were up and the tape player going."

"Then what is the sound?"

"That is weird, isn't it? In the dream, it's the sound that panics me more than anything."

"You described it as a clunk?"

"Sort of a hollow thud. A little like . . . Jeez. Is it like . . . ? No, not really. I was thinking it reminded me of the sound of a basketball bouncing, but that's not it. Other than a sort of hollowness. Brief, final—God, Min, I don't know. Why does it matter, anyway?"

"Okay, Lauren, take a couple of deep breaths. The tissues are on the table next to you."

I'm crying, Lauren realized with a shock. *Why am I crying? What the* fuck *is going on, a stupid frightened cat causing some damned psychosis or something.* "Why is this so awful?" she pleaded. "I mean, I could understand if I'd watched a person get run down, that would be enough to haunt you, but cats get killed all the time. And it wasn't even me that hit him!"

One of the things she had always liked about Min Henry was that the doctor actually answered her patients' questions instead of turning the questions back around. Now she said,

"Lauren, you are assuming this scene with the cat has triggered off some traumatic episode or emotion that you've hidden from yourself. That may be so, or it may simply represent some state of mind you're having trouble acknowledging. In either case, the key may lie with that anomalous sound. You say it doesn't belong with your memory of the actual cat incident; if that's the case, then it must have snuck in from elsewhere."

"But where? I told you that my mother had no idea of a trauma with a cat."

"Could it have been something other than a cat?"

The simple question reverberated softly through Lauren's mind, stirring up an odd and unidentifiable series of feelings, excitement and confusion and a peculiar stillness, as if she were a rabbit hiding from a circling hawk. She blinked, and found that the therapist was watching her closely.

"We're running short on time today," Min Henry told Lauren, "but I can see that sparked something off."

"I don't know."

"Think about it, for next time."

"How about trying hypnosis?" Lauren blurted out. "This not knowing—it's making me crazy."

"Lauren, I'd rather see if your memory can loose this on its own. We can try hypnosis, but let's give the mind a while longer to work it out."

"How much longer?"

"Give it a month, two at the most. Your doctor gave you the prescription for sleeping pills, didn't he?"

He had, although they left Lauren feeling as groggy as sleeplessness did. Two months?

But in the end it didn't take anywhere near that long.

The week passed. Wednesday a conversation with her

mother, Friday a session with Min, two more practices, four broken nights, and all the while Lauren's mind fretted over the question.

Could it have been something other than a cat?

Oh, yes. But what?

Saturday dawned, four endless weeks after the cat had fallen from the sky and into Lauren's mind. There was a game this morning, and Lauren dragged herself reluctantly from bed, made herself a pot of forbidden coffee, and drove to school. The girls were excited, the new uniforms looked good, the other team was strong enough to challenge but with definite exploitable weaknesses, and the bleachers were full of enthusiastic supporters. Lauren's own problems, for once, retreated.

It happened in the last quarter, the blow that hammered the wedge all the way home and split her memory clean up the middle.

The score was 47–45, the home team hanging on to its slim lead through the quarter, when the visitors called a time-out and sent in three new players, girls who separately were a threat, but together bonded into something formidable. A tipped-in rebound tied the score, a gorgeous shot from what seemed like center court put Lauren's girls three points behind. They made up two, the others matched it, then got two more, and with ninety seconds left on the clock, the struggle was in earnest. As the visitors brought the ball down, Marisol's hand darted out to slap it away; Juana was there as if by magic, and the two girls flew down the court with a stampede on their heels. The crowd stood and roared as Juana leaped up to drop the ball through the hoop. Then the other team had possession, sprinting down toward the basket with the determination of aristocrats threatened by the lower classes. They slammed into the home players, tried for a shot, missed, and as Marisol struggled to position herself for a rebound, the opposition's six-two forward rose past her, spiked the ball in, and came down again with her elbow centered squarely over the top of Marisol's skull.

The crack must have been more imagined than actual, since the noise level in the auditorium was so high only a gunshot would have risen above it, but the impact was nearly as great. Marisol's knees turned to water and she staggered back into the girls behind her, collapsing slowly until she was sprawled flat on her back, her short hair spiky with sweat, eyes wide, mouth in an astonished "O." Three hundred throats went abruptly still as the girl lay briefly stunned, then Lauren, in a narrow gap between two players, saw the comprehension come back into Marisol's eyes, saw the girl's focus snap onto the clock to see if she had time, saw the determination to regain those points, to get back into play, to *win*.

The tall forward was nursing her elbow with stifled curses and the other coach was racing across the court to see if either girl was badly hurt, but Lauren stood rooted in place. *Thud;* bewilderment; spiky hair; a determined struggle to rise. The faint lapping of waves against wood reached Lauren's ears. Marisol sat up, the opposing forward stopped hugging herself to reach down and pull Marisol to her feet, the crowd applauded its relief, and players from both sides gathered around the two girls.

Nobody was expecting one of the coaches to collapse. No one even noticed Lauren at first, standing rigid on the sidelines, both hands clapped over her mouth, her face as bleached as the team's new shorts. She stared at Marisol, who was rubbing her head and shrugging off the concern of her teammates, and then Lauren's knees gave way and she dropped to the court, completely limp. It was Lauren for whom the paramedics came.

* * *

In the hospital emergency room, with the curtains drawn and a call in to Min Henry, Lauren saw it again and again, a twenty-six-year-old movie playing itself out in her mind's eye.

The bench beneath her had been the unpadded seat of an old wooden skiff, her tiny shoes dangling free of the boards; the gray expanse of concrete was really the cold surface of a wooded river in winter. The young man in the water had been, she could only assume, Arty. She had adored him—that she remembered—not just his fragrant cigars, and he had gone into the river with a huge and bewildering splash, to surface, spluttering, head bolt upright and eyes popping at the shock of cold, a look of astonishment on his face. He had shaken his head like a dog, making his dark hair go spiky; his naked hand, surprisingly delicate without the glove, had reached up, in supplication or to ward off the next blow of the upraised oar. His eyes had been frantic, locked into a determined search for support, for haven from the icy water. He had been about to lunge for the boat when the oar hit him a second time, with a weird, hollow thunk.

She had been little more than a baby, too immature to make any sense of what her eyes had witnessed, too young to remember this confusing event in a confusing world. Until the cat had dropped in front of her and shaken loose her father's deed.

Lauren looked up at the rattle of the curtain being pulled back. Min Henry's kind face was pinched with concern.

"The sound was an oar," Lauren told her without preamble, reaching out for the therapist's hand. "I was too young to make any sense of it, but it was an oar, hitting the head of a man in the water. A man named Arty, my father's manager, whom I loved, and used to follow around like a shadow. I think my mother was having an affair with him. My father set him up, made it look like Arty was the one who stole the company into bankruptcy. When Arty was never found, everyone assumed he had fled to Mexico."

It explained an awful lot, Lauren thought, about what I became. When I was two and a half years old, a young man with spiky hair passed in front of me, and was gone.

MRS. CASH

Mike Lupica

They were inside the blue and white Academy tour bus, on their way down Fifth Avenue from the Pierre, on their way to the Garden, and Billy Cash was talking about Monica again.

Somehow it always came back to Monica these days, even when he was talking about all the other girls in his life, the ones Billy said he wanted to fuck, not have it be the other way around. Didn't matter where they were, either, or who was listening. They could be talking about whether or not the Magic—Billy's team—could hold off the Nets and Sixers for home court in the playoffs. Or whether Billy could score enough points the last two weeks of the season to hold off that little tattooed shit from Memphis, Taliek Moore, to win another scoring title, which would make it only ten in a row.

Billy didn't even seem to pay much mind to his injured foot, that fascia deal he had going, whether or not he could mess himself up good by playing on it between now and when the playoffs started.

He was fixed on his wife. Mrs. Cash, he called her most times. At least when he wasn't calling her "that bitch." The former Monica LaGuerre. Most times Billy talked about her like she was some defender he couldn't shake, not even with the famous step-back move he liked to use right before he shot his patented fade jumper. Or that move he'd make starting to his right, then planting his right foot—the one hurting him so bad now—so that the guy guarding him would go flying past just before Billy'd make another fifteen-footer, the ball usually hitting the net like hair hitting a pillow.

"You see that guy in the lobby last night, we got back from the club?" he said to Gary Hall.

Gary said, "Course I saw. You pay me for that, right, dog? To see shit?"

Billy Cash leaned back in the first seat on the left, behind the driver, the one that was always his seat, on the way to a shootaround or a game or to the airport in the night. Gary was where he always was, across the aisle.

"He coulda had a camera on him," Billy said.

"Yeah," Gary said, "he coulda. So could the room service waiter. Or the woman from housekeeping they keep on call twenty-four hours a day when you're in town, in case you decide your pillow feels as hard as your dick or some such. Or the bellman brings your brushed suedes back looking all new after you smudged them someplace and they've been botherin' you ever since."

Only Gary could talk to him that way. Not even the Magic coach, Tommy Clayton, could. There'd never been a coach Billy Cash had in his life, all the way back to Wake Forest, who had any real juice with him. Or any coach Billy trusted. But he trusted Gary Hall, his bodyguard, the man in charge of what

Billy liked to call his all-around situation, the ex–undercover cop from New York City he'd hired to permanently have his back, in season and out, work his surveillance, watching out for Billy Cash the way he had when he was chasing bad guys, going over every single hotel room Billy stayed in like it was in one of those crime scene shows on television.

Only the job was more than that now, Gary knew. All of a sudden, these last months, the full-time job was listening to this nonstop shit about Monica and how he was sure she was having him followed so it would be no problem when she divorced him to get half.

That and taking care of the girls.

Billy Cash said, "That your way of tellin' me you checked him out? The guy in the lobby?"

"I talked to security. They said he was just a driver, wanting to be right there when *his* man, some Saudi asshole, came off the elevator, probably coming down from doing the same bad things in his suite you were about to go up and do in yours."

"Speaking of," Billy said. "We good for later?"

"With the MTV girl?"

"Uh-huh."

Billy Cash leaned back, smiled. "MTV," he said. "Maybe we'll make our own damn video." Then he closed his eyes and with them still closed said to Gary, "You see that driver guy in the lobby again, the one with the towel-head, you act like you're with hotel security, check him out your own damn self."

"After I get Miss MTV squared away," Gary said. "As part of my ever-expanding duties."

Billy wasn't even listening, Gary saw that he'd put his headphones on, was probably listening to some of that thump-thump-thump rap he said got him going.

So this was another time when Gary stopped short of telling him that he didn't sign on to be a pimp, that he didn't know when he signed on with Billy Cash that his job would turn into getting the girls into the hotel and then out, after Billy had finished his business.

That and watch out for all the private eye shit Billy was sure Monica was putting on him, looking to have him by the balls when she filed, something Billy was sure was going to happen soon.

Billy took the headphones off and said, "You ought to get yourself a girl of your own, you wouldn't act so fucking pissed off all the time."

"So I can be as happy as you and Monica?" Gary said.

"I'm talkin' about one who'll love you for yourself, not for the cold cash," Billy said. Always looking for another play on words when it came to Monica.

The Academy ran into some traffic, turned right on Forty-fifth, on its way over to Broadway.

"My life's complicated enough," Gary said, "watching out on your life."

"I sound paranoid about her sometimes, don't I?"

It made Gary smile, he couldn't help himself "Ya *think*?" he said. Trying to remember a time when there wasn't this kind of standoff between Billy and Monica, her holding on to the title of Mrs. Cash, the celebrity it gave *her*, the way he held on to his money.

"You know what they say, dog," Billy Cash said. "Just 'cause you're paranoid don't mean the motherfuckers ain't out to get you."

*   *   *

Billy Cash was Jordan after Jordan. Not the Michael who couldn't stay unretired and came back and retired wearing the funny Wizards uniform. The *Chicago* Michael, the one who won everything and made all the money. Billy said he'd gone to Wake, not North Carolina, where Michael'd gone, or Duke, because those schools didn't need him, they'd already won all their national championships. So he went to Wake, in the same neighborhood down there, and won his Deacons two NCAAs, his sophomore and junior years, came out before his senior year to play for the Magic, even though everybody'd known he was ready for the pros after high school. Only he said he'd win more titles in college than Michael, so that's what he went and did. Now it was Billy Cash on the Wheaties box, Billy selling his cell phones and his Gap clothes and those high-def TVs and Suburbans. It was Billy in the Disney commercials, more visible for Disney than the fucking mouse.

It took him a while to win in the pros, six years, but then the Magic had finally broken through and he had won two titles in a row there. Then some of the guys he played with got tired of being his "supporting cast," which he'd accidentally called them one time same as Michael had with the Bulls, started leaving for free agency, moving on for cash of their own. So the people running the Magic had brought in a younger supporting cast and Billy kept scoring and finally, the year before, they'd won again. And were on their way to another, all the TV experts agreed, as long as that sore foot of Billy's made it to the end of June. It should have been enough, Gary Hall knew, to have Billy Cash feeling as if he had his skinny-assed self sitting on top of the world, keeping his eye on the prize.

Problem was, he kept looking over his fucking shoulder for Monica.

He'd met her at the Guest Relations desk at Disney, some

appearance he made right after the Magic had drafted him and the mouse-ear people had signed him up to be their smiling pitchman, shooting the first commercial the day the Magic had picked him first in the draft. *Where you goin', Billy Cash? I'm goin' to Disney World!* One of those deals. Gary wasn't with him yet, having just made detective, assigned to a surveillance detail with the Seventeenth Precinct, Manhattan. But he'd heard the story about how Billy and Monica had met so many times he could recite it by now like he could the Pledge of Allegiance.

"I'm Cash," he said to Monica that day, a snappy little dish in her Disney colors and Disney clothes, giving him a look.

"Fast Cash?" she said.

"Hard Cash."

Then Monica had said, "Your next question should be where I'm gonna be after you get done waving from the back of your convertible in the afternoon Disney parade."

They went out that night and every night that week and when she told him she'd missed her period two months into his rookie season, they eloped to Las Vegas on an off-day between playing the Clips in L.A. and the Kings in Sacramento, like they were just a couple of crazy kids. "Just so's the math would be close enough for all them at Disney corporate later on," Billy said.

They had a boy and then a girl the year after that and became the happy *People*-magazine-cover couple—sitcom Negroes, Billy liked to say to Gary—even though the whole time, from the day they got married in the tacky Vegas chapel just for laughs, Billy Cash was still fucking everybody who'd stay still long enough. If Monica knew, at least in the first years Gary'd gone to work for Billy, she never let on to him. She was into the full swing of being Mrs. Cash by then, working the charity circuit hard, fighting for Afghan women and land-mine victims with that pretty blonde that Paul McCartney'd married, the one with one leg; somehow putting herself in the middle of all the 9/11 shit even though she'd been having her picture taken with the kids at Splash Mountain when the planes hit; going up to the White House what felt like every couple of months to Gary for another luncheon or photo op with the First Lady.

Little Monica from Guest Relations, living large.

"She sure as hell knew what she was doin' when she had her relations with this guest," Billy bitched all the time. " 'Specially when she forgot to take that damn pill she swore she was on and just didn't work that one time."

Gary had met Billy in New York one night when the Magic were in to play the Knicks. Billy'd gone clubbing with some of his teammates, a lot of the ones who'd move on later, and they'd picked up some girls who wanted to go to Elaine's and see if there was any movie stars up there eating fried calamari. They got there about one in the morning. Gary was drinking with some other cops at the bar, because for all the shit you read in the papers about Woody Allen and movie stars and other celebrity dinks going to Elaine's, it was a cop bar, too, especially late at night. Elaine liked her celebrity crowd because it was good for business, but liked drinking and hanging around with cops just as much, from the commissioner on down.

Gary saw Billy Cash's crowd come in the Second Avenue door, watched the fuss everybody made, saw the stroke the room gave him once he got his big table, the one Woody liked in those days, back there where you made the men's-room turn. Then Gary went back to his drink and the two waitresses from

Hanratty's up the block he was talking up didn't pay Billy Cash any more mind until the fat drunk actor decided to call Billy out.

The actor, some guy who used to be in the movies but was working on some ABC soap—all this time later, Gary couldn't remember whether or not it was *All My Children* or *One Life to Live*—had some drunk friends with him. So it made him whiskey-brave enough to tell Billy that they should take whatever it was had started between them outside. And Billy, who Gary would find out later usually laughed assholes like this off, didn't think it was so funny this time.

Plus, the girls he was with wanted a show.

Gary, leaned on the bar near the front window, thought it was all bullshit, that it was a playground face-down and nothing more, and once the air hit them they'd settle it before anybody threw a punch. But then he watched through the window as the actor set his hands as if he'd boxed some in his life. Or maybe played a boxer in the movies. And before Billy Cash knew it, he'd been hooked solid on Second Avenue above his ear and was down on one knee.

The fat actor was lighter on his feet than Gary thought he could be, as much gut he was showing against his white shirt, and as Billy started to get up the actor clipped him again, another left, same place above the ear. Gary couldn't hear what was happening, just saw the guy's friends laughing and cheering him on and probably telling him to finish Billy off.

It was then that Gary excused himself from the Hanratty's girls, came through the door as Billy was getting to his feet, finally having enough sense to get his hands up.

One of the friends said, "Oh, look, the faggot brought a playmate."

Gary took a fistful of the friend's long stringy hair with his left hand, pulled out his badge with his right, then pulled the guy close to him and said, "Give us a kiss."

The fat actor said, "This is between me and him."

"Unless I say it's not," Gary said. "That would be another way of looking at things."

The actor took a step at Gary now, like he was going to do something about it, badge or not, and as soon as the left hand came forward Gary caught it the way you would a softball in a mitt and said, "The next move anybody makes here will be me breaking that pretty nose of yours."

It ended right there. The actor and his buddies got into a cab. Billy told the girls to get back inside with his teammates, who somehow managed never to leave the table. Billy started to introduce himself to Gary that night and Gary said, "I know who you are." Billy told him to come in, join the party, and about a half hour later he said, "How much you make? With the cops, I mean." Gary couldn't think of a reason not to tell him, so he did, right down to the thirty-seven cents at the end of it after everything got taken out. And right there, straight out that night, Billy said, "How'd you like to come work for me?"

Gary asked him what that meant, and Billy pretty much laid out what the job would be. Leaving out the parts about the girls. And Gary Hall said yes, just like that, the answer coming out of how tired he was of counting off the days and months and years to his pension, setting up his cameras across the way from some club where the mob boys had watched too many movies, life with Billy Cash sounding like more high life than Gary had ever known, all the way back to growing up under the el on Roosevelt Avenue in Corona.

After that, nobody fucked with Billy Cash and got away with it.

Excepting Monica.

In the early times, those first years, Billy never treated Gary like an employee, some kind of walk-around guy. "My brother," is the way Billy would introduce him, "just from another mother." That would be when they were clubbing or riding around in a limo or playing gin in the back of the team plane. It only changed over time, subtle at first, gradual, Gary not really noticing it, Billy helping himself to as many girls as he ever did but worrying about it more as he got older, as he started to lose a step even as he still kept getting his points, worrying more and more about his sponsors, letting them run his goddamn life as though playing ball had become some kind of moonlighting deal with him, some kind of side thing, that all that really mattered to Billy Cash now was the money.

Now he just wanted to hold on to as much of that money as possible when Monica and her lawyers came after it, sure that Monica was secure enough in her own celebrity now, her own deal, to think she could stand alone as Mrs. Cash without him now.

Once she got her half, what people said could be close to half a billion.

It was why the last couple of years Gary's main job had become organizing all the logistics of the girls, setting up this whole elaborate floor plan with the three rooms at every hotel they stayed at, it never occurring to Billy to slow down. He just thought he needed to be more damn careful.

The fool losing a step on the court, but obsessed with staying one step ahead of Mrs. Cash.

★ ★ ★

There was a reporter from that new ESPN magazine Billy Cash ran with sometimes, a sharp-dressed young guy about forty, shaved head, named Jayson Miles. Miles also did some on-air work for ESPN and managed to act like an insider without busting balls the way some of the other TV experts did. Over time, he had managed to get tight with the right stars in the league, especially the hip-hop do-rag kids with their hair and their tattoos, gaining their trust in a way most other guys couldn't, white or black. It was Miles being on television that allowed him to lamp with the ballplayers the way he did, nobody gave a shit what he wrote in some magazine. By now, hanging with Billy Cash as long as he had, seeing Billy Cash's world from the inside, Gary understood that the only ones in the media who had any status with players were the ones they knew from the TV. The only time some player cared about the newspapers was when one of his boys—and they all had their boys—told him some writer was trying to mess with him.

Gary had seen Jayson Miles a few times on one of those shows where they all sat around and argued about everything. And when it came down to it, and the others were yelling about how these kids made too much money and didn't give a rat's ass about anything except themselves, Jayson Miles, in his cool way, would find a way to stick up for the young stars of the league, say they weren't all that different from basketball stars all across history, it was just that the fat white guy sitting there watching with his beer and his Cheez Doodles didn't like all the graffiti up and down their arms, and their Sprewell hair. So Miles was officially on the inside now, dressing like a dude, talking the talk even if he had been to Stanford as an English major, moving through this world as easily as if he were the one knocking down the midrange Js.

Gary was standing with Miles now in the hallway outside the visitors' locker room at Madison Square Garden, Gary leaning against a wall next to this big mounted color photograph of Frank Sinatra. Miles was wearing a camel sports jacket, beige mock turtleneck sweater, two-toned shoes that probably cost as much as everything Gary had on, Gary's black jeans and black leather jacket and gray pullover sweater.

Miles said to him, "Word is, your boy's getting careless."

Gary shrugged. "He keeps saying he's all worried about Monica stalking him with her investigators and her picture-takers, having me do everything except sweep the room for bugs before he'll even walk through the door. But he still thinks he can turn himself invisible every time his dick gets hard."

"You remember what it was like in the old days," Miles said. "He had so many of his logistics getting the girls in and out of hotels, I wondered if he forgot sometimes what room the one he was supposed to fuck was in."

"I'm the one invented those logistics," Gary said.

"Forgot."

Gary said, "What are you hearing?"

"He got seen in the men's room in that new club down in D.C. You know it? Jump, it's called. Last time in New York, one of the waiters saw him getting it on, no shit, in a function room at the '21.' That's the short list, trust me."

"He gets his urges, tells me he's going to go walk around, smoke one of his Cubans. Winking, telling me it's one of his long ones, one of those hour smokes he likes so much."

Gary felt the buzzer on his cell go off, took it out of his jacket pocket, saw the callback number, ignored it.

"When he does come back, in a half hour, hour, whatever, all cleaned up, happy-looking, he right away asks if I saw anybody suspicious while he was gone."

"You think Monica's having him followed?"

"Yeah. I think."

"But following the boy and getting the goods on him are two different things."

"So he keeps telling himself."

Miles said, "You think she's really ready to give it up? Being Mrs. Cash?"

Gary said, "I'm just surmising, okay? Knowing her the way I do. But she might be thinking like this here: Let me get my two hundred million, or whatever it is, and I don't give no never-mind to whether I still got him in the house or not. On account of, I've got his money and his name. And the kids. *And* the house. And whatever. Then she can finance a real nice search for a new man, one who doesn't want to fuck around on her soon as the car pulls out the driveway."

On the other side of the locker room door they could both hear the kind of cellblock yelling you always heard from Billy and the rest of the Magic right before it was time for them to take the court.

"You guys leaving right after the game?" Miles said.

"In the morning."

"He got something lined up for after?"

"I'm picking her up," Gary Hall said.

★   ★   ★

Gary didn't even catch her name right when she got into the backseat of the limo with him. Alicia? Nykesha? And even if he heard it right, he knew he'd have no idea how to spell it, the way they all jacked around with the way they spelled their names now. It didn't matter, anyway, he knew that, too. She was just another one with too much makeup, the girl light-skinned black this time, long straight hair, another one thinking that looking as skinny as a scaghead was a good look for her.

Short skirt on her. Long legs. Spiky heels. No eye contact. If she was much more than twenty-one or twenty-two, Gary was missing his guess.

All he knew for sure, in his ever-expanding role as pimp, is that they kept getting younger.

He'd already picked up younger than Alicia or Nykesha or whoever she was for his man, Billy Cash.

"Where'd you meet Billy?" Gary said, talking just to talk, so he didn't have to think too much on his own all-around situation, where it was at and where it was going.

"Club," she said, checking her nails, painted the same bloodred color as her puffed-up lips.

"Ray's?" he said, meaning the club they were on their way to right now.

"Was with some friends," she said. "When Orlando was in last time? Billy was with somebody else, but the manager handled it for me."

"Got him your number, you mean."

"Uh-huh."

It worked that way a lot. They'd be in L.A., out having lunch after a shootaround, and every good-looking woman in the place would somehow find an excuse to stop by Billy's and his table. Half the time giving Billy a lot of made-up shit about how they had met him in Vancouver or Alaska or at the Jamaica Inn one time. Then they'd leave and Gary would say to Billy, "When were you in Jamaica, I must've forgot."

Billy would say, "Never, that's when I was in Jamaica."

Then he'd smile and say, "Aw, man, you know what it is by now. They're just trying to come up with creative ways to say 'Please fuck me.'"

The car pulled up to Ray's, the new hot club, at least for the time being, this one way down in the West Village. They sat down at the table they had reserved for Billy and Gary ordered one of those nonalcoholic beers that tasted like real. The girl ordered a Cosmopolitan that came in a huge martini glass. They sat there feeling the loud beat of the music as much as listening to it until Billy made his big entrance about an hour after the Magic had beaten the Knicks, which Gary knew already from making a call when he'd gone to the men's room, knowing the final was 112–100 and Billy had gone for forty-three on them. Now Billy did his usual at Ray's, kissing on a few please-do-me girls at the bar, giving the manager his Billy hug even though you could barely notice him stopping him to do it, bopping his head in a cool way to some inner beat, acting as if he had all the time in the world before he got to the table where Alicia or Nykesha or whoever the hell she was was watching him with this heavy-eyed dreamy look, like she was ready to go right now.

"Hey, fine thing," Billy said, leaning down to kiss her hair.

It came out "thang," the way it did sometimes when Billy wanted to brother himself down a little.

Gary wondered if he called them "fine thing" as much as he did because he wasn't sure of their names, either.

"Hey," he said to Gary.

"Big man," Gary said.

To the girl, Billy said, "My man Gary treatin' you good like I told him?"

His man.

One that brought the girls.

Shit, Gary Hall thought.

The girl tried to look sexy as she looked at Gary and took a sip of her Cosmopolitan and then licked her big lips.

"He's nice," she said.

"The best," Billy said. "Like my own Secret Service."

Now Billy said to Gary, "You want to go wait at the bar? Or go someplace your own self? I'll call you on the cell by and by, you can meet me outside the hotel?"

"I know the drill," Gary said.

"We got it down, don't we, dog?"

"There's a jazz club not too far. I may go over there, have a real drink, kick back for a little bit."

"Keep the phone on," Billy said, "I don't know how long I'll be."

He always got more bossy at this hour of the night, not even hearing the snap in his own voice.

Gary shook his head on the way to the door, thinking about what he'd talked about with Jayson Miles, how Billy obsessed on Monica the way he did, then thinking he could be out and about like this, grab-assing his way through life, telling people the girl just wanted to have a drink with him, or have her picture taken with him, if somebody did take a picture and it ended up in the papers.

Gary didn't go to the jazz club, just walked into the first quiet bar he saw, on Horatio Street, nursing a Scotch until the phone buzzed about one. Gary paid his check and got into a cab and got to the Pierre before Billy did, shot the breeze a little bit with the guy from security who helped him set things up, then walked up Central Park South, past Mickey Mantle's, where he knew the limo would pick him up.

When the car showed up, he got into the front, then it eased its way east on Fifty-ninth, uptown on Madison, back over to Fifth, and the front entrance to the Pierre. Gary got out and opened the back door for the girl, and the two of them walked through the lobby like a happy couple, Gary even putting his arm around her. There were simpler ways to do this, Gary told Billy that all the time, but he didn't give a rat's ass, this way was his way now, and his way was all that ever mattered.

Thinking he was being as careful as he was with the ball with ten seconds left.

Billy showed up a few minutes later in what was supposed to be the safe room, the one between his and Gary's, the one he was sure was safe, tonight's do-me girl getting herself ready for him in the bathroom.

Gary checked the room one last time, made sure everything was all right, then he was out the door as soon as Billy was in, Gary not even bothering to say good night.

*   *   *

They clinched home court for the playoffs, the Magic did, with a week to go in the regular season. Mostly, Gary knew, the rest of them watched as Billy did it, that was the truth of things, Billy doing it to the Wizards all by himself in that new MCI Center in downtown Washington, part of one of those urban fix-ups that mostly fixed up the owner of the team moving into a place like MCI. Billy Cash went in there and dropped his fifty-eight points on the Wizards and gave the Magic the best record in the NBA, east or west, carving those points into the young guys trying to stay with him the way you'd carve your initials on the side of some tree.

Billy didn't want to go out after the game, even though D.C. was one of his favorite cities to go clubbing in the whole league. "Gary, my brother," he said in the locker room, "I believe I'm just gonna take my shit back to the Do-It Room over there to the Four Seasons." That's what he liked to call his fuck room at these expensive hotels. The Do-It Room. He'd been out in L.A. one time when he was a kid, visiting Wilt Chamberlain's famous house in Bel-Air, and he'd come up on a room that was just water bed and mirrors, no real floor to it, and outside was a little plaque, next to the door, saying THE DO-IT ROOM.

Billy told Gary to go pick up Sharon, the girl from Alcohol, Tobacco and Firearms he'd met at lunch after the shoot-around, bring her over there.

Billy said, "And tell her not to worry, the only illegal weapon I'm packin' is the one I got right here," he said, grabbing himself under his towel.

Gary said he'd be sure to pass that along.

Sharon. At least he had a name to put to the girl this time. Went outside where the limo was waiting next to the players' entrance, drove to the address nearly all the way out of town, got her back to the hotel in Georgetown a little bit before Billy would be showing up after finishing with his media and whatnot. Took her up there, showed her around, called room service and ordered some of the champagne Billy liked, his big fruit platter. And whipped cream. Fresh-whipped and kept on ice. Lot of it.

Gary smiled.

The shit you did for love.

★   ★   ★

The second-to-last game of the regular season was in Philadelphia, so the Magic were just going to bus up there in the early afternoon, Thursday afternoon, since they weren't playing until Friday night.

The phone rang in Gary's room at the Four Seasons a couple of minutes after eleven.

"Get down here now," Billy said. "I got a situation."

"Your room or the other?"

"Mine."

"You still got the girl here?"

"Got Monica here," Billy said, and hung up.

Billy was wearing a white Magic T-shirt, baggy gym shorts. He was on one couch in the living room of his suite. Monica was across from him on the other couch in the room. She wore a sharp-looking navy-blue pantsuit, one leg crossed over the other, showing off some big heels on her black shoes. She had a black leather purse next to her. On the coffee table between her and Billy was a thick manila envelope and the kind of thick binder you used to carry to school. And a shoe box that had PRADA written on the side.

By now, Gary knew that Monica would rather go barefoot than wear something other than Prada on her size 7 feet.

"Monica," Gary said.

"Gary Hall."

He hung back, over where the room service table was, pouring himself a cup of coffee. Waiting to see how it would play out, now that they were all finally down to it.

Here, Gary thought, in the real Do-It Room.

"She's servin' me," Billy said in a dead voice.

"Just a different kind of serving than went on next door," Monica said. "Kind always goes on next door."

"This is how you do it?" Billy said. "Blindside me this way?"

Monica said, "One of us was blind, Billy. From the start."

"You said the papers were in the envelope," Billy said. "What's the rest of it?"

"Aren't you even a little bit curious?" Monica said.

"You'll tell me," Billy said. "You always did like being the smart one, even when you were little Miss Congeniality behind your Disney desk, unbuttoning enough buttons on your blouse to show yourself off."

Monica said, "The binder's my black book on you, Billy. You got your black book, with all your little whores in it? Now I've got mine. The shoe box has got cassettes in it, you can keep them if you want, watch yourself instead of the dirty hotel movies. All of it's why we're going to do this nice and easy, which means you can take that pre-nup you had me sign and throw it right out that window over there. I could've had somebody else serve you, but I wanted to do it myself. Put it all on the table, so to speak. We'll call it irreconcilable differences. Maybe throw in a little mental cruelty on the side, just so it sounds more official. Then we smile and call it painful but amicable." Monica smiled now. "Before I get my half."

Billy opened up the binder, saw that some of the pages had black-and-white pictures under plastic.

He took the picture out, stared at it.

"Goddamn," he said. "This here is Charrisse. From last week in New York. The one from MTV."

Billy looked over to Gary and said, "How'd somebody get a fucking camera in the room?"

"It's easy, you know where to hide it," Gary said. "If you can't have a practical application of all they made you learn with surveillance from the cops, what's the point?"

All you could hear now in the suite was the hum of the air conditioner, some kind of soft music playing from the bedroom.

"You?" Billy said to him.

From the couch, Monica said, "Us."

Billy turned and stared at her, then back to Gary, then back at the picture of him and Charrisse in the Do-It Room at the Plaza. Dropped that and pulled out another one. "Selena," Billy said. Kept going through them and not saying the names now, just saying Cleveland and San Antonio and Phoenix and Detroit. Like he remembered the cities better than he remembered the girls.

Billy Cash stopped finally and looked hard again at Gary, more hurt now than sad, or at least playing it that way. "Why?" he said.

"Got tired of being the boy bringing the girls. Once you do that, all you are is somebody's boy."

Monica stood up and said, "You know what they say, don't you, Billy? My people will call your people."

Gary Hall walked over then and put his arm around her.

"You two . . . ?" Billy said.

"Us," Monica said.

Gary Hall said, "Remember you're always telling me to get my own girl? I did."

"Rich one, too," Mrs. Cash said.

WHITE TRASH NOIR

Michael Malone

Ll of a sudden Dr. Rothmann, the foreman of my jury, says she wants to talk to the judge. She gives me a look when she walks by the defendant's table, straight in my eyes, and I nod back at her but I can't tell what she's thinking because there's so many different feelings in her face. But behind me my Mawmaw stands up and bows her head to her. The judge and the jury get up too and they crowd each other out of the courtroom and just leave us sitting here. My lawyer leans over and says, "Charmain, you have got to change your mind and take the stand." And I tell him, "No thank you."

Mr. Snow goes, "This is Murder One, Charmain. You just cannot kill your husband in the state of North Carolina if he played ACC basketball."

I go, "Well, this is Charmain Luby Markell and I'm not talking about my personal private life to a bunch of strangers in a court of law and have them turn it all into lies against me and mine."

I got this lawyer? He's young, just two years more than me, and halfway through our first talk in the jail I can tell he hasn't had a lot of Life Experience, which, between you and I, I've already had way too much. Tilden Snow's his name, Tilden Snow III, and I think it's lazy for a family to use a name three times in a row when there're so many nice new names out there you can choose from. They even got little *Names for Your Baby* books at the checkout counters, which is where I got my Jarrad's name. That's what I call my little boy, Jarrad Todd Markell, even though his birth certificate says Kyle Lewis Markell, Jr., totally because my husband's mother worships the ground her son Kyle walks on. Well, did walk on before I shot him.

So Mr. Snow wanted me to get up on the witness stand and tell why I shot my husband in the head and set him on fire in our backyard.

Mr. Snow chews at a cuticle; his nails are a mess. He sighs a long deep sigh and shakes his head at me. "Please won't you help me here, Charmain?"

Please won't I help him? Who're they trying to give a lethal injection to, me or Tilden Snow III? I go, "Mr. Snow—"

He holds up his hand like a safety patrol. "Tilden. I keep asking you, please call me Tilden. Mr. Snow's my Daddy's name." I think he was trying to make a joke so I smiled and said I'd try to call him Tilden but I wouldn't take the stand and tell why I shot Kyle.

"Oh, Jesus," he says. "Well, you better hope your friend Dr. Rothmann's telling the judge she's going to hang that jury."

I say, "What does that mean, she's going to hang the jury?" But he just pulls on his ears like he wishes they were longer and he runs off with the other lawyers after Dr. Rothmann and the judge and leaves me to sit and wait, which is what I've mostly been doing since Kyle died. Which I admit he did do when I shot him.

I'm used to it now but the first time they hauled me into this courtroom, I was crying and grabbing onto my grandma Mawmaw so hard they had to prize my fingers from around her neck. I saw the way it was upsetting her how they had my hands and feet both hooked up to a chain. But Mawmaw whispered at me, "Don't you cry, baby doll, don't you let those folks see you cry," and I tried hard to stop and I did. The only other time I ever went to pieces was when Mawmaw brought Jarrad into the back of the courtroom and held him up for me to look at (he's two and a half now and he was nineteen months last time I seen him). He had a little toy basketball in his hands and I swear he looked like his daddy, maybe because he started to cry and his face turned purple the way Kyle's did when he got mad.

The first day I was in court the whole jury kept staring at me like somebody was going to test them in the morning. Right off I noticed this one lady on the front row, a soft pretty lady, small, with a sharp smart face. From day one, she looked right at me with her head cocked over to the side like a little hawk, sort of puzzling about me. They said her name was Mrs. Nina Gold Rothmann, except they called her Doctor. She got to be the foreman of the jury even though she wasn't a man. And for two whole weeks of the State's making its case against me, she's about never took her eyes off me.

Now the State's done and it's time for our side to "shred them to pieces," according to Mr. Snow, except I'm not going to take the stand so there won't be much shredding likely to get done. Maybe that's why Dr. Rothmann's made them all go off to talk to the judge now. Maybe she's in there telling the judge just give Charmain Markell the death penalty so the jury can go on home. They must be about as sick of hearing about that gun and kerosene and Kyle's eleven points against Wake Forest as I am.

The first day of my trial I didn't like Dr. Rothmann. It's rude to stare the way she does. But after a while I kind of felt like we was almost talking to each other. I heard all about her life at what they call the vow deer, I believe. She had to tell about herself to get on the jury, or get off it, which a lot of them tried to because of their jobs or kids or whatever. They said she was a big doctor at the Research Center. She told how she was working on what we're all made up of, genomes, something like that. When you know their genomes, you can tell people what they're going to die of someday. Well, but I guess I don't need a research center to tell me that. Lethal injection. Least if the District Attorney, Mr. Goodenough, gets his way. Anyhow, this foreman lady's job of sorting out our genomes sounded hard but interesting and I could tell she cared a lot about it from the way she talked. At first I smiled at her just to be polite, but later on it was sort of personal because she was divorced and had a boy in college. And I thought that was kind of like me—I mean, I've got one little boy and no husband anymore too. So a lot of days went by in court with me and Dr. Rothmann looking at each other. I started figuring out some beauty tips I could of given her if she'd come in Pretty Woman. She had three suits that didn't do much for her; the sleeves were too long so she just had them rolled up. Her hands were nice though; somebody did a good job on her nails, but not us—I never saw her in Pretty Woman and I do all their hands.

After a while I decided her eyes weren't mean, she was just thinking hard all the time, not like some folks on my jury that were taking naps with their eyes open. Not that I blame them.

All that State's evidence was boring *me,* and it was *my* life. But Dr. Rothmann, she hung in there even with that old fat Mr. Goodenough mumbling about ballistics this and ballistics that for four solid hours. Isn't it something? I could not make myself listen.

After a week or so Dr. Rothmann got to be somebody I could kind of talk to in my mind in my cell at night, like maybe explain things to her that were all balled up inside me like string in a junk drawer, like she'd be smart enough to see how they'd look if they got untangled. When I looked at her over there in the jury box, I felt like she could see what was true. I tried to explain it to my lawyer, Tilden Snow, but he said, "I don't trust Rothmann." He figured the D.A. must know something or he wouldn't have let her on my jury because he said usually the State avoids these Ph.D.'s like the plague on account of they are soft on crime.

Yesterday I told Mr. Snow in the visiting room how, deep down, I thought the foreman lady was kind of sweet and he snorts at me, "She's about as sweet as a jar of pickled okra." I said I was surprised somebody rich as him even ate pickled okra but he tells me, "Charmain, I've got a grandmama same as you and she loved pickled okra."

I say, "I know you do because my grandma used to clean her house and your mama's house."

He says, "I know. Your grandmama was the White Tornado."

"Yes, she was and still is. She quit your mama," I say.

He wants to know why but he's not surprised.

I tell him. "Your mama called her a servant and said how she had to iron your daddy's boxer shorts. And Mawmaw's like, 'No thank you, Mrs. Snow, I am not your servant and I am not about to put my hands in a strange man's underpants.'"

Mr. Snow—I'm sorry, I don't want to call him Tilden—laughed. He says, "I didn't know that. And here's something I bet you don't know. I remember you. Your grandmama brought you to the house with her one time while she was cleaning—"

I nod. "She brought me with her to a lot of houses because I helped her clean till I started at Pretty Woman."

"Well, one time when I was there visiting my grandma and I guess I was about six or seven, I asked you if you wanted to swing on my swing and then I asked you if you'd marry me. Do you remember that?"

"No."

"You don't remember that?"

"I'm sorry."

He shook his head like he couldn't believe I'd forget he wanted to marry me when I was four or five years old. Then he stacked up all his papers to go. He says, "Well, my grandmama was a bitch on wheels. And I bet the same can be said for your sweet Dr. Nina Rothmann."

People think you can't be nice and smart both but I don't see why. Mawmaw used to tell me and my brother Tanner, "I'd rather have sweetness and niceness in a child than a report card full of As," but why couldn't she get both? Course the last A she ever saw was the one I got in algebra in tenth grade. But I blame that on going out almost every night with Kyle, who was a senior and the star of the basketball team. Rich as Tilden Snow was, even he wasn't popular like Kyle. So my grades slipped. Meanwhile my brother Tanner would probably still be stuck in first grade if all his teachers hadn't passed him along to get him out of their classrooms. I bet he's the only boy ever flunked conduct in a elementary school.

Our grandma Mawmaw raised me and Tanner after Daddy and Mama got killed trying to beat a Food Lion truck through an intersection. She said they wasn't cut out to be parents anyhow, due to drugs, drink and the NASCAR tracks. They dropped us off at Mawmaw's almost every night even before they got killed. Mawmaw said my Mama was the only thing my Daddy ever met that was as fast as him. He loved speed and speed killed him in the long run. And he took my Mama along for the ride. Only twenty-four, both of them, which is how old I am now, so I guess twenty-four is just a real unlucky year for the Lubys in general, since that's how old my brother Tanner was three years ago when he held up the ABC store while still on parole.

Poor Mawmaw, she used to tell me with my brother Tanner it was déjà vu right back to our daddy only worse. Daddy was Mawmaw's only child and she said he was one too many. Plus she said she didn't have her strength like she used to. But she never quit. Thirty-five years at the job and she's still cleaning houses. Because of her I was never cold and I was never hungry and I was never made to feel no good. And I know my little boy Jarrad never will be either, if Mawmaw can just hold on to him against Kyle's mama's, Mrs Markell's, lawsuit. Kyle's mama getting her hands on Jarrad scares me more than a lethal injection. I mean, look how Kyle turned out. So bad his own wife shot him.

Way back when Daddy was fourteen and he robbed Mawmaw's purse, stole her car and drove it down to Mardi Gras in New Orleans, she asked her minister at Church of the Open Door if the devil could of got her pregnant while she was asleep at night, 'cause she'd started wondering if Daddy was the son of Satan. But the minister said the Devil don't make personal acquaintanceships in the modern world. Well, that minister never met my husband Kyle Markell. And I wish I could say the same. When Mawmaw came down to the hospital after they pumped out my stomach, she told me the only way somebody *wouldn't* have killed Kyle sooner or later was they never met him. But I sure don't think Mawmaw figured it'd be me. I never was a violent person, never yelled, never cursed, and I never could stand blood. I couldn't even cut up a frog in biology. And when that Clemson guard whammed his elbow into Kyle's nose his freshman year and they couldn't stop the bleeding, I fainted dead away in the stands. I fainted other times too, like when Kyle had JuliaRoberts put to sleep just because of her seizures. That was my dog that had eyes like Julia Roberts. I'm convinced Kyle ran over her with the van and swore he didn't. I never wanted to hurt anything in this world till the day I picked up that gun and told Kyle to put down that basketball and shut the fuck up.

Anyhow, the reason I wouldn't go on the stand in my own defense was the samples Mr. Snow gave of what the District Attorney would likely ask me. I wouldn't tell that sort of thing to Mawmaw on my deathbed, much less testify on a Bible about it to everybody in my hometown. Like the weird disgusting stuff Kyle heard on the Internet that he kept trying to make me do in bed. And Mr. Snow said how they'd twist things all around so lies would look true and the true things sound like lies. So I kept telling the lawyer the same thing I used to tell Kyle. No thank you. He got real upset. The lawyer, I mean. To be honest it was nothing much compared to the way Kyle used to freak out on me when he was alive, which I guess it's my fault he's not anymore. All my lawyer does is grumble how I'm tying his hands behind his back. One day early on in the trial

he said I had a sympathetic personality and was young and petite and pretty—the way his eyes shifted around behind his
glasses when he said that, I had the feeling he was coming on
to me without even knowing it, which would be pretty strange
considering, but he wouldn't be the first man that got strange
on me at the wrong time. His idea was if I took the stand and
started crying I could maybe win over the jury to go easy on
me even if Kyle had played in the Sweet Sixteen.

Three weeks back, the night before my trial started, my
lawyer goes, "I don't want to scare you, Charmain"—(Sure!)—
but he explains how unless I testify so he can bring up about
the drug stuff and weird sex stuff and the 911 and the rest of
it, I could get Death.

I'm like, "Well, okay, then, I'll take Death. But I won't take
the stand."

He's like, "Great. You know who's gonna love this? The
District Attorney. You know why? Because you just lay down
in the death chamber, Charmain, handed him the needle and
said stick it in!" He shakes this bunch of papers in my face.
"Look at this, look at this, look at this!"

I say, "Excuse me but I heard you the first time."

"This is State's evidence. These are exhibits the State's
gonna be showing to the jury and you don't think they're not
going to have a seriously deleterious impact?"

Well, I didn't know what "deleterious" means but from the
twitch in his mouth I could tell it wasn't good. I looked at the
papers. Stuff like:

STATE EXHIBIT #7. One desert eagle mark VII .44-caliber
Magnum pistol, black matte finish. Six-inch barrel. Fingerprints of defendant on grip.

STATE EXHIBIT #13. Eight-round clip of .44 Magnum shells. Two rounds fired.

STATE EXHIBIT #28. Emptied kerosene can. Fingerprints of defendant on handle.

STATE EXHIBIT #51. Two .44 Magnum slugs taken from cranium of the deceased.

STATE EXHIBIT #85. Five-page letter of confession to shooting on Marriott stationery signed by defendant.

STATE EXHIBIT #97. ACC tournament basketball with bullet hole.

STATE EXHIBIT #103. Photographs of partially burned corpse of the deceased.

I said it did look like they had plenty of exhibits. Tilden Snow just nodded like his head was on a spring. But he was right about them making the most of what they had. For two weeks mornings and afternoons that sour-faced District Attorney, Mr. Goodenough, kept shaking plastic Baggies with those exhibits in them in front of the jury's faces. He made it all sound like I was the original black widow spider. The worst was the pictures of Kyle's body. I didn't look at them. But the foreman lady, Dr. Rothmann, turned gray as a old dishrag when Mr. Goodenough shoved them at her, and I'm not sure how much she even saw because she turned her head so fast.

I'd rather be dead anyhow probably. I mean, I already tried. And failed flat as I did Algebra II when I was going out with Kyle every night, which was a shame, I mean the algebra 'cause it was kind of interesting. But at the time, I'm sorry to say, not as interesting as Kyle, who was already such a big basketball star at Creekside High he was on the news just about every week, leaping and dribbling and dodging and tossing. He could

WHITE TRASH NOIR • 183

have had any girl he wanted in Creekside High and I was such an idiot I was glad he picked me.

Anyhow, I tried to die after I killed Kyle but I didn't. I woke up alive in the ICU and I could just hear Kyle laughing that snuffling way he had about how Charmain Luby never could do a single thing right. But I did try. I bought a shelf's worth of every pill Wal-Mart's had on display, then I went to the Marriott and got most of them down with a bottle of vodka which tasted terrible because I'm not much of a drinker. I propped my letter to Mawmaw against the ice bucket and took out my silver-framed picture of my baby Jarrad (that Mrs. Markell got named Kyle, Jr., on the certificate) and I lay down with the picture on the bed and cried myself to sleep. I felt like I was dying and they said I would of too if it hadn't been for the highway patrol knocking the door down and rushing me to the emergency clinic.

It was my brother's Mercury Cougar got the police there, which I didn't know was a stolen vehicle at the time I parked it out in front of the Marriott on Old 89, not that anything Tanner did would surprise me anymore. They had a whatever-you-call-it out for his car and it was a easy color to spot, Light Sapphire Blue, plus had a Pirates of the Caribbean flag from Disney World hanging on the antenna, plus Florida plates. They weren't even looking for me yet. So they saved my life and went for the death penalty.

I always wanted to stay in that Marriott. Or any Marriott. Even on our honeymoon Kyle took me to a Motel 6 at the beach. "I'm not paying good money for a bed in the dark." He wouldn't eat in nice restaurants either. "I'm not paying good money for something that's going to turn to shit in three hours." Kyle always called it good money and I guess what was good about it was he never spent it on me. He spent it on drugs and what he called Antique Vehicles. He collected old junk motorbikes, cars and trucks, and anything else crappy that used to move and now couldn't anymore. He claimed their "value" was "going through the roof" someday and then he'd fix them and sell them for a fortune on the Internet. But he never did, surprise surprise. All he did was leave them there turning to red rust and weeds I couldn't get at to pull. Between his antique vehicles and his basketball court, he used up all the space in my yard so I couldn't grow a vegetable garden. He squashed my peonies under a 1952 Ford truck and he shot free throws standing on top of my tulip bulbs. Mostly up Kyle's nose is where the good money went. And I got Motel 6.

Where I really always wanted to stay at was the Polynesian Resort at Disney World. But considering what's happened, it don't take the Psychic Hotline to tell me Disney World's not in my future, because even if I don't get Death, I'll get Life.

My brother Tanner went to Disney World. Drove down to Orlando right after he got out on the ABC store thing. I wish he'd taken me with him. At least I would have seen the Magic Kingdom. Or I wish he'd never come back with that Mercury Cougar that stopped me from dying at the Marriott. Or I wish he hadn't come back at all, so I wouldn't have gone over to his trailer and seen his Desert Eagle Mark VII .44-caliber Magnum pistol I shot Kyle with. (Mr. Goodenough has been talking for weeks about that gun, like it was the most important thing in my life, so that's how I know so much about it now, because believe me at the time I borrowed it from Tanner, all I knew was it was black and heavy and if you pulled the trigger a bullet came out.) Most of all I wish I'd never eloped with Kyle.

I picked the Marriott because I figured as far as me and a nice motel goes it was sort of now or never, since I planned on meeting my Maker after those medications took hold—if there's even Anybody up there *to* meet, though I'd hate for Mawmaw to hear me wondering something like that. And you know what's funny—not really funny but freaky—is at first I was thinking, Ha ha, wait'll Kyle gets this Visa bill, he'll turn totally purple, because on top of $129 at the Marriott, I had tore through Wal-Mart, looking like Kyle used to on the basketball court before they found out he was using cocaine. After I loaded up on medications, I bought Mawmaw a Hoover Deluxe because she brings her own equipment to the job, plus $326.59 worth of toys for her to put out under the tree next Christmas for Jarrad. It took me a long time to choose the toys and it was like I forgot I didn't have a long time. That's what was funny. I had completely forgot I'd killed Kyle, shot him in the head and drug him out in the yard and set fire to him right under his basketball hoop with a big pile of brush and a gallon can of kerosene.

Then when I was lying on the king-sized bed in the Marriott swallowing those pills, it hit me how there was no way Kyle was ever going to pitch another fit over the Visa bill or the other million things he blamed me for, like his whole entire life, which I used to be dumb enough to think was my fault. And then it hit me how it was Mawmaw that was gonna get stuck with that huge Visa bill. And how it was Jarrad that was gonna get stuck with his friends saying his mama had murdered his daddy, which is worse than what I had to put up with in school because of my name and that was bad enough, calling me Toilet Paper and "Please don't touch the Charmain." Plus jokes about my parents being trash and roadkill. Trying to write a letter for Jarrad to read when he was old enough was the last thing I remember.

My lawyer said a suicide attempt didn't look good for me in some ways, and did look good in others. The way it did look good was it showed I wasn't in my right mind and was full of remorse and confusion and maybe had acted "on impulse" and wasn't trying to get away with something. The way it didn't look good was I'd left a note for Mawmaw asking her to apologize to Mr. and Mrs. Markell for me and say I hoped they could forgive me for killing their son but not saying anything about how shooting Kyle was a accident, or self-defense, or spur-of-the-moment, or too much to drink, or some other reason why it wouldn't be Murder One. Plus setting fire to Kyle with kerosene—my lawyer said that had the look of a cover-up.

I guess it was a cover-up, just not enough of one. But it's true, I couldn't stand the idea of Mawmaw and Jarrad (when he was old enough) thinking I killed anybody, much less my husband, and I guess that's why I tried to get rid of his body. I figured if Kyle was just gone and everybody thought he'd run off to Hawaii or something, then Mawmaw wouldn't get her life ruined and Jarrad would have, I don't know, a chance, I guess. When I tried to explain my reason to Mawmaw in the hospital, she said my Mama and Daddy hadn't had half a brain between them but she had used to think I did have some brains. But I'd handed them over to Kyle to wipe his feet on. She said there *wasn't* no reason for acting the way I had, and I had to accept I'd acted crazy and move on from there.

But I will swear this on a Bible. I *never* thought Mr. and Mrs. Markell would drop by our house that afternoon (which is something they never did, and Kyle sure never told me he'd asked them to supper) and find Kyle only half burnt up. I fig-

ured that brush pile would burn on through the weekend—
nobody lives near us and besides Kyle liked to keep trash burning out back so you couldn't smell his marijuana. I'd figured by
the time anybody showed up, I'd be gone to Heaven or probably Hell, considering, and Jarrad would be at Mawmaw's safe
and sound, and when Kyle wasn't at Creekside Ford on Tuesday, because he had Monday off, somebody would call the
house, and then one of his coworkers would come over and
think he was gone. I *never* figured Mr. and Mrs. Markell would
be wandering through my kitchen by four o'clock on Sunday,
and they'd see the smoke and walk out to that brush pile. Because that is something parents should never have to see. Their
son burning up in his backyard. And I do apologize for that.

Another thing that didn't look good for me was my brother
Tanner and the fact that I'd borrowed Tanner's gun three
whole days before I used it to shoot Kyle with. My lawyer
called it "our elephant in the kitchen." Before Tilden Snow got
to be my lawyer, I admitted in my statement that I took the gun
out of Tanner's refrigerator and brought it home with me.
"That gun implies premeditation, Charmain, which is why
Goodenough's going for first-degree homicide." He (I mean
Tilden Snow) couldn't stop trying to get me to say something
that wasn't true about that gun. "Charmain, go back to that
time frame. I want you to let me know when I say something
that correlates to your motivation." I swear that's the way he
talks; sometimes even the judge looks at him like he's nuts.

But when Mr. Snow says, "Okay, go back," I say I'm not
going anywhere. He doesn't listen any more than Kyle did.
"Maybe you took the gun because you didn't want your brother
Tanner to get in trouble with it."

I say, "No, I didn't."

"Maybe you took the gun because there'd been crime in the isolated rural area you lived in and you felt afraid to be in the house with Kyle gone."

I say, "All I *wanted* was to be in the house with Kyle gone."

He jumps on this. "So maybe you felt afraid to be in the house *with* Kyle and wanted that gun for self-defense."

I shake my head.

He sighs. "Maybe you weren't even aware you took the gun."

I say, "Now, Mr. Snow—"

"Tilden."

"How could I not know I took it? That thing weighs a ton."

He never did ask me to tell him why I *did* take the gun out of Tanner's refrigerator. But he made that a rule from the very start. The day we met, he said, "Charmain, don't answer any questions I don't ask you. Don't tell me anything I don't tell you I want to know. Do you understand?"

I shrug. "Sure." And that was the end of honest communication. That's what the marriage counselor I got for me and Kyle two years ago said good relationships was based on. Honest communication. But that marriage counselor was a moron, plus started hitting on me every time Kyle went to the toilet (which was pretty often and the reason why good money got sniffed straight up his nose). All I hope is, that moron's marriage-counseling business has already gone bust. It can't be real good for business when one of your patients shoots her husband in the head and sets fire to him. I told Mawmaw back when I quit the marriage counselor, "That man didn't respect me any more than Kyle did."

That's when she said the thing that was haunting me from right then till a year later when I pulled the trigger on Kyle. She took my hands in hers that were like tree bark they were so rough, and none of the paraffin wax dips I give her could do a thing for them. She said, "Charmain, you listen to me. Since I was eleven years old I been cleaning out other people's toilets and the only way I can stand it is, I get the respect of the folks I work for and if I don't, I don't work for them no more. Listen to me, you got to *earn* respect. But when you do earn it, you make sure they give it to you. They can't make you turn any which way they want to. You got to learn that, honey. You're my only hope that thirty-five years on my knees with a scrub brush wasn't just a gob of spit in a week of rain. You got to learn that."

I said, "Mawmaw, I'm trying."

She said, "I know, baby. You're my hope. Because the Savior knows your brother Tanner is nothing but your daddy born again to torment me."

My lawyer felt about the same way about Tanner as Mawmaw. He said Tanner looked bad for us. First of all, he had a record of crime and violence that Mr. Goodenough could use to show a bad family background or bad genes or whatever. Second of all, Tanner had told the police he'd *advised* me to shoot Kyle and had said he'd be glad to shoot Kyle himself if I didn't want to. After he blabbed this total lie at the police station (and Tanner would always say any wild thing he could think of to get attention), for a little while the police got the idea in their heads that Tanner *had* shot Kyle. They kept trying to get me to admit I was just pretending I was the one had killed Kyle, instead of my brother. They accused me of lying to protect him because he had a record and I didn't. The police chief came to the hospital after my suicide attempt, questioning me about that.

I go, "I'm sorry. But I am not a liar. And I wouldn't lie for my brother about something like this."

The police chief, a nice man, with a little smile like life was one big joke, said, "Wouldn't you lie to protect him, Mrs. Markell? Isn't that a Luby family trait? I remember when your brother shot ya'll's cousin Crawder Luby in the chest at point-blank range following an argument over a girl in the parking lot of Lucille's Steak House."

I say, "Tanner was never charged with shooting Crawder."

"That's exactly right. Tanner drove Crawder to Piedmont Hospital and tossed him out in front of the emergency entrance. Now, when we came to interview your cousin Crawder, he claimed he had no idea who'd shot him. That's why we never could charge Tanner with that crime because his cousin that he *shot* stood by him. So, yes, Charmain, I think you Lubys will lie to protect each other."

"Well, I won't," I said.

Pretty soon they had to believe me because it turned out Tanner was off with Crawder the day I shot Kyle. They'd gone deep-sea fishing off of Wrightsville Beach and had run out of gas and had to be rescued by the Coast Guard. That's why Tanner'd given me his Mercury Cougar to keep till he came back. At least I thought it was his. Now I see he was hiding it out.

So then the police believed *I* shot Kyle and wanted to know why. Was it for money? Was there another man in my life? But by then Mawmaw had got Tilden Snow III to represent me and every time I'd open my mouth he'd say, "Don't answer that, Charmain." Mawmaw got him because she knew he and his daddy and grandpa were all lawyers, and they knew her from back when she was the White Tornado in their house. He took my case on what he called pro bono.

According to my cousin Crawder, Tilden Snow III only did it because it was a good way for him to make his name as big as his Daddy's, since newspaper and TV people were crawling all over us at my trial. That was a little bit because they said I don't look like your regular-type killer, plus had been a Teen for Christ, even if some big snoots in town called my family white trash, and Mrs. Markell didn't think I was good enough to marry her son Kyle since he'd been a big basketball star in high school and started out that way in college and scored eleven points at the NCAA tournament Sweet Sixteen game. He could of kept on playing too if he hadn't got caught using cocaine.

But the other thing was two people in Creekside besides me had murdered somebody this same year and it's not that big a place. So we were getting a reputation. A Mexican man used rat poison on his wife, which folks thought was a accident at first because that part of town did have rats you couldn't kill with a pitchfork unless you hit them with a sledgehammer first. But then they found the rat poison in his wife's Maalox. Then Lucas Beebee (who was crazy and everybody in town knew it) used a chain saw on a Jehovah's Witness and put her toes and ears in a flower arrangement on his mother's dining room table. A friend of the victim was there for the Beebee Easter buffet and recognized this woman's earbobs in the ears and called the police. So Kyle's murder was number three in a year and instead of Creekside, North Carolina, which is our real name, they started calling us "Homicide, U.S.A." for a joke.

So Mr. Goodenough the D.A. said he was going to make an example out of me and he sure has tried. He's been elected District Attorney in Creekside for twenty years running and they say it's mostly because of his name. I remember those campaign billboards from when I was little: HE'S GOODENOUGH FOR YOU.

At my trial the D.A. said I had broke every vow I took in church when I promised to love and honor Kyle till death do us part. He said I was a black mark on the holy name of "Wife." Every chance he got he told the jury how Kyle had been a basketball star and played for the ACC because around here that's like saying you taught Jesus how to walk on water. He held up that souvenir basketball Kyle had from the Sweet Sixteen game that I'd shot a hole in and he carried on about it almost like it was worse I'd shot the damn basketball than shot Kyle in the head. That's when I could see Dr. Rothmann on the jury start to fidget in her seat like she wanted to tell the judge to make the D.A. stop talking so much about how this was the very same basketball that Kyle had shot that three-pointer with, with two seconds left in overtime. Dr. Rothmann even rolled her eyes at the ceiling when the D.A. said how I'd cut short a promising young man's great career in pro basketball when even the newspapers knew it was drugs cut short Kyle's career when he had to drop out of college his sophomore year and no pro basketball team had given him the time of day since. He couldn't even have held on to his job at Creekside Ford if his uncle hadn't owned it.

Now, my brother Tanner is so dumb he figured it would look better for me if he told the police he gave me the gun to take home because Kyle hit me all the time and I was scared of him. The truth is, I don't believe Tanner even knew I took his pistol out of his refrigerator that day.

And Kyle didn't hit me. Oh, he said he was going to hit me all the time, but he didn't have the guts. His style was more stuff like kicking my dog JuliaRoberts when I wasn't looking.

Or pouring nail polish on my new winter coat and saying Jarrad did it when Jarrad was so little he couldn't even walk yet. Or making fun of me in front of his stupid buddies at Creekside Ford. Or smacking Jarrad in the face when he was a tiny baby, which is the one time I ever slapped anybody in my life, when I slapped Kyle as hard as I could except it mostly just got his shoulder and he laughed at me.

So I couldn't help Tilden Snow with his plan to use the "battered wife syndrome." The only 911 ever got called from our house was me getting the ambulance for Kyle when he sniffed too much cocaine and knocked over his trophy case and almost bled to death from broken glass. Course if I'd let him die that time maybe me and Jarrad would be in Disney World right this minute, staying at the Polynesian Resort.

I don't mean to make it sound like I wanted a fancy life. And maybe this is what I would of tried to explain to Dr. Rothmann if there'd been a way for her and me to talk. I could of took not having things, easy, no problem, if I'd had somebody that loved me, even liked me. Because you can hit somebody without laying a hand on them, which is what Kyle kept doing to me. That's why I couldn't stop thinking about what Mawmaw said about how I was her only hope and had to earn respect. So I told Kyle he had to respect me more and not make me feel small. But he laughed at me and said, "Yeah, well, maybe I would if you stuck a gun in my face."

So that's really why it all happened. That's why when I was over at Tanner's trailer and I saw that black pistol of his in the refrigerator, all of a sudden I got the idea I'd do just what Kyle said. Next time he was making fun of me, I'd stick a gun in his face.

So that Friday when Tanner carried Jarrad down to the

pond to look at the ducks, I took his gun and hid it in my purse. Then on Saturday Mawmaw watched Jarrad for me and I worked all day at Pretty Woman. That night was bad because Kyle was trying to make me do stuff in bed I didn't want to. Sunday morning he's mad at me. He's sitting on the couch in his underpants and wearing his old college basketball shirt, Number 56, click-clacking with that straight razor blade at his cocaine. I'm trying to get me and Jarrad dressed to go pick up Mawmaw for church and I'm late. Then Kyle tells me to nuke him a cup of coffee and when I can't get the microwave to go off Defrost, he starts laughing about "No-Brain Charmain." Then pretty soon he starts bouncing his souvenir Sweet Sixteen basketball off the living room wall like he was in a gym and not our living room.

Then he starts in on me about the Visa bill and what was I buying shoes for "that kid" for anyhow when he was so dumb he couldn't even walk yet so he must take after me? I'm looking at Kyle bouncing that basketball while I'm standing there crying, and Jarrad's crying too because I'm crying. I'm thinking, How dumb was I marrying this man when I was just sixteen when Mawmaw begged me to at least finish high school? How dumb was I not knowing maybe he was a freshman in college and a big basketball player, but he was still, excuse me, a total asshole?

So I'm standing in the living room, holding Jarrad. Kyle's yelling about the Visa bill, and my whole body fills up with the idea that year after year after year for the rest of our lives Kyle'll do the same kind of meanness to me and he'll do it to Jarrad too if I don't make him respect me starting now. And that's the first time I think about Tanner's gun since I took it. So I walk down the hall to our bedroom and I put Jarrad in his crib. Now he's crying at the top of his lungs, and I can hear Kyle yelling from the living room, "Shut him the fuck up!" I go get the pistol out of the bottom drawer of my bureau where I hid it and I walk back in the living room and I stick it in Kyle's face and I say, "*You* shut the fuck up."

He's surprised and his mouth falls open. But he's not scared. And then he laughs. "Hey, where'd you get that thing?" he says, pointing at the gun. "You planning to shoot some-body?" I don't say a word, I just keep looking at him. He says, "Well, No-Brain, if you're planning to shoot a pistol you got to take the safety off." He laughs some more and then he snatches the gun right out of my hand. He waves it in my face and says, sarcastic, "Here you go." He snaps this little lever on the side of the handle. "That's the safety." Then he hands the pistol back to me. "Knock yourself out."

Off in our room, Jarrad's bottle falls out of his crib and he cries harder.

All of a sudden Kyle starts throwing the basketball against the wall close to me. He breaks a lamp. Down the hall Jarrad screams like the world's gone crazy and Kyle turns purple. "I told you, shut that stupid kid up!"

I say, "You're scaring him."

Kyle screams, "I'll scare him okay!" And then he throws the basketball hard right at me and hits me in the head with it. Then he grabs the ball back and spins around to run down the hall. And that's when I pull the trigger. The pistol goes off. The noise was so loud it hurt. Most of the back of Kyle's head flies away. But he spins around and it goes off again and then it flings out of my hand. His knees bend, and it's weird, it's just like he's at the free-throw line and is going for a basket. But then he drops the ball, which is all crumpled because I shot it, and his knees give way like the floor fell out from under him. He jerks over sideways and lands hard. The whole room shakes. Down the hall Jarrad keeps screaming. All I can think about is, at least Jarrad didn't see it but the noise must have scared him. I run and go pick up my baby and I hide his eyes against me so he can't see Kyle lying there and we run out of the house. I drive Jarrad to Mawmaw's and tell her I can't go to church. I say I had a fight with Kyle and I can't talk about it now. Then I go back home and Kyle's still lying there with blood oozed out all around his head and his stomach. I have to run to the bathroom 'cause I'm sick to my stomach. I don't know what to do. I just keep wishing I could make it go away. After a while I get an old blanket and wrap him in it. He's cold but I try not to touch him. I think I fainted. I don't remember the rest but I must of drug him out to the backyard and poured the kerosene on him and lit it.

That's the truth. If I could take the stand and tell Dr. Nina Rothmann the truth, the whole truth and nothing but, that's what I'd tell her.

But Mr. Goodenough made out how I'd plotted and planned to kill Kyle for his insurance policy and how I sneaked up on him and shot him in the back of the head from behind. Like I would *plan* for Jarrad to hear that gun go off so loud! The D.A. claimed how I tore up my own house to make it look like burglars so people would think I wasn't anywhere around and it was the burglars that set fire to my husband. But how I was so dumb I used my own brother's gun and left my fingerprints on it and on the kerosene can too and left them both right at the scene. The D.A. said I never meant to really commit suicide in the Marriott. It was a "ploy."

Mr. Goodenough spent a lot of time telling the jury,

"Imagine the horror and anguish" of Mr. and Mrs. Markell when they saw their only son smoldering on a brush pile. Then he'd hold up the crime scene photos (that my lawyer tried to get excluded but he lost) and wave them right at the jury and shout, "Ladies and gentlemen of the jury, just imagine!"

Both the Markells testified against me. They were the State's last witnesses. Mr. Markell slumped and looked beaten down. Mrs. Markell could scarcely sit still on the stand she hated me so much. Course that was true even before all this. I didn't like her either. She had spoiled Kyle so bad he told me himself how when he was little he would kick and slap her and she wouldn't do a thing about it if they were in public except give him what he wanted. On the stand Mrs. Markell said it didn't surprise her at all that I'd killed her son and she wouldn't rest easy till I had paid the price. They had to haul her off the chair she was shouting at me so loud even after she was excused. Her face looked just like Kyle's when he was yelling.

I'll tell you how I could rest easy even strapped down in the death chamber. That's if I knew Priscilla Markell had lost her case trying to get my baby Jarrad away from Mawmaw. I can't stand the thought of her screaming at Jarrad until he turns into a screamer too. And Tilden Snow has promised me he won't let that happen even if I do get the maximum. Which he's worried I'm going to get if all he's got on the defense side is character witnesses and the emergency doctor saying I really did try to kill myself judging from my stomach.

But some things you can't do. And letting Mr. Goodenough ask me sarcastic personal questions and twist my answers around into lies and make fun of me and say I don't deserve to be Jarrad's mama is one of them.

So that's all the far we'd got to in my trial by this morning.

And that's when all of a sudden Dr. Rothmann calls over the bailiff and hands him a note and then the judge studies it for a minute at the bench and then the judge says we're taking a recess and he calls Counselor Goodenough and Counselor Snow to "come in my chambers," and they all leave us sitting here, waiting and waiting.

About an hour later, Tilden Snow comes back looking surprised but sort of smug. He motions for Mawmaw to lean forward and he whispers to us all this stuff about how Mr. Goodenough was backing down and dropping Murder One because otherwise he's going to get a hung jury and how if they could work it out would I agree to say I'd shot Kyle but I didn't plan to. Would I say I did it without premeditating and when I'd gone to pieces for a minute. I look at Mawmaw and she pats my hand. I tell him yes I will say that because it's the truth. Tilden Snow says I ought to thank my stars he got Dr. Rothmann put on my jury! I swear I think he even believed it was his plan all along, after he'd told me I was wrong for trusting her. He runs back off to the judge's chambers, all puffed up like a little rooster in a tan suit.

So we wait some more. After a while Mawmaw leans over again from the row behind me and every now and then I can feel her hand patting me on the back. Right through my blouse I can feel the stiffness of her fingers and the calluses and rough spots on her hand like each one had a memory in it like a electric spark. I can see her mopping the kitchen floor of this house, and me helping her make the beds in that house, and us walking in the rain to the bus stop from this other house, dropping off the trash bags on the way. I can see her fingers working to tie the bow on my dress the day she took me to Tilden Snow's grandma's big house that they called Heaven's Hill.

That was the day the little boy ran out the front door and hollered, "That's my swing. Get off of it." It was only after his grandmama came out with Mawmaw and told him to be nice to me because I belonged to the cleaning lady that he said, "I'm Tilden Snow. You want to marry me?"

I said to him, "No, I don't." And I looked over at Mawmaw 'cause I was worried she'd be mad but she was smiling like I had said the right thing.

So I'm feeling all these memories in Mawmaw's hand while she rubs my back. Then the jury comes back with the judge and all, and Dr. Rothmann stops in front of me for a second and looks right in my eyes. And I nod at her and behind me Mawmaw stands up and gives her a little bow.

After a lot of talking, the judge tells me to stand up and I do and say I'm guilty and I get fifteen years. The first thing I think is, I'll get out in time for Jarrad's high school graduation. Then they come over to take me out. I turn around and I grab both of Mawmaw's hands and I kiss them. I say, "I'm sorry, Mawmaw, I'm sorry, I'm sorry."

She says, "You hang on, baby."

So I do.

GALAHAD, INC.

Joan H. Parker
and
Robert B. Parker

The lettering on the door said GALAHAD, INC. When Jamal Jones opened the door and went in, there were two white people. The woman was blond with big blue eyes and a wide mouth. Jamal stared at her for a moment. Bitchin' body. The man was tall and had a mustache. They both smiled at him. Having entered, Jamal didn't know what to do next.

"I'm Nick West," the man said. "This is my wife, Holly."

"Jamal Jones."

"Come in," Holly said. "Have a seat."

Jamal sat. They looked like money to him. White money. Good clothes. Nice perfume. View of the harbor. He felt uneasy. It made him aggressive.

"You ever hear of me?" he said. "I play basketball at Taft."

"You been suspended," Nick said.

Jamal had cornrows and baggy clothes and tattoos on his neck.

"Tha's a bad rap, man," Jamal said.

"Which is why you're here," Holly said.

"I read that article about you in the paper," Jamal said.

Nick grinned at him.

"The Couple of Last Resort," Nick said.

"Huh?"

"That was what the paper called us," Holly said.

"Yeah," he said, "well, I got suspended for groping some broad at a party and I don't even know the bitch . . . excuse me, ma'am."

Holly smiled. "What's the bitch's name?" she said.

"Tricia Clark," Nick said.

They both looked at him.

"She says at a party you came up behind her and put your hand down the front of her jeans."

"I never even seen her," Jamal said.

"How do you know all this?" Holly said to Nick.

"I read the sports pages," he said.

"Sports pages are boring," Holly said.

"Only to the unenlightened," Nick said. "Anybody believe your story?"

Jamal shook his head.

"White girl," he said.

Nick nodded.

"And a black boy with cornrows and tattoos," Nick said.

"It's my look, man. It's Jamal Jones, and I gonna be Jamal Jones and fuck anybody don't like it."

"Temperate and well spoken as well," Nick said.

"You raggin' me, man?" Jamal said.

Nick nodded. "A little," he said.

"Nick rags everyone a little," Holly said. "But there's a point there."

"I didn't come here to take no shit," Jamal said.

Lotta times you could give a white guy the angry-brother look and he get scared. Nick didn't seem to.

"Thing is you look like Whitey Suburban's worst nightmare," Nick said. "You're black. You look black. You sound black. Of course you'd feel up a white coed at a party."

"Fuck you, man," Jamal said.

"So what's your side of it?" Nick said.

"Huh?"

"What's your side of the story?" Holly said.

"I got no side, except I didn't do it. Nobody believes it. Soon as the A.D. heard the story he had Coach suspend me. They takin' 'way my scholarship. I don't get money I can't go to school. I don't go to school I got no shot in the pros."

"Kids your age are playing in the pros," Nick said.

"Sure, like LeBron. Well, I ain't no LeBron. I'm pretty good, but I'm not ready yet and I know it. Couple years, Division I, make a name for myself, I be ready."

Everyone was quiet. Nick and Holly looked at each other.

"Okay," Nick said. "You didn't do it, we'll prove it."

"You gonna represent me?"

"Yep."

"I ain't got no money."

"Pay us when you make the pros," Nick said. "Besides, Holly's rich."

"We have money," Holly said. "We do this because we like to."

"You know what you doing?" Jamal said.

"Nick was a police detective for twenty years," Holly said. "I was a prosecutor."

"You a lawyer?" Jamal said.

"Uh-huh."

She looked so hot Jamal couldn't imagine her *being* something.

"So how you get rich?" he said.

"My daddy," Holly said.

"Your daddy give it to you?"

"In a trust fund."

Jamal wasn't entirely sure what a trust fund was. It was a white thing.

"How you gonna help me?" Jamal said.

"We'll go over it," Nick said.

"Tha's it?" Jamal said. "You gonna go over it? You got a ghetto black man accused of feelin' up Miss White Sorority Prom Queen. And you gonna go over it."

"You were at the party?" Nick said.

"Yeah."

"Anyone see you do it?"

"Course they didn't see me do it," Jamal said. "I didn't do it."

"And it's pretty hard to find somebody who saw you not it," Nick said.

Jamal gave Nick another hard look. Was Nick putting him down?

"Jamal," Holly said. "Getting tough with Nicky doesn't work. It has no effect on him. It's like he doesn't notice."

Jamal looked at her. She smiled. He almost smiled back before he caught himself. She was money for sure. Everything she wore was probably silk.

"Hell," Holly said. "Even I don't scare him."

Jamal nodded. She was something.

"So it's your word against hers," Nick said.

Jamal nodded.

"And you don't know why she would lie about this?"

"No, man. I don't even know the bitch."

"Okay," Nick said. "We'll talk with her. Here's what I need from you. You go home. You stay there. You don't get drunk or do dope or get laid or have a fight or do anything but homework and sleep."

"I be keepin' the low profile," Jamal said.

"The best kind," Nick said.

★ ★ ★

The sun flooded into the atrium breakfast room. It intensified everything. The orange juice in the emerald glasses. The yellow plates and cups. The persimmon chairs and the green glass table. Nick's shirt was whiter than possible. Holly's hair was bright gold. She was sipping orange juice and looking at a notepad. She put down her glass.

"Okay," Holly said, "here's what I found out in a mere three days."

"I was hoping someone would find out something," Nick said.

"I can find out anything," Holly said.

"I'll keep it in mind."

"Jamal is a communications major," Holly said. "Two point seven grade point average."

"That's like what, B minus?" Nick said.

"Uh-huh. No trouble in school. No police record. Same for high school."

"He Muslim?" Nick said.

"Apparently."

Nick nodded. He helped himself to some shirred eggs from the sunflower-yellow serving dish.

"What's on these eggs?" he said.

"A reduction of sherry finished with butter," Holly said.

"My mother used to give us Pop-Tarts," Nick said.

"We've never doubted that you married up," Holly said.

"I'll say. Three days and already you know his grade point average."

"What do you know?" Holly said.

"Jamal's the oldest of seven kids. Father's whereabouts unknown. Mother is a court officer. Jamal's a point guard. His coach says he doesn't see the floor well enough yet, and he needs to work on his outside shot. But he's six feet four and strong and quick and works his tail off. The coach thinks he has a legitimate shot at the pros if he stays in school."

"Does his coach think he did this?" Holly said.

"Coach is staying low," Nick said. "I think it wasn't his idea to suspend the kid, but Coach is a team player."

"How about the other players?" Holly said.

"They claim he doesn't drink."

"He has a Muslim name," Holly said.

Nick shrugged. "Lot of sexual groping is alcohol-driven," he said.

"I've noticed," Holly said.

"Mine is hormonal," Nick said.

"Uh-huh. What else from the teammates?"

"He's a good guy, a good teammate, a winner, blah, blah. It's pretty much see no evil, say no evil. They've obviously been told to shut up."

"And they obey?"

"They have a lot at stake," Nick said, "and they've had team player drilled into them since grade school. What about Tricia Clark?"

"Sophomore at North Atlantic University. Honor roll last year. Member of Omega Omega Nu sorority. No record of trouble. Parents divorced, father has money."

Nick broke the end of a croissant and ate it. "Nothing wrong with a rich father," he said.

"You should know," Holly said.

"We've never doubted that I married up," Nick said.

"You married me for my money?" Holly said.

"Your ass, actually," Nick said. "You talk with Tricia?"

Holly shook her head. "I tried but we couldn't seem to get a time."

"Talk to anyone?" Nick said.

"I talked to the president of Omega Omega Nu."

"Every time you called?"

"Yep."

"Odd," Nick said.

"What do you know about sororities?" Holly said.

"As little as possible," Nick said.

"The prez says Tricia's in seclusion. Have you talked to the campus police?"

"They seem to be in seclusion too," Nick said.

Holly put some lime marmalade on the end of her croissant and took a bite. "So we don't have a transcript of her interview with campus police?"

"No. All I know is what I read in the papers."

Holly nodded. There was a glisten of lime marmalade on the corner of her mouth. She wiped it carefully away with her pale yellow napkin. Behind her in the atrium window the cityscape stretched to the water.

"I read the clippings," she said.

"You remember what she was wearing when molested?" Nick said.

"She was at the party alone," Holly said. "He came up behind her, put his left hand on her breast and slid his right hand down inside her jeans in the front and touched her, ah, flower."

"Flower?"

"It's what she called it," Holly said.

"Flower," Nick said.

Holly nodded.

"Do you have jeans you would wear to a frat party?" Nick said.

"I have clothes to wear to anything," Holly said. "You know that."

"What kind of jeans would they be?" Nick said.

"The ones that I wore wet for several days so that they shrunk to my body so tight that I'd have to lie down to get them on."

"Tricia look like she could wear something like that?"

"Pictures of her say she's slim and pretty," Holly said.

"You got jeans like that?"

"Of course."

"Go put them on."

"Now?"

"Uh-huh."

"Are we going to a frat party?"

"Just put them on," he said.

Holly left the breakfast room. Jake poured himself a fresh cup of coffee from the silver carafe. He added cream from the matching silver pitcher and sugar from the matching silver bowl. It made him smile.

Long way from the brickyard, Nicky.

Holly came back in wearing low-slung slate-colored jeans and a cropped T-shirt, the color of amethyst, that exposed her navel. Nick nodded in approval.

"As long as I'm not required to breathe," Holly said.

Nick stood and walked around behind her.

"Don't get jumpy now," he said. "We're going to reenact the crime."

"Reenact? Are you sure you're not just trying to cop a feel?"

"Pretty sure," Nick said.

He stood behind Holly and put his left hand lightly on her left breast, then put his right hand around her and tried to slip it down the front of her jeans. They were too tight. Nick couldn't get his hand down the front of Holly's jeans.

"No flower," Holly said.

"Of course maybe Tricia's jeans were looser fitting," Nick said.

"And maybe it don't rain in Indianapolis in the summertime."

"They'd be tight," Nick said.

"Like a glove," Holly said.

"So if it don't fit," Nick said, "you must acquit."

They were still for a moment.

"You figured that out?" Holly said.

"I've often been thwarted by jeans," Nick said. "It was a thought."

"Are you still thinking?"

"Well, yes."

"About Jamal Jones and Tricia Clark?" Holly said.

"Well, no."

"But since we're here in this compromising position, anyway . . ."

"Exactly," Nick said. "When's the last time we had spontaneous sex in the middle of the morning?"

"Yesterday," Holly said. "On the living room rug."

"Oh," Nick said. "Yeah."

"This time," Holly said, "could we at least use the bedroom?"

★　★　★

Nick pulled the car in beside some shrubs outside the Omega Omega Nu house in the east quadrangle at North Atlantic University. He looked at Holly in the front seat beside him. She wore a tailored blue suit with an open-necked white shirt and a red silk scarf around her neck. She had on too much makeup.

"Perfect," he said.

"I look like the traveling secretary of Omega Omega Nu?" she said.

"Exactly."

"Have you ever seen a person from the national headquarters of a sorority?"

"No."

"Are you sure it's in Tulsa?"

"I looked it up," Nick said. "You look just right."

"If I had on any more makeup," Holly said, "I'd have a stiff neck."

"Remember, your name is Elinor Gilmore," Nick said. "I looked her up too."

"What if they ask me for a secret handshake or something?"

"Dismiss it haughtily," Nick said.

Holly gave him an air kiss, took her big handbag and got out of the car.

They met downstairs in the sorority chapter room: Holly; Tricia; the president of Omega Omega Nu, whose name was Wilma Trent; and an Omega Omega Nu alumna named Evelyn Akers, who was an attorney and served as chapter adviser. There was tea and scones.

"How may we help you, Ms. Gilmore?" President Trent said.

She was slim and pale with a lot of blond hair, and she spoke with dignity and reserve, a kid pretending to be a grown-up.

"We at national," Holly said, "are very concerned about what happened to Tricia. If a sorority means anything, it means sisterhood."

Would she get away with that line?

"And a sisterhood cares equally for every sister."

Everyone nodded.

"Is there," Holly said, "anything we can do to help you?"

Everyone looked at Tricia. She looked startled.

"I don't know. He groped me."

"At a party."

"Yes."

"Were you wearing anything provocative?"

"Ms. Gilmore!" the lawyer said.

Holly shook her head and gestured the lawyer to be quiet.

"National needs the answer," Holly said. "Just for the record."

"No," Tricia said. "I wasn't. I had on jeans and a good T-shirt like everyone else."

Holly smiled. "I remember," she said. "I always wore jeans to parties. They were so tight I could barely sit."

Tricia found herself on more familiar ground. "I know," she said.

"Is that what you were wearing?"

"Yes. I stood up the whole time."

They all laughed, except the lawyer, who glanced at Tricia and frowned.

"Trying to breathe," Holly said, chuckling.

"I know," Tricia said. "What we do to look good."

"So how'd he get his hand down the front?" Holly said.

"Excuse me?"

"How could he get his hand down the front of your jeans when they were that tight?"

"I don't know," Tricia said. "He just did."

"Must have been a struggle," Holly said.

"It was."

"And no one noticed?"

"No. Everyone was drunk. People were making out."

Evelyn Akers suddenly leaned forward and put her hand on Tricia's arm. "That's enough talking," she said.

"He did it, she can't say he didn't."

"Stop talking, Tricia," the lawyer said.

"We could re-create the scene," Holly said.

"No. I'm not talking to you anymore. What kind of traveling secretary are you?"

"What are you implying?" the president said.

"Sisterhood requires trust," Holly said. "Trust requires truth."

Will I get away with that one?

"He did it," Tricia said. "He really did. He pushed his hand down the front of my jeans. He did it." She began to cry.

"Ms. Gilmore," Evelyn Akers said, "this is very strange. Could you leave us alone for a moment?"

"Of course," Holly said. "I assume my purse is safe here?"

"No one will steal it," the lawyer said.

Holly left the room and stood in the small hall outside it.

Is there anything in the world as silly as sororities?

Holly looked at her watch. Two minutes.

Yes, fraternities.

She leaned against the wall and made a mental list of silly things.

After fifteen minutes Evelyn Akers came to the door and

gestured for Holly to come back. Tricia was still sniffling when Holly sat back down.

"We are all Omega Omega Nus," the lawyer said.

Holly's purse was where she'd left it. It hadn't been stolen.

Holly nodded.

"Omega Omega Nu is, of course, a secret society," Evelyn Akers said. "And we have all agreed to that."

Holly nodded again.

"So what is said here stays here?"

"Absolutely," Holly said. "I will need to report to the national council. But, of course, it will go no further."

"I have learned some things recently that modify the original events, and we will need to consider an action."

Holly didn't say anything.

The lawyer studied her for a moment, then she looked at Wilma Trent.

"Go ahead, Wilma," the lawyer said.

Wilma looked straight ahead. No eye contact.

"It was a sorority initiation," she said.

"Really?" Holly said.

"Taft is, as you may know, our archrival. The Chowder Kettle tournament is coming up. And it will be between us and Taft."

"Exciting," Holly said.

"When Tricia pledged Omega Omega Nu, her initiation quest was to do something that would increase North Atlantic's chance to win the Chowder Kettle."

"So Tricia decided to get Jamal Jones suspended," Holly said.

"He is their best player."

"Did the sorority suggest it?" Holly said.

"No. Tricia was required to think of the prank."

"And it was a prank, Tricia?"

Tricia nodded her head.

"Did Jamal put his hands on you?" Holly said.

Tricia shook her head.

"I want to hear you say it," Holly said. "The truth. Sisterhood."

"Jamal never touched me," Tricia said.

"And the sorority knew this?" I said.

"We never knew," Wilma said.

"Was she credited with fulfilling the quest?"

There was silence.

"Truth," Holly said. "The sisterhood is strong only if it is truthful."

"We accepted it," Wilma said.

Wilma's pale cheeks had two red splotches. Her bony hands were clasped tightly in her lap. She was wearing a cashmere sweater and tweed shorts.

For God's sake, she even wore pearls.

"So you were willing to flush Jamal Jones's life," Holly said. "To pledge Omega Omega Nu?"

"I don't condone this," Evelyn Akers said. "Mistakes were made. But these are still kids, and the mistakes were kids' mistakes. I'm hoping we can find a way to work this out so that it doesn't impact negatively on Tricia or Omega Omega Nu."

"It just got out of hand, Ms. Gilmore," Wilma said.

"Nowhere near as far as it's going to," Holly said.

"Excuse me?" Evelyn Akers said.

Holly picked up her purse and took a small electronic device from it and set it on the table.

"That's a transmitter," Holly said. "My husband is outside in the car with a receiver recording everything we say."

The three Omega Omega Nu women stared at her. Holly smiled at them. Then silence.

"You can't do that," Evelyn Akers said. "You have no right to record us without our permission. We had a reasonable expectation of privacy. You'll never be able to use that in court."

Holly nodded.

"Court, shmourt," Holly said. "We can use it in the press and at Taft. And maybe in the dean's office here at good old North Atlantic U."

Tricia started to cry again. The red blotches spread on Wilma's pallid cheeks. Evelyn Akers opened her mouth and closed it and opened it again.

"Who the hell are you?" she said.

"My name is Holly West. I'm a detective. And I represent Jamal Jones."

"You're not from the national," Wilma said.

"No."

"You are here under false pretenses," Evelyn Akers said.

"Very," Holly said.

"What kind of deal can we make?" Evelyn Akers said.

"No deal required," Holly said. "I have what I need."

She put the receiver back in her purse. And stood. And walked out of the room.

★   ★   ★

The rain against the big picture window was persistent. They sat in the quiet bar looking through the rain at the water, gray and uneasy and dappled by the rain. Nick had on a dark suit and Holly wore a small black dress. His shirt gleamed whitely in the dim bar. She was wearing her hair down today and it moved softly when she nodded.

"A goddamned sorority prank," Nick said.

"Did you talk to Jamal after he was reinstated?"

"Yeah."

"Was he grateful?" Holly said.

"No."

"Maybe he was," Holly said, "and didn't know how to say it."

"Maybe."

The cocktail waitress brought martinis. Straight up with olives for Holly, on the rocks with a twist for Nick. They clicked glasses.

"Galahad," Holly said.

Nick smiled.

"There's still a lot of trouble," Holly said.

"There should be," Nick said. "But our guy's okay."

"Yes, we fixed his part of it."

"That's what we agreed to do," Nick said.

"Be nice if we could fix everything," Holly said.

"Which we can't."

"No."

They sipped the clear drinks from the bright glasses. The rain traced down the glass beside them.

"It's what ground me down as a prosecutor," Holly said.

"The amount of stuff you can't fix?"

"Yes," Holly said. "How do you deal with it?"

"I think about you," Nick said.

Holly looked hard at him. There was none of the usual mockery. He meant it.

"That's sweet," Holly said.

Nick grinned and raised his glass.

"Martinis are good too," he said.

She smiled and put her hand out on the table. He put his on top of hers. And they sat and drank their martinis and watched the rain wash down the window.

STRING MUSIC

George Pelecanos

WASHINGTON, D.C., 2001

TONIO HARRIS

Down around my way, when I'm not in school or lookin'
out for my moms and little sister, I like to run ball. Pickup
games mostly. That's not the only kind of basketball I do.
I been playin' organized all my life, the Jelleff League and
Urban Coalition, too. Matter of fact, I'm playin' for my school
team right now, in the Interhigh. It's no boast to say that I can
hold my own in most any kind of game. But pickup is where I
really get amped.

In organized ball, they expect you to pass a whole bunch,
take the percentage shot. Not too much showboatin', nothin'
like that. In pickup, we ref our own games, and most of the
hackin' and pushin' and stuff, except for the flagrant, it gets allowed. I can deal with that. But in pickup, see, you can pretty
much freestyle, try everything out you been practicing on your
own. Like those Kobe and Vince Carter moves. What I'm
sayin' is, out here on the asphalt you can really show your shit.

Where I come from, you've got to understand, most of the time it's rough. I don't have to describe it if you know the area of D.C. I'm talkin' about: the 4th District, down around Park View, in Northwest. I got problems at home, I got problems at school, I got problems walkin' down the street. I prob'ly got problems with my future, you want the plain truth. When I'm runnin' ball, though, I don't think on those problems at all. It's like all the chains are off, you understand what I'm sayin'? Maybe you grew up somewheres else, and if you did, it'd be hard for you to see. But I'm just tryin' to describe it, is all.

Here's an example: Earlier today I got into this beef with this boy James Wallace. We was runnin' ball over on the playground where I go to school, Roosevelt High, on 13th Street, just a little bit north of my neighborhood. There's never any chains left on those outdoor buckets, but the rims up at Roosevelt are straight and the backboards are forgiving. That's like my home court. Those buckets they got, I been playin' them since I was a kid, and I can shoot the eyes out of those motherfuckers most any day of the week.

We had a four-on-four thing goin' on, a pretty good one, too. It was the second game we had played. Wallace and his boys, after we beat 'em the first game, they went over to Wallace's car, a black Maxima with a spoiler and pretty rims, and fired up a blunt. They were gettin' their heads up and listenin' to the new Nas comin' out the speakers from the open doors of the car. I don't like Nas's new shit much as I did *Illmatic,* but it sounded pretty good.

Wallace and them, they work for a dealer in my neighborhood, so they always got good herb, too. I got no problem with that. I might even have hit some of that hydro with 'em if they'd asked. But they didn't ask.

Anyway, they came back pink-eyed, lookin' all cooked and shit, debatin' over which was better, Phillies or White Owls. We started the second game. Me and mines went up by three or four buckets pretty quick. Right about then I knew we was gonna win this one like we won the first, 'cause I had just caught a little fire.

Wallace decided to cover me. He had switched off with this other dude, Antuane, but Antuane couldn't run with me, not one bit. So Wallace switched, and right away he was all chest out, talkin' shit about how "now we gonna see" and all that. Whateva. I was on my inside game that day and I knew it. I mean, I was crossin' motherfuckers *out,* just driving the paint at will. And Wallace, he was slow on me by, like, half a step. I had stopped passin' to the other fellas at that point, 'cause it was just too easy to take it in on him. I mean, he was givin' it to me, so why not?

'Bout the third time I drove the lane and kissed one in, Wallace bumped me while I was walkin' back up to the foul line to take the check. Then he said somethin' about my sneaks, somethin' that made his boys laugh. He was crackin' on me, is all, tryin' to shake me up. I got a nice pair of Jordans, the Air Max, and I keep 'em clean with Fantastik and shit, but they're from, like, last year. And James Wallace is always wearin' whatever's new, whatever it is they got sittin' up front at the Foot Locker, just came in. Plus Wallace didn't like me all that much. He had money from his druggin', I mean to tell you that boy had *every*-thing, but he dropped out of school back in the tenth grade, and I had stayed put. My moms always says that some guys like Wallace resent guys like me who have hung in. Add that to the fact that he never did have my game. I think he was a little jealous of me, you want the truth.

I do know he was frustrated that day. I knew it, and I guess I shouldn't have done what I did. I should've passed off to one of my boys, but you know how it is. When you're proud about somethin', you got to show it, 'specially down here. And I was on. I took the check from him and drove to the bucket, just blew right past him as easy as I'd been doin' all afternoon. That's when Wallace called me a bitch right in front of everybody there.

There's a way to deal with this kinda shit. You learn it over time. I go six-two and I got some shoulders on me, so it wasn't like I feared Wallace physically or nothin' like that. I can go with my hands, too. But in this world we got out here, you don't want to be getting in any kinda beefs, not if you can help it. At the same time, you can't show no fear; you get a rep for weakness like that, it's like bein' a bird with a busted wing, sumshit like that. The other thing you can't do, though, you can't let that kind of comment pass. Someone tries to take you for bad like that, you got to respond. It's complicated, I know, but there it is.

"I ain't heard what you said," I said, all ice-cool and shit, seein' if he would go ahead and repeat it, lookin' to measure just how far he wanted to push it. Also, I was tryin' to buy a little time.

"Said you's a bitch," said Wallace, lickin' his lips and smilin' like he was a bitch his *own* self. He'd made a couple steps towards me and now he wasn't all that far away from my face.

I smiled back, halfway friendly. "You know I ain't no faggot," I said. "Shit, James, it hurts me to fart."

A couple of the fellas started laughin' then and pretty soon all of 'em was laughin'. I'd heard that line on one of my uncle's old-time comedy albums once, that old Signifyin' Monkey shit or maybe Pryor. But I guess these fellas hadn't heard it, and they laughed like a motherfucker when I said it. Wallace laughed, too. Maybe it was the hydro they'd smoked. Whatever it was, I had broken that shit down, turned it right back on him, you see what I'm sayin'? While they was still laughin', I said, "C'mon, check it up top, James, let's play."

I didn't play so proud after that. I passed off and only took a coupla shots myself the rest of the game. I think I even missed one on purpose towards the end. I ain't stupid. We still won, but not by much; I saw to it that it wasn't so one-sided, like it had been before.

When it was over, Wallace wanted to play another game, but the sun was dropping and I said I had to get on home. I needed to pick up my sister at aftercare, and my moms likes both of us to be inside our apartment when she gets home from work. Course, I didn't tell any of the fellas that. It wasn't somethin' they needed to know.

Wallace was goin' back my way, I knew, but he didn't offer to give me a ride. He just looked at me dead-eyed and smiled a little before him and his boys walked back to the Maxima parked along the curb. My stomach flipped some, I got to admit, seein' that flatline thing in his peeps. I knew from that empty look that it wasn't over between us, but what could I do?

I picked up my ball and headed over to Georgia Avenue. Walked south towards my mother's place as the first shadows of night were crawling onto the streets.

SERGEANT PETERS

It's five a.m. I'm sitting in my cruiser up near the station house, sipping a coffee. My first one of the night. Rolling my head around on these tired shoulders of mine. You get these aches when you're behind the wheel of a car six hours at a stretch. I oughta buy one of those things the African cabbies all sit on, looks like a rack of wooden balls. You know, for your back. I been doin' this for twenty-two years now, so I guess whatever damage I've done to my spine and all, it's too late.

I work midnights in the 4th District. 4D starts at the Maryland line and runs south to Harvard Street and Georgia. The western border is Rock Creek Park and the eastern line is North Capitol Street. It's what the newspeople call a high-crime district. For a year or two I tried working 3D, keeping the streets safe for rich white people basically, but I got bored. I guess I'm one of those adrenaline junkies they're always talking about on those cop shows on TV, the shows got female cops who look more beautiful than any female cop I've ever seen. I guess that's what it is. It's not like I've ever examined myself or anything like that. My wife and I don't talk about it, that's for damn sure. A ton of cop marriages don't make it; I suppose mine has survived 'cause I never bring any of this shit home with me. Not that she knows about, anyway.

My shift runs from the stroke of twelve till dawn, though I usually get into the station early so I can nab the cruiser I like. I prefer the Crown Victoria. It's roomier, and once you flood the gas into the cylinders, it really moves. Also, I like to ride alone.

Last night, Friday, wasn't much different than any other. It's summer; more people are outside, trying to stay out of their unair-conditioned places as long as possible, so this time of year we put extra cars out on the streets. Also, like I reminded some of the younger guys at the station last night, this was the week welfare checks got mailed out, something they needed to know. Welfare checks mean more drunks, more domestic disturbances, more violence. One of the young cops I said it to, he said, "Thank you, Sergeant Dad," but he didn't do it in a bad way. I know those young guys appreciate it when I mention shit like that.

Soon as I drove south I saw that the avenue—Georgia Avenue, that is—was hot with activity. All those Jap tech bikes the young kids like to ride, curbed outside the all-night Wing n' Things. People spilling out of bars, hanging outside the Korean beer markets, scratching game cards, talking trash, ignoring the crackheads hitting them up for spare change. Drunks lying in the doorways of the closed-down shops, their heads resting against the riot gates. Kids, a lot of kids, standing on corners, grouped around tricked-out cars, rap music and that go-go crap coming from the open windows. The farther you go south, the worse all of this gets.

The bottom of the barrel is that area between Quebec Street and Irving. The newspapers lump it all in with a section of town called Petworth, but I'm talking about Park View. Poverty, drug activity, crime. They got that Section 8 housing back in there, the Park Morton complex. What we used to call the projects back when you could say it. Government-assisted hellholes. Gangs like the Park Street and Morton Street Crews. Open-air drug markets; I'm talking about blatant transactions right out there on Georgia Avenue. Drugs are Park View's industry; the dealers are the biggest employers in this part of town.

The dealers get the whole neighborhood involved. They recruit kids to be lookouts for 'em. Give these kids beepers and cells to warn them off when the Five-O comes around. Entry-level positions. Some of the parents, when there *are* parents, participate, too. Let these drug dealers duck into their apartments when there's heat. Teach their kids not to talk to the Man. So you got kids being raised in a culture that says the drug dealers are the good guys and the cops are bad. I'm not lying. It's exactly how it is.

The trend now is to sell marijuana. Coke, crack and heroin, you can still get it, but the new thing is to deal pot. Here's why: In the District, possession or distribution of marijuana up to ten pounds—*ten pounds*—is a misdemeanor. Kid gets popped for selling grass, he knows he's gonna do no time. Even on a distribution beef, black juries won't send a black kid into the prison system for a marijuana charge, that's a proven fact. Prosecutors know this, so they usually no-paper the case. That means most of the time they don't even go to court with it. I'm not bullshitting. Makes you wonder why they even bother having drug laws to begin with. They legalize the stuff, they're gonna take the bottom right out the market, and the violent crimes in this city would go down to, like, nothing. Don't get me started. I know it sounds strange, a cop saying this. But you'd be surprised how many of us feel that way.

Okay, I got off the subject. I was talking about my night.

Early on I got a domestic call, over on Otis Place. When I got there, two cruisers were on the scene, four young guys, two of them with flashlights. A rookie named Buzzy talked to a woman at the front door of her row house, then came back and told me that the object of the complaint was behind the place, in the alley. I walked around back alone and into the alley and right off I recognized the man standing inside the fence of his tiny, brown-grass yard. Harry Lang, sixty-some years old. I'd been to this address a few times in the past ten years.

I said, "Hello, Harry," Harry said, "Officer," and I said,

"Wait right here, okay?" Then I went through the open gate. Harry's wife was on her back porch, flanked by her two sons, big strapping guys, all of them standing under a triangle of harsh white light coming from a naked bulb. Mrs. Lang's face and body language told me that the situation had resolved itself. Generally, once we arrive, domestic conflicts tend to calm down on their own.

Mrs. Lang said that Harry had been verbally abusive that night, demanding money from her, even though he'd just got paid. I asked her if Harry had struck her, and her response was negative. But she had a job, too, she worked just as hard as him, why should she support his lifestyle and let him speak to her like that . . . I was listening and not listening, if you know what I mean. I made my sincere face and nodded every few seconds or so.

I asked her if she wanted me to lock Harry up, and of course she said no. I asked what she did want, and she said she didn't want to see him "for the rest of the night." I told her I thought I could arrange that, and started back to have a talk with Harry. I felt the porch light go off behind me as I hit the bottom of the wooden stairs. Dogs had begun to bark in the neighboring yards.

Harry was short and low-slung, a black black man, nearly featureless in the dark. He wore a porkpie hat and his clothes were pressed and clean. He kept his eyes down as I spoke to him over the barks of the dogs. His reaction time was very slow when I asked for a response. I could see right away that he was on a nod.

Harry had been a controlled heroin junkie for the last thirty years. During that time, he'd always held a job, lived in this same house and been there, in one condition or another, for his kids. I'd wager he went to church on Sundays, too. But a junkie was what he was. Heroin was a slow ride down. Some folks could control it to some degree and never hit the bottom.

I asked Harry if he could find a place to sleep that night other than his house, and he told me that he "supposed" he could. I told him I didn't want to see him again any time soon, and he said, "It's mutual." I chuckled at that, giving him some of his pride back, which didn't cost me a thing. He walked down the alley, stopping once to cup his hands around a match as he put fire to a cigarette.

I drove back over to Georgia. A guy flagged me down just to talk. They see my car number and they know it's me. Sergeant Peters, the old white cop. You get a history with these people. Some of these kids, I know their parents. I've busted 'em from time to time. Busted their grandparents, too. Shows you how long I've been doing this.

Down around Morton I saw Tonio Harris, a neighborhood kid, walking alone towards the Black Hole. Tonio was wearing those work boots and the baggy pants low, like all the other kids, although he's not like most of them. I took his mother in for drugs a long time ago, back when that Love Boat stuff was popular and making everyone crazy; his father—the one who impregnated his mother, I mean—he's doing a stretch for manslaughter, his third fall. Tonio's mother's clean now, at least I think she is; anyway, she's done a fairly good job with him. By that I mean he's got no juvenile priors, from what I know. A minor miracle down here, you ask me.

I rolled down my window. "Hey, Tonio, how's it going?" I slowed down to a crawl, took in the sweetish smell of reefer in the air. Tonio was still walking, not looking at me, but he mumbled something about "I'm maintainin'," or some shit like that.

"You take care of yourself in there," I said, meaning in the Hole, "and get yourself home right after." He didn't respond verbally, just made a half-assed kind of acknowledgment with his chin.

I cruised around for the next couple of hours. Turned my spot on kids hanging in the shadows, told them to break it up and move along. Asked a guy in Columbia Heights why his little boy was out on the stoop, dribbling a basketball, at one in the morning. Raised my voice at a boy, a lookout for a dealer, who was sitting on top of a trash can, told him to get his ass on home. Most of the time, this is my night. We're just letting the critters know we're out here.

At around two I called in a few cruisers to handle the closing of the Black Hole. You never know what's going to happen at the end of the night there, what kind of beefs got born inside the club, who looked at who a little too hard for one second too long. Hard to believe that an ex-cop from Prince Georges County runs the place. That a cop would put all this trouble on us, bring it into our district. He's got D.C. cops moonlighting as bouncers in there, too, working the metal detectors at the door. I talked with one, a young white cop, earlier in the night. I noticed the brightness in his eyes and the sweat beaded across his forehead. He was scared, like I gave a shit. Asked us as a favor to show some kind of presence at closing time. Called me Sarge. Okay. I didn't answer him. I got no sympathy for the cops who work those go-go joints, especially not since Officer Brian Gibson was shot dead outside the Ibex Club a few years back. But if something goes down around the place, it's on me. So I do my job.

I called in a few cruisers and set up a couple of traffic barriers on Georgia, one at Lamont and one at Park. We diverted the cars like that, kept the kids from congregating on the street. It worked. Nothing too bad was happening that I could see. I was standing outside my cruiser, talking to another cop, Eric Young, who was having a smoke. That's when I saw Tonio Harris running east on Morton, heading for the housing complex. A late-model black import was behind him, and there were a couple of YBMs with their heads out the open windows, yelling shit out, laughing at the Harris kid, like that.

"You all right here?" I said to Young.

"Fine, Sarge," he said.

My cruiser was idling. I slid under the wheel and pulled down on the tree.

TONIO HARRIS

Just around midnight, when I was fixin' to go out, my moms walked into my room. I was sittin' on the edge of my bed, lacing up my Timbies, listening to PGC comin' from the box, Tigger doin' his shout-outs and then movin' right into the new Jay-Z, which is tight. The music was so loud that I didn't hear my mother walk in, but when I looked up, there she was, one arm crossed over the other like she does when she's tryin' to be hard, staring me down.

"Whassup, Mama?"

"What's up with *you*?"

I shrugged. "Back Yard is playin' tonight. Was thinkin' I'd head over to the Hole."

"Did you ask me if you could?"

"Do I *have* to?" I used that tone she hated, knew right away I'd made a mistake.

"You're living in my house, aren't you?"

"Uh-huh."

"You payin' rent now?"

"No, ma'am."

"Talkin' about *do I have to.*"

"Can I go?"

Mama uncrossed her arms. "Thought you said you'd be studyin' up for that test this weekend."

"I will. Gonna do it tomorrow morning, first thing. Just wanted to go out and hear a little music tonight, is all."

I saw her eyes go soft on me then. "You gonna study for that exam, you hear?"

"I promise I will."

"Go on, then. Come right back after the show."

"Yes, ma'am."

I noticed as she was walkin' out the door her shoulders were getting stooped some. Bad posture and a hard life. She wasn't but thirty-six years old.

I spent a few more minutes listening to the radio and checking myself in the mirror. Pattin' my natural and shit. I got a nice modified cut, not too short, not too blown-out or nothin' like that. A lot of the fellas be wearin' cornrows now, tryin' to look like Iverson. But I don't think it would look right on me. And I know what the girls like. They look at me, they like what they see. I can tell.

Moms has been ridin' me about my college entrance exam. I fucked up the first one I took. I went out and got high on some fierce chronic the night before it, and my head was filled up with cobwebs the next morning when I sat down in the school cafeteria to take that test. I'm gonna take it again, though, and do better next time.

I'm not one of those guys who's got, what do you call that,

illusions about my future. No hoop dreams about the NBA, nothin' like that. I'm not good enough or tall enough, I know it. I'm sixth man on my high school team, that ought to tell you somethin' right there. My uncle Gaylen, he's been real good to me, and straight-up with me, too. Told me to have fun with ball and all that, but not to depend on it. To stick with the books. I know I fucked up that test, but next time I'm gonna do better, you can believe that.

I was thinkin', though, I could get me a partial scholarship playin' for one of those small schools in Virginia or Maryland, William and Mary or maybe Goucher up in Baltimore. Hold up—Goucher's for women only, I think. Maybe I'm wrong. Have to ask my guidance counselor, soon as I can find one. Ha, ha.

The other thing I should do, for real, is find me a part-time job. I'm tired of havin' no money in my pockets. My mother works up at the Dollar Store in the Silver Spring mall, and she told me she could hook me up there. But I don't wanna work with my mother. And I don't want to be workin' at no *Mac*-Donald's or sumshit like that. Have the neighborhood slangers come in and make fun of me and shit, standin' there in my minimum-wage uniform. But I do need some money. I'd like to buy me a nice car soon. I'm not talkin' about some hooptie, neither.

I did have an interview for this restaurant downtown, bussin' tables. White boy who interviewed kept sayin' shit like, "Do you think you can make it into work on time?" and do you think this and do you think that? Might as well gone ahead and called me a nigger right to my face. The more he talked, the more attitude I gave him with my eyes. After all that, he smiled and sat up straight, like he was gonna make some big announcement, and said he was gonna give me a try. I told him I changed my mind and walked right out of there. Uncle Gaylen said I should've taken that job and showed him he was wrong, for all of us. But I couldn't. I can't stand how white people talk to you sometimes. Like they're just there to make their own selves feel better. I hired a Negro today, and like that.

I *am* gonna take that test over, though.

I changed my shirt and went out through the living room. My sister was watchin' the BET videos on TV, her mouth around a straw, sippin' on one of those big sodas. She's startin' to get some titties on her. Some of the slick young niggas in the neighborhood been commentin' on it, too. Late for her to be awake, but it was Friday night. She didn't look up as I passed. I yelled good-bye to my moms and heard her say my name from the kitchen. I knew she was back up in there 'cause I smelled the smoke comin' off her cigarette. There was a ten-dollar bill sittin' in a bowl by the door. I folded it up and slipped it inside my jeans. My mother had left it there for me. I'm tellin' you, she is cool people.

Outside the complex, I stepped across this little road and the dark courtyard real quick. We been livin' here a long time, and I know most everyone by sight. But in this place here, that don't mean shit.

The Black Hole had a line goin' outside the door when I got there. I went through the metal detector and let a white rent-a-cop pat me down while I said hey to a friend going into the hall. I could feel the bass from way out in the lobby.

The hall was crowded and the place was bumpin'. I could smell sweat in the damp air. Also chronic, and it was nice. Back Yard was doin' "Freestyle," off *Hood Related,* that double CD they got. I kind of made my way towards the stage, careful not to bump nobody, nodding to the ones I did. I knew a lot of young brothers there. Some of 'em run in gangs, some not. I try to know a little bit of everybody, you see what I'm sayin'? Spread your friends out in case you run into some trouble. I was smilin' at some of the girls, too.

Up near the front I got into the groove. Someone passed me somethin' that smelled good, and I hit it. Back Yard was turnin' that shit out. I been knowin' their music for like ten years now. They had the whole joint up there that night, I'm talkin' about a horn section and everything else. I must have been up there close to the stage for about, I don't know, an hour, sumshit like that, just dancing. It seemed like all of us was all movin' together. On "Do That Stuff," they went into this extended drum thing, shout-outs for the hoodies and the crews; I was sweatin' clean through my shirt, right about then.

I had to pee like a motherfucker, but I didn't want to use the bathroom in that place. All the hard motherfuckers be congregatin' in there, too. That's where trouble can start, just 'cause you gave someone some wrong kinda look.

When the set broke, I started to talkin' to this girl who'd been dancin' near me, smilin' my way. I'd seen her around. Matter of fact, I ran ball sometimes with her older brother. So we had somethin' to talk about straight off. She had that Brandy thing goin' on with her hair, and a nice smile.

While we was talkin', someone bumped me from behind. I turned around and it was Antuane, that kid who ran with James Wallace. Wallace was with him, and so were a coupla Wallace's boys. I nodded at Antuane, tryin' to communicate to him, like, "Ain't no thing, you bumpin' me like that." But Wallace stepped in and said somethin' to me. I couldn't even really hear it with all the crowd noise, but I could see by his face that he was tryin' to step *to* me. I mean, he was right up in my face.

We stared at each other for a few. I shoulda just walked away, right, but I couldn't let him punk me out like that in front of the girl.

Wallace's hand shot up. Looked like a bird flutterin' out of nowhere or somethin'. Maybe he was just makin' a point with that hand, like some do. But it rattled me, I guess, and I reacted. Didn't even think about it, though I should've. My palms went to his chest and I shoved him back. He stumbled. I saw his eyes flare with anger, but there was that other thing, too, worse than me puttin' my hands on him: I had stripped him of his pride.

There was some yellin' then from his boys. I just turned and bucked. I saw the bouncers started to move, talkin' into their headsets and shit, but I didn't wait. I bucked. I was out on the street pretty quick, runnin' towards my place. I didn't know what else to do.

I heard Wallace and them behind me, comin' out the Hole. They said my name. I didn't look back. I ran to Morton and turned right. Heard car doors opening and slammin' shut. The engine of the car turnin' over. Then the cry of tires on the street and Wallace's boys laughin', yellin' shit out. I kept runnin' towards Park Morton. My heart felt like it was snappin' on a rubber string.

There were some younguns out in the complex. They were sittin' up on top of a low brick wall like they do, and they watched me run by. It's always dark here, ain't never no good kinda light. They got some dim yellow bulbs back in the stairwells, where the old-school types drink gin and shoot craps. They was back up in there, too, hunched down in the shadows.

There was some kind of fog or haze out that night, too, it was kind of rollin' around by that old playground equipment, all rusted and shit, they got in the courtyard. I was runnin' through there, tryin' to get to my place.

I had to cross the little road in the back of the complex to get to my mother's apartment. I stepped into it and that's when I saw the black Maxima swing around the corner. Coupla Wallace's boys jumped out while the car was still movin'. I stopped runnin'. They knew where I lived. If they didn't, all they had to do was ask one of those younguns on the wall. I wasn't gonna bring none of this home to my moms.

Wallace was out of the driver's side quick, walkin' towards me. He was smilin' and my stomach shifted. Antuane had walked back by the playground. I knew where he was goin'. Wallace and them keep a gun, a nine with a fifteen-round mag, buried in a shoe box back there.

"Junior," said Wallace, "you done fucked up big." He was still smilin'.

I didn't move. My knees were shakin' some. I figured this was it. I was thinkin' about my mother and tryin' not to cry. Thinkin' about how if I did cry, that's all anyone would remember about me. That I went out like a bitch before I died. Funny me thinkin' about stupid shit like that while I was waitin' for Antuane to come back with that gun.

I saw Antuane's figure walkin' back out through that fog.

And then I saw the spotlight movin' across the courtyard, and where it came from. An MPD Crown Vic was comin' up the street, kinda slow. The driver turned on the overheads, throwing colors all around. Antuane backpedaled and then he was gone.

The cruiser stopped and the driver's door opened. The

white cop I'd seen earlier in the night got out. Sergeant Peters. My moms had told me his name. Told me he was all right.

Peters was puttin' on his hat as he stepped out. He had pulled his nightstick, and his other hand just brushed the Glock on his right hip. Like he was just lettin' us all know he had it.

"Evening, gentlemen," he said easylike. "We got a problem here?"

"Nope," said Wallace, kinda in a white-boy's voice, still smiling.

"Somethin' funny?" said Peters.

Wallace didn't say nothin'. Peters looked at me and then back at Wallace.

"You all together?" said Peters.

"We just out here havin' a conversation," said Wallace.

Sergeant Peters gave Wallace a look then, like he was disgusted with him, and then he sighed.

"You," said Peters, turnin' to me. I was prayin' he wasn't gonna say my name, like me and him was friends and shit.

"Yeah?" I said, not too friendly but not, like, impolite.

"You live around here?" He *knew* I did.

I said, "Uh-huh."

"Get on home."

I turned around and walked. Slow but not too slow. I heard the white cop talkin' to Wallace and the others, and the crackle of his radio comin' from the car. Red and blue was strobin' across the bricks of the complex. Under my breath I was sayin', Thanks, God.

In my apartment everyone was asleep. I turned off the TV set and covered my sister, who was lyin' on the couch. Then I went back to my room and turned the box on so I could listen to my music low. I sat on the edge of the bed. My hand was shaking. I put it together with my other hand and laced my fingers tight.

SERGEANT PETERS

After the Park Morton incident, I answered a domestic call over on First and Kennedy. A young gentleman, built like a fullback, had beat his girl up pretty bad. Her face was already swelling when I arrived and there was blood and spittle bubbling on the side of her mouth. The first cops on the scene had cuffed the perp and had him bent over the hood of their cruiser. At this point the girlfriend, she was screaming at the cops. Some of the neighborhood types, hanging outside of a windowless bar on Kennedy, had begun screaming at the cops, too. I figured they were drunk and high on who knew what, so I radioed in for a few more cars.

We made a couple of additional arrests. Like they say in the TV news, the situation had escalated. Not a full-blown riot, but trouble nonetheless. Someone yelled out at me, called me a "cracker-ass motherfucker." I didn't even blink. The county cops don't take an ounce of that kinda shit, but we take it every night. Sticks and stones, like that. Then someone started whistling the theme from the old *Andy Griffith Show,* you know, the one where he played a small-town sheriff, and everyone started to laugh. Least they didn't call me Barney Fife. The thing was, when the residents start with the comedy, you know it's over, that things have gotten under control. So I didn't mind. Actually, the guy who was whistling, he was pretty good.

When that was over with, I pulled a car over on 5th and Princeton, back by the Old Soldier's Home, that matched a description of a shooter's car from earlier in the night. I waited for backup, standing behind the left rear quarter panel of the car, my holster unsnapped, the light from my Mag pointed at the rear window.

When my backup came, we searched the car and frisked the four YBMs. They had those little-tree deodorizers hangin' from the rearview, and one of those plastic, king-crown deodorizers sitting on the back panel, too. A crown. Like they're royalty, right? God, sometimes these people make me laugh. Anyhow, they were clean with no live warrants, and we let them go.

I drove around, and it was quiet. Between three a.m. and dawn, the city gets real still. Beautiful in a way, even for down here.

The last thing I did, I helped some Spanish guy try to get back into his place in Petworth. Said his key didn't work, and it didn't. Someone, his landlord or his woman, had changed the locks on him, I figured. Liquor stench was pouring out of him. Also, he smelled like he hadn't taken a shower for days. When I left him he was standing on the sidewalk, sort of rocking back and forth, staring at the front of the row house, like if he looked at it long enough the door was gonna open on its own.

So now I'm parked here near the station, sipping coffee. It's my ritual, like. The sky is beginning to lighten. This here is my favorite time of night.

I'm thinking that on my next shift, or the one after, I'll swing by and see Tonio Harris's mother. I haven't talked to her in years, anyway. See how she's been doing. Suggest to her, without acting like I'm telling her what to do, that maybe she ought to have her son lie low some. Stay in the next few weekend nights. Let that beef he's got with those others, whatever it is, die down. Course, I know those kinds of beefs don't go away. I'll make her aware of it, just the same.

The Harris kid, he's lucky he's got someone like his mother, lookin' after him. I drive back in there at the housing complex, and I see those young kids sitting on that wall at two in the morning, looking at me with hate in their eyes, and all I can think of is, where are the parents? Yeah, I know, there's a new curfew in effect for minors. Some joke. Like we've got the manpower and facilities to enforce it. Like we're supposed to raise these kids, too.

Anyway, it's not my job to think too hard about that. I'm just lettin' these people know that we're out here, watching them. I mean, what else can you do?

My back hurts. I got to get me one of those things you sit on, with the wood balls. Like those African cabdrivers do.

TONIO HARRIS

This morning I studied some in my room until my eyes got sleepy. It was hard to keep my mind on the book 'cause I was playin' some Method Man on the box, and it was fuckin' with my concentration. That cut he does with Redman, called "Tear It Off"? That joint is tight.

I figured I was done for the day, and there wasn't no one around to tell me different. My mother was at work at the Dollar Store, and my sister was over at a friend's. I put my sneaks on and grabbed my ball and headed up to Roosevelt.

I walked up Georgia, dribblin' the sidewalk when I could, usin' my left and keeping my right behind my back, like my coach told me to do. I cut down Upshur and walked up 13th, past my school, to the court. The court is on the small side and its backboards are square, with bumper stickers and shit stuck on the boards. It's beside a tennis court and all of it is fenced in. There's a baseball field behind it; birds always be sittin' on that field.

There was a four-on-four full-court thing happenin' when I got there. I called next with another guy, Dimitrius Johnson, who I knew could play. I could see who was gonna win this game, 'cause the one team had this boy named Peter Hawk who could do it all. We'd pick up two off the losers' squad. I watched the game and after a minute I'd already had those two picked out.

The game started kind of slow. I was feelin' out my players and those on the other side. Someone had set up a box courtside and they had that live Roots thing playin'. It was one of those pretty days with the sun out and high clouds, the kind look like pillows, and the weather and that upbeat music comin' from the box set the tone. I felt loose and good.

Me and Hawk was coverin' each other. He was one of those who could go left or right, dribble or shoot with either hand. He took me to the hole once or twice. Then I noticed he always eye-faked in the opposite direction he was gonna go before he made his move. So it gave me the advantage, knowin' which side he was gonna jump to, and I gained position on him like that.

I couldn't shut Hawk down, not all the way, but I forced him to change his game. I made a couple of nice assists on offense and drained one my own self from way downtown. One of Hawk's players tried to claim a charge, doin' that Reggie Miller punk shit, his arms windmillin' as he went back. That shit don't go in pickup, and even his own people didn't back him. My team went up by one.

We stopped the game for a minute or so, so one of mines could tie up his sneaks. I was lookin' across the ball field at the seagulls and crows, catchin' my wind. That's when I saw James Wallace's black Maxima, cruisin' slow down Allison, that street that runs alongside the court.

We put the ball back into play. Hawk drove right by me, hit a runner. I fumbled a pass goin' back upcourt, and on the turnover they scored again. The Maxima was going south on 13th, just barely moving along. I saw Wallace in the driver's seat, his window down, lookin' my way with that smile of his and his dead-ass eyes.

"You playin', Tone?" asked Dimitrius, the kid on my team.

I guess I had lost my concentration and it showed. "I'm playin'," I said. "Let's ball."

Dimitrius bricked his next shot. Hawk got the 'bound and brought the ball up. I watched him do that eye-fake thing again and I stole the ball off him in the lane before he could make his move. I went bucket-to-bucket with it and leaped. I jammed the motherfucker and swung on the rim, comin' down and doin' one of those Patrick Ewing silent growls at Hawk and the rest of them before shootin' downcourt to get back on D. I was all fired up. I felt like we could turn the shit around.

Hawk hit his next shot, a jumper from the top of the key. Dimitrius brought it down, and I motioned for him to dish me the pill. He led me just right. In my side sight I saw a black car rollin' down Allison, but I didn't stop to check it out. I drove off a pick, pulled up in front of Hawk, made a head move and watched him bite. Then I went up. I was way out there but I could tell from how the ball rolled off my fingers that it was gonna go. Ain't no chains on those rims, but I could see the links dance as that rock dropped through. I'm sayin' that I could see them dance in my mind.

We was runnin' now. The game was full-on and it was fierce. I grabbed one off the rim and made an outlet pass, then beat the defenders myself on the break. I saw black movin' slow on 13th but I didn't even think about it. I was higher than a motherfucker then, my feet and the court and the ball were all one thing. I felt like I could drain it from anywhere, and Hawk, I could see it in his eyes, he knew it, too.

I took the ball and dribbled it up. I knew what I was gonna do, knew exactly where I was gonna go with it, knew wasn't nobody out there could stop me. I wasn't thinkin' about Wallace or the stoop of my moms's shoulders or which nigga was gonna be lookin' to fuck my baby sister, and I wasn't thinkin' on no job or college test or my future or nothin' like that.

I was concentratin' on droppin' that pill through the hole. Watching myself doin' it before I did. Out here in the sunshine, every dark thing far away. Runnin' ball like I do. Thinkin' that if I kept runnin', that black Maxima and everything else, it would just go away.

MAMZER

R. D. Rosen

My grandfather was Sidney Fogelman.

To basketball fans of a certain age, his name will still evoke memories of a time when they played the game in a cage through which the other team's less inhibited fans might stab your leg with a lit cigar or a hatpin. When professional basketball was the college sport's ugly little sister. A time before it occurred to anyone that you could shoot with one hand from the outside, when you played for fifteen or twenty-five bucks a game on your way to a career coaching or running a bar or selling real estate.

Grandpa Sidney was there in the early days of professional basketball and he was there thirty-five years later, after World War II, when, having nurtured basketball through decades of rough, raw regional play, he helped conceive the National Basketball Association. By then, of course, the number of Jewish players, who had been a dominant force on the court, had begun to dwindle. After the war, Jews began clambering out of the ghettoes that have always spawned most of our hungriest and best athletes. But Sidney had always been a short, dumpy coach and front office guy—ironically, he'd never been that good at the game—and in the late 1940s he had a visionary businessman's belief in the game that would someday give Wilt Chamberlain, Larry Bird, and Michael Jordan a forum for their special skills.

When I was a little boy, he started at last to make some real money from the game. Since he was not a materialistic man, he decided to invest some of it for my sister and me, his only grandchildren. Twenty years later, that decision put Beth through law school and me through the Jewish Theological Seminary.

Back in the 1970s, when Grandpa Sidney was in his seventies, the National Basketball Association employed him to provide a variety of services of which he was uniquely capable. Among these jobs was the annual making of the league schedule, which, in the days before computers, required Sidney to hole up in a New York City hotel room with fistfuls of airline schedules and arena calendars. Miraculously, he would emerge a week or two later, like Moses with the tablets, clutching a handwritten plan. When the first computers came along, the league took the job away from Sidney and gave it to a machine. However, the computers of the day were unable to accomplish in any amount of time what Sidney Fogelman was able to do in a week or two on a legal pad, and so they gave the job back to him until they made better computers.

Grandpa Sidney thought his only grandson—me—would make a crafty point guard, quick off the dribble and able, as they say, to see the floor. (Sidney's only son, my father, had disappointed him in this area by proving to be no more gifted on the court than he had been.) After Grandma died, Sidney came to live with our family and he taught me the game in endless conversations, as well as on our suburban playground, where he would stand on the sidelines in a brown double-breasted suit and stained fedora, barking intructions at my friends and me as he had once screamed himself blue in the face coaching his most famous team in the 1920s and '30s, a team composed entirely of Philadelphia and New York Jews.

Because Sidney had the gift of making others want to please him, I devoted far more time to the game than my talent warranted, and only gave it up in high school when even my own loving parents had to admit I was no good, and Sidney himself, now in his eighties, was beginning to retire from the affairs of the world and lose the aura of biblical authority that made me practice my jump shot long after I'd given up any hope it would go in the basket with any frequency.

Grandpa Sidney held on for several more years, body slowly failing but mind terrifyingly intact. In his last years, I'm quite certain he still would have been able, if called upon, to make up the NBA schedule. Although Sidney Fogelman himself was a barely observant Jew, he was so proud a product of first-generation American Jewish culture that the formal aspects of Judaism seemed almost beside the point. He may not have attended shul with any regularity, but he understood Hebrew and spoke Yiddish and he could effortlessly drop a quote from the Bal-shem Tov into a sentence about the pick-and-roll off the high post. His spiritual gene found its way to me, and around the time I went off to college, I decided I wanted to become a rabbi.

This pleased him enormously because his own father had been a poor but religious man in Poland. He was the shammes—the caretaker—of a small synagogue, whose job it was to sweep the sanctuary after service, dust the Torah, fold the yarmulkes and the tallises. In his last two or three years, when I was at the seminary in the city, Sidney would sit with me at my parents' kitchen table, and after a few perfunctory comments about the triangle offense or the approaching NCAA basketball tournament, we would settle into a discussion about Israel, moral relativism, destiny, or a number of other topics that I, as a future rabbi, was ravenous to explore.

It was during one of these visits toward the very end of his life that Grandpa Sidney told me the story that only now, years later, do I feel safe in relating. I can see him now across the speckled Formica expanse of kitchen table, his face deeply furrowed, his nostrils dense with thick black hairs my mother would trim for him every few weeks.

"Did I ever tell you the story about the '37–'38 season with the Planets?" he said, referring to the Philadelphia Planets, the all-Jewish professional basketball team that he owned and coached, which won numerous Eastern League championships in that faded, sepia-toned era.

"Which story?" I asked.

"The one I'm about to tell you."

"I have no idea whether you've already told me the story you're about to tell me."

He waved a liver-spotted hand in my direction. "What do *you* know?" he said. This was his favorite rebuke—"What do *you* know?"—as if the listener were an idiot who couldn't be trusted to understand what Sidney was telling him. Often the phrase would be accompanied, for emphasis, by a light backhanded slap against my chest.

"It's impossible that I told you this story before, because never before have I told it to a single soul. You, Ronnie, my favorite grandson, are the first."

"I'm your *only* grandson. Why am I so lucky?"

"Because you I like," he replied.

This was a high compliment. Sidney often said about others, including people he might have led you to believe he liked: "Him I wouldn't give you a nickel for!" or "I wouldn't give you a penny for the whole lot of them!" To be liked by Sidney Fogelman was a particular honor, especially in his own mind. It was really hard to say what gave him this power, the power to make you infinitely glad that he approved of you, but you accepted it because people like Sidney, as I've learned over the years, are what give life its shape and its deeper meanings.

"Let me hear it," I said, plucking a Marlboro from the pack in my pocket.

"No smoking," Sidney said with coachlike command. I put the cigarette away.

"Now, in 1937, Ronnie, I had perhaps my best group of boys ever. Every one a Jew. Which wasn't so unusual in those days because I'd had many Planets teams that were every one a Jew. Just like the other teams were all micks or dagos or"—he seemed to pause here in deference to some particular racial sensitivity—"Negroes. We had Gordy Metzger, Vic Fine, Ted Morris, Leon Skolnik, Bakey Gumbiner. You name it."

On his fat fingers he counted off some of the great Jewish ballplayers of that era, not one of them taller than six foot three, names familiar to me from the Philadelphia Planets' memorabilia he kept in a box under his bed in the spare room: programs, newspaper accounts, autographed team photos. The team jerseys were emblazoned with Stars of David. They were proud to be Jews, these immigrants' meaty kids, and tough enough to stand up to anyone who objected.

"And Al Newberger," Sidney went on. "God, that young

man could shoot the ball. Two-handed set shots. High-arcing sons-of-bitches. They used to hit the rafters in that Union City dump the Arrows played in. But he hardly ever said a word. Even on the court he used to take his licks with a quiet smile. Then he'd give it back to the guy two quarters later when his back was turned. And, Ronnie, I'm not talking about a time when your eight-million-dollar-a-year *putz* whines to the ref about a tap on the chin under the basket. Back then, you'd get clocked and the ref wouldn't even blink. No blood, no foul. Sometimes it was like a prison yard riot.

"And Al was a good-looking guy," he went on. "Could've been a movie star, except, as I said, he never opened his mouth. But he saw more pussy than a pair of ladies' panties. Which is why I never understood why he was shacking up with this girl Vera, who made her living as a whore."

"Al Newberger lived with a whore?" I said.

Sidney lunged across the table and backhanded me on the left breast. "What the hell do *you* know? Of course he was living with a whore!"

"What do you mean, *of course?* You just said you never understood it yourself."

"That's what I'm saying!" Sidney said. "He lived with her!"

It's tempting to say that Sidney's exasperating conversational logic had been brought on by old age, but, sadly, it appears to have been a permanent fixture of his temperament.

"He lived with a girl who made her living *shtupping* other men," Sidney said, shaking his head at the peculiarity of it.

"Maybe he was afraid of commitment," I suggested.

Sidney looked at me as if I were out of my mind. Psychological speculation was not a hobby of his, while I, who was already in therapy—no doubt partly because of growing up around infuriating Jewish men—loved nothing more than speculating about the complexities of human relationships.

"I'll tell you what he was afraid of, Ronnie. He was afraid of not getting a first-class blow job, that's what he was afraid of. If you want a job done well, get a professional—that's what I've always said. I hope you don't mind my plain speech."

"I can take it," I said. I not only loved his salty language— I loved hearing about these Jews who didn't talk so much, who beat the shit out of their opponents, who lived with whores.

"Still," Sidney said, "what kind of man wants to sleep with a lady you don't know where her pussy's been? What am I gonna do? He's my best ballplayer. What's the worst could've happened? The clap. Al even brings her around the National Hotel—you remember, don't you, that we played our home games in a hotel ballroom?—and all the guys know her, and she's a classy kind of whore, always with the tailored suits and a nice hat."

It was dawning on me that Sidney was working up to something. Although I had no idea where the story was going, he didn't seem merely to be trolling the past for glimmering little glories, as old men do, as Sidney had started to do the last few years. This story was already longer than most of them.

"So we're leading the league by a game or two over the Bronx Black Stars, and it's March, maybe two or three weeks to go before the playoffs. Now, we've won the championship two out of the last three seasons, five of the last seven, so everyone's gunning for us. You should've heard the crowds at our road games, Ronnie: 'We'll get you, you bunch of kikes' and 'You fuckin' sheenies!' But we loved it. 'We may be sheenies,' I'd yell back, 'but we're the sheenies who are kicking your ass!' I've got to tell you, Ronnie, it was a great time to be a Jew who could put a ball in the hoop. A great time. You should've been there."

Like many American Jewish boys who had known only the suburbs growing up, who had never served in the military, I had gone through life feeling untested, but not especially eager to pass any of the tests I had in mind. Our energies had been rerouted, like traffic around a bad accident, to the world of intellectual pursuit. Through Sidney and his stories, I vicariously enjoyed the tough ethnic brothers I admired from afar. Not the thugs like Mendy Weiss, Arnold Rothstein, Bugsy Siegel, or Gurrah Shapiro. The good Jews, like Sidney.

Sidney yanked a hanky out of his pants pocket and mopped his brow, then ran the soiled cloth over his balding head, as if he were polishing it. "So what happens? What happens is Al Newberger's home one night in the apartment he shared with Vera when he hears a car pull up outside and there's an argument going on in there between Vera and one of her johns. Apparently, the guy couldn't perform and he's saying he shouldn't have to pay, and she's telling him there're no free samples and that she won't get out of the car till he forks over the two bucks. And Al's watching from the window and sees this guy get out, come around, and pull Vera out of the car and throw her on the ground and give her a kick for good measure.

"Well, Al's out of the apartment building in no time flat— you gotta understand how quick he was, Ronnie—and Al picks up Vera, makes sure she's all right, and sends her into the apartment. Then he and the guy have a few words. Before the other guy knows it, Al Newberger is kicking the crap out of him. By the time Al's through with him, the guy's face looks like a *tsimmes.* So Al throws him in the back of the guy's car and then drives the car to the old railroad yard and leaves him there and walks back home, fuming.

"I forgot to tell you one thing, Ronnie. While Al was beating this john up, a gun, a five-shot revolver of some kind, falls out of the guy's camel-hair coat, and now Al's got it. He doesn't know what to do with it, but he sure as hell isn't going to leave it in the back of the car with the guy, so he goes home, wraps it up in some rags, and hides it up on a ledge inside the fireplace chimney."

"How do you know all this?" I ask.

"Because Al told me later. I got it out of him later. Get me a glass of water, Ronnie, no ice. I'm not used to doing this much talking."

He waited until I returned from the kitchen sink to resume the story. He took occasional, incongruously dainty sips of water. "So a couple of days later, after our next home game, Al's walking home from the National when a guy falls in step with him. Spiffy-looking gentleman in his late thirties wearing a nice chalk-striped, double-breasted suit and rimless glasses. He looks like a well-dressed accountant, which, I happen to know, is what his mother once hoped he would be. But his father, who used to launder restaurant linen for the mob, seemed to get the upper hand with Irving. That's this guy's name, Irving Levchuck, but he introduces himself to Al as just Irving, and when Al tells him to get lost, Irving says very calmly that Al beat up an associate of his the other day, a guy named Itchy Weintraub. That's the name of the guy Al left bleeding in the Packard in the railroad yard."

"Is everybody a Jew in this story?" I asked.

"Yes. Absolutely. So Irving says to Al as they're walking along that he's in a position to propose a resolution to their squabble that will leave Al Newberger physically unharmed. So Al says, 'I'm supposed to worry about some guy named Itchy hurting me?' So Irving says, 'Look, Al, you shoot basketballs for a living, and you're pretty good at it. Well, Itchy Weintraub shoots people for a living, and he's got an even higher shooting percentage than you.'

"Now Irving Levchuck has Al Newberger's attention. Irving tells Al that this guy Itchy's a *schlammer* who used to work for the Matteo brothers, who used to control South Philadelphia when the Italians were in charge. So if you were a little *schmeggege* like Itchy and you liked to shoot people, and you wanted to get paid for it, you worked for the dagos."

"So why's this guy Irving involved?"

"Do I interrupt you when you're in the middle of a story?"

"Yes."

"So here's what Irving says to Al. He says if you're good enough to make a basket, which you are, then you're good enough to miss. Al knows just where this is going, of course, and tells Irving to take a hike. Why shouldn't he? After all, Al Newberger's a hero in Philly. He's the biggest thing going. There's only one professional basketball team in Philly and that's us. For Jews, he's like Michael Jordan. Whole families would come to the National on Saturday night to watch us play. After, there was a dance, with Ted Morris conducting his orchestra. Ted was one of our starting guards, fast as hell, but he had a band and they'd start up right after the game. Ted didn't even have time to shower. He'd get out of his uniform and right into his tux. Ten minutes after the game's over and the ballroom's a sea of dancing Jewish couples. You never saw anything like it. This was before television, Ronnie—"

"I know that, Grandpa," I said.

"What do *you* know? Where was I? You made me lose my place."

"Al Newberger was telling Irving what's-his-name to take a hike."

"Thank you, Ronnie. So Al tells Irving to take a hike and Irving, very gentleman-like, explains that if Al doesn't 'play ball,' something terrible could happen to him or, worse, Vera.

"Now Al's even more interested, because he can't figure out how this guy would know Vera's name. But he's still not giving in to Irving, and when Irving says Itchy wants his gun back, Al pretends like he doesn't have it. 'Cause how's Itchy going to shoot Al if he doesn't have his gun?" Sidney laughed ruefully and went on. "I can laugh now, Ronnie, it's a long time ago, but you can imagine that this encounter with Irving Levchuck, however inconclusive, would begin to play with Al Newberger's mind. He should've come to me right away, of course, but it wasn't Al's nature.

"So a couple of days later, after a game, Al and some of the guys are drinking at a place in South Philly that they used to go to, called the Two Deuces or the Forty-two Queens, one of those. Al leaves to go home and that guy Itchy Weintraub— with his face all bandaged and fucked up—jumps out of a car parked at the curb, grabs Al, and throws him in the front seat. Irving is behind the wheel."

"Itchy, Irving," I said. "It's a little hard to keep these guys straight, Grandpa."

"Do your best," Sidney said. "So Itchy gets in the backseat and before Al knows it, he's pointing a pistol at the back of Al's head and Irving's saying, 'Look, Al, Itchy's got a new gun.' Then he tells Al that they're spreading a lot of money around town that says the Planets won't beat the Union City Arrows by more than two points at the National Hotel on Saturday night. Al tells him he's not going to do it, not going to shave points, and before he knows it, now Itchy's got a piano wire around Al's neck and he's choking him to death and that seems to do the trick. Al's in the tank.

252 · R. D. ROSEN

"So, wouldn't you know it, on Saturday night we beat the Arrows by a single point. Instead of killing the clock at the end of the game with a three-point lead, Al takes a bad shot and gives the Arrows the ball and then lets his man waltz past him for an easy bucket. I figure Al's having a bad night. He's too proud to come to me with his problem. But somebody else isn't.

"A few days later, Vera comes to see me at my office. An exceptionally good-looking girl, Ronnie. She tells me how Al beat this guy up who used to work for the Matteo brothers and how Itchy's going to pay him back. I ask her if Al knows she's coming to see me and she says no. So I ask, 'How do you know what this guy Itchy's going to do?' She says, 'Because everybody knows how these bums operate.' You following me so far?"

"Yes."

"Good. Then you'll understand my problem. Because I can tell that Al hasn't told her anything. He never talked to nobody in general. So Vera knows more about this on her own than she's letting on. So I ask her, 'What's your relationship with these monkeys, anyway?' Because I figure—"

"—that she's tied in with Itchy and knows exactly how much trouble Al's in."

"When I want some information I'll consult the encyclopedia. So I thank Vera for her concern and figure it's time to make some inquiries. Meanwhile, Al's up to his *pupik* in trouble. I can use this like a hole in the head. We already got a Depression that won't end. We got the German American Bund parading around the city in swastikas and jackboots.

"Al gets another visit from Irving, who tells Al that when the Planets go up to Harlem in a few days, the Rens are going to win by four. Al tells Irving no, I'm through, that's it. So Irving whispers an address in Al's ear, 'That's where my mother lives,' Al says, and Irving says, 'And it's where she's gonna die if the Rens don't win by at least four.' So Al says, 'You can't make me do this,' and Irving says, 'You'd be amazed by what I can make you do.'

"But the next day I buy Al dinner at the old Horn and Hardart and I tell him I know he's in the tank. I don't say it was Vera who told me. He admits some guy named Irving says some guy named Itchy is going to shoot him. I've got to take care of this problem, right? So I take Al down to Atlantic City to see Mo Mo Scharf."

"Mo Mo?"

"Big bootlegger I knew 'cause he was the moneyman for a team I coached in the late twenties. Not that I knew he was an *untervelt mensch* at the time. Now he's semiretired, living on the boardwalk, and I figure he might do us a favor. He was always doing business with the Matteo brothers. But I'm in for a couple surprises. First of all, he's become a schlump. He's a nobody now, an old man in slippers with a bad memory. But he does know one thing, and that's the second surprise. He tells Al and me the Matteo brothers are no longer running things in South Philly. Who, then? A guy named Levchuck, Mo Mo tells me. Irving Levchuck."

At this point, I recall clearly how Sidney's demeanor changed. He no longer seemed to be telling me a story at all. The light in Sidney's face dimmed slowly, as if on a rheostat, and his voice became quieter and more determined, as if he was now being forced to tell the story. "Now, Ronnie, you understand that, until this point, I have no idea that the guy who's got his claws into Al is Irving *Levchuck*. Al knows him only as

Irving. Let me tell you, this throws me for a loop, because I grew up with the guy."

"You grew up with him?"

"What did I just say? Our mothers were in the same canasta club. Even then I hated him. He was a little goniff. When we were about twelve or thirteen, he stole some athletic equipment from the Jewish Community Center and sold it to some Negroes across town. I ratted him out. From then on, he hated me. I wasn't surprised that he became a bookkeeper for Mo Mo when he was still in his twenties. He was always good with numbers. But did I know the little goniff had moved up to run organized crime in Philadelphia? What did I know from the workings of the underworld? I was shocked when Mo Mo tells me this, but I don't let on to either of them that I grew up with the *mamzer*.

"Because now I know why Irving Levchuck has Al by the balls and won't let go. First of all, he's getting back at me for ratting him out twenty-five years before. But the real reason? Owning a piece of the Planets was like owning a piece of God. We were the force of good, Ronnie, and Irving was the kind of guy who had to take a shit on everything he couldn't control. And without knowing it Al had just handed him the opportunity of a lifetime.

"So we drove back from Atlantic City in silence and when we played our last regular season game in Harlem a couple of nights later, I kept Al on the bench. And that fucking Itchy had the balls to come down to the bench near the end of the game and yell at Al. I was right there and I heard him ask Al, 'You got a death wish, Al? You got a death wish?' His face was right down next to Al's, and Vic Fine, who's sitting next to him on the bench, throws an elbow right in Itchy's face. Itchy opens his coat and shows them his semiautomatic. 'I got something better than elbows, you pricks.' I remember this like it was yesterday, Ronnie. I thought he was going to use the gun then and there. But I point a finger at him and order him back to his seat, and you know what? He goes. But after the game, since I figure these *mamzers* are going to be waiting for Al, we got him out of the Renaissance Ballroom with the Harlem team."

Out of his pocket Sidney took the soiled hanky again and ran it around his forehead and skull. "But nobody had to tell me this story didn't look like it was going to have a happy ending. I put Al and Vera up in the Rittenhouse Hotel. The next day, or the day after that, Vera pays me another visit at my office and says that if Al doesn't play and do what they say, they're gonna kill him. You don't have to be a genius to know this is a distinct possibility. But how come she's so sure? Well, since I last saw Vera I've been asking about her around South Philly, and now I know she's been peddling her puss for Irving and his crowd since she was a teenager. *This* is the broad my best ballplayer chooses to shack up with?" Sidney clapped his hand against his forehead. *"Gott in himmel!*

"It took me about a minute and a half to turn her, Ronnie. I told her she had to choose sides. I told her from now on she was my spy. To let Irving's people know Al wasn't going along with them and I wanted Vera to let me know exactly what they were going to do about it. The playoffs are about to start and Vera reports back to me that Al won't make it out of the National Hotel Ballroom alive if he doesn't go in the tank—the Planets win by two points in the first game, no more.

"If she's telling me the truth, all I got to do is frisk all three thousand people who show up for the game. I hire every tough Jew I know to guard the doors that night. Irving and Itchy and their broads waltz right in, but not until we've patted them down. I put Al in the game. Only problem is, they smuggled a gun in somehow and Itchy comes out of his seat at the end of the game and tries to shoot Al as he's leaving the floor. Some of my guys get to Itchy first and nobody gets hurt, but Itchy gets away.

"An hour after the game, Al goes back to his suite at the Rittenhouse, the one I got for him and Vera, and he walks in and there's Vera asleep in the bed with the covers pulled up over her chin. She doesn't wake up when he comes in, so Al goes over and pulls the covers down. Vera's throat has been slit from ear to ear. Poor girl. And me, I figure I'm responsible for it because when Irving and Itchy saw all the security at the game, they must've figured Vera was talking to me, had tipped me off. And she paid a terrible price.

"So now it's war. I'm ready to break Itchy in two when one of my guys who was watching the stands during the game tells me that it was Irving's seat that was empty since the middle of the game. Are you sure? I ask. Sure I'm sure, says my guy. So it's Irving, who used to kill kittens when he was a boy. Now he's killed a grown-up kitten named Vera."

"This is quite a story, Grandpa," I said.

"You haven't heard nothing yet."

"Is it true?"

"What're you talking about?" Sidney said, genuinely enraged this time. "What do *you* know? Of course it's true! Sit and listen. I'm trying to tell you something!" His eyes started to glisten with tears of old grief. "I make a few calls, people I know, and I set up a meeting with Levchuck. I knew he'd see me. The kid who made good and the kid who made bad. So we meet on a bench by the Schuylkill River, where there can be no surprises. He's got three or four of his guys stationed all around, just like in the movies. Touching their weapons through their clothes.

"Let me tell you, I'm disgusted. I *know* the guy's murdered Vera, but he's blaming Itchy. Saying, 'Sidney, I can't control him. For ten bucks, he'd shoot himself!' I can't say anything to him, because I've got to protect Al. Got to protect my team. I got to get Al and the team out of this alive. So I plead with this goniff to call the whole thing off.

"I say to him, I say, 'Don't you have bigger things to worry about?' And he says to me, 'Sidney, what could be bigger than having you come to me on your knees?' See? That's what it was all about for him, Ronnie! Making me come to him on my knees begging for Al Newberger's life.

"So he purses his lips and decides to change the terms. Doing me a big favor. Irving says the money on the street is swinging the Jersey Reds' way now, saying we can't beat 'em in the series. So Irving wants to put his money on us now, the underdogs."

"So Al Newberger's gonna have to bet his life that the Planets take the Reds," I said.

"'I'll take your boys, Sidney,' he tells me, pleased with himself. 'All they've got to do is win. Everything's kosher. You win, I'll win, we'll all win.' What can I do, Ronnie? I've got to take the terms. At least Al's not shaving points now, and he's in charge of his own destiny. But the whole thing's making me sick. That's what I remember saying to Irving. 'Guys like you make me sick.'

"And he says, 'There aren't any guys like me, Sidney. There's just me.'"

"I think I've read about this guy Levchuck," I said.

"Of course you have! He was a big *k'nacker*! Listen to me!

I take Al aside and tell him what the deal is now: we win the series and everything's copacetic. But he's out of control. Irving's murdered his girlfriend and now he's supposed to go out and win the championship? To save his own life? Being owned by Levchuck all because he beat up his scrawny *schlammer,* and now this? He's out of control and he's throwing things around the hotel room. I have no doubt he'd kill Irving if given half a chance.

"I know what I've got to do. I ask him where the gun is, the gun he took off Itchy two or three weeks before. He says he's stashed it up his chimney at his apartment. So I drive him over there and make him give it to me. He hands it over, but first he takes the bullets out. 'Give me the goddamn bullets,' I say, because, sure, I figure he's thinking he'll get another gun and use the bullets. But Al says, 'Fogey, I'm just taking them out because I'm afraid you might hurt yourself.' You can imagine me handling a gun, Ronnie, right? So he hands me the bullets separate and now I feel a little bit safer that Al's not going to do something stupid. And I tell him that we'll be all right, that all we've gotta do is beat the Reds in seven, which is what we were gonna do anyway.

"Well," Sidney said with a long sigh and a sip of water, "to make a long story short, the Reds beat us up and before we know it, we're down two games to one. Now we're shitting bricks. If we don't win three of the next four, I don't know how I'm gonna keep Al alive. The fourth game's at the National, so I get every tough kid in the neighborhood to watch the doors and stand around the court, watching the stands, just in case. I tell 'em we're expecting trouble. The place is all *kocked up* with people. Every Jew and half the Italians in Philadelphia are there, and none of them knows we're playing for our lives. Just Al and me.

"Well, we lose by three in front of our own fans. We're down three games to one now, with two of the next three in Jersey City, and I'm thinking of asking the league on the q.t. to move the rest of the series to an undisclosed location. I'm thinking of how to get Al out of Philadelphia, maybe out of the country.

"Then it happens, like manna from heaven. Sometime after midnight on the night of that fourth game, somebody pops Irving Levchuck in the alley behind the candy store where he likes to conduct his business. Ran his operation out of the storeroom in the back. Old Irving takes one right in the *punim*. Dead. It's front page in all the papers the next day. No one can figure it out. There's talk that the Matteo brothers sent some-one to do it. That somebody in Atlantic City thought Irving was taking too big a piece of the heroin racket.

"And, of course, there's talk that Al Newberger might've had something to do with it, because it turns out that Al hasn't kept his mouth completely shut about his predicament, espe-cially after Irving slit Vera's throat. After Irving gets popped, it's not long before the cops know that Al's got a reason to kill him. Also, thanks to Vera, who knew these guys, that Al prob-ably knows about Irving's comings and goings."

"Wait a second," I say. I disappeared into my parents' den, where it took me only a minute to find a Time-Life illustrated history of organized crime, one of those volumes they used to advertise on television; when you signed up, they'd send you one a month. I used to be fascinated by this particular volume and brought it back to the kitchen table, where I quickly found what I was looking for and turned the book around so Sidney could see it.

It was a wire service photo of Irving Levchuck's body in a South Philadelphia alley. He lay on his back, limbs akimbo, his hat sitting on its crown a few feet away. In the photo, a dark smudge on his cheek indicated where the bullet had entered. Blood, rendered black by the film, pooled behind his head on the alley's gravel surface. The caption read: "On April 14, 1938, in a slaying that was never solved, Philadelphia mobster Irving Levchuck was gunned down in an alley near the candy store out of which he ran his various enterprises."

"While you were telling me the story, I kept thinking it sounded familiar," I said.

Sidney stared at the photo for a long time as he passed his hanky over his face and forehead. "That's him, all right," he said. "I haven't seen that photo in a long time, Ronnie." He looked up with that sad, hound-dog face in which the eyes still burned bright. "All right. So the cops were all over Al for a day or two, but Al had an alibi. He said he was drinking at the Two Deuces with some of the guys after the game and then they went to Horn and Hardart for eggs and bacon about three in the morning. The guys told the cops Al was never out of their sight until well after Irving had been shot. They had the time of death, you know, because a newsie at the end of the alley heard the shot and went immediately to tell a cop.

"Now the cops back off finally because none of the guys on the team will break and, frankly, the cops are glad Levchuck's been rubbed out, maybe even the ones whose pockets he's been lining. Everyone figures that it was a gangland slaying and they leave it alone. Except that one fact doesn't quite fit. Irving's wallet's gone, assuming he was carrying one, but he's got a money clip with a couple hundred dollars in it still in his front pocket. That's like walking around with a few grand today. Why would someone go to the trouble to take his wallet, but not his money?"

"The killer wanted a souvenir," I suggested.

"Souvenirs are for tourists and children. At least the guy could've taken Irving's walking-around dough. Anyway, so Irving's suddenly out of the way, but who can predict what's gonna happen to the deal now? Is it still in effect? We figured we could breathe a little easier, but Itchy Weintraub, that crazy bastard, might take the whole thing on himself. Who knows? So as the series goes on, Al doesn't go nowhere without half a dozen boys from the neighborhood protecting him. But you know what? Itchy disappears. Without Irving, he shrivels up and dies. Al's a new man. As I know you know, the Planets win three straight to beat the Reds and take our third championship in four years. And Al scores six points in the last period in the seventh game to win it for us." With that, Grandpa Sidney leaned back in his chair and took a long swallow of water.

"Wow, Grandpa, that's quite a story. You lived through some amazing times."

Sidney yawned. He consulted the old Benrus on his wrist. "It's late." But he made no move to get up and pad off to the guest room he'd occupied for a few years now.

"So, Grandpa," I said, "do you think Al did it?"

"Naw."

"Then it was an incredible stroke of luck that Levchuck was murdered when he was."

"Luck had nothing to do with it."

"You don't think so?"

Sidney was rummaging around in one of his pants pockets. He pulled out something wrapped in a white cloth, like a piece of an old undershirt, and said, "I'm an old man, Ronnie. It all goes so fast."

"You're good for ten more years," I said.

He pushed the undershirt-wrapped package across the table, keeping his hand on top of it for a moment before leaving it in front of me.

"It's for you."

"What is it?"

"Open it, Ronnie."

It finally occurred to me what it was, and when it did, tears filled my eyes. To this day, I can't say whether they were tears of pride that he was my grandfather, tears of mourning because he was going to die soon, or tears of fear because of all I would have to do in my lifetime to feel worthy of him. Probably a combination of all three.

"Go ahead, Ronnie. It won't bite."

"I can't."

"Don't be a *putz*. Open it."

"No."

"You're telling me you can't even open it?"

I opened it. I unfolded the cloth and there it was. A wallet, a brown rectangle of leather, remarkably well preserved.

"Go ahead, Ronnie. Take a look."

Gingerly, I flipped the wallet open and took out the folded papers, one by one, soft with age. A Pennsylvania driver's license describing Irving Levchuck as five foot ten, with brown eyes. A membership card to something called the Miracle Club. A Blue Cross card signed by Levchuck in faded blue fountain pen ink. A business card that read: "Detective Lieutenant John McGuire, Homicide, Philadelphia Police Department," with a phone number. A folded piece of vellum on which Levchuck had written a series of initials in blue fountain pen ink followed by phone numbers. A hundred-dollar bill tightly folded into quarters. Four business cards that read: "Irving M. Levchuck, Accountant," with a phone number.

A killer's wallet, given to me by the killer's killer, who happened to be my grandfather. My father's father, who loved my father and me, but who also loved his "boys," the long stream of brilliant Jewish basketball players for whom he would do anything. And had.

"So that someone should know," he said.

"Jesus, Grandpa." I looked down at the wire photo of Levchuck lying in the South Philadelphia alley, then at the wallet that had been taken from his pocket, then at Sidney. "You?"

He just looked at me.

"The gun you took from Al?" I said.

Sidney didn't say anything.

"What do you want me to do with this, Sidney?"

"That's *your* business, Ronnie. Whatever you want."

"Jesus," I said.

Then he coughed lightly into his fist, took a sip of water, and said, "We won that series in seven, Ronnie. We won that last game with a cute little play we had, springing Al loose in the corner coming off a double pick by Gumbiner and Morris. Fine got Al the ball right where he liked it and he turned and let go one of his high-arcing sons-of-bitches and put that game away for us. You should've been there."

SHOTS

S. J. Rozan

I'd been following the Knicks all season, but I didn't see Damon Rome's last game. I was down at Shorty's that December evening, with a beer and a bunch of guys who, like me, could have been drinking at home, where the liquor's free and the TV tuned to whatever you want. But the liquor's the excuse, not the reason. And at Shorty's, the TV over the bar is on so the silent drinkers have something to keep their minds off whatever brought them here alone, and the ones who want to talk to each other have something to talk about.

It was late in the football season, still plenty of time left for basketball, so the TV was tuned to the Giants and the talk was interceptions, rushing, bad knees and bowl chances. Close to halftime, waiting for a commercial to pass, someone ordered another Rolling Rock and brought up the Knicks, how hot they were, and other guys, working on their own beers, shook their heads over it. Who'd have thought? The Knicks unstoppable heading for the playoffs, a real shot this year at taking it all, in a season when Nathaniel Day played only ten games.

It was that new kid, Rome, one guy said, nobody liked him

but everybody knew it, damn punk, ball hog, head case, but shit, he could play. Knicks should have grabbed him up when he came into the league two years ago, they'd have their rings by now. Grabbed up an asshole like him, what are you, crazy? said someone else. What they're paying him, they could have gotten three veterans, guys who want to play ball more than they want to see their name in the papers. A third guy said, Ah, Rome's just the spark plug anyway, he just embarrassed them, they've been riding Nathaniel's coattails for too long and now he's hurt they've all got to step up, play the game for a change. Nathaniel, by him being so good he might actually be bad for the Knicks, anyone ever thought of that?

But you can't knock Nathaniel Day in a bar in New York without half a dozen guys telling you you're full of shit. Day's the franchise, one guy said, and another said he'll be back next year and the Knicks can't go anywhere without him, watch, they'll fold in the playoffs. The anti-Nathaniel guy downed a handful of peanuts and said, Hell, they been folding in the playoffs for eight years *with* him, and come on, a guy who's coached by his sister?

But the sister thing didn't fly. Everyone knew it was Nora Day, five years older than Nathaniel and barely three inches shorter, who'd gotten him through Christ the King as an All-American, through Seton Hall as the most draftable center in the college game, through his first, stunning season with the Knicks, when he was unanimous choice for Rookie of the Year. From then on, Nora had sat courtside, with a shrewd eye to what was missing from the Knicks' game and how she could coach Nathaniel to provide it: rebounding, foul shooting, the fade-away jumper that made him as big a threat from the outside as the inside. She made him indispensable and she made him the franchise; the coaches organized the offense around him and he did the work, pre- and postgame practices, off-season conditioning, weight training, whatever it took, with his sister his personal coach. And, one of the pro-Nathaniel forces said, *and* you know he wouldn't have without her pushing him all the time. Natural talent like that, but too nice a guy for his own good, you see it all the time. No killer instinct, that guy. *I* had that kind of skills, catch me helping other teams' players back up, after I knocked 'em on their ass. *You* had any skills at *all,* another guy said, you wouldn't be sitting here right now on *your* ass. Yeah, well, you watch, the guy without skills said, she'll have him in rehab the minute the cast comes off, he'll be better than ever next season.

That was the way of it and everyone knew it: Nathaniel was who he was because Nora was who she was, and Nathaniel was the first to say so. Nathaniel could afford to be a nice guy, easygoing, because Nora was driven. Nora didn't take vacations, Nora didn't spend time in the country until the off-season—though Nathaniel had bought her a house, because she liked gardens—and as far as anyone knew, Nora didn't date. Nora had a full-time, overtime, all-the-time job, and that was Nathaniel.

The other thing everyone knew was that Nora Day would have been twice the player Nathaniel was if there'd been a woman's pro game when she left college. But there wasn't and hey, one of the beer drinkers said, that's how it goes, too bad for her, but guess Nathaniel and the Knicks lucked out, huh?

The anti-Nathaniel guy just shook his head and drank his beer. Still, someone said, be something if the Knicks finally got their rings in a season with Nathaniel on the bench. Yeah, well, you got that right, someone else said. It's a damn shame, almost, and a worse shame we were gonna have to be grateful to a trash-talking, cornrowed, skirt-chasing asshole like Damon Rome. And another guy said, Yeah, but he's *our* asshole now. Everyone laughed, and the commercial ended, and the Giants snapped the ball.

I didn't see the Knicks game and I didn't hear who won, and I didn't hear until I hit the diner for breakfast the next morning that after the game was over, after the fans had all filed out and the players had left and the Garden was deserted and silent, someone who was not grateful had stepped in front of Damon Rome on an empty New York street and put a bullet through Damon Rome's heart.

I read about it in the papers and talked about it with the other guys at the diner counter as I drank my coffee, with the waitress as I ordered eggs and, as I paid my check at the register, with the owner, a Greek who'd first learned English from baseball radio broadcasts forty years ago. I talked about it, but I didn't get into it until, on the street on my way home, my cell phone rang.

"Smith." I stopped in the cold, clear light, moved closer to a building to get out of the way.

"Tony Manelli, man. How you doing?"

It had been maybe a year since I'd heard from Tony Manelli, longer since I'd seen him, but that didn't mean anything. Young, sharply muscled, an ex-marine, Tony had worked for me years back. He was working investigation because he needed the state license, but his goal was protection; I'd worked both and gave him what help I could. In the years since, our paths sometimes crossed, more often didn't, but the few times I'd needed someone to fill out a security detail I'd hired Tony and had no reason to complain.

Right now, on this bright December morning, his voice sounded strange to me: tight, strained. "Hey, Tony, long time," I said. "I'm okay, what's up with you?"

"I'm in trouble," Tony said.

Twenty minutes later I was giving my name to a receptionist who gave me back a practiced, impersonal smile, and a minute after that, I was being led through the high-rise maze of a Midtown law firm to a partner's glassed-in office. The paralegal who'd brought me closed the door and retired with the gravity of a butler.

Tony and his lawyer, a dark, quick man named John Sutton, both stood when I came in, shook my hand, thanked me for coming. Tony was blond and broad-shouldered and usually looked better than this: his face was ashen under his skier's tan, the skin around his eyes tight, like a man trying hard to focus because he didn't understand what he was seeing. Tony was shorter than I and Sutton was shorter than both of us, jacket off, shirtsleeves rolled up, ready for some serious work here. He pressed a button on his desk, asked someone to bring us coffee, and I found out what the work was about.

"Damon Rome," Tony said. He leaned back in his chair, crossed one leg over the other, uncrossed it right away. "You heard about it?"

"I heard. Everybody in New York heard."

"Yeah," said Tony. "Well, until last week, I did his security."

I glanced from Tony to Sutton. "You're not saying you think that makes you responsible?"

"Christ, no." Tony shook his head, sounded despairing, as though I'd missed the point entirely, might be no use after all.

Sutton leaned forward on his big glass desk. "Tony's about to be arrested for Damon Rome's murder."

A young woman came in with a coffee beaker, mugs, cream

and sugar. She left them on a space Sutton cleared on his desk. We each took our coffee, did what we wanted to it, sat back again.

"Did you kill him?" I asked Tony.

"I don't want—," Sutton began.

But Tony said, "Jesus, John," and then to me, "No. Goddammit. No. Good enough?"

"If it's true. If you did, I'd want to know why."

"I didn't. He was a fucking asshole. But you've had this gig. Sometimes you work for assholes."

"So what do they have, then?"

"All circumstantial," Sutton said promptly. "None of it any good. They just need an arrest, fast."

"If none of it were any good," I said evenly, "you wouldn't have called me."

"Hey, John," Tony said wearily. "Save the speeches for the jury, okay? Bill's on our side. I think?"

I nodded. "Tell me."

Sutton leaned back in his desk chair, leaving it to Tony but ready to jump in and protect him from his own mistakes, if he made any.

"He fired me," Tony said.

"Why?"

"I was fooling around with his wife."

Yvonne Rome: a former model who, in the months since Damon Rome had been with the Knicks, had burst like fireworks upon New York's black-tie charity scene. You'd see her photo two or three times a week on the society pages, at parties and galas, on the arm of her famous husband or, if he'd had a game, flashing her wide smile at whichever of his close friends had gallantly escorted her.

I said, "That was stupid."

"Tell me about it." Tony rubbed his eyes. "But some-times . . . you know?"

I let that go. "What happened?"

"A week ago, in that bar he owns, Shots? After the game."

"That's where he was leaving last night, when he was killed."

"Yeah. It's mostly where he goes."

"Okay. So a week ago . . . ?"

"Yvonne came to meet him, like sometimes she does. He was waiting. Turned out he was setting me and her up."

"How'd he know?"

"I guess we weren't real careful."

"Both of you weren't? Or one of you was and the other screwed up?"

Tony shrugged. I read: he'd been careful, Yvonne Rome had screwed up.

"Go on."

"He started in on us as soon as she got there. Man, that s.o.b. knew words I never heard."

"What did you do?"

"Told him to calm down. Stood there and took it as long as I could. Whole freakin' bar was watching. Ended up, four other guys had to keep me and Damon from punching each other's lights out."

"You threaten to kill him?"

"We threatened to kill each other."

"And he ended up dead first."

Sutton, at his desk, nodded. Tony said, "Yeah. Damon said, he ever saw me and Yvonne together again, he'd waste us both. I said, he laid a hand on her, he was a dead man. He fired my ass, told me to beat it out of the bar. I asked her to come, but she stayed. Next day, Seattle comes to the Garden, she's not there."

"Where was she?"

"Lenox Hill, getting her arm set. Broken in three places."

"Did you mean it? That you'd kill him?"

"When I said it. If I'd known about Yvonne, maybe I would have. But I didn't."

"Didn't kill him?"

"Didn't know. No one told me." He shook his head. "Wish to hell someone had."

"Why? So you could have killed him?"

He stared. "Because I'm in love with the lady."

"That true? Or you were just fooling around with Damon Rome's wife?"

"What the hell does that mean?"

I shrugged. "She's classy, gorgeous, rich, married to a pain-in-the-ass basketball stud who expects everyone, including you, to jump when his fingers snap. You're a bodyguard."

"Hey!" Tony started, but the deep red color in his face told more truth than whatever he could have said.

"Forget it," I said. "Doesn't matter. What do you want me to do?" I asked Sutton that, not Tony, because strategy was the lawyer's, not the client's.

"Last night," Sutton said, "Tony was home. Alone. All night."

"That's hard to prove."

"We have the night doorman saying he didn't see him go out after eleven. That's good but it's not enough. Tony was heard threatening Rome and he had what could sound like a motive to kill him. I didn't know Rome, but from what I've heard, there must be a dozen other people who did, too."

"You want me to find them?"

"Right. As I said, everything the D.A. has is circumstantial. If the same circumstances—motive and opportunity—also apply to other people, they'll have a lot more trouble indicting. Right now they have it in their heads it was Tony, so they've stopped looking. I want to kick-start them."

I finished my coffee. "They have the weapon?"

"A Smith & Wesson .38. The number had been filed off. No prints. They found it in a Dumpster up the block."

"In your face, NYPD." To Tony: "What do you carry?"

I thought he'd be insulted by the question, but he just looked surprised, as though I should have known the answer. "A .38, man," he said, pulling back his jacket, showing me. "It's what you taught me."

★   ★   ★

John Sutton gave the NYPD detective on the case a call. I spoke to him first, just to find out what he had, to let him know what I was doing. His name was Mike Beam and he was a young guy but his words were ageless cop words: "Don't screw up my case."

"We think you have the wrong man," I told him.

"No, you think you can keep me from proving I have the right man. Don't mess with my witnesses, keep out of my way." He said that, but without any teeth, because I was working for the defense and as long as I stayed on the right side of the line, he knew he couldn't stop me. He told me they had witnesses to the near-brawl in Shots last week and that the widow and Tony had both admitted to the affair. He said Tony had no alibi for last night, and the recovered gun was Tony's weapon of choice, though he couldn't prove it was Tony's. I knew all that, and then he told me something else I knew. "The whole city is watching this, Smith. Whoever shot Rome shot up the Knicks' chances, and people are pretty much pissed off about that. Including," he added, "me."

I told him, "Me, too."

Then Sutton took the phone, arranged, now that they'd hired me, to bring Tony in. His last call, before we all left his office, was to a bail bondsman.

★ ★ ★

My first stop was Yvonne Rome. The battered wife, publicly humiliated, her lover canned by her abusive husband. She should have plenty of motive, and opportunity.

I called, used Tony's name and problem to get past an assistant who thought I was press. Yvonne Rome received me in a duplex high in Trump Tower. A gray-uniformed housekeeper asked me to wait and I did, looking around.

Abundant sprays of flowers and baskets of fruit gave the cream-carpeted living room the look of a Renaissance still life. The scattering of subdued people drinking coffee added to the effect. *Still Life with Moors,* I thought. Very tall Moors: of the seven guests in Yvonne Rome's living room, four were Knicks, including Nathaniel Day, and a fifth was Nathaniel's sister Nora. It's not all that rare for me to be the only white person in a room, this being New York, but at six-two I don't often get the chance to be the short guy.

The view through the floor-to-ceiling windows was terrific, south down Fifth Avenue, west to the Hudson. Dirt and traffic, trouble and noise stayed on the far side of the glass. The romance of rooftops and the glitter of sun on the river were all the New York you could see from here.

When Yvonne Rome separated herself from her guests and came to the door, though, I thought maybe she'd stopped buying that romance and glitter some time ago.

It wasn't only the cast on her arm or the lump on her forehead, not just the startling white patch of bandage against the ebony skin of her jaw. It was a flatness in her eyes, an indifferent distance in her voice as she said, "So you're the detective who's supposed to get Tony out of it?"

"Bill Smith," I said. "I'm sorry for your loss. But Tony says he didn't kill your husband."

"Loss." Yvonne Rome cocked her head, as though considering a new thought. Then she shrugged, the strap of her sling rising, dropping back. "Come with me."

I followed her elegant model's slouch into a small room filled with sunshine and wicker furniture, gauze curtains and lush potted plants and watercolors of children handing each other flowers. The air was tinged with a spicy scent rising from crystal bowls of potpourri. Brick paved the floor as though this were a sunroom, a place you could just walk out into the garden from, be on solid ground, but of course it was thirty stories above Manhattan and the windows were sealed.

"Damon hated this room," Yvonne Rome told me, crossed her long legs as she sat on a wicker chaise. "He wouldn't come in here. You know Tony and I were having an affair?"

"He told me."

"The whole world probably knows, because Damon made that scene at Shots. Damon loved scenes. When he made one everyone looked at him." She leaned across her cast to slip a cigarette from a silver box beside her, held it in a languid hand. I stood, lit it for her, lit my own. Her eyebrows rose. "You smoke? No one smokes anymore. This was the only room in this whole place I was allowed to smoke." She shook her head, streamed out a plume. "Allowed. In my own house. How pathetic is that?"

"Where were you last night?"

"Where was *I*?" Her eyes widened with amusement. "This is Tony's plan, to find someone else to pin it on? *Me?*"

"My plan. Tony wouldn't do that. He says he loves you."

She shot an arrow of smoke into the room. "He'll get over it."

"Do you love him?"

"Of course not."

"Did you love Damon?"

"When I married him. You know," she said, "when we were dating he never hit me. Not once. Isn't that interesting?"

"When did he start?"

Tapping the cigarette into a silver ashtray, she said, "On our wedding night. He couldn't get it up. Not"—she gave me a sly smile—"that that was the first time. But now that we were married, it was my fault. Damon Rome," she said, leaned back on the rose-patterned cushions of the chaise, "superstud. The truth is, he wasn't very good in bed. In fact, there were times I thought about shooting him because he wasn't. You think maybe I did?"

"If I were you I might have shot him because he wasn't very nice."

She looked steadily at me, pulled on her cigarette again. "Well, you're not me," she said. "I was here last night. Ask Maria."

"That was Maria who answered the door? Would she know if you went out late?"

"My," she said, lifted her head, sank back again. "I have no idea. But ask the doorman. Ask the kid at the garage. Go ahead, ask whoever you want."

"I will. Tell me, what would have been Damon's routine, after the game?"

She used her good hand to wave away any interest in the question. "Dinner."

"At Shots?"

"Sometimes. Sometimes he'd grace some other lucky place with his glamorous presence."

"Alone?"

"Are you serious?"

"With other guys from the team?"

"Some. Most of them don't like him, you know. I believe 'grandstander' was one of the kinder words they used. Hot dog? Is that something basketball people say?"

"If it fits. Who went with him, then?"

"The really important people in Damon's life. His agent, Sam Landau. Those whores from the halftime show. I'm sorry, dancers. I think one of them is here right now, as we sit here and speak. And Randall Lee." She flashed the famous smile, made up of teeth too perfect for anyone to have been born with.

"Who's Randall Lee?"

"He's right out there." Again the indolent hand. "Go ask him."

"But not Damon's teammates?"

She shrugged. "Some of them sometimes. Nathaniel didn't mind Damon. Nathaniel's too nice a guy for this world, if you ask me, but of course you didn't."

"His sister Nora?"

"Sometimes. More to make sure that Nathaniel left at a decent hour and didn't drink too much than because she enjoyed the company."

"She didn't like Damon?"

A faint smile lifted her lips. "First of all, no one really liked Damon. Second, Nora doesn't like any of them, except Nathaniel. She's permanently angry at God and the world because they're playing and she's not. I understand she was as good as her brother. I mean, I don't know anything about basketball, of course, but that's what I've heard."

Being married to Damon Rome, I imagined, you'd have to go pretty far out of your way not to know anything about basketball. "She was better," I said.

"Oh. Well, then, I suppose it's a shame. Maybe the Knicks should try her out. To replace Damon? If she's that good. They'd still have a shot then. Everyone would be so pleased." Her tone said everyone but Yvonne Rome, who couldn't have given less of a damn.

"She was a point guard when she played," I said. "Damon was a forward."

Yvonne Rome shrugged off such petty distinctions. She tapped her cigarette against a crystal ashtray. "I thought, when I first came here," she began, but trailed off.

"You thought . . . ?"

She pinched a tiny brown leaf off an otherwise perfect ivy. "The other wives and girlfriends, they're really into the game. I have nothing to talk about with them. But Nora, I'd heard she liked flowers." She pulled her hand back into her lap and looked at me. "But she's more into the game than anyone else. Even with Nathaniel out, the team's chances are all she cares about. I should have known." She took a draw on her cigarette, blew a smoke ring. It drifted past a drawing of two bonneted little girls walking arm in arm.

I ground my own cigarette out. "Did you go to dinner with Damon?"

"Sometimes," she said.

"Did you go last night?"

"No."

"You didn't see him after he left for the game?"

"Or before. I've been avoiding him. I know it's hard to believe, avoiding someone as exciting and magnetic as the great Damon Rome. But, you know, he did break my arm."

Motive and opportunity: that was my job. Nothing Yvonne Rome had told me eliminated her from my list. I left her among the wicker and the plants and joined the somber crowd in the living room. Two more Knicks had arrived, raising the average height of the population another few inches.

At a table spread with sweets, I poured myself a cup of coffee and looked around. I spotted two unfamiliar faces. One was sweet, toffee-colored, smoothly perfect. That face was on a thin young woman in a black suit that would have been appropriate to the occasion if the skirt had been more than two inches long. She was tossing glossy curls and sharing sad thoughts about Damon Rome, or at any rate sharing something, with Luke McCroy, the Knicks' rookie shooting guard just out of Georgetown. The other strange face was much darker, belonged to a walnut-skinned man who stood alone by the window in a black suit, black silk shirt, black tie. The corner of a black handkerchief rose from his breast pocket, and his black shoes shone. His hair and mustache were salt-and-pepper. I had three or four inches on him, and he had ten or fifteen years on me, which made him the shortest and oldest man in the room. But his look held its own. I took my coffee and headed over.

"Randall Lee?" I asked.

"Well, now, that's right." He turned from the vast view, gave me a smile and raised eyebrows. "Who might you be?"

"Bill Smith. I'm investigating Damon Rome's death."

"Well, now," he said again, "that would make you not an officer of the law, wouldn't it? From what I hear, the official investigation is over and done and the bodyguard's been fingered."

"There are still some questions."

"He doesn't confirm, he doesn't deny," Lee mused, as though talking to a third person. He bit into a white-frosted petit four from a plate of them he held. "So I'm right. And you've come to talk to me. Look out, Randall Lee, you're being investigated."

"I just want to know what happened last night."

"Last night I lost seventy-eight thousand dollars."

"Sounds like a bad night."

"Average. My goal is to win more than I lose, but there are those other nights."

"We all have them."

"My stroke of good fortune was that Damon had no bets down, so of the pitifully small pile of money I did win, none of it was his. Seeing the kind of night Damon had, *that* would have been a bad night."

"Damon Rome was a gambler?"

Lee grinned. "Shocking, right?" He stuck out his hand. "Randall Lee, oddsmaker."

"You were his bookie?" I said as we shook.

"You," Lee said, "are right on top of things. I like to see that."

"Why would it have been a bad night if you'd won Damon's money?"

Lee frowned. "Could it be I was wrong about you? Think, sonny. Damon's gone. The missus feels very little sense of ob-

280 • S. J. ROZAN

ligation about Damon's debts, and I'd hardly be one to lean on her in her tragic circumstances."

"Sensitive of you."

"To my own good name, my boy. Word would get around. It wouldn't do. Nonetheless, I'm already in the unenviable position of writing off twelve thousand dollars in Damon's paper. Damon, you see, had very little sense of obligation either."

"He died owing you money?"

"If I stretch my imagination I can think of it as a marketing expense. Sadly, I don't have the imagination to handle much more than twelve thousand."

"Twelve thousand dollars sounds like a lot of marketing expense to me."

"It most certainly is. I'm not happy about it. But I suppose your next question would be, did I shoot Damon because I was sick and tired of his deadbeat ways? Did I do him dirty because he wouldn't pay up?"

"I'm not sure I would have asked that. But go ahead and answer it."

"Let me tell you something about my business, sonny." He leaned close, as though I was about to hear a trade secret. "Dead men don't pay."

Lifting his eyebrows to indicate our new brotherhood of esoteric knowledge, Randall Lee bit into another petit four.

I said, "But if Damon's debt was no good anyway, I could see writing him off, too. That way other people would have gotten the message."

Randall Lee wagged his finger. "That's the old way. In my business we have new paradigms now. Like I mentioned, Damon's debt was a marketing expense."

"Meaning?"

"Another secret you might want to know is, people are sheep," Randall Lee told me. "Randall Lee partied with Damon Rome. We ate and drank and fondled the girls. People saw us and said, 'Who's that?' and when they found out, they said, 'I want to lay off money with the guy Damon Rome lays off money with.'"

"Were you the only one?"

"Only bookie Damon had? Odds are, I am."

"Why do you say that?"

"Damon bet dumb and lost. Then he didn't pay up. I made it back in exposure: I took in more in sucker bets from his groupies than Damon owed me. Who else was hanging around? Who else was getting a public relations benefit—or anything else—from Damon, to make it worth putting up with his cavalier attitude towards his responsibilities?"

"Who was?"

"Well, now," Randall Lee said, "because you're a hardworking boy, and because I didn't kill Damon, I'll tell you who wasn't, lately."

"Okay."

He spread his arms. "Sam Landau."

"Damon's agent?"

"You see him here?"

"I wouldn't know him."

"Exhibiting good taste on your part. But his client's dead and he's not here to pay respects. I rest my case."

"Was he at dinner with Damon last night?"

Randall Lee peered at me. "A sneaky way of asking was *I* at dinner with Damon last night?"

"Were you and Landau at dinner with Damon last night?"

"Yes. Both of us. And Nathaniel." He indicated an ivory leather sofa across the room supporting Nathaniel Day's broad-shouldered bulk, his leg in its high-tech brace resting on a matching hassock. "And Luke McCroy," Lee said, pointing, "and Holly March." He nodded at the thin young woman in the skimpy skirt. "When she was an exotic dancer she called herself Holly Ivy. Personally, I prefer to think of her as Holly Cow. But brave, to show up in the widow's own lair. Where is the widow, by the way?"

"In the garden," I said. "Nora Day wasn't there? At dinner?"

"Nora wasn't a regular at Damon's table. She doesn't suffer fools gladly, and Damon was a fool. It's a shame, because I rather enjoy her company. She's a decisive young woman, and surrounded as I am in my professional life by waverers, doubters, coin tossers, and second-guessers, I find her a breath of fresh air."

I asked Randall Lee another question or two, and his answers didn't cross him off my list. He'd been the first to leave after dinner last night, had taken a cab to his Upper West Side apartment, where he lived alone. If he was fibbing about the bookie business being run along new paradigms these days, he could be said to have had both motive and opportunity. I thanked him and left him by the window admiring the view.

I wanted to talk to Sam Landau, who wasn't here, and to Nathaniel, and to Holly March and Luke McCroy, and, one by one, to the rest of Damon Rome's teammates. Nathaniel, on the sofa beside his sister, was talking to the Knicks' backup center, Shawan Powell. Powell had racked up more minutes these last two months with Nathaniel out than he had in his first three years in the NBA. He wasn't bad, but no one thought for a minute he had anything but a supporting role in the Knicks' run at the playoffs, a run that had starred the now-gone-forever Damon Rome.

I figured Nathaniel and Powell would keep for a while, and turned my attention to Holly March and Luke McCroy, he on a leather recliner, she on the arm. He said something and she gave him a soft, teasing smile. She poked him in the shoulder and said something and he laughed. He was handsome and she was beautiful and they both seemed to be admirably handling the death of Damon Rome.

They handled my approach well, too, with polite, interested looks, handshakes as I offered my name and my errand. There being no other chair in the vicinity, McCroy swung his long legs off the hassock and I sat there. Holly March stayed where she was. A sweet scent floated on the warm air, the complicated delicacy of expensive perfume.

"I understand you both went to dinner with Damon after the game last night," I said.

"That's right," said McCroy. Holly March nodded, her mahogany eyes wide to show sincerity.

"Can you tell me about it?"

"Not much to tell," said McCroy. His shaved head reflected the sunlight. "We went to Shots for some of those good steaks they have there—"

"Except for me," Holly March put in, her voice breathy and high, like a little girl's. "I had pasta. I'm a vegetarian."

I nodded; McCroy waited, eyebrows raised, in case she had more to say, but she smiled at him and looked down, as though to apologize for usurping his storytelling prerogative.

He took her hand, went on. "Then we left. Damon stayed to finish his conversation with Landau."

"Sam Landau? His agent?"

"Yeah. Damon said he needed to talk to him, privatelike."

"You know about what?"

"Uh-uh. Damon and me, we wasn't close like that."

"Can you tell me who else was at dinner?" I asked that, though I already had Randall Lee's list, just to see what McCroy would say. He said the same. Holly March used wide-eyed silence to signal agreement and traced her scarlet fingernail across the back of McCroy's hand to signal something else.

"From what I hear, not many of Damon's teammates hung out with him," I said.

"Not many liked him," McCroy said simply.

"Why?"

McCroy shrugged. "He was the man. He was the great Damon Rome. With Damon, wasn't about the game."

"What was it about?"

"Damon's stats. Damon's picture in the papers. Damon's endorsement deals. He was a damn ball hog, worse than guys on the playground."

"Doesn't sound like much of a teammate."

"Damon didn't never understand the word 'pass,' wasn't coming out of his own mouth. Dude could say, 'Give me the damn ball,' but someone else said it, he couldn't hear it."

"But you went to dinner with him. And so did Nathaniel."

"Nathaniel, he hangs with the new guys. Thinks it's his job, show us the ropes. Hangs with me, with Damon. Don't nobody piss Nathaniel off, off the court."

"And you? Damon didn't piss you off either?"

"Sure he did. I like the ball, too, sometime."

"So why did you go?"

McCroy smiled up at Holly March. "Other considerations."

"I'm sorry," I said, "but I have to ask this. I was under the impression, Ms. March, that you were seeing Damon Rome?"

She smiled. "Who told you that?" she asked gently, as though she was worried my feelings would be hurt when I found out how wrong I was.

"It's just something I heard."

"Well, we did date a little bit. A while ago. But Damon wasn't faithful. I like faithful men." She smiled again at Mc-Croy, dipped her head so her curls hid her face.

Feeling very much like I was cutting in on their dance, I said, "You dated Damon Rome before he got married?"

She looked up at me, tilted her head like she was trying to figure out where I'd gotten that idea. "No," she said. "This fall, when the season started."

It seemed it hadn't occurred to her that a married man who'd date her was by definition not a faithful man. "Was it a problem for you two, when you . . . became interested in each other?" I asked them both. "I mean, did Damon object?"

"Well," Holly March said, "maybe if Damon had known."

"He didn't?"

"That's why I went to dinner with him, and things," she explained. "He thought we were still seeing each other."

Holly March's definition of "faithful" was, I decided, fairly unique. I turned to Luke McCroy to see if he had anything to add.

Luke McCroy stared at me in silence, and then, once again, he shrugged. "Ball hogs," he said, "they don't share well."

I asked a few more questions: when had they left Shots, where had they gone? They'd left within minutes of each other, not together, they said, but had hooked up as planned in a hotel lobby on the next block. From then on until the next morning they were each other's alibi. Holly March smiled gently at me and Luke McCroy beamed at her. They seemed to have run out of things to say to me, and they obviously had a lot to say to each other. I thanked them and stood.

I was thinking to talk to Nathaniel next and I had just started over there when the housekeeper opened the door to let in someone: a white man shorter than the tall-tree Knicks around me, taller than I, with a face I knew. When he'd played, Dan Wing had been as big as you'd expect, six-four, average for the NBA in his day. But his day was twenty years ago and the players were bigger now. If he were still playing he'd be a little guy, but he was the head coach of the New York Knicks and that made him as big as anyone in the league.

I watched as Wing strode into the room, his jaw thrust forward, his brows knit, wearing that glowering look you saw courtside during the games and in front of the banner at the press conferences afterward. It was the look he'd worn as a player, too, pure concentration and intimidation. I'd always thought of it as his game face, and maybe it was, but it occurred to me now that there were people who never took their game faces off.

When Wing came in, a change seemed to come over the players, tiny shifts in stance and expression, a sense of sharpened alertness. They greeted him, nodded in his direction, went back to the conversations they'd been having, but I got the feeling that each of them knew where he was all the time, and the air became electric. Wing was a famous disciplinarian, a my-way-or-the-highway kind of coach who had taken a team of talented but not, with the exception of Nathaniel Day, brilliant players and pounded them into fiercely loyal troops, championship contenders every year he'd coached them. He put up with Nora Day because Nathaniel's contract said he had to, but he made no secret of the fact that she was a thorn in his side.

Damon Rome, acquired over Wing's objections by the Knicks' management as soon as it was clear Nathaniel was out for the season, had been another.

I waited for Wing to ask about the widow and be told she was resting. I met him at the sideboard. He poured himself a cup of coffee, picked up a crustless cucumber sandwich and glared at it.

"Coach?" I said.

Wing snapped me a suspicious look, devoured the sandwich in one bite. "Who're you?"

"Bill Smith. I'm investigating Damon Rome's death."

That didn't seem to improve his mood. "You a cop?"

"No."

"Then what are you doing?"

"I'm working for Tony Manelli's lawyer. We think they've got the wrong man."

"You do? Who do you think the right man is?"

"I don't know."

"Smith." He picked up another sandwich. "Don't fuck with my team."

"Is there a reason I should?"

"No, there's a reason you shouldn't. I can still pull this out but I'll need the men focused. They think someone thinks one of them killed Damon, they lose focus. You get it?"

"What if one of them did?"

Wing gulped some coffee. "Would have been a public service."

"You didn't like him?"

"You read the papers?"

"I understand he was disruptive."

"He was fucking uncoachable. He was a goddamn time bomb that kept going off."

"The price of a shot at the championship?"

"Screw that. I'll tell you something. Papers this morning are screaming without Rome we got no chance this year. I say with him we never had one. These guys"—he waved his coffee cup to indicate the men around us; one or two of them turned their heads—"they make a fuck of a lot more money than I do but they know who's boss. Even Nathaniel and that head-case sister of his know. Rome never knew. He thought he was paid the big bucks because he could think, not because he could shoot and rebound and mow guys down. He was pissing the other guys off and this team would have shaken itself apart before the playoffs if he kept on. I didn't want him, I won't miss him, and I don't want you fucking with anybody's head."

Wing's famous glower burned through me. "If I didn't know better," I said, "I'd think that was a motive."

"To kill him? Are you crazy?"

Wing's voice had gotten louder and a couple of Knicks turned their heads to see what was up with their coach and this stranger.

"Can you tell me where you were last night?"

He gave me the red-faced, unbelieving stare I'd seen him give refs when the call went against the Knicks. "Where *I* was? I was at the Garden until two o'clock in the fucking morning, going over game tapes, is where I fucking was."

"Anyone with you?"

"Douglas and Pontillo"—two of the assistant coaches— "left around midnight. You can't be serious?"

"No one saw you after that?"

"I got home about three. My wife and kids were asleep. I can't believe I'm even talking to you about this."

"I appreciate it, Coach," I said. "My job is to make sure Tony Manelli doesn't get nailed for something he didn't do. I'm going to keep at it. But," I added, "I'm a Knicks fan. Have been for years."

Dan Wing's glare made it clear that he'd have benched me now and traded me tomorrow, if only he could. He stalked away. A couple of players stared at me. I tried a cucumber sandwich myself, decided the bread was too soft. I checked the room again, in case someone new had arrived while I was talking to Wing.

Someone had, and he stood out even more than I did. As white as I was, as old as Randall Lee, balding and chubby, he glanced at his watch when Maria told him the widow was resting and not to be disturbed. I thought he might turn and leave, but he narrowed his eyes, peered around the room, headed for the coffee urn. I waited for him to arrive.

"Sam Landau?"

He gave me a once-over, stirred sugar into his coffee and said, "Who wants to know?" When I told him, he said, "What's to investigate? I hear Tony did it."

"Tony's been arrested for it. There's a difference."

"Not to me. Yesterday I had ten percent of Fort Knox. Today I got ten percent of bubkes. You know what's bubkes?"

"Chickpeas?"

Landau snorted. "Only looks like chickpeas. It's goat turds. Listen, Tony wants to tell his story, have him call me." Landau handed me his card.

Just what Tony wants, I thought, but I pocketed the card. "Can I ask you about dinner last night?"

"The cops already asked me. New York's Finest."

"Just to clear a few things up."

Landau picked some cookies for his saucer. "Why not? Go ahead, ask."

"Who was there?"

By now I knew the litany, but I waited to hear it. "Lee. Nathaniel. McCroy. That pretty little girl." Landau pointed people out one by one with a chocolate biscotti, then dipped it in his coffee.

"Anyone seem unhappy to you? Any tension?"

Landau bit off the biscotti's dripping end. "Damon stole Nathaniel's headlines. McCroy stole Damon's girl. Lee was out a pile of dough and Damon said yeah, yeah, he'd get around to it. Sound like a happy party to you?"

"What about you?"

"What about me?"

"You and Damon stayed after everyone else left, to talk. About what?"

"Business."

"I hear business wasn't so good."

"You hear that where?"

"From a little bird."

"I fucking hate birds. You know what's the trouble with birds? They shit all over."

"Business was fine?"

He sighed. "You any good?"

"As an investigator? Fair."

"Should I bother to lie to you?"

"It would save time if you didn't."

"Okay, then. Business stank. We just inked a deal, Nike, terrific, I'm talking multiyear, multo dinero. Suddenly, Damon's telling me Adidas makes a better shoe. Springier, he tells me, more bounce to the ounce, who the hell knows?"

"Well, if it's better—"

"Better? Shoe? Nothing to do with the shoe! Look at these feet." He waved his biscotti around again, this time at the gleaming loafers and wingtips holding down the carpet. "Guys that size, feet that size, they custom-make the shoe. Damon wants more bounce, more grip, he wants the thing to squeal like a pig or sing like a canary, Nike'll put it in for him. Had nothing to do with the shoe. It was extortion."

"He was holding Nike up?"

"Goddamn right. Add a few million or I sign with Adidas."

"Didn't he have a contract?"

"Oh, sure, he had a contract. But you're Nike, you don't want to be on the short end of a news story that the great Damon Rome wants out of an endorsement deal because he doesn't like your fucking shoe."

"So it would have worked?"

"Yeah, for him."

"Not for you? Ten percent of a few more million doesn't sound so bad."

"It would have fucked me over, is what it would have done for me. I got other clients, you know. I represent major players, all sports. Who's gonna sign a deal with any of my guys, Damon pulls this shit? No point in negotiating with Landau, he can't control his clients: it would be everywhere."

"And last night you tried to talk him out of it?"

"Right."

"And?"

Sam Landau gave me a long look. "You ever pee in the ocean?"

"Uh-huh."

"Made you feel better, right? But it didn't matter a damn to the ocean."

I asked Landau the same question I'd been asking everyone else: where he was when Damon Rome died.

"On my way home."

"You and he left Shots together?"

"Are you kidding? I was so pissed I got up and stomped out. Small satisfaction but you get 'em where you can."

"Anyone see you on your way home?"

"How the hell do I know? I drove, probably not."

"Where was your car?"

"Right there. Garage around the block."

Landau ate a few more cookies and I asked a few more questions. His answers put him right where I'd been hired to put people, right where I'd been able to put the others. He had a reason to be furious with Damon Rome and no alibi for the time of his death. He didn't give any more than a philosophical shrug to the implications of my questions, but he didn't seem sorry to see me walk away either.

Nathaniel Day hadn't stirred from the white sofa, nor had his sister, but the seat next to Nathaniel was empty. I went over, offered my hand.

"Bill Smith," I said. "I'm investigating Damon Rome's death. I'd like to ask you a few questions. But first I want to tell you what a big fan I am of yours." I turned to Nora Day. "And of yours. I watched you play in college."

Ice in her voice, Nora Day said, "Long time ago."

Nathaniel Day was not a handsome man, but his wide smile and crooked nose had dominated the sports pages, and occasionally the front pages, of New York's newspapers for so long that it was hard not to think of him as someone I knew, could just sit down and chat with, talk plays and ball handling, ask for tips on my hook shot. Nathaniel's nose had been broken, fa-

mously, in a high school tournament game he'd refused to come out of. He'd claimed it didn't hurt, was just a bump. Then, because he was afraid a doctor would forbid him to play, he put off seeing one until the tournament was over. The first time New York had seen that wide smile was two weeks later, when Nathaniel Day, a sophomore at Christ the King and already a star, waved the trophy over his head.

He gave me a smaller version of that smile now, offered the seat on the sofa beside him. His sister gave me a cold look, one that said easygoing friendliness was not a coin with much value in her realm. I was familiar with that look, too, had seen it on TV, as Nora Day followed the games.

I sat, shifted to face the two of them. Nora Day, her voice as chilly as her look, said, "I thought I heard they arrested Tony Manelli this morning."

"I'm working for his lawyer. We think they have the wrong man."

"Why?" She sipped her coffee. She was darker skinned than her brother, and better looking, but even seated, her height and her don't-mess-with-me eyes created the sense of more space around her, perhaps, than there actually was.

"For one thing, he says he didn't do it."

She gave a scornful laugh. "Do people often say they did?"

"Sometimes. Sometimes they find they didn't count on the guilt."

"Well," she said, "maybe Tony doesn't feel guilty."

"Maybe. Or maybe he's not. Can I ask you some questions?"

Nora sipped more coffee, didn't answer.

Nathaniel said, "Don't mind her." He grinned good-naturedly, a younger brother who'd known, and shrugged off, his older sister's moodiness all his life. "What do you want to know?" Nora rolled her eyes, an older sister who'd known, and been short-tempered with, her younger brother's affability since he was a baby.

"You went to dinner with Damon last night?"

"Sure."

"And you," I said to Nora, "didn't?"

She turned her icy gaze on me, said, "I don't go out after the games."

I nodded, said to Nathaniel, "Luke McCroy and Holly March were there? And Randall Lee and Sam Landau?"

"That's right."

"Anyone else?"

"No."

"Did Damon have a new security detail?"

"No. He said bad enough a guy tried to beat your time, you didn't have to pay him for it."

"What happened after dinner?"

"After? I went home kind of early. Had to put my damn leg up. Holly left, and Luke, just before me. Randall Lee was long gone."

"Anyone see you after you left?"

Nora cut into her brother's answer. "Wait—what are you saying?"

"My job is to find out what happened last night," I said.

"You cannot—can*not*—be saying Nat may have shot Damon?"

"No," I said. "I'm asking if anyone saw him after he left. Did you?"

"Me?"

"Don't you have apartments in the same building? Did you see him coming home?"

"I didn't stay in New York last night," Nora admitted grudgingly. "I went to Connecticut, to my house. But there's no way Nat—"

"Come on, calm down, Nora. It's the man's job," Nathaniel said soothingly. Nora, her glare fixed on me, didn't seem soothed. Nathaniel turned to me. "I took a cab, went straight to my place," he said.

"You take down the cab number, keep the receipt, anything like that?"

"No. But you want to, I'll bet you could find the driver. I'm a little hard to miss." He gave me the grin again.

I had to grin back. "That's true. Okay, tell me more about dinner. Was anyone acting strange? Upset, on edge?"

Nathaniel shook his head cheerfully. "Only me."

"Oh, for Christ's sake, Nat!" Nora snapped.

"Hey, it's true."

"Why were you?" I said.

Nathaniel lifted his aluminum cane, pointed to his immobile leg. "Sometimes I get pissed off."

"Must be frustrating," I agreed.

"Frustrating?" Nora Day looked at me as if I'd told her that water was wet or fire could burn. "He's out for the season," she explained carefully, as though I must not have known that or I'd never have said anything so patronizing and dumb.

"It's not that bad," said Nathaniel calmly. "I'll be back next year. Could've been worse, could've been serious. Just sometimes I get pissed off."

"Yeah," I said. "I saw you fling a chair the other night."

Nathaniel's smile turned abashed. "When Shawan missed that alley-oop?"

"You'd have made it."

"That's why I threw the chair. Told him I was sorry, later. Wasn't him. He said he knew that. Nice guy, Shawan."

"What about Damon? I hear he wasn't a nice guy."

"Damon was okay. He was just young. He just needed to understand what it is about a team."

"Meaning what?"

"My brother," Nora Day said between clenched teeth, "thinks it's his job to make Knicks out of jackasses."

"I'm sorry?"

Nathaniel said, "Some young guys, they come into the league, they think it's all about them. Damon was a great player. So far he was carrying us, nobody even missed me."

"That's just wrong, Nat!" His sister's coffee cup rattled as she put it down. "You're the man. You're the one they need!"

"I think she's right," I said. "Everyone's waiting for you to come back."

"Well, thank you." He grinned again, and Nora looked at me as though, in a move that had caught her completely off guard, I'd finally said something intelligent. "But what I mean," Nathaniel went on, "Damon loved the spotlight. If he kept on the way he started, hogging and hotdogging, team was going to fall apart, right around the playoffs. I wanted to make him see that."

"Did he?"

"He was coming around. I was working on him for a while. He was getting better."

"I just talked to Coach Wing. He doesn't think so. He said Damon was ruining the team."

"Great coach, Coach Wing. Guess he can be a little blind sometimes, though. Damon was coming along. You saw that, right?" He turned to Nora.

"Damon," she said, "was a nasty, selfish, ball-hogging child. That's all he was."

Nathaniel turned back to me, winked. "Coming along."

"Well, thanks," I said. "Anything else you can tell me?"

"No. Got to say Tony's okay, though. I'd be surprised, turned out he did kill Damon."

"Is there anyone you wouldn't be surprised to find that out about?"

After a hesitation Nathaniel shook his head. "Surprise me, anyone I know *does* turn out to be the one. Walk up to a man, middle of the night, pull a trigger on him? That's cold."

Nora snorted. "*You* think. Most people wouldn't have trouble with that."

"Anyone in particular?" I asked her.

"I barely knew him," she told me. "But it seemed to me a lot of people wanted a lot of things from Damon, and everywhere except on the court, he was a big disappointment."

★   ★   ★

I stayed at Yvonne Rome's for a few hours more. People came and went, and I talked to them all. Most of them had disliked Damon Rome, some mildly, some intensely. Most of them didn't have much in the way of an alibi for the middle of the night. After the game the players had gone to get dinner or driven back to their suburban homes or taken limos or cabs to their city apartments. Some had walked, the way Damon was doing when he was killed. Some had no doubt been seen, but it wasn't my job to find the people who'd seen them. On my way out I talked to Yvonne Rome's doorman and garage attendant, and I went over and talked to the guy at the garage where Sam Landau's car had been. I called Dan Wing's wife and went up to Randall Lee's building and later that night I spoke to the concierge at the hotel where Holly March had hooked up with Luke McCroy. I checked gun registrations: two of the Knicks owned .38s, though neither was a Smith & Wesson, and five others owned other guns, and those were just the New York permits. I looked at arrest records, too, and found one assault, a few drunk-and-disorderlies, one or two DWIs. No convictions except for Shawan Powell, thirty days' suspended sentence on one of the D&Ds from his pre-Knick days. I called John Sutton the next morning, gave him a preliminary report.

"Sounds like a lot of people wanted a lot of things from Rome that they didn't get," he said.

"Seems to have been Rome's specialty," I agreed.

"Also seem to have been a lot of people who didn't like him, wandering around loose in the middle of the night."

I followed the preliminary up with a detailed package by the end of the day. Sutton called me that evening to say charges against Tony Manelli had been dropped, "pending further police investigation." Which, according to Sutton, had started up already, cops swarming the Garden, interviewing Knicks and trainers, wives and girlfriends. Beer guys and janitors, too, probably.

"You want me to stay on it?" I asked. "I've got a list of things I didn't do yet, stuff I'd have gone into deeper if I'd been looking to solve the case, not just muddy the waters."

"I'll let you know, but I don't think so. I don't really care what they find as long as they don't come back at Tony again. We embarrassed them, let's leave them alone for now. Go ahead and send your bill."

"Forget it. Professional courtesy, for Tony."

"That won't make him happy."

"Someday I'll need him, he can do the same."

When I hung up I did some paperwork, cleaned up some loose ends on other cases. About eight I went down to Shorty's, sat at the bar, drank bourbon and listened to the talk. The Knicks game, on the TV over the bar, was the topic, and the opinion of everyone was the same: they stank.

They were at the Garden, playing Indiana. They wore black ribbons on their shirts and Dan Wing wore one pinned to his lapel. The dancers, including Holly March, wore them on their spangled leotards. I wondered if Sam Landau and Randall Lee were wearing black, too.

The Knicks were bad. They fell apart. Some of the fans wore black ribbons or black armbands, and one of the guys at the bar wondered aloud if those were for Damon or for the Knicks. The team had been built around Nathaniel Day, guys pointed out to each other, and they hadn't had much trouble learning to feed Damon Rome and get out of his way, but now they had no star and Wing's adjustments, his furious coaching, the players' hunger, it just wasn't enough. Without a franchise player they didn't know what to do; they were lost, and it showed.

I didn't know what to do either; I was lost, too.

It wasn't good enough, this business of finding other people with as much motive and opportunity as Tony Manelli had. Good enough for Tony and his lawyer; they just wanted Tony free. And good enough, it seemed, for most of the people I'd spoken to. None of them seemed particularly bothered about the question of who'd killed Damon Rome. His death had consequences in everyone's life and they were all handling those as they had to, but no one had liked Damon enough that they were burning with a need to know what had happened to him.

I hadn't known him, and I probably wouldn't have liked him. But I didn't like walking away in the middle like this.

Not your job, Smith, I told myself. I sipped my drink, tried to settle back, tried to watch the game. I saw the Knicks falter, surge forward, fail. They were never really in the game; they lost. I finished my drink, said my good-byes, went upstairs.

The Knicks began a road trip the next day, three games in four days, and I saw the games, watched them lose two of the three, pull the last one out as a squeaker against an under-.500 team they hadn't lost to in three seasons. I wondered whether the NYPD sent cops along to question potential suspects or just waited for the team to come back to town, because at what these guys were being paid to play they weren't much of a flight risk. I wondered how the young detective, Mike Beam, was doing under the ferocious glare of Dan Wing. The day the Knicks came back to town I called him, to ask.

"You're not a guy I'm happy to hear from," he told me.

"I'm feeling guilty."

"Why? Your guy did it and you're ready to give him up now?"

"He didn't. But I know Wing worried a long investigation would make the players lose their focus and I'll bet you're even less popular at the Garden right now than I'd be in your squad room."

"That would be a toss-up."

"You getting anywhere?"

"You call just to give me a hard time?"

"No," I said. "You may not buy this and there's no reason you should, but this thing is eating me. Nobody liked the guy

and the only ones who miss him are Knicks fans, but somebody walked up to him on the street and shot him. It wasn't
Tony Manelli but I'd like to know who it was. If I can help, let
me know."

In a guarded voice he said, "I have the report you gave
Manelli's lawyer. You know anything that's not in it?"

"No."

"Then you've been enough help, thanks."

"Sorry."

"Listen," he conceded, "you could be right. Rome seems to
have let down a lot of people on a lot of fronts. When I find
the one fed up enough to kill him, that'll be my guy. *Your* guy's
not out of the running, by the way."

"Yeah," I said, "I figured. Okay, just thought I'd call."

We hung up, neither of us sure what I'd wanted. Beam went
back to the business of investigating Damon Rome's murder
and I went back to the business of doing other things. That
night when the game came on I didn't go down to Shorty's. I
poured myself my own bourbon and sat on my couch and
watched the Knicks take on Houston. It was no contest; they
were disorganized, had no rhythm, nothing worked for them,
and by halftime they were getting slaughtered. The cameras
showed Wing glowering, Nathaniel on the bench shouting and
pounding chairs. Nora Day, behind him, silently followed every
play, as usual. Luke McCroy had stepped up and was playing
well, and so were Shawan Powell and a couple of others, but it
wasn't enough. The dancers, led by an almost frantic Holly
March, tried to get the crowd into it, but the crowd saw what I
saw and wasn't having any. I watched the start of the third
quarter, the miscommunicated passes and the turnovers, heard
the boos from the crowd at the rushed shots that wouldn't

drop, the easy layups missed, and all of a sudden, in the kind of shift that makes figure become ground, ground become the sharp center of focus, I knew what had happened.

It wasn't what I'd been told and it wasn't what I'd said. Damon Rome hadn't been killed because of what he didn't do. He'd been killed because of what he did.

* * *

I didn't sleep well that night. The next morning, I went back to the list I had of things I hadn't done yet, people I hadn't spoken to. Carefully, I started doing some of those things. I checked more gun registrations, went and talked to more doormen, more garage attendants, prowled the streets near Shots and near the Garden again. I talked to winos and losers and cold-eyed kids looking for the main chance. I was hoping to be wrong but I was right. That night I watched the game, and when it was close to finished—the Knicks again in the hole— I grabbed my jacket, headed to the Garden.

Once there, I didn't go in; I set myself at the players' door, the place where autograph hounds wait, missing the end of the game for a chance to get near their heroes.

About an hour after I got there the heroes started to come out. Powell, McCroy, the others who'd played. Nathaniel, with his cane, surrounded by the largest crowd. Because of what had happened to Rome, security was tight, but each player had the chance to sign autographs or refuse to, to talk to his fans or duck into a waiting limo. I watched them make their choices according to their nature, watched guys sign a few and then wave as they left, or scowl and walk right past their fans, while Nathaniel stayed and signed as long as there were fans who wanted him.

When the crowds thinned out I stepped forward. Not to speak to Nathaniel, who, with the famous smile, climbed into a white limo and was gone. The fans drifted away then, and the players' door opened again, and I was left alone with the person I'd come to see.

Nora Day, six inches taller than I, pushed through the deserted doorway and strode quickly along the sidewalk. Dawdling and daydreaming were not part of her game; she'd been tall for a point guard but magically fast in sizing up situations, creating plays, making opportunities for her teammates where you'd swear none could be found.

She did that now: I was the situation, and she sized me up, fixed me with that icy glare as I stepped into her path. "What do you want?" she asked, but I was sure she already knew.

"Team's not doing well," I said. "Championship shot seems to be gone this year."

"They never had one. Not without Nat."

"That's not true, is it? They had a damn good shot without him and that was the problem."

Nora Day's eyes flashed. "What the hell do you want?" she asked again.

"Were those Damon's last words?" I said. "Did he say, 'Nora, what the hell do you want?' just before you shot him?"

She regarded me silently. When she finally answered, it was in a voice as cold as the winter night we stood in. "No. No, he said, 'This team's mine. You and your gimp brother ought to be looking around for someplace else to play.'"

"And that's it? You were afraid Damon would replace Nathaniel as the Knicks' go-to guy?"

"Afraid?" From her height she looked down at me as she always had at the world. "No, I wasn't *afraid*. New York loves

Nat. When he comes back no one will remember Damon Rome ever existed."

"Then why?"

Nora Day looked up at the darkened Garden, out at the empty street. "That ring is Nat's," she said. "For eight years we've been promising New York a championship. We'll deliver."

"You'll deliver." I nodded. "Not Damon Rome."

"That ring is Nat's," she repeated.

"He'd have had one if they'd won this year. He's a Knick, playing or not."

"He wouldn't have earned it. He wouldn't have been the one to bring it home."

"And New York would have known that. Everyone would have known the Knicks could do it without Nathaniel."

Lights in the stairwells of the Garden began snapping off, now that the players and the fans were gone. I hunched into my jacket; a wind had come up. Nora Day said, "Everyone? You really think I care about everyone and what they know?"

I didn't answer. A car rolled by; at the end of the block a drunk staggered, not sure where he was going. Nora said softly, "Nat would have known."

"Would have known what? That other people can play the game, too? I got the feeling he knows that already. It doesn't seem to bother him."

"He would have known," her words came slowly, "that he was expendable."

I looked at her eyes. In my mind I saw those eyes, over the years, fixed on the weaknesses in the Knicks' offense, the holes in their defense. I thought about how, over each season, those weaknesses had been covered and those holes filled by skills Nathaniel polished up.

"You were a great player," I said. "A legend. But when you came out of school, you had nowhere to go."

She stared at me steadily. A sheet of old newspaper brushed the sidewalk as it blew up to us, and then swirled past.

"Get out of my way," Nora Day said. She cut around me, strode down the block.

I kept pace, said nothing, until finally, without slowing, she asked, "What are you going to do?"

"I don't know."

"You have nothing."

"That's not true. My fault, I didn't check you out the first time around, but I did today: you have a permit for a Smith & Wesson .38. The one they found has no numbers, but still, where's yours? Could you produce it if you had to?"

She wheeled on me, glaring.

"And your car," I said. "Everyone in New York knows you don't go up to the house in Connecticut during the season, but you went that night. So your doorman here wouldn't see you come in late, right? But the car—you took it out of the garage right after the game. And then parked it on the street two blocks from here. The police can get your E-ZPass records. They'll show what time you actually left New York."

"You're bluffing."

"I have a witness. A kid who was considering jacking your car, until he saw you walking toward it. About two a.m."

"It's still nothing. All of this, it's nothing."

"That won't take you far. The police can see what I saw, once they look. They'll figure it out, too."

I said that, but I wasn't sure it was true, if I didn't point them in the right direction. Nora Day's face stretched into a cold smile. She turned, walked away without looking back. I stopped where I was, watched her stride, arrow-straight, down the empty sidewalk. I wondered what it felt like to know, absolutely know, what the right play was.

I never found out. At the diner the next morning I heard the news: in the middle of the night, on her way to her secluded Connecticut home, Nora Day's SUV, running much too fast over a deserted stretch of highway, had jumped off the road, hit a tree, smashed like a tin can. Another tragedy for the Knicks, people said; my God, what are they, cursed? And it's strange, said the guy at the counter next to me, I thought she stayed in the city during the season, only used the country place during the All-Star break, the summer, things like that. Yeah, said the waitress, pouring us both more coffee, and I read once she was a real careful driver. Nathaniel used to go nuts anytime they had to go someplace together, because of how slow and careful she took it, that's what I read. Well, said the other guy, lucky they weren't together last night. You can write off the Knicks this season, he said, but with Nathaniel healthy next year, they'll be back. This'll be hard on him, but he's got the stuff. You think? said the waitress. I mean, she's his sister. Well, sure he'll miss her, the guy said, but he'll find out he don't need her, as a coach, I mean. They both looked at me, but I was busy with my coffee. From the cash register by the window, the owner nodded his agreement. Yeah, he said. Yeah, she was great. But she wasn't indispensable.

IN THE ZONE

Justin Scott

Scottie Pippen elbowed him in the grill when the ref wasn't looking, busted him so hard that Shorty felt tears swarming into his eyes like he was still a little kid playing B-ball back in the projects.

"Wha'd you do that for?' Shorty yelled, but the pack was already kickin' downcourt and Pippen never heard. Must have been an accident. Scottie was his friend. Besides, who played for blood in a charity National Basketball Association All-Star Game at Madison Square Garden?

They were all his friends. All the stars. Chris Webber, Shaquille O'Neal, Karl Malone, Allen Iverson, Kevin Garnett, John Stockton, Allan Houston, Latrell Sprewell. The top of the top, the best of the best. ESPN called them the finest ten players ever in one game. Webber, O'Neal, Malone, Iverson, Garnett, Stockton, Houston, Pippen, and Shorty O'Tool, who had come a long, long way from hooping ratball in the hood.

Some guys bitched about wasting their downtime on charity. Said they needed the rest. Who wanted to tear his ACL or bust a finger for nothing? But their agents said do it, their business managers said do it, and their publicity guys said do it. Even Shorty's mother said do it: take folks' minds off the gambling thing.

Besides, All Stars got tons of TV face time; and dinner with the mayor; and lunch with the president. Then, down in Florida, the whole Disney World wide open for them and their folks. Just for playing for free for fifty million fans national and twenty thousand screaming in the Garden.

Loose ball! Shorty floated through the pack, scooped it like an orange in his huge hand. Too far out to shoot? Think so, Latrell? He faked right, like he was heading in. Think so, Chris? He faked right again, like he was fading back.

> *Psyched 'em out so far away,*
> *Two by two, like Dr. J.*

Sprewell and Webber were still guarding air when Shorty powered off the floor. Jumper. In!

Karl Malone banged him on the butt. "All right, kid!"

They called him kid—not because he was the littlest, not at seven feet two inches—but the youngest. Always the youngest. Always all-world game. Youngest varsity at Clinton, youngest starting center at St. John's, youngest captain of the Knicks, youngest All-Star ever.

He took a pass from Karl, passed to Allen Iverson, drove toward the basket, and went up to meet Allen's pass back to him. In!

"All right, kid!"

Youngest and dumbest. No denying Shorty O'Tool was newjack. The gamblers knew. They'd seen him coming.

What did people expect? Seeing his daddy gunned down,

right before his eyes, when Shorty was ten years old. Try and forget, his mama always said. He did try. Playing hoops made it seem so long ago. But off the court, it still dragged him down. Off the court, bad memories stayed sharp as knives.

Dirty yellow Electra 225 ghetto sled rolling up. Driver doing a gangsta lean, low over the passenger seat. Shoulda known. Shoulda warned Daddy. But he was too busy boasting how the teacher said he was so good in school. Besides, the scarface in the Buick's backseat wasn't even wearing shades. No cap, no skully, nothing covering his face. Looked like just another permafried crackhead grinning big and laughing loud. And Shorty grins back at the man, thinking it's a joke, never knowing it's a hooptie ride, until the Tec-9 is pointing out the window.

Daddy holding his hand. Tec-9 sprays *bayaka-bayaka*. Still holding Shorty's hand when the slugs thud into him, shaking his huge, hard body like kicks and punches. Still holding Shorty's hand as he starts to fall.

The scarface sees Shorty's seen him. Opens up again to spray the kid, too. *Bayaka-bayaka*. Slug plucks Shorty's sleeve. Another sears his cheek. But Daddy's pushing him down, falling on him hard and heavy, protecting him under his chest.

Bayaka-bayaka. Daddy twitching and shaking, taking the bullets until the thunderous *boo-yaa* of a Mossberg twelve-gauge slams him to pieces like an earthquake.

What'd you see? said the boys in blue.

Nothin', he saw nothin', says Shorty's mother.

"Yes, I did! I saw him, Mama, I saw him."

The cops get a lady with a computer and when Shorty tells her what he saw, damn! the scarface is staring from the screen like he was looking out his window.

Everybody sees them come home to Grandma's in the police car. Grandma says, "Don't you worry, child. You'll be safe.
God will protect you on angels' wings."

"Like they protected his daddy?" Mama cries, bent over the
table, her face all wet.

Grandma puts him to sleep on her couch, hugs him close
and explains. "Your mama's very sad. She doesn't know what
she's saying. Don't you listen to her. You listen to me and listen
hard. God will protect you on angels' wings."

"Why didn't angel wings protect Daddy?"

"Your daddy was a great big man. Too heavy to lift. Angels
protect little boys, like you, who done no wrong." She passes
her hand over his eyes. "Sleep."

That same night, when the boys in blue are still sitting outside the building in their car, a guy comes pounding Grandma's
door. "They gonna getcha! They gonna wetcha!"

Mama and Shorty bail out, run for it before the gangstas
cap him for a witness. Hiding out in men's apartments. Couldn't
go to family. The gangstas were waiting. They knew who's
Shorty's grandma. They know his aunts. Ran all the way to the
Bronx.

Scarface came to the Bronx.

Cops didn't care. Court didn't care. Social worker didn't
care. Maybe God cared. Maybe it was God who gave Shorty
the eyes to scope their rusted old deuce-and-a-quarter in time
to drag his mother down into the subway. C train. A train. All
the way to Brooklyn.

L train. Caught sleeping on the late train. Cops dump them
at the homeless shelter. Gangstas *own* the homeless shelter.
PATH train over to Jersey City. Chilltown. Mama doing what
she had to for any man who didn't know them, just to give

them a room to hide. Men who think she's nothing but a skeegers giving sex for dope.

Finally there came a day when Shorty knew he couldn't stand running anymore. And that very night, God sent a fire on angels' wings, burned down a crack house and fried the gangsta who shot his father.

Like magic, all is well. Shorty and Mama go home. Shorty back to school, scared no more, back to B-ball—Clinton High, summer leagues. No more jumping at shadows. No more seeing Mama afraid.

Told the St. John's scout that he believed in God and owed Him and His angels big-time. Full scholarship! Turned pro in his freshman year. Knicks. Champs. All-Stars.

Gamblers. Scarfaces following him around again. Just like when the gangstas shot his father, all those years ago. Wouldn't believe how much you could lose before they said, Pay up. Pay up. Pay up or die. Pay up—hey, relax, kid. No die. Shave a point.

Shave a point? *Shave a point.* This was the NBA, not some peckerwood college league. Shave a point? You crazy.

Three points. One missed jumper, for chrissake, Shorty. White guy named Joey. What's the big deal? One little shot off the rim. Wipes out a million bucks. You go home free, buy your mom another house.

He was newjack. Young and dumb. Maybe he shouldn't have clocked the gambler. Couldn't stop himself. All that stuff came up about his daddy and he just clocked him.

Blood bubbling from his lips, white boy screaming he'd have Shorty killed. Shorty laughing, "You gonna kill a twenty-million basketball star?" Busts Joey again. Feels so good he waxes the floor with him. Erased the past with the gambler's face.

"I kill you," Joey screams, spitting teeth. "You're one dead nigger."

Shorty laughs. He's so far above this.

But *damn* if next day four hard-rock diesel dudes in a Lincoln Navigator don't roll by the big house he bought his mama in Great Neck. *Great Neck! Strong Island!* Could not believe that he was looking over his shoulder again. Seemed so long ago.

But finally, today, all is well again. Things is dope. Because today Shorty's playing with the All-Stars in Madison Square Garden. No way Joey Cascone is moving on Shorty in the Garden. No way dudes in a Navigator are popping him anywhere, anytime, nohow. Now Shorty's rich. Now his manager hires security guys, guys with legal guns and headsets and earpieces watching his back. Used to be Secret Service, said his manager. Watched the president's back. Now they watch yours. You too valuable to get smoked. So chill. Gambler Joe's ass is waxed, says Shorty's agent. All you got to do is get in the zone. Hold on to the game. Everything's cool. Just stay in your zone.

All is well, said his mama. Things is dope, at last.

Sprewell shot, missed. Shorty popped up for the rebound and the fans hollered as he wiped the glass.

Boom. Another elbow. Shaquille O'Neal's, so hard it felt like he'd cracked a rib.

"What are you doin'?" Shorty gasped. "It's the lousy All-Stars!"

He wrestled the ball from Shaq, thinking, I'll send you back to school, nigga, front of the whole damn Garden. He went around him like Shaq's dogs were nailed to the wooden floor.

Fast break!

Malone goes, "Gimme the rock!"

Shorty, Malone, Shorty, Iverson: pass, receive, pass, receive. Barrel down the lane. Up! And jam a deep, deep *dunk*!

The fans went wild. It felt like they'd shake down the Garden walls with their stompin' and hollerin'. Folks had seen those elbows—even if the ref was blind. They were rooting for Shorty O'Tool, who could take a hit and keep playing.

But it was getting harder to stay in his zone. His ribs ached. His lips stung. He could taste blood. And here Latrell Sprewell came humming, like he was looking to bust him again. And the damn ref was looking the other way.

"What are you doing? Latrell?"

Latrell goes, point-blank, "Your mama's a strawberry."

"Oh yeah? Your mama's a bag bride."

"Your mama's a buffer."

"Your mama's a skeegers."

Then Shaq nailed him right to the floor:

> *"You wish you was taller,*
> *you wish you was a baller."*

Hard to remember he was playing Madison Square Garden instead of ratball, cold hoopin' it on busted asphalt.

"Shorteeeeeee!"

The ref was blowing his whistle. Manager was calling time.

"Your mama's calling," mocked Shaq. "She back at the fence again, going, 'Shortee, Shortee, Shortee.'"

Shorty O'Tool screwed his eyes shut and tried with all his might to get back in his zone. But when he listened for the fans it was the trucks and buses on Ninth Avenue that filled his ears. When he opened his eyes the rippling sea of fans in the bleachers had hardened into the housing project walls. Down at his feet, hoping for Nikes on gleaming hardwood, he found tattered sneakers on cracked asphalt.

Shorty walked slowly to the chain-link fence that separated

the narrow playground from Ninth Avenue. His mother was standing stiff and scared with the social worker. And there was absolutely no denying that he was still only ten years old and tired to death of running.

★ ★ ★

The social worker was all his fault. He'd begged and begged his mother could he go to school. No one knew them in this neighborhood. It was safe—the project was surrounded by rich people in fancy houses with iron garden gates and bushes and Christmas wreaths hung on the doors.

School was safe, he pleaded. They'd never look for him in a school with rich kids. Finally his mother relented. And damn if in two days there isn't a social worker all over his mother bitchin' that the teacher says Shorty is "depressed."

The social worker came at him with questions, right through the playground fence. He stared at his sneakers. Water running along the sidewalk smelled of fish from the wholesaler next door. He spoke when he had to.

Yes, ma'am. No, ma'am. Yes ma'am. No ma'am.

She kept humming at him. "How often do you see your father?"

Shorty looked carefully at his mother. She stuck a tissue through the chain-link fence and dabbed a drop of blood from his lip. Her eyes were dead, a silent warning. Running so long, they could say what they were thinking with a look. "Don't tell. Don't trust her. Don't trust no one."

He hung his head. "No, lady. He don't come 'round no more."

"When did you last see him?"

Again his mother's warning.

"I don't remember."

"Last year," said his mother.

"Yeah. Christmas. He came by." This was lies. It was making his father sound like he hadn't held his hand when they walked down the street. Like he didn't come home almost every night. Like they didn't watch B-ball on TV. Like his father wasn't gonna take him to a Knicks game the day they shot him. Like he couldn't buy two tickets to Madison Square Garden.

"Go back to your game," said the social worker. "I have to talk to your mother."

Like his mother would hear her, while she was twirling her head looking everywhere to make sure they were okay.

Round ball! Coming at him. Hustling downcourt, the Garden a wall of hollering faces. Shorty O'Tool, fast break down the lane. Takes it to the rack.

Shaq yells, "Your daddy was a zoomer."

"You lying. You don't even know my daddy."

"My cuz at Queensbridge tole me."

Home. The Queensbridge project. Shorty wanted to give up and die. No way to get away. Seemed like everybody knew somebody somewhere. He looked over at the fence. The social worker was talking. His mother's head was ducked down like a turtle. But she was watching the street.

"Cuz tole me your daddy was a zoomer."

"My daddy never sold fake rock."

"How you know that?" said Shaq.

"Mama told me he was a thoroughbred."

"Thoroughbred?" Shaq laughed in his face.

Shorty's shoulders sagged even as he forced himself to step close to the taller boy. "I'll bust you in the grill, Shaq. My mama don't lie."

"Why you callin' me Shaq? My name's Junior."

"Knuckle up!"

Junior Brown laughed again. "Knuckle up? Who you kidding, Shorty? You can't scrap a lick."

"I can't care how big you are, Junior. Knuckle up. My mama don't lie."

"Oh yeah? Well, tell me this, before I clean your clock. If your daddy was a thoroughbred that sold good dope, how come he got popped?"

Shorty couldn't speak. It was like the wind got kicked out of him. And suddenly he needed help so bad he could cry. He looked around.

The ref was curled up under a broken bench, hugging an empty bottle of Colt 45. He looked at the other kids, looked for a friend. But he was newjack, and they didn't know him. They were scoping his tears and gasfacing him, waiting to watch Junior Brown wax his ass. Junior stood a head taller. He had fists all knuckly, sharp-edged like crushed beer cans.

"My mama don't lie," Shorty said. Trembling, he raised his fists.

A big kid rolled up. Twelve years old, too old for B-ball with the little guys. He had a smooth round face and a kind smile. He'd had his head shaved for lice, bald as Michael Jordan. "Yo, Junior, give the little guy a break. All of you. Just play ball and chill."

All the kids stared at him. Nobody moved. Till Michael Jordan lifted Junior Brown off the court by his shirt and said in his face, *"Get out there and hoop!"*

Junior, Lester, Enrique, and Shawn ran onto the court. Shorty hung back, trying to see where his mother had gone. Michael Jordan nudged him, whispered, "Go on, get out there.

I got my eye on you. Me and Magic Johnson are starting a new squad. All-Star All-Stars.

> *"The best of the rest.*
> *They dream on my team."*

"All right!"

Shorty pulled the game back around him like putting on a coat. Fans were hollering, getting wild. Up in the project walls, the windows were melting into a cheering blur. Roaring, louder than the bus and the fish trucks.

Round ball! Coming at him, fills his hands like his hands and basketballs were made in the same factory, like computers shaped them to fit, like he was born to *jump.*

Missed. Rim ball. Shorty's there for the rebound, drives around Shaq, takes Scottie Pippen to the rack. Up and . . . *Dunk!*

Can't hear himself think over the cheering. "Shorty!" they're hollering. "Shorr-tee! Shorr-tee!"

He waves up at the stands and sees twenty thousand fans going wild. All but one. One's just staring.

"Mama!" He looks for his mother. She's watching the other way.

One out of twenty thousand is still as ice. Watching, tracking him, tracking Shorty O'Tool like he's a cat and Shorty's a rat. A face so still that all the other faces seem to dissolve and blend into one thin sheet of cloth, like curtains blowing from an open window.

Shaquille O'Neal yells, "Look out. Where he going?"

The big Lincoln Navigator is circling the court, rolling right through the stands. People are running and screaming. It bounces over the guardrail onto the court. "Run, Shorty! Run!" Shaq throws an arm over his shoulder, screaming, "Run, run." But Shorty is frozen to the floor. It's not possible. This can't be happening. Right here in the Garden.

"Shorty! Run!"

His mother screams. He sees her on the edge of the court, clawing the chain-link fence, screaming, "Run, run," so hard that she doesn't see another scarface creeping up behind her.

The fans throw themselves under the broken benches, yelling, "Gun! Gun! Gun!"

The ref sinks into the body of the drunk again. Shorty's friends the All-Stars—Shaq and Webber and Houston and Pippen—scatter with Junior, Lester, Enrique, and Shawn. And Madison Square Garden goes dark as a busted TV as the big Navigator turns into a rusty yellow deuce-and-a-quarter Buick filled with the gangstas who killed his father.

"Run, Shorty, run."

"Mama!"

When at last Shorty runs he runs toward his mother. He hears the Tec-9 going *buyaka-buyaka*.

Just like when they capped Daddy. The bullets hit like punches, knock his eighty pounds through the air, smash the air out of his chest. The asphalt's jumping at his face.

But suddenly the fans are going crazy, screaming, lifting him with their cheers. He's flying, rising over the court, over the garden, searching for that open place.

Something happening behind the chain-link fence. Frantic, desperate motion. Then the *boo-yaa, boo-yaa* thunder of the twelve-gauge Mossberg pump. Then cops all over, running, shooting.

The boys in blue too late for you.

Too late for us.

But his mother is rising, too. She's coming with him. The court's wide open. He sees his shot.

Gimme the rock.

Shaq to Magic to Michael Jordan.

To Shorty.

Jumper.

In!

BUBBA

Stephen Solomita

The way it goes down, I'm more than ready. The moron's been riding me since the first minute of the first quarter. He does not shut up, not for a minute. *You got nothin', you white bread bitch. You can't handle my shit. You slow. You old. You ain't now and you never was.*

And me, Bubba Yablonsky, I'm trying to keep the game close because at the end, when we make our move, I want everybody worked up. So I'm letting the moron go by me and I'm missing my shots and this inspires him to even greater rhetorical flights. *Where's yo game, white bread? You leave it with yo mama? Ah think she done stuck it down her panties. 'At's 'cause it stinks.*

I put up with it because I'm basically a goal-oriented guy and because I've learned to control my anger.

We're well into the fourth quarter, the game tied at 38, when their point guard takes a jump shot that comes off the far side of the rim. I box out the moron, who compensates by twisting his knuckles against my spine, then go up for the rebound. The ball drops into my hands, but I don't catch it. I tip it, instead, toward the sideline.

Spooky Jones, our small forward, is closest to the ball and he tears after it, leaping over the sideline and into the third row of benches. While he's in the air, I slam my elbow into the moron's chest, then scrape the heel of my Nikes against his shin. As expected, the moron begins to throw punches, and a moment later both benches empty. Now all eyes are on the combatants, all eyes except those of Road Miller's wife, Louise. Her eyes are on her work as she yanks at the waist of Spooky's shorts and jams a small package down into his crotch. The package is bound with double sided tape and molds so nicely to Spooky's abdomen that when he finally pulls himself up and dashes off to the locker room, nobody notices a thing.

I don't see the rest of it, of course, because the moron has me by the throat and one of the screws is pounding on my back like I'm the one who won't let go. But the plan is for Spooky to dump the package beneath a pile of dirty towels in the hamper, then come back on the court. Later, Freddie Morrow will push the hamper to the prison laundry, remove the package, and bring it to yours truly.

It's an eminently workable prison hustle, brilliantly conceived and elaborately planned. The package contains two ounces of powder cocaine which sells on the inside for two hundred dollars a gram. As there are twenty-eight grams in an ounce and the two ounces are costing me and my partners twelve hundred dollars . . . well, the math speaks for itself.

I let myself be pulled away from the moron and back to the sidelines where my teammates are already gathered. Spooky Jones isn't there. That's because he's lying in a shower stall, his throat slashed and the product vanished. He's still bleeding when we find him, his heart still fluttering. His breath whistles through the hole in his throat while a deputy warden screams into the phone for a doctor; his eyes remain open and imploring until the doctor rushes into the locker room. Then Spooky's breathing stops, for good and forever.

★ ★ ★

I can't help it. I'm a criminal. I don't mourn Spooky. Yeah, he was a good guy and we'd split many a joint during our stay at the Menands Correctional Facility, a minimum security joint with a spectacular view of the Hudson River. But if there's anything a thief can't stand, it's being ripped off. Somebody took my coke and I want it back. As for Spooky Jones, he's past caring.

Deputy Warden Ezekiel Buchanan rakes me over the coals. Him and Coach Poole, who's also, technically, a deputy warden.

"You started the fight," Buchanan tells me. He has a thin face and a long nose and unnaturally red lips. "Can we agree on that?"

I'm thinking, *If I was still in Attica, the screws would be working me over with ax handles.* I'm thinking, *That's exactly where you're going, dickhead, back to Attica, where your life is on the line every minute of every day. Say good-bye to paradise.*

"Coach," I finally respond, "I didn't have anything to do with . . . with what happened to Spooky. I was on the floor every minute, which you know because you were there. For me, that's an alibi."

Coach Poole doesn't respond. He looks devastated, like a jilted lover. His ebony skin has a grayish cast and his small chocolate eyes are shot through with jagged red veins.

"You wanna answer me, Bubba? Answer the question I asked you?" Buchanan's a patient guy, a twenty-year man who's worked a dozen institutions, and he also thinks he's been betrayed. That's because he personally recruited the Menands' basketball team from some of the worst prisons in the system, choosing very carefully from the pool of eligible talent. In the process, he'd put his reputation on the line.

"The only point I wanna make," I say, "is that the entire team was on the court when this went down. I don't see how you can blame us."

"I asked you if you started the fight."

"It was the moron threw the first punch."

"After you elbowed him."

"This is prison basketball, Deputy, which, as you know, is characterized by aggressive defense. You want us to play nice, you tell the officials to start callin' fouls. They're your officials, right?" Again, I'm thinking, *If you talked like that to a deputy warden in Attica, they'd find pieces of your body in Montreal.*

Now I've got two goals. I want my coke back and I want to finish my bit at Menands, where life is easy, where the food is edible, where there are no rats, where the screws don't begin every conversation with *Hey, you piece of shit.*

"Jones flies into the cheap seats. You start a fight. Jones disappears into the locker room, where he gets killed. Am I supposed to believe this is all coincidental?"

"I didn't start the fight, Deputy. And I didn't see when Spooky took off for the locker room. But anybody in the stands could've followed him and nobody would've noticed."

We go around and around for another hour. I'm polite and respectful, but I stick to my guns. Fights, I insist, are common under the best of circumstances and this was the New York Prison League's championship game. High feelings were to be expected and the refs were allowing us to play. Thus, when the very predictable confrontation finally went down, person or persons unknown had taken advantage of the resulting chaos.

Coach begins to perk up toward the end. I'm giving him an out and he knows it. Sure, Menands is a minimum security prison, but it's still a prison. Assaults among the populace are uncommon, but they happen. Murders are quite rare, but they also happen. I mean, if a murder occurs in the dining hall, do you blame the cook?

When Buchanan finally dismisses me, I plant a seed. "Coach, we're gonna play a makeup game, right? This is for the championship and we were tied."

* * *

I'm back in living unit 8, locked down, me and the rest of the starting five. Hafez Islam, our starting two-guard, is busting my balls, which I don't need. Hafez is a prison-converted Black Muslim, the only one at Menands, which has a majority-white population. I've never seen him when he wasn't angry about something, and from time to time (when that anger was directed at me) I was tempted to slap his mouth shut. Unfortunately, our stay at Menands depends as much on our nonviolent behavior off the court as on our game-day ferocity. Which meant that I mostly have to eat it.

"I know you up to somethin', Bubba," he tells me. "You coulda took that rebound, only you tipped it out. What's up wit' that? You fuckin' wit' us?"

"What I'm up to is none of your Allah-damned business, Hafez. In fact, you're disrespecting me by asking the question." I pause long enough to let the message hit home. "And you better think about something else. If Warden Brook decides that we had anything to do with Spooky gettin' capped, he's gonna ship us back where we came from. In your case, if I remember right, that was Green Haven."

I gather my troops for a team meeting and explain that there had to be five hundred people watching us when Spooky was killed. "You all are just feeling guilty because you're criminals and you expect to be accused of any crime that takes place in the neighborhood. I want you to put that kinda thinking outta your minds because a week from today we're most likely gonna be playing a makeup game. And this game, my brothers, we'd best not lose. Understand what I'm tellin' ya? We cop the trophy, Warden Brook ain't gonna send us nowhere. But if we lose, we'll be on the bus before we take a shower."

Somber nods, sober looks. Now we're all on the same page.

★　★　★

At eight o'clock, before I have a chance to meet with my surviving partners, Roger "Road" Miller and Hong "Tiny" Lee, I'm called to the office of Warden Odell Brook. Brook was a Notre Dame shooting guard who'd been drafted in the second round by the Detroit Pistons, only to blow out his knee in a schoolyard game before he signed a contract.

"You start that fight, Bubba?"

It was the same question Deputy Buchanan had asked, but this time I put a different spin on it. "I had a bad game, Warden. Real bad. And the moron was in my face from the opening tip."

"I saw that," Brook admits. "He was disrespecting you big-time."

"And I didn't answer back, right? Even though I was tossing up bricks. Even though he was goin' right by me."

"Yeah, fine. You were an angel." He waves a long blunt

finger in my direction. "But that rebound, Bubba. You coulda taken it down. You know that."

I nod agreement, then feed him the line I should have fed Hafez Islam and which I'd made up on the way to the warden's office. "It was late in the game and we were tied. I wanted to start a fast break, see if we could get some numbers on the other end."

"Bubba, there was nobody within ten feet of that tip-out."

"What can I say, Warden? I mean, nothin' went right for me the whole game. Somehow I thought Spooky was there. I thought I saw him."

"You're so full of shit it's leaking out of your ears. I can smell it, Bubba. It's stinkin' up my office."

Ever the humble convict, I lower my head before disagreeing. "Swear on my mother, Warden. When I saw the tip go out of bounds I flipped out. Like, it's the championship game and I've been fucking up and now I fucked up the worst of all." I raise my eyes, meet his gaze. "You know what I'm sayin' here because you been there, too. I took it out on the moron, all my frustration, everything he said." I ball my fists, don the most fearsome scowl in my repertoire. "I wanted to kill him, Warden. I wanted to put the motherfucker *down*."

I'm six inches taller than Warden Brook's six-three, and, at 270, eighty pounds heavier. Still, he's unimpressed by my ferocity. "You gonna have a bad game next week, Bubba? You gonna tip the ball to a phantom teammate?"

"Does that mean we're playing?"

"If Spooky . . ." He pauses, starts again. "If the incident had nothing to do with the basketball game, I don't see why we should punish the players and the fans. It doesn't make sense." He contemplates his hands for a moment. "As for the fight . . .

well, you say *he* threw the first punch and he says *you* did. The officials didn't see what happened and neither did anyone else who counts. I think the league's gonna be inclined to call it a wash."

So far, the conversation's gone pretty much the way I expected. Menands is populated mainly by white-collar crooks: lawyers who raided a client's trust fund, bankers who robbed their own banks, doctors who plundered Medicaid, boiler room operators who hung around a little too long. These are folks with money; they love to bet on sports and the persistent rumor is that the cons making book in the yard pay off to a certain deputy warden who pays off to Warden Brook. I don't know if the rumor's true, but when I finally respond, I'm definitely hoping.

"If you're worried about the game, Warden, there's something you might wanna try. You know, to help the team along."

"And what would that be?"

"Well, you could put a little bug in the ears of the officials. I'm not talkin' about high pressure here. I'm talkin' about very low-key so it doesn't get around."

"Bubba, you wanna make your point."

"Okay, Warden." I lean a little closer, drop my voice. "The way it looks right now, what with all the bad attitude out there, the first hard foul next week and somebody's gonna go off. *Unless* the officials take control of the game in the first two minutes. Unless they call a few touch fouls, a few offensive fouls. Unless they send a clear message." I lean back. "Later on, the refs wanna let us play, that'd be great."

Though Warden Brook says, "Bubba, you don't have a redeeming bone in your body," his smile, as I read it, is purely admiring.

★ ★ ★

It's after midnight when I'm finally hunkered down with Road Miller and Tiny Lee in the day area of our housing unit. There's a forty-watt bulb over the door, enough light for the three o'clock count, but not enough for me to read the messages in my partners' eyes.

"Talk to me," I tell Road. "Tell me what's on your mind. 'Cause I know you been thinkin' about it all night."

Roger "Road" Miller is our starting power forward. He's a little too light for the position, especially on the defensive end, but he can elevate on the jumper and he rolls to the basket with determination. I've always wondered if Road's mother deliberately named him after a white country singer. Road is ebony-skinned and proud of his heritage, but he'd once admitted to me that his nickname was derived from the Roger Miller hit "King of the Road."

"Freddie is what's on my mind," he tells me. "As in Freddie fucked us."

Freddie Morrow is the team drudge. He does everything from stacking the equipment to washing our dirty uniforms. I knew when I recruited him that he was the weak link in the chain, but I had no other way to get the coke out of the locker room.

"Freddie was sitting on the bench when Spooky went down," I point out. "Plus, he hasn't got the balls of a canary."

"I didn't say nothin' to nobody," Road insists, "and Tiny didn't say nothin' neither. We ain't stupid enough to brag on our business, not when we ain't done it yet."

"What about Spooky?"

"No way."

"And me? What about me?"

"Don't be an asshole," Tiny Lee declares. Tiny's our point guard. He's five-eight and doesn't weigh more than 150 pounds. Meanwhile, he fears nothing. "If Spooky got whacked over some beef with another con, the coke would still be there. It wasn't and that means somebody had to tell somebody else. There's no way around it."

We're sitting at a rectangular plastic table bolted to the floor, on gray plastic chairs, also bolted down. We're supposed to be in our bunks, but we're the basketball team and the screws won't bust us for petty violations.

"I don't know about you guys," I say, "but I want my coke back."

Tiny says, "That or somebody's blood."

"No, Tiny. I want the coke, which, if you recall, we still haven't paid for." I rub my fingertips together, then sing, *"Money, money, moneyyyyyy."*

I came into the deal as part of an effort to turn my life around, an effort which included my anger-management and computer classes. Though I'd been incarcerated for a crime of violence, then passed four years in a very violent prison, my short stay at the Menands Correctional Facility presented me with an inescapable truth: when it comes to white-collar crime, the profits are long and the sentences short. And what I figured, when Tiny first approached me, was that if I sacrificed and worked very hard, I could accumulate enough capital to buy into a top-tier boiler room operation when I finally made parole.

"Oh, man," Road moans. "I'm gonna catch hold of Freddie and rip his arms off." It was Road's Aunt Louise who stuffed the coke into Spooky's shorts and it was Road who arranged to have the coke fronted. And it was Road, of course, whose ass was on the line.

"Nobody talks to Freddie," I tell him, a calculated act of disrespect. I'm Road's partner, not his boss. "Let's take a little time, take a look around. We got nothin' but time, right? Time is what we're doin'."

Road smiles, cheered, perhaps, by my attitude. "Wha'chu thinkin', Bubba? I know you schemin' somethin'."

"Look around you, Road, next time you're in the yard. How many cons you think you're gonna see out there with the heart to cut Spooky's throat? Because Spooky was *spooky*."

Tiny has a terrible burn scar on the right side of his face, and he scratches it when he's lost in thought. He's scratching away now, and I lean in his direction as I continue. "You see Spooky's hands, his wrists? You see any cuts? Spooky came down from Clinton, where you can get your ass shanked for brushing up against somebody's shoulder. There's no way he'd let anyone he didn't trust get close enough to take him out before he could put up his hands."

By this time, I have a pretty good idea who capped Spooky. What I don't have is a way to get the coke back. I don't know where it is, and this particular individual can't be approached directly. I can't lay my suspicions on my partners either. I have to keep them under control, especially Tiny, who's liable to go off, do something stupid, get us all shipped out.

"Like I said, let's take a few days, look around, see who's out there. Meanwhile, come Tuesday's practice, we'll send Freddie a little message."

* * *

I go to my computer class on Monday. I'm learning how to keep books using Windows NT and Lotus. Hafez Islam is there, and a few other cons, but more than half the desks are empty because most of the prisoners at Menands are familiar with computers. Though I'm also on good terms with the technology, I'm an avid student, more often than not staying after class to work directly with my instructor, Clifford Entwhistle. Cliff came to Menands via one of Manhattan's most prestigious accounting firms. In class, he teaches me to keep the books. After class, he teaches me to cook them.

"You holding?" he asks. Cliff will put virtually anything down his throat or up his nose. He's an incredibly hairy middle-aged man with a beard that starts at his cheekbones and runs all the way to his ankles. In the shower, he looks like a bear with an ass.

I shake my head. "Look, I need you to do me a favor. And I need you to keep it quiet."

"What's that?"

"I want you to get me the name of the screw who worked the door to the locker room last night."

Cliff is a very soft guy with a very hard mind and he gets it right away. "You think a screw killed Spooky?"

"That's the wrong question, Cliff. The question you're supposed to ask is, *What's in it for me?*" I shift my chair closer to his, until our knees are touching. I can see the fear in his eyes and address myself directly to it. "One other thing, my friend. You're gonna have to keep this to yourself. That's because if anybody finds out, I'm gonna kill ya."

Cliff's lips curl into a little pout. All along, he's thought us, if not friends, at least comrades. Now he knows better. "You didn't have to say that," he says.

"Yeah, I did, Cliff. I had to say it because I meant it and because it's very, very important. You fuck up, you're gonna die."

I give him a second to absorb the information, remembering that I'd issued the identical threat to Freddie Morrow and it hadn't stopped him from shooting his mouth off. For a moment, I wish I really meant what I said, but then my anger-management training kicks in, and I move on.

The central computer that runs Menands cannot be reached via the computers available to inmates. But Cliff works in the accounting office, where he routinely processes the Menands' payroll. From there, he once explained to me, it was just a matter of looking over Deputy Warden Monroe's shoulder as Monroe entered his password.

When I'm sure he's not about to put up even a token resistance, I put my hand on Cliff's shoulder and say, "You do this for me, I won't forget it. I'll keep you high for as long as we're in Menands. You have my word on that."

I offer my hand, just as if I hadn't threatened him, and he takes it because he has no choice, sealing the pact.

* * *

There are eight or nine serious bookmakers in population, and maybe double that number of contraband dealers who peddle everything from dope to steroids to pornography. I'm sure they had nothing to do with stealing our coke because all the inmates—players and spectators—were subjected to a very intrusive strip search before returning to their cells. But the dealers do figure on the other end. Sooner or later the coke will have to be sold off and one (or more) of them will have to do the selling. As a group, they're not nearly as vicious as their counterparts in Attica, but they're not punks either.

I watch these players as Road, Tiny, and I walk along a jogging track that frames the yard at Menands. Wondering if one of them has already taken delivery. If my coke is already disappearing up some rich con's insatiable nose.

"No sign of Freddie Morrow," Tiny observes.

"As expected." I want to tell my partners what I think and what I'm doing about it, but I still can't risk either (or both) of them blowing their cool. "We need eyes and ears," I say. "Anybody starts moving coke, we have to know right away."

My partners solemnly agree and we break up a short time later. I stroll across the yard, graciously accepting the adulation of my fans and the advice of my critics. By this time, everybody knows we're going to make up Sunday's game and the question of the day is how we're gonna do. The Menands' bookies originally made us ten-point favorites to win the championship, but not only didn't the Menands Tigers (and especially yours truly) meet expectations, Spooky's loss at the small forward position has weakened the team. All of that was okay with me because I intended to get a bet down (through a third party, of course) on the Menands Tigers. That was another reason I'd kept Sunday's game close, why I'd let the moron have his way. With a little luck, the makeup game will be pick 'em by the time we step on the court. Maybe we'll even be underdogs.

I help my luck along, as I make my way across the yard to where Clifford Entwhistle stands with his back against the outer wall of D Unit, by sticking to the party line. I had a bad game, but I expect to get it together. Though we all miss old Spooky, Bibi Guernavaca can do the job for us at small forward.

The last part is pure bullshit, and though I'm shown no disrespect, everyone I speak with knows it. Bibi, our sixth man, is a good point guard and a decent shooting guard, but he's too short and too light to play small forward. Somebody else is gonna have to have a big game and I expect that somebody to be me. I'd faced the moron for the second time in yesterday's game and I knew I could take him. Especially if Warden Brook convinced the officials to call the game tight in the opening quarter.

As I approach, Cliff pushes himself away from the wall and we begin to walk. I don't say anything, just wait for him to get to the point. The sun has dropped to the ridgeline of Blue Top Mountain at the western edge of the Menands Valley. It sparkles in the chain-link fence surrounding the prison, in the razor wire that tops the fence. Prisoners huddle in small groups. They speak softly, their collective conversation an insectlike hum, a swarm of bees heard at a distance. Suddenly, I feel very good about myself. I've set goals and I'm moving toward them and I'm not letting obstacles throw me off course.

"Percy Campbell," Cliff tells me, "was manning the door outside the locker room last night. He's the one who found the body."

Cliff is wearing a Brooklyn Dodgers baseball jacket and I slide a small package into his pocket, a down payment (and all the payment he's likely to get) on my promise. "Now remember," I tell him, "the only way to keep a secret is not to tell anybody. *Any*body."

* * *

Coach Poole begins Tuesday's practice with a moment of silence in Spooky's honor, then declares that because we played so poorly on Sunday, every starting position is up for grabs. "It's preseason all over again. It's training camp. You wanna play, you gotta make the team."

I'm not particularly worried because I know that if the Tigers blow the championship, Coach Poole will have to answer to Warden Brook, and the Tigers can't win without me.

Nevertheless, because I'm a team leader and I don't want Coach to lose face, I practice hard. By the time we begin our regular scrimmage two hours later, my knees are aching. Both knees, so I don't know which one to limp on first.

"You ready?" I ask Road as I take the ball out of bounds a few minutes later.

"Yeah. Past ready."

I toss the ball in, nod to Tiny, then set a pick at the top of the key. Tiny goes by, dribbles to the baseline, then passes back to me. As I receive the ball, Road, posted in the opposite corner, takes off for the hoop. I fake left, then put everything I have into a pass that misses Road's outstretched fingertips by a good six inches before slamming into the side of Freddie Morrow's traitorous head.

We catch a break here. Freddie's ear is torn halfway off and the doc ships him to the infirmary for an overnight stay. That evening, I pay him a visit, but I don't tell him how sorry I am for my errant pass. Instead, I sit at the foot of his bed, take his hand in mine, and say, "Who'd you blab to, ya little fuck?"

"Bubba, I . . ."

I'm an ugly man. I have a jaw like the prow of a ship, a pronounced underbite, a small flat nose with perfectly round nostrils, tiny eyes overhung by a slab of a brow. For most of my life, I've been extremely self-conscious about my appearance. It's only recently, since coming to Menands, that I've made a more positive adjustment. Everything in life, I now understand, has its uses. You just have to look on the bright side.

The bright side here is that I don't have to lay a finger on little Freddie. All I have to do is stare at him.

"You snitched us out, Freddie. You ratted on us. I just wanna hear it from your lips."

"Bubba, I . . ."

"We're not gonna kill you, Freddie. We're not even gonna hurt you any more than you've already been hurt. That's because you're gonna help us get our product back." I pull him toward me, until we're nose-to-nose. "Take the first step," I tell him, my voice steady, my tone encouraging. "The first step is always the hardest. You take the first step, the rest is easy."

"Bubba . . ."

"No, don't start with *Bubba*. You've done that three times and it hasn't gotten us anywhere. Start with somebody else's name, like the name of the screw you told about the coke." I give his hand a playful squeeze. "You confess, maybe we can dream up a way to protect you."

I can hear the little switches in Freddie's mind as they click into position. With Spooky dead, he's now the weak link on two chains.

"You know what I think, Freddie? I think it was pure accident. I mean, we didn't run the scam until near the end of the fourth quarter and the screw had to be in and out before the end of the game. Most likely, when he snuck into the locker room, he figured Spooky was already back on the court. 'Turn around,' is what I would've said in his place. 'Face the wall. I'm gonna search you.' Then out comes the knife and it's judgment day for Spooky Jones."

"Bubba . . ."

"Start with the name, Freddie. You're gonna feel so much better when you tell me the name."

"Percy Campbell," he finally blurts.

Freddie may feel better, but he looks terrible. He's gasping for breath and he's bright red from his forehead to his throat. When I let go of him, he falls back onto the pillow and brings his hand to his chest. Freddie's twenty-two years old, a computer nerd who created a virus that shut down six of the biggest Web sites on the Net.

"How long have you been Campbell's snitch?"

"Since I got here. He grabbed me the first week and took me to his office. You know about the office?"

I shake my head. Campbell is a middle-aged muscle brain who's been walking a tier for three decades. A veteran of the worst prisons New York State has to offer, he generally manages to restrain himself at Menands. Still, his personal violence surrounds him, a sour stink detectable by an experienced con at a distance of a hundred yards.

"That's what Campbell calls it: my office. It's behind the main furnace, a coal room. You know, from the time when they heated with coal. It's not used for anything now, and when you're inside, the furnace is so loud nobody can hear you even if there's someone around. Which most of the time there isn't." He pauses long enough to wipe his nose, then jumps back in. "Campbell told me things . . . things he'd do to me if I didn't . . . I was scared, Bubba. I was never in trouble before I came here. For all I knew, Campbell could do anything he wanted to and get away with it. I didn't know where to turn."

Now that I see a way to get my coke back and exact a little revenge for Spooky at the same time, I can't even fake being mad. I stretch, yawn, take a breath. "I'm gonna need you, Freddie, so I want you to stay alive for a few days. Don't be alone, no matter what. Stay in a group and Campbell won't be able to get to you. Remember, it's only for a couple of days."

"What about tonight?"

"I'll talk to the trusty on the floor, see that he watches your back." I get up, take a step, then turn back to Freddie. I'm smiling now, a genuine smile. "Was I right?" I ask.

"Right?"

"Do you feel better? Now that it's out in the open."

"Yeah," he tells me, "I do."

*   *   *

Coach Poole makes an announcement after Wednesday's practice. The league's championship game will be made up on the following night with no civilians present. This is good news for me because there won't be a practice on game day and I'll have enough time to get to the coal room unseen. Unlike Attica with its many checkpoints, Menands runs mostly on the honor system. The fence and the razor wire surrounding the prison are there to reassure the community, not to prevent an escape. The population is controlled by a very simple and very potent threat: you fuck up, you get sent to some horrible place where your survival (not to mention your sexuality) is anything but assured. Most prisoners at Menands aren't willing to risk their privileged status.

Later that night, Tiny and Road press me, but I don't reveal much. I tell them to be patient and to stay clear of Freddie Morrow. I tell them I hope to recover the product soon and that I don't need their help. They don't care for the underlying message, but they seem to accept it. Nevertheless, within a few days, should I fail to deliver, I know they'll begin to suspect a double cross.

I wake up on Thursday, take a shower, then skip breakfast and head for the locker room. Freddie's already there, hanging our pressed uniforms in our metal lockers. Once upon a time, the lockers were a uniform gray, the color of pewter, but they've tarnished over the years and now have a mottled overgrown look, as if the victim of some exotic fungus.

"You ready, Freddie?" I ask. "You ready to go to work?"

"Bubba, I . . ."

"Don't start that *Bubba* shit again. I have something I need you to do."

"What is it?"

"This afternoon, two o'clock, Campbell is gonna be workin' in the library. I want you to go there, talk to him, tell him that I know you snitched us out."

"He'll kill me."

"For Christ's sake, you're gonna be in the library. You even cough, you get eighty-sixed."

"Then he'll get me later."

"He's *already* gonna get you later." I put a foot up on the bench that runs in front of the lockers. "It's your chance, Freddie. Your chance to be a man for the first time in your miserable life, your chance to stand on your own two feet." I hold up a finger. "Plus, you can help yourself at the same time. Because I'm telling you, when Campbell hears what you have to say, he's gonna be a lot more worried about me than you."

Freddie thinks it over for a moment, the possibility of deflecting Campbell's wrath onto me obviously appealing. If he gains an ally in the process, so much the better. "Whatta ya want me to say?"

"Tell Campbell that I put the pieces together on my own. I know he killed Spooky and snatched my product because he was the only one who had the opportunity. I know you snitched because . . . well, I know you snitched because you're you. Likewise, because you're you, when I threatened to shank your ass, you confessed. Those stitches in your ear and that bandage oughta be proof enough that I meant business."

"And that's it? Just that I admitted talking to him?"

"Yeah, you opened up because you were in fear of your life

and now you're trying to make it good by telling him the truth." I put my arm around his shoulder, let my voice drop. "Campbell's gonna ask you a lot of questions. He's gonna want to know everything you said to me and everything I said to you. It's only natural, right?"

Freddie nods. "Right."

"So you tell him everything you told me about his threats and where he took you before he delivered them. The only thing you don't tell him, Freddie, is that I asked you to come forward. That's the one teeny-tiny thing you keep to yourself." I give his shoulder a squeeze. "That's gonna be our little secret."

★   ★   ★

I go from Freddie to Warden Brook's office. He tells me that he's spoken to the two refs, and I guarantee him a win. We're one-point underdogs by now.

"You're not worried about losing Spooky?"

"You remember when you brought me here, Warden? You remember I promised you a championship? Well, tonight I'm gonna keep that promise."

I know the warden bets on every game, always on the Tigers, even when I tell him the team's so worn-out we'd get our asses kicked by the Menands High School Barracudas. He's a fan is what he is, a former athlete who lives through his favorite team, which is us.

"So make room in the trophy case," I declare, "because we're bringin' the cup home."

My next stop is in the computer room, where I find my teacher, Cliff Entwhistle, hard at work. Cliff is a big-time gambler, but unlike Warden Brook, he's willing to wager against the

Tigers. Though I only bet with the team (and once threatened to crush the fingers of a skinny point guard I thought was shaving points), I don't bet every game.

"What's the word?" I ask him. "Out on the yard?"

"Without Spooky, Menands doesn't have a chance."

"Good, because I want to get a bet down." I retrieve a pair of C-notes from their resting place in the crotch of my underwear and hand them over. If the coke deal had gone down as planned, it'd be a lot more, but I'm doing the best I can. "I guarantee a win here," I tell him. "You can take it to the bank."

Cliff nods. "Thanks, Bubba."

"Don't thank me. There's something I need you to do. Like, right now."

An hour later I make my way down a long flight of stairs to the furnace room. Two stories high and at least a hundred feet long, the room houses a state-of-the-art, fully automated boiler the size and shape of a diesel locomotive. It being May and warm, the unit is only producing hot water. Still, the steady hiss of the flame is loud enough for my purposes. I work my way along the north wall, the route taken by Campbell when he recruited Freddie, avoiding a pair of cameras mounted on the ceiling. The cameras use heat-sensitive film and are in place to detect fires.

The coal room, Campbell's office, is not as Freddie described it. I expect a large empty space, but the room is cluttered with discarded desks. There are desks upside down, on their sides, on three legs, desks piled one on top of the other. Desk drawers, heaped in a corner, rise halfway to the ceiling.

It's now one o'clock. Freddie's scheduled to make his confession at two. That leaves me an hour to find my product. Assuming it's here at all, that Campbell doesn't have another hideaway, that he didn't take his prize home with him, maybe peddle the weight to a street dealer.

I begin to search, at first systematically, then more and more frantically as time passes. A pair of overhead lights don't respond to a switch next to the door, and the only illumination splashes in through the open doorway. The desks are extremely dusty. The dust coats my throat and mouth as I work. When I run my fingers over my brush cut, it feels like I'm dragging them through mud.

Somewhere around one forty-five, I force myself to slow down. I tell myself I have one of those unforeseen problems that crop up from time to time, no matter how carefully I try to plan my activities. I tell myself they happen to everybody. It's not God getting me, like I sometimes thought before I learned to control my anger.

I set out to draw ten deep breaths, each one slower and deeper than the last, just the way I've been trained. I don't get past the fifth before I realize there's another way, and if I'd only taken a moment to think before I started ripping desks apart, I could have saved myself a lot of work.

I'm standing just to the left of the door, looking for a good place to hide, when Campbell walks into the room. He is not alone. A dealer named Redmond Mitchell is with him. At the tail end of a ten-to-life bit, Red is also a veteran of New York's maximum security institutions. His stay at Menands is theoretically the final step in his rehabilitation.

Coming from the intensely bright furnace room, neither Red nor Campbell sees me until I step in front of them.

"What's up, guys? You lookin' for me?"

Campbell is maybe five-ten. A layer of fat covers a much thicker layer of muscle on his heavy boned frame. At one time,

I suppose, he was quite the brawler, an upstate redneck who would have been a convict if he hadn't become a screw. But now he's nearing fifty, a hard drinker who maintains his self-image by terrorizing inmates, like Freddie Morrow, who are in no position to fight back.

Red is another matter. He's younger, in much better condition, a man who maintained his personal dignity over many years in many prisons. I see Campbell glance at him, smiling, convinced that Red is an ally in this war. He's wrong.

"Red," I explain, "what I gotta do here is convince this dumb-as-shit screw to show me where he's hidden my cocaine. Most likely, it'd be better if you weren't here to see it."

I know that Red's not afraid of me. I also know that he's got a release date for the end of the summer and the last thing he needs is a serious beef. "No harm, no foul," he says. "I'm not out no money and I ain't got a dog in this fight." He backs through the door, then asks, "You gonna win tonight, Bubba?"

"I guarantee it."

"Thass good, man. 'Cause I took the points big-time."

Red steps into the furnace room and his footsteps are instantly masked by the hiss of the boiler. He might be lingering a few feet from the open doorway, or he might be on the moon. Campbell stares up at me and I stare down at him. I wonder if he's looked through my file, tried to get an idea of who he was up against. But, no, careful is not his style. Freddie told him about the coke and he wanted it and that was all she wrote. When he found Spooky in the locker room, he could have backed off, or busted Spooky and taken the credit. But he was already counting the money, already holding it in his sweaty palm.

"Where's my product, Percy?"

The shiny white surface of his bald scalp slowly reddens. Most likely, in his entire career, no con ever spoke to him this way. But then, in times past, he always had plenty of backup. Now he's on his own. He can't call for help, even if he could make himself heard over the din of the furnace, without everything coming out. Spooky, Freddie, the cocaine, everything. Officer Percy Campbell is helpless.

"I don't know what you're talking about, Yablonsky."

"You can do better than that." I watch his hand inch toward his back pocket. It's pathetic, really. "You wanna go that route, Percy, it's all right, but I don't see how it's gonna do you any good." I step forward until we're less than an arm's length apart.

Credit where credit is due, Campbell's right hand dives into his pocket and he snarls, "See you in hell, ya Jew bastard."

Despite the epithet and the made-for-TV dialogue, death is not on today's agenda. First because I'm not a killer, and second because Officer Campbell's body would draw far too much attention. Most likely, he's already a suspect in Spooky's murder.

I grab his wrist, pin his hand in his pocket, then put all 270 pounds into a looping right that makes a sound like a bat slammed into a watermelon as it crashes into his chest. His eyes roll up, his legs wobble, then fail him altogether. He drops to the floor and stops breathing.

For a minute, I think I'm gonna have to give him CPR, maybe catch some fatal screw disease, but then his eyes snap into focus as he rises to a sitting position, draws a painfully ragged breath, and begins to gasp.

I squat down, remove the knife from his pocket and a can of pepper spray from a holder on his belt. I toss them into the furnace room where they can be easily recovered.

"Time for a reality check, Percy. First, you're completely on your own here. You couldn't call for help even if there was someone to hear you. Not without risking a murder charge. Second, you're a middle-aged, out-of-shape, alcoholic sadist who's been caught with his hand in the cookie jar, while I'm a hardened, merciless criminal who wants his cookies back."

I grab him by the collar, yank him to his feet, deposit him on one of the few upright desks. Campbell probably goes about 220, but I handle him easily enough. Last time I was in the weight room, I benched 350 for the first time.

"Where's my coke, Percy?"

There's no more fight in Campbell's eyes. There's hate in abundance, and fear, but no fight. He points up, to a ventilator shaft in the wall. "Behind the grille."

A moment later I'm holding the package in my hand. It's a joyous moment, even triumphant, but it's not enough.

"Now you gotta pay for Spooky," I tell him.

"What?" He seems honestly confused, as though I'd brought up the name of a mutual acquaintance he can't quite recall.

"Spooky was my teammate and my friend. You killed him and now I'm gonna punish you, and there's not a fucking thing you can do about it. You've already been checked out on the computer, by the way. You're on sick leave."

I push him backward off the desk and onto the floor. I expect a struggle, but Campbell's eyes reveal only a rapidly enveloping panic. He slides away as I approach, until he comes up against an overturned desk. "Please, please," he moans. "Please don't." I wonder how many times he's heard those words from the mouth of a Freddie Morrow. I wonder how many times he's shown mercy in the course of his long shitkicker career.

A long wet stain runs along the inside of Campbell's thigh,

from his crotch to his shins. As I kneel beside him, he rolls onto his side and curls into a fetal position. "Please, please, please."

* * *

In the locker room, before the game, I tape my knees using a pair of Ace bandages that haven't been washed since the season began. The bandages are still damp from yesterday's practice and they feel slighty gritty against my skin. They stink, too, stink something nasty. The bandages are part of a ritual that started five years ago when my legs began to give out. As I wind them around my knees, I put on my game face. No mercy is what I tell myself. Take the moron's game, take his heart, crush his soul.

I flex the knuckles of my right hand. Though I kept well away from Campbell's head and face, both hands are a little sore.

"Bubba?"

"Yeah, Road?" I've already spoken to Road, Tiny, and Hafez Islam about the officials calling the game close. I left out Bibi Guernavaca because he's a Pentecostal and begins every encounter with the words *Cristo salva.*

"You found our product, bro. You the best, you the baddest. You saved our asses. I love you, man."

A poignant moment, by prison standards. I rise, thump Road's chest. "Forget that bullshit," I tell him. "You wanna show your gratitude, hit the jump shot when I pass out of the double team."

* * *

I let the moron win the opening tip. A few seconds later, when the ball comes to him maybe fifteen feet out, I let him drive by me. The packed stands, ablaze with energy a moment before, grow silent. I hustle up the court and plant myself just outside the paint and Tiny gets the ball to me before the double team closes down. I fake left, then spin to the baseline, where the moron checks me with his hip, as he did twenty times in the first game. From fifteen feet away, the senior official, a screw called Dashing Dan Thomas, blows the whistle as I toss the ball in the direction of the basket.

I make both free throws and the crowd wakes up. Red Mitchell, sitting four rows back at midcourt, grins and shakes his head. The moron sets up fifteen feet from the basket, well outside his range. I know he'll go right and that he'll bump me with his shoulder on his way across the court. I know because he bumped me in the first game and got away with it. This time, however, Dashing Dan . . .

The moron goes ballistic, launching a string of epithets at Dashing Dan, who, very predictably, tees the moron up. Satisfied, I watch Tiny make the free throw while the moron's coach drags him over to the bench.

By the end of the first quarter, we're up 25–9. The fans, even those who bet against us, are on their feet with every play. I've scored thirteen points, most of them against the moron's sub, who's slow and short, but at least knows when to keep his mouth shut.

As a high school senior, at seventeen, I was already six-six. My knees were coiled springs and injuries were catastrophes that happened to somebody else, somebody smaller and weaker. I was never tired in the last quarter. No, fatigue was what I felt after the party that followed the game, at six o'clock in the morning, with my equally spent girlfriend lying beside me.

I experience all of that again. Just as if I hadn't thrown it away in a moment of rage. My body is sweat-slick. Sweat drips from my headband into my eyes. I'm completely alive in my flesh now. Flesh is the only reality I have. I measure time in the thump of the ball on the floor. I'm unstoppable.

The moron comes back at the start of the second quarter. By that time, the refs are letting us play again. Meanwhile, the moron backs off when he should be aggressive, then complains bitterly when I hand-check him in the post. I'm being triple-teamed now, the minute I touch the ball, and I'm passing out to Road Miller, who's draining fifteen-foot jumpers, one after the other.

It's all over by the middle of the third quarter. We're up by twenty-two points and the crowd is on its feet, chanting *Bub-BA, Bub-BA, Bub-BA.* Warden Brook can barely contain himself. He's dancing around, smacking his fist into his palm. Coach Poole is standing with both arms in the air. He's shouting instructions, calling a play, but I can't hear him as I sprint up the court. It doesn't matter anyway, because Tiny steals the ball and we're off and running. I'm the trailer on the play with Road coming up fast on the right. Tiny fakes a pass to Road, fakes a layup, then flips the ball over his left shoulder. I receive the pass at the head of the key, take a step to the foul line, then elevate. From a distance, I hear myself scream and I hear the screaming of the fans, a great roar only a half-step removed from utter madness. Then I'm coming down, slamming the ball through the hoop, slamming the palms of my hands into the rim. The backboard jerks forward, then back, then finally shatters, burying me in a sparkling wave of broken glass.

God, I love this game.